A
TALENT
FOR
MURDER

A
TALENT
FOR
MURDER

An
Everett Carr
Mystery

Matthew Booth

To Mum and Dad,
With thanks for all the love, laughs, and support

Chapter One

S ir James Ravenwood placed the dagger into its exhibit case and poured himself a congratulatory glass of his very best whisky. A little early, perhaps, for such an indulgence but Ravenwood felt it was both justified and deserved, in equal measure. Deserved, because the period of negotiation which had resulted in the final purchase of the weapon had been long and tortuous; justified, because possession of the dagger was of such importance to a collector like himself that the toasting of the fact could be done with nothing less than the most luxurious of drinks. And yet, Ravenwood could have no idea that, within a matter of days, the dagger would be used to commit murder.

The knife was a broad-bladed weapon, its edge serrated, the hilt made from bone and encrusted with a selection of jewels set in gilt cases. It had been well preserved, a fact for which Ravenwood was grateful, and he could imagine that its dark history might prompt any owner of it to ensure that its condition was nothing less than immaculate. A distinguished and intriguing provenance to an item seemed to Ravenwood to demand it be treated with care and respect. Certainly, Ravenwood anticipated doing so and, by placing it in an exhibit case set into its own plinth, so that it rose above those treasures surrounding it, he felt that he was making a statement about the awe in which he expected it to be held. No doubt some of the people to view it would do so with suspicion and Ravenwood supposed that he was obliged to excuse any such doubts. After all, he had no proof that the knife's legend had any basis in fact, simply because it was impossible to say for certain whether any blade had truly been used to stake

1

a vampire, but it was this very uncertainty which excited Ravenwood. It was the possibility of the story behind the dagger which intrigued the collector and any certainty on the matter would have dimmed that enthusiasm almost entirely. People may be entitled to their scepticism on the existence and execution of vampires, but Ravenwood felt equally permitted to embrace the possibility of both.

He took a further look at the dagger through the glass of its exhibit case and allowed himself a small sigh of satisfaction. He looked around the museum room in its entirety, feeling that familiar sense of pride which his extensive collection of curiosities always instilled in him, and made a circuit of the room. The vampire dagger was not the only item which was rooted in mystery and superstition. He owned a small leather pouch said to contain charms and poppets manufactured by one of the Pendle witches from the 17th century. There was a shawl, moth-eaten and bloodstained, which it was said had been used by Jack the Ripper to clean his knife. Not all of the collection was steeped in myth and legend, but none of it was without an element of darkness. A scold's bridal, a heretic's fork, a confession of treason scrawled in an illegible and broken hand by one of the Gunpowder plotters, an operational iron maiden: these and similar sinister artefacts from the history of mankind's more violent episodes were all placed in their own glass cases, each with a neatly printed card declaring the name of the exhibit and offering something of its background. It was a collection of some significance, one which was largely praised and admired by experts in the field, and Ravenwood knew that his pride in his private museum was not misplaced.

He walked out of the museum room and into the hallway, locking the door behind him. He crossed the chessboard flooring and pushed open the door of the drawing room. Lady Mary Ravenwood was sitting in an armchair, a small leather volume open on her knee. She looked up at her husband as he entered and smiled gently. To Ravenwood, despite the years of their marriage, she seemed not to have aged. Her eyes retained the same fire of youth which had impressed him at their first meeting and her skin maintained that pale, flawless delicacy which gave her the impression of a finely painted portrait. Ravenwood knew that of all his treasures, Lady Ravenwood was the finest, and, as if to show her that he knew it, he bent over and kissed her on the cheek.

"Have you put that awful thing on display?" she asked.

Ravenwood sat down in a chair beside her. "Awful isn't the word, my dearest. Fascinating would be better."

"If you say so." She looked across at him. "Fascinating enough to have a whisky before tea?"

He nodded without contrition. "Without question."

"Do you think it appropriate to greet a guest by breathing whisky into his face?" asked Mary, her voice a blend of amusement and reproach.

"Guest?"

"Your author fellow."

Ravenwood groaned and the overlooked appointment now returned with burning fire to his memory. "I'd forgotten about him. What time is he due?"

Mary looked at the small clock on the marble fireplace. "In an hour."

Ravenwood rose from the chair and kissed his wife once more on the cheek. "You're the very best asset a man could have. I'd forget to wake up in the morning without you."

"Don't forget to tell him that we have other guests this weekend, so he's going to have to share you with them. And don't tell me that you've forgotten about those other guests too, since inviting them was your idea."

"I haven't forgotten. Oh, and I might have asked one more chap along. Sorry, I meant to mention it to you."

Mary slammed shut her book and sighed. "Who is it?"

"Just a fellow I know. A collector of mysteries, like I am myself."

"I do wish you'd keep me updated on matters, James." She rose from her chair and walked across the hearthrug to stand by his side. "Any other skeletons in the cupboard?"

He shook his head. "No."

She took one of his hands in hers. "If you allowed this young author fellow to slip out of your head, does that mean you haven't read that book of his I gave you?"

3

Ravenwood creased his brow in distaste. "I've never cared for detective stories. All too unlikely and convoluted for my taste."

"It's polite to know something about a man's work before you meet him, James. You've an hour to spare before Mr Deville arrives. Go and fetch his novel and immerse yourself in it. Without any whisky to accompany it, mind you."

It was an unnecessary rebuke, but Ravenwood accepted it without complaint.

In the library, the hour spent in the company of *The Corpse Feld By Moonlight* by R.P. Deville passed as excruciatingly and as slowly as Ravenwood had feared. He was irked not so much by the quality of the writing, which he found surprisingly impressive, but by the unnecessarily circuitous and improbable plot mixed with the insufferably pompous central character of the aristocratic sleuth. He felt he might have been able to cope with one or the other, but their combined effect was too suffocating to tolerate. Finally, his mind awash with bizarre clues and outlandish twists of plot, Ravenwood put the book to one side and rang the bell for Fenton. The butler arrived with customary alacrity.

"Fenton, a guest is arriving in a few moments. Be so good as to bring along a decanter of sherry and a couple of glasses, would you?" Mary had prohibited whisky, after all, not sherry.

"Certainly, sir. Might I ask whether this guest is Mr Deville, the writer, and whether his room can be prepared now, sir? I have been waiting for confirmation."

Ravenwood nodded. "Correct, on both counts. See to it, would you?"

The butler inclined his head and departed wordlessly. Within moments, the sherry had been delivered and the announcement of the arrival of R.P Deville himself was made.

Ravenwood was not sure what he had expected of the author of detective novels but he was nevertheless surprised by the youth of the man. Deville seemed to be not yet forty years of age, his face free of those lines of experience which marked Ravenwood's own features. Deville's hair was fair, slightly too long to meet the older man's approval, but the latter supposed that such unruliness was common amongst artistic types. His suit was far from expensive and it was filled with the very type of crease which was missing from his face. His eyes were bright with intelligence, shining from behind the lenses of horn-rimmed spectacles which sat unevenly on his long nose. He carried with him a notebook and pencil and, when he shook Ravenwood's hand, the ink stains on his hands did not go unnoticed.

"I must thank you for allowing me to intrude into your weekend, Sir James," said Deville. "I very much appreciate it."

Ravenwood handed the author a glass of the sherry. "I don't pretend to understand what use it can be to you, I must say."

"Research is invaluable, sir. I find it almost impossible to write convincingly about a place or a person unless I have visited or met a real-life example. It adds a certain amount of authenticity to what can often be a highly artificial situation."

Ravenwood thought back to the novel he had battled with. He had been unable to discern anything approaching verisimilitude of character or place but there had been no doubt in his mind about the implausibility of the scenario presented by the story. Fearing that his face might betray his thoughts, he tried to cover his feelings with evasion.

"I've been reading one of your things as a matter of fact," he said, indicating the upturned novel with his sherry glass.

Deville's face flushed with pride. "I'm so very honoured, Sir James. One of my more elaborate plots, I see."

Ravenwood thought it prudent not to comment. "Might I ask what the R.P stands for?"

"Roderick Pettigrew, sir," replied R.P. Deville. "I chose to use the initials to add mystery about myself. A stupid idea, I see now, but it seemed like a good one at the time. A mystery about the author as well as about the stories."

"And you're working on a new caper at the moment, are you?" asked Ravenwood.

Deville nodded. "It's set in an apparently haunted mansion, which is why I thought of Warlock's Gate."

Ravenwood frowned. "We're not haunted, you know."

Deville laughed. "No, that part will be added colour from my own head. No, no, I thought Warlock's Gate's history might be of some use to me, that's all."

Ravenwood knew now what was behind Deville's request for an interview. "You are referring to Abraham Dyer, of course."

Deville's voice lowered. "Do you believe he was a black magician?"

"I think he believed it."

"So did his peers, did they not? They burned him after all."

Ravenwood had walked to the window of the library and pointed out over the extensive lawns of the grounds. "In the adjacent field yonder, if you are prepared to accept such things. There is no actual evidence of the burning."

Deville joined his host. "Forgive me, Sir James, but your reputation suggests that you yourself are more inclined to believe such things than the average gentleman. I am looking forward to being shown your little black museum, for example," he added, his voice heavy with suggestion.

"I enjoy the romance of the occult, of myths, legends, and folklore," replied Ravenwood. "That is different entirely to believing it."

"The name of the house, though," persisted the author, "suggests that Dyer was a warlock, surely. It would be irrelevant otherwise, wouldn't it?"

Ravenwood smiled. "It might suggest equally that Abraham Dyer was a man with a sense of humour and a talent for self-advertisement. That uncertainty is what I find so fascinating. In a similar vein, have you ever heard of Baron Tethran of Lamianbad?"

Deville was not a man who enjoyed confessing his ignorance. "I seem to recall the name."

If Ravenwood was fooled by this ambiguous display of knowledge, he did not show it. "He was a marauding, dissolute nobleman of the last century. A profane villain, a man who lived only for the excesses of life. More than that, he was widely believed to have been a vampire. Whether you believe such a thing or not is immaterial, Mr Deville, because what truly matters is that the people who murdered Tethran believed it. So much so that they plunged a jewel-handled, serrated knife into his heart."

The author's eyes glittered with excitement. "They staked him?"

"Right you are, my boy."

"And what is the connection to Abraham Dyer?"

Ravenwood shrugged his head. "None at all, except to show that whether a thing is true or not is secondary to whether it is captivating in its possibilities. I am much more interested in whether Dyer could have been a warlock or whether Tethran might have been a vampire than whether either of them actually were those things. For that reason, I bought Dyer's house and I bought the dagger which was plunged into Tethran's breast."

"You mean you have the dagger here?" stammered Deville.

"It is the latest addition to my black museum, as you called it."

"This sort of detail and perspective is exactly the sort of colour I need for my book," enthused the author, his cheeks filled with a crimson excitement.

Ravenwood seemed not to have noticed the effect of his boasting on the younger man. "As a matter of fact, Deville, there's something I should tell you. Before you got in touch with me about this research of yours, I had already invited some people over for the weekend to see the dagger. A sort of unveiling party, if you will. I hope you don't mind but you will have to fit in with it all. Not a problem, I trust?"

Deville was unable to suppress a snort of satisfied laughter. "Of course not, Sir James. It will be enthralling in itself and, you know, it might prove to be excellent inspiration. I only hope I will not be in the way."

Despite himself, Ravenwood found that he was warming to the fulsome eagerness of the young man. He patted him on the shoulder. "Good man. Treat the place as your own, of course. If you want some peace and quiet for your scribbling, Fenton can find you a quiet corner of the place, I have no doubt. Speaking of Fenton, shall I call him and he can show you to your room?"

"If you please, Sir James. I think a splash of water on the back of the neck and across the face would be welcome. The journey was rather tiring."

Ravenwood touched the bell. There was only the smallest of delays before Fenton escorted Deville out of the library, leaving the baronet alone. He poured a second sherry for himself and sat back down in one of the leather armchairs. He picked up Deville's novel once more. Somehow, having met the author, his previous prejudices seemed to evaporate. The unlikely complexities of the plot now seemed to intrigue rather than irritate and, for almost an hour, Sir James Ravenwood found himself lost in the dark mysteries of murder.

Chapter Two

Jack Truscott stepped off the train onto the small platform of the country station and breathed deeply. The country air was crisp and fresh, its coolness seizing his lungs with an unexpected chill. As if afraid that the air was too clean for his health, or perhaps to provide himself with some comfort and security, Truscott lit a cigarette and inhaled. He watched the steam of the departing engine merge with the smoke from his mouth until both had dispersed into the air.

The station was one of those quaint, provincial buildings which give the immediate impression of efficiency whilst simultaneously reminding a weary traveller that he is as far from the city as he might wish to be. It was workmanlike, consisting only of those features which were necessary for its existence, without any superfluous embellishment. The platform was only as long as it needed to be and the ticket office was perfunctory but competent, only selling tickets and offering advice on times of the services which pass through it. There was no waiting room and no refreshment facilities. Truscott doubted that the traffic through the station was sufficient to make either necessary or worth the expense. The surrounding countryside was so impressive, however, that the size of the station might have been a deliberate attempt not to offend it. The hills rolled towards the horizon, their greens and browns both vibrant and refreshing after the grey slates of the town, and the winding roads which decorated them were untouched by modern conveniences. It struck Truscott that the roads and lanes might not have looked any different to his Neolithic ancestors than they did to him. It was a fanciful thought, but one which he found impossible to resist amid the natural beauty of the landscape. Despite the chill in the air, the sky was blue and without any blemish of cloud, which increased Truscott's impression that the scenery had been untouched for centuries and every effort had been made to limit any interference with it.

In other circumstances, Truscott would have been enamoured with the little hamlet of Vale Thorn, but even its undoubted charm was incapable of entirely alleviating his mood. Perhaps it was the isolation of the place which emphasised his own feelings of loneliness. Or it might simply have been that those feelings were still capable of haunting him and that no amount of England's pleasant land could lift them. It had been a year since Jane had died and yet, in his darker moments, Truscott could feel the loss as acutely now as he had on the day when she had left him. The illness had been long and cruel but, with the unreasonable selfishness of those who are left behind, Truscott had felt it was nothing compared to the pain of having to survive without the woman he had loved.

The months which followed Jane's death remained blurred in his memory. They had been soaked in alcohol, the pain only ever temporarily numbed by the glasses of wine and whisky, to the extent that Truscott had begun to lose all sense of himself. There had been no diverting him from his course of self-destruction, certainly not in those initial months of despair, and any attempt to do so had been viewed as unwanted interference and treated accordingly by him. He had been unable to realise that his conduct was isolating him from those who cared about him and, looking back, he doubted he would have cared even if he had been able to realise it. His increasing reliance on alcohol had become severe enough to ensure that his perception was suitably distorted not to care about any attempt to help him. Now, looking at the countryside which surrounded him, Truscott could contemplate his past with a sober clarity and he could appreciate how close he had come to ruin.

Surprisingly, it had been Jane's mother who had saved him from himself. Until the death of her daughter, Mrs Evelyn Addison had not been impressed with her daughter's choice of prospective husband. She was a woman whose opinion of herself was rather higher than it ought to have been, so that the prism through which she viewed others was forever slanted against them. Truscott had not been offended by Mrs Addison's derisory opinion of him, because he had understood very swiftly that her assessment of anybody who was not landed gentry like herself or, preferably, undeniably aristocratic would have been unfavourable. A journalist who specialised in crime was never likely to meet Mrs Addison's expectations of a suitable man for her daughter and, when faced with a losing battle, Truscott knew well enough not to engage in the fight. Instead, he satisfied himself that Mrs Addison would raise no serious objection to the marriage as long as she understood and could see that Jane herself was happy and, in that, Truscott was both willing and able to comply.

Jane's death shifted the focus of Evelyn Addison's relationship with Jack Truscott. She had never explicitly said as much, but Truscott thought that his obvious pain at the loss of his bride might have demonstrated to Evelyn the depth of his love and devotion to Jane. He might not have expected her to change her opinion of him, and to presume to do so would have been too arrogant for Truscott's nature, but he knew that Evelyn had come to realise what her daughter had meant to him and, perhaps for that alone, she had begun to view him with less distaste.

"You need to clean yourself up, Jack," she had said on that day when his life had changed. She had taken his hand in hers, a gesture of uncommon tenderness, and one which had surprised but not offended him. "I know how hard it is," Evelyn had continued. "God help us, we both know better than anyone how it feels to have lost her, but we have to keep hold of ourselves."

In retrospect, his reply had been unwarranted. "You find it that easy to let her go, do you, Evelyn?"

If she had been offended, and he failed to see how she could not have been, she did not show it. "We may never entirely have been at ease with each other, Jack, but I have no wish to see you kill yourself. And nor would Jane."

It had been those words, coming after a pertinent pause, which had cut deepest. He had not come to a decision to clean up his life in that precise moment, but those words had lingered in his memory and they had refused to dislodge themselves from his conscience. Over the coming weeks, they had soured the taste of the whisky, they had sickened his desire for wine, and they had shamed him out of bed in the mornings. Gradually, Truscott dragged himself out of his misery, out of the peculiar apathy which only grief can produce, and he had begun to see the world in colours more vivid than the blacks and greys of his own mind. Evelyn had not said anything to him about his progress, but when he learned that he had not lost his job on the paper as a result of her discussions with the editor, he came to appreciate the depth of debt which he owed to her.

"I know what you've done for me, Evelyn," he had said to her on one of their lunches together. "I don't want you to think I don't appreciate it."

She had not replied, but she had poured him more tea. It was sufficient acknowledgement.

"I miss her," he had said. "I would hate for you to think I don't."

"I don't think anything of the sort." She had watched him drink the tea. "Are you feeling fully recovered?"

He had shrugged his shoulders. "How does one know that? I know that I can look at a glass of wine and not feel it consume me. I know that I can look at photographs of Jane, read her letters, remember her voice, and not want to throw myself into oblivion. Does that mean I am fully recovered?"

"I think it is a start," Evelyn had said. And then: "Have you ever heard of a place called Warlock's Gate?"

It had stirred something of a memory inside him. "Owned by an occultist, is it not?"

Evelyn had clucked her tongue in disgust. "Sir James is not an occultist. He is a historian and a collector."

"Of some fairly odd things, if rumour is to be believed."

She had dabbed the corners of her mouth with her napkin. "His tastes are somewhat esoteric, no doubt, but he is a thoroughly charming man."

"You mean to say that you know him?"

"Socially," she had replied. "Well enough to know that he is hosting a weekend at Warlock's Gate for a select number of people. He has acquired a new piece for his museum and he is having some sort of informal unveiling of it."

"Sounds fascinating," Truscott had said without irony.

"I am pleased you think so, because I have secured you an invitation."

"Evelyn—"

"Don't argue, Jack. The country air, the surroundings, and the company of others will do you the world of good. It might even complete the recovery which you have begun so well."

"I don't want to spend my weekend with strangers, Evelyn. Thank you and all that, but I don't think I can face it."

She had been silent for a moment, her eyes drifting out of the restaurant window into the traffic outside, her lips quivering despite her efforts to control them. Then, she had looked back at him and her words had come very softly, yet earnestly, to him. "Please, Jack, go."

All of which was why he was standing at Vale Thorn railway station, breathing in cold but refreshing air, and admiring the hills and iced peaks which rose above him.

He finished his cigarette and picked up his luggage. Slowly, without much enthusiasm but not entirely without purpose, he walked out of the station and onto the small road which stretched out away from the small, brick building. He had been assured of a ride from the station, presumably courtesy of Sir James Ravenwood's driver, but there was no sign of any delivery of the promise at present. Truscott wondered what he was supposed to do, balancing the unsatisfactory choice of walking and missing the car or waiting indefinitely for it to arrive, when the voice behind him startled him out of his deliberations.

"You are a little out of your way, surely, Mr Truscott?"

He turned to find himself staring at a familiar face. It had aged, without question, from the last time Truscott had seen it but he found it impossible not to recognise the sharpness of the dark eyes which stared out at him under the heavy, grey brows. The moustache and Imperial beard had been as black as the eyes the last time Truscott had seen them, but now they were white, although it seemed to Truscott that the change was not caused by age, because the man could have been only a few years over his fiftieth. Truscott wondered whether it was a specific experience rather than natural progression of age which had changed the man's appearance. Something of Truscott's own sadness returned to him and, whether touched by it or not, Truscott felt sure he could see some tragedy behind the darkness of those eyes which now glared at him. The man was carrying a cane and he walked with a defined limp, something which Truscott did not remember seeing before, and he found himself wondering whether the whitening of the beard and the tragedy in the eyes was linked to whatever injury had been suffered to the leg. Having noticed these differences in the man, Truscott was struck almost immediately afterwards by those aspects which were as familiar as the changes were alien. The black suit was still immaculate and the matching tie and handkerchief were still so vibrant in their contrasting brightness as to be almost gaudy by comparison. The expensive grey gloves matched the band of ribbon around the base of the hat, which was set at a reassuringly familiar angle on the head. These touches convinced Truscott that he could be assured of the presence beneath the heavy, fur-lined overcoat of the watch chain across the man's stomach and the ruby-eyed skull pin fixed into the button hole of the jacket's left lapel.

Truscott shook the man by the hand. "Good Lord, Mr Carr, what are you doing here?"

Everett Carr smiled, stretching the moustache and Imperial. "I rather thought I had asked you that question."

Truscott stammered an apology. "You're the last person I should have expected to meet in this out of the way place."

Carr smiled warmly. "Are you not impressed by the solitude and beauty of it? I suppose it does not concur with your journalist's practical and urban mind."

Truscott smiled, but there was very little happiness behind it. "I've not done much journalistic work recently, Mr Carr."

Carr lowered his head discreetly. "No. I had gathered as much."

"How?"

"Your name disappeared from the pages of the newspapers. Even to an old man like me, such things do not go unnoticed."

Despite himself, Truscott smiled. Carr's reference to his age was nothing more than a self-deprecating exaggeration. Like the darkness of the eyes, it was a familiar, almost comforting trait which recalled itself to Truscott.

"Do you still sit on the Bench, sir?" he asked.

Carr shook his head. "I have retired."

"I remember covering many of your trials."

"To return the compliment, I remember you doing so."

"You were always good copy for us. Does that sound grossly cynical?"

"It does," smiled Carr, the moustache bristling with amusement. "But I am happy to have been in the spotlight. Barristers and judges are all failed actors, don't you know?"

Truscott offered no reply. "And yet you have turned your back on it all?"

"I had my reasons. As I presume you did for abandoning your own life."

"I lost my wife," Truscott said, surprising himself more than Carr with its suddenness. Then, as if conscious of his potential indiscretion, he added: "I'm sorry, I don't know why I said that so bluntly."

Carr placed a hand on his arm, the fingers slowly and gently applying a comforting pressure. "Life can be cruel."

Truscott had no wish to dwell on his own misery. He pointed to Carr's cane. "It seems to have been painful to you too."

Carr waved away any suggestion of offence. "As I say, life can be cruel. For us both, it seems, because of a woman we loved," he added, giving a brief smile, of which his eyes did not seem to approve.

Feeling a need to change the subject, Truscott let out a breath of air. "I assume you are heading to Warlock's Gate, Mr Carr. I can't see any other reason for you to be standing here with me."

"And I cannot deny it," said Carr, giving a slight bow of his head. "But I had no idea you knew Sir James Ravenwood sufficiently well to receive an invitation to his gathering."

"And I don't," replied Truscott. "I'm here because someone thinks I need a break from myself."

Everett Carr did not reply, nor did he look into the eyes of Jack Truscott. His response was simply to smile to himself and give a delicate hum of understanding from under his moustache. There might have been more to be said, but they were denied the opportunity by the late arrival of a Lagonda and the apologies of the chauffeur as he jumped down to the road to greet them.

Chapter Three

"He will be there, Richard, that's all that matters."

"That doesn't mean he's going to do anything."

Alicia Ravenwood pulled herself out of his arms and twisted herself towards the edge of the bed. As if conscious of her nakedness for the first time during their lovemaking, she pulled part of the bedsheet around her slim frame. She was aware of the chill of the room and she suspected that it was exacerbated by the cold fear which seized her spine.

Richard Prentice sat up in the bed and kissed his fiancée's shoulder. She tensed at the touch but Prentice barely registered her response. "He's going because your dear papa has invited him. It's to do with this knife your father has bought. We won't be foremost in Lynch's mind, my darling, I promise you."

Alicia twisted her neck, so that she was looking at him over her shoulder. Her eyes were fierce, so evidently hostile that they presented a harsh contrast to the intimacy of the promise of the naked shoulder. "Don't make me promises you cannot keep, Richard."

Prentice sighed. He shifted his position so that he was sitting next to her on the bed. He did not bother with the propriety of concealing his dignity. Alicia forced herself not to look at his natural state, however much she admired and desired it. As if in a reaction against it, she pulled the sheet tighter against herself.

"We have to face facts, darling," said Prentice. "We have to be there because of your father, so we have very little choice on that front. And we have no control over who he invites or does not. So, you see, we're rather stuck

17

between Scylla and Charybdis."

"We are trapped," spat Alicia. "That's what you're saying, isn't it, Richard? We have to suffer Daddy's weekend, always wondering if Lynch is either to torture us further or to expose us."

"We have to roll the dice," said Prentice. "Think about it. Would Lynch want to embarrass himself when he's so close to your father?"

She considered his words with the sulky petulance of the young when they have heard common sense but refuse to want to accept it because doing so proves them wrong. At last, she gave a slight nod of her head and wiped away a stray tear from her delicate cheek. She rose from the bed and slipped on a silk dressing gown. Declaring she was going downstairs to make some tea, she left the room.

There was something comforting in the process of boiling the kettle, filling the pot, and assembling the tray. It could not entirely erase her anxiety, but it seemed somehow to alleviate its pressure. She took the tray into the sitting room and sat down. Richard had not followed her downstairs and she was grateful for the temporary solitude. They had been together for over a year now, but the passage of time had seemed to her to be a mere fraction of itself. From their initial meeting at the party of a mutual friend, she had found Richard Prentice captivating. There was something exciting about him, a knife blade of danger behind the charming smile, and Alicia had never experienced anything like it. The young men who had attended dinners and functions at Warlock's Gate in the past had been attractive in their own fashion but they were beyond anaemic in the wake of any comparison with Richard Prentice. His dark hair and the coldness of his blue eyes were intoxicating in themselves but they seemed to reflect the sense of iced danger which so stimulated her. Her parents had disapproved, but they had not forbidden the match. Alicia supposed they had reasoned that she would make her own mistakes and they would be obliged to pick up the shattered pieces of her heart at a later date; or it might have been the knowledge that she would only have moved closer to him if they had in any way sought to keep her away from him. Whatever the truth, they had not interfered. That was not to say that Richard had been welcome at Warlock's Gate. Far from it; he was accepted with typical but suffering politeness by both Sir James and Lady Ravenwood. Alicia could not fail to wish that matters were different, naturally, but she was sensible enough to allow them to continue as they were, not least because the alternative was impossible to contemplate.

Alicia poured some tea. It was strong, hot, and soothing. For a moment, she consoled herself with it, freeing her mind of those shadows which had plagued it for the past few months. Her memory of that night her life soured was twisted now, but she knew that she had been laughing at a party, drinking champagne and dancing without care, when Sebastian Lynch had approached her. He had been smiling at her, but it was more sinister than ingratiating, the beads of sweat on his temples making him look even more unpleasant. He had smelled of whisky and cigars when he had talked to her, his mouth uncomfortably close to her ear. Even now, she felt she could smell his breath close to her, just as she felt she could hear his words hissing on the air between them.

Richard Prentice broke in on her thoughts. "Is there enough in the pot for me?"

Alicia found herself grateful for the interruption and she smiled up at him. She poured him a cup of the tea and he sat down opposite her. "Are you all right, Alicia?"

She allowed him a smile. He reached out a hand and she took it, the fingers tightening around his own. It was enough of a reply for him. Alicia bit her lip. As if sensing that she had something important to say to him, Prentice leaned forward in his chair.

"I should never have started it," Alicia said. "I must stop it. It's bad enough Lynch knowing about it, but if anybody else found out it could finish us."

"Everything will be all right." Prentice's words were seriously spoken.

"I can't live like this anymore, Richard." Her tears were free from their prisons now and her voice broke into violent sobs.

Prentice got up slowly from the table and moved across to her. His arms were around her in an instant and she found herself melting into them. He allowed her to cry herself into silence before he released her. Then, kneeling in front of her, his cold eyes like diamonds, he straightened her hair, brushing a lock around her ear.

"Don't worry about Lynch, my lovely," he whispered. "He won't trouble us anymore."

When Alicia Ravenwood looked into the eyes of her lover, she thought she could recognise the cold glare of determination. Gently, slowly, she began to weep once more.

Chapter Four

Sebastian Lynch knew what would be inside the package even before he cut the string which was tied around it.

It had arrived on the morning of the day on which Lynch intended to travel down to Warlock's Gate. It was the third package of its kind which he had received. The packages had all been similarly plain, ordinary cardboard boxes. Inside each of them, there had been a layer of tissue paper, as if the contents of the parcels were of extreme value and importance. They never were, and Lynch had come to expect as much. The contents were always the same: a small, wooden figure, carved into a simplistic representation of the human form. Smooth limbs, narrow shoulders, with no particular detail to the torso and abdomen nor any discernible facial features. None, of course, other than the painted image which had been applied to the carved head of the figure. The image was crude, but there was no mistaking what it was meant to represent. The entire head of the figure had been painted white, with a pair of black circles applied as eyes and two smaller black spots representing a nasal cavity. The teeth were designated by a horizontal line across the bottom half of the face, with smaller vertical lines running across it at regular intervals. Rudimentary, perhaps, but there was no scope for mistake. It was a death's head: a skull.

The painted, skeletal face was not the only suggestion of death. Around the necks of each of the dolls, there had been a small length of cord, fashioned into a noose, the excess length of cord hanging loosely down the figure's wooden back. There had never been any note. It was as if the dolls were supposed to speak for themselves and, for his own part, Sebastian Lynch had felt that no further words were necessary.

He was sure he could recognise a death threat when he received one.

It was not simply the dolls. There had been the telephone calls which he had received which had consisted of nothing more than breathing down the line or, very often, the sound of sobbing. Then there had been the time when he had returned to his Daimler after dinner to discover what he thought was acid had been thrown across the bonnet. The paint had blistered and split, the damage being both extensive and expensive. As a campaign against him, it had never approached actual physical violence, but there was something about the deliberate malice behind it which struck Lynch as more dangerous than any physical attack. It was as if the suggestion of malevolence, and now of actual death, was more unnerving than a confrontation in a dark alley. Lynch felt he would be able to handle any direct confrontation in the shadows. He was not a cowardly man and he had never been a man who was afraid to take on any enemy. But when the enemy was unknown and the motives unclear, Lynch was not able to act and this inability to control the situation frustrated him as much as the threats against him had unsettled him.

There was never any indication of the identity of the culprit. The postmarks on the packages were never from the same location and, when he enquired at the telephone exchange, he discovered that the anonymous calls had come from public boxes on street corners and in different public houses across London. It could hardly have come as a surprise to Lynch. He had not expected to discover anything from his enquiries. Anonymous callers and poison pens were not prone to leaving clues to their identities. What Lynch had not anticipated, however, was how much more acute these failed investigations would make his fear. Whenever he walked around London, passing telephone box after telephone box, or pillar box after pillar box, he wondered whether any one of those boxes had been used to further this persecution against him. Worse, he began to wonder whether any of the people he passed on the street, or sat beside on the train, or stood next to at a public house bar was the one responsible for his anxiety and fear.

In his moments of clearer thought, Sebastian Lynch knew that the likelihood was that his torment was the work of someone closer to him than a stranger in the street. It had to be true: strangers did not tend to plague other strangers. The reason for these nuisances which had now elevated their danger to almost certain threats of death had to lie in some personal vendetta. Lynch was not a man who felt able to lie to himself and, as a result, he had to confess that there were many people who might consider themselves to have a personal reason to do him harm. Whether he could imagine any of them undertaking this campaign against him seemed to Lynch to be something of a vexed question. What mattered to him was that one of them had begun to persecute him and, for that, Lynch demanded some retribution. He was not a man who allowed any challenge to go unheeded.

Lynch took the latest doll out of its tissue paper shroud and stared at it. Identical to the other two, down to the noose around the neck and the painted skull. For a moment, Lynch allowed his thoughts to accumulate and the memories of the six months which had elapsed since the torture began to swell within his mind. His initial scorn, his developing fear, and his intensifying sense of futility against it all came back to him, as if the last half year had been played over again at increased speed. So intense were the recollections that his reaction to them could not have been any less violent. He squeezed the doll in his hands and finally, with a roar of outrage, he threw it across the room. It struck a shaving mirror, dislodging it from the chest of drawers upon which it stood, so that it fell onto the floor with a clatter, the delicate tinkling of the broken glass seeming somehow anticlimactic after the ferocity of Lynch's gesture. Ignoring the mess, he strode out of the room and slammed the door behind him.

For the remainder of the morning, he went about his business and attempted to put the whole business out of his thoughts. He was not entirely successful, even in his own mind, until he was in the Daimler and was leaving the greys of London behind him. He drove at speed, as was his wont, but not with any invitation of danger, and he found himself enjoying the rolling hills of the country suburbs which raced past him. He was not a sentimental man, but he could not fail to be impressed by the change in both the landscape and the air. It was a reminder to him that he should leave

London more frequently in the future. It was too simple to allow oneself to become trapped by the city, to forget that a world existed beyond its limits. Only when the green shrubs and the tapestries of the fields beyond London were stretched out into the distance could somebody like Lynch appreciate what the poets meant when they talked about a green and pleasant land.

As he drove, Lynch thought back to the telephone call which had resulted in his motor ride to Warlock's Gate. It had come through one afternoon and it had been both unexpected and entirely welcome. Lynch had been acquainted with Sir James Ravenwood for several months now. He doubted either man would be presumptuous enough to call it a friendship, but it was amicable and it was based on a mutual respect.

"How are you, Sir James?" Lynch had asked. "I trust all is well with you."

"I have got it, Lynch." The baronet had been almost adolescent in its excitement. "They accepted the price."

"The Tethran Dagger?" Lynch's voice had been hoarse with enthusiasm but he spoke with sincerity. "I congratulate you, sir. I cannot say that I am not envious, but I salute you."

"Thank you, my dear fellow! You must come down to Warlock's Gate for a celebration. I am having a weekend party, old lad. Friends and family. Call it a celebration and an unveiling! And, of course, as a fellow collector, I would very much like you to be there, Lynch."

If Lynch had suspected there was any degree of gloating behind the invitation, he had not expressed it and, looking back now, he doubted he would have resented it. He was fully able to understand the collector's desire to show off his treasures. He was able to understand it, because he suffered from it himself. Had their roles been reversed, Lynch doubted he would have been able to resist making the very same telephone call to Ravenwood, which he had made to Lynch. And so, he had accepted the invitation.

Almost as soon as Ravenwood had mentioned Lynch visiting Warlock's Gate, the idea that Alicia Ravenwood and Richard Prentice would also be there had come into Lynch's mind. He had not allowed it to linger for very long. Lynch felt secure about his position, so much so that he allowed himself a small, satisfied smile. It occurred to him that Prentice might be behind the dolls. It was the sort of cowardly attack a man like him would launch. If his idea was correct, Lynch would make it his business to find out and the weekend visit to Warlock's Gate would provide him with the prime opportunity to find out.

And to do something about it, if required.

Chapter Five

Truscott had settled in and unpacked before he decided to investigate the grounds of Warlock's Gate. He had been struck by the size of the estate as he and Carr were driven up the winding pathway which led from the front gates and the groundkeeper's lodge up to the gothic mansion itself. Now, he walked down the landing from his room to the main stairway and jogged down the stairs into the hallway. There was nobody about and Truscott allowed himself a moment to enjoy the splendour of it. The chessboard floor was striking without being ostentatious and the oak panels which lined the walls were rich in colour and effect. The portraits which hung above them, most of them being of Ravenwood's ancestors, peered down with aristocratic pride, the features reserved rather than arrogant.

Truscott opened the front door of the house and stepped onto the front terrace. He walked to the left, following the structure of the house. Turning a corner which took him along the east wing of the house, he passed a series of broad windows, each looking out onto the terrace along which he now walked. From the brief, discreet glances into each of the rooms he passed, he could see that he was passing the library, the drawing room and, finally, the room which he knew was Sir James Ravenwood's private museum. As he reached the back of the house, the terrace opened up into a large patio, upon which there was a set of garden furniture and a small series of stone steps which led down onto the lawns themselves. From here, Truscott could see a folly set onto a small knoll surrounded by imposing and dense oaks. Separated from the folly by a summerhouse, there was a stone fountain set on a disc of gravel and fringed with brightly coloured flowers whose identities were unknown to him. It was idyllic, a place almost beyond time, and Truscott had the distinct impression that he was as far away from the city as he could ever remember being and farther out of his own existence than he had ever felt.

"Admiring the view?"

The voice was a woman's, but it was deep and luxuriant. Truscott turned to greet it and discovered that it belonged to a girl of extraordinary beauty. Her hair was very dark, almost black, reminding Truscott of raven's wings. Her features were suitably delicate to complement the colour, but the eyes were the deepest green which Truscott had ever seen. The contrast served to give her an exotic mystery which it seemed impossible to solve. She was smoking a cigarette and her eyes squinted at him through the smoke. It was a gently mocking stare, interested without being insolent, but with sufficient control of itself not to encourage any unnecessary optimism on his part.

"It's beautiful," Truscott said. "I've never been anywhere like it."

The girl, smiling, came to stand beside him. "It once belonged to a necromancer, you know."

"Abraham Dyer, yes."

"You've done your research."

Truscott shrugged. "Occupational habit. I'm a journalist," he added by way of explanation. He held out his hand and she took it with a cool but elegant grip. "Jack Truscott."

"Helena Garrick," said the girl. "Don't tell me you've come to do a story on Sir James and his collection of morbid curiosities."

"Is that how you see his museum?"

"Exhibiting instruments of torture, pieces of the clothes of dead women, ghoulish relics of past executions - what would you call it?" She did not give him time to reply. "You know why we're all invited this weekend, don't you? So that Sir James can show off a knife which was said to have staked a vampire in the early Victorian era."

"You sound scornful."

She smiled at him. "I don't share my host's taste for the lurid and the macabre, Mr Truscott."

He breathed in some of the afternoon air. "I'm surprised you bothered accepting the invitation."

She laughed. "I always accept a Ravenwood invitation. I've been coming here since I was a little girl. Alicia Ravenwood and I are old friends. None of which means I have to like the chamber of horrors, but the food and wine are never to be missed."

Her laugh was infectious. It was harsh, husky without being obscene, but it was so genuine that it reached the dark eyes and seemed to warm them. Truscott found he was unable to resist complimenting it with laughter of his own.

"You're a friend of the family?" he asked.

"Of Alicia, particularly," she said, with a nod of her head. Then, when she saw that the name was unfamiliar to him: "The daughter. What about you, Mr Truscott?"

He wondered for a moment how to reply. It would be inappropriate to tell her the full truth of his reason for being there; somehow, it seemed to him to be a betrayal of himself to explain his grief to a stranger, no matter how attractive she was. He became conscious suddenly that he was not speaking and his silence seemed to be demanding further explanation.

"I'm here for a rest," he said. It seemed a compromise without being an untruth. "Clear the old head."

"Overwork?"

"Over-indulgence."

She might have said something else, but for a long moment, she simply stared at him. He wondered what she thought of the face which looked back at her. Could she see the recent past in the broken veins in his eyes? Could she detect something of his unhappiness in the pale cheeks? Or would she see beneath the effects of his period of self-destruction and see the man he hoped he was underneath?

If Helena Garrick was ever going to explain what she saw in his face, or what she felt about him, it was not to be in that moment. A man had approached them and, instinctively, Truscott had resented the intrusion. The man was older than either of them, it seemed to Truscott, but only by a few years. A little closer to his middle forties than earlier, possibly, but he was undeniably a handsome man. His hair was dark, swept back from an intelligent forehead, the eyes a clear, almost transparent blue. He was dressed in a dark suit, the tie precisely tied at his throat, a scarlet thread of elegance against the black of the jacket and waistcoat beneath it. He was smoking a pipe, the stem clenched between regular and well-kept teeth which were exposed by the lips being stretched into a smile.

"Hello, Helena," said the man. "Early afternoon stroll?"

"Idling away the time until dinner, Dr Gilchrist."

The doctor looked at Truscott. "I hope she's not maligning our host too much."

"Not at all," replied Truscott. He introduced himself.

Dr John Gilchrist accepted the offered hand and shook it with a firm, determined grip. "Welcome to Warlock's Gate."

"Have we met before, Doctor?" asked Truscott.

"I don't believe so."

"I could have sworn it…"

Truscott said the words aloud but they were meant only for himself. When he looked back to the doctor's face, the feeling of recognition was even more acute. Gilchrist was watching him carefully, the blue eyes darkening with something which Truscott could only say was concern.

"I would have remembered," said the doctor, finally. "I've a fine memory for faces, Mr Truscott."

"Perhaps I'm mistaken."

"Must be," smiled Gilchrist. And then, with rather more speed than seemed entirely natural, as if the subject needed to be changed as soon as possible, he said: "Come to see the Tethran Dagger, Truscott?"

"The what?"

Gilchrist gestured aimlessly with his pipe. "This new knife Sir James has spent a ridiculous amount of money on. Said to have dispatched a blood-sucker."

Truscott was nodding. "I've heard about that but, no, I've not come here especially for it."

"I hope you don't expect to escape Sir James' unveiling ceremony tomorrow night." Gilchrist laughed to himself. "Precious little chance of that."

"I think I'll find it rather interesting," confessed Truscott.

"The first experience often is," replied the doctor. "After a while, you get a little tired of them. Likes talking about himself, old Sir James, but likes talking about his collection of murder trophies even more. Am I right, Helena?"

Helena Garrick was smiling, but it was obvious to Truscott that she was merely tolerating the presence of the doctor. "Don't be obnoxious, John. It's too early in the day for it. Let's at least have the benefit of a couple of drinks inside us before you begin all that."

Gilchrist was laughing but he obeyed her. He walked to the low balustrade which lined the terrace and perched himself on the end of it. "Is Alicia bringing that dreadful fiancé of hers, Helena?"

"You could hardly expect her to do otherwise."

Gilchrist looked at Truscott. "Richard Prentice is a chancer, Mr Truscott. The sort of man who would happily drink champagne all day without ever being able to afford it. Wants to be a member of the elite, but he's never quite sure which way to pass the port."

Truscott felt it prudent to remain silent. Helena, as if sensing his unease, hissed a warning to the doctor. "You're embarrassing Mr Truscott."

"I'm only speaking the truth. You may be right though. We should watch our step this weekend."

"Why is that?" asked Truscott.

"There's a damned detective novelist in our midst. Down here doing a spot of research for a book, apparently. I can't see what sort of research a detective story writer can need to do. I would have thought it was simply a case of making up a poison nobody's ever heard of, ensuring your detective is too eccentric to be credible, and starting to tap away on the typewriter. What do you say, Helena?"

It seemed she had nothing to say in return.

"Who is it?" asked Truscott.

"You will have heard of him. R.P Deville."

Truscott's eyebrows raised. "I've heard of him, but I've never read any of the books."

"I've read a couple of them," said Helena. "Cleverly done, rather well written, too. And I didn't guess the killer."

"It must take a tortuous mind to work out plots like those," said Gilchrist. His manner had soured significantly, his voice lowering and his eyes hardening. "Murder is hardly a topic for entertainment."

"I tend to agree," said Truscott.

"Know something about murder, do you?" asked the doctor.

"I know enough." Truscott fell silent. He became conscious of Gilchrist staring at him and he felt some sort of qualification of his agreement was required. "I'm a journalist, a crime reporter."

Gilchrist kept his gaze on Truscott. There was something in his eyes, a glimmer of suspicion or possibly even fear, a flicker only perhaps but it was so intense that the smile across the doctor's lips was incapable of extinguishing or even disguising it. Again, Truscott had the impression that the two of them had met before, but the memory refused to surface. It seemed to Truscott that they stared at each other in uncomfortable silence for an unnaturally long period of time. It was as if they were two wild animals circling each other, waiting for the other to strike.

It was Helena who broke the tension. "I think I shall have a walk around the grounds before tea."

Gilchrist checked his watch. "You had better be quick, my girl. You know that Lady Ravenwood likes to have tea promptly."

"If you don't detain me here with aimless warnings any longer, I shall be back in time." She smiled at him briefly and turned her attention back to Truscott. "Nice to have met you."

"And you."

He watched her walk along the terrace in the direction from which she had come. She walked with an easy elegance, as if she knew that he would be watching, and he found himself wondering whether she would look back at him. Whether he wanted her to or not, he was unable to say, but he knew that he could not avert his gaze without knowing for certain whether she would look back or not. As it was, she turned the corner of the terrace with only her own thoughts for company and it seemed that there was no room in those thoughts for Jack Truscott.

"Fascinating woman," Gilchrist said.

Truscott nodded. "Incredibly so. Have you known her long?"

The doctor shook his head. "Only from gatherings like this. She's been friends with Alicia Ravenwood since they were girls. She's as much a part of Warlock's Gate as the family itself."

"Does she live here?"

"No, no. I don't know where she lives." Gilchrist rose to his feet. He began to walk away from Truscott, smiling to himself, as if he knew something which nobody else did. "As you get to know our Helena, Mr Truscott, you'll come to learn that she is not only fascinating, but intensely secretive. I wouldn't like to guess at the skeletons she keeps behind closeted doors."

His smile broke into a laugh as he turned his back on Truscott.

For a long moment, the stranger to Warlock's Gate stood alone. His mind was filled with Helena Garrick and the words of the doctor sang a dark melody in his brain. But his thoughts were not exclusively intoxicated by the girl whom he had met. They were also engrossed with Gilchrist himself. His memory of where he had met the doctor before maintained a stubborn refusal to come into focus in Truscott's mind, but he felt certain that it was not only Helena Garrick who might be keeping dark secrets of the past to herself.

Chapter Six

Sir James Ravenwood pulled off the black silk shroud which hung over the display case and flicked the switch to illuminate the dagger. The light of the small bulb glinted across the broad, serrated blade and the stones in the handle flickered into life like the stars in a clear, night sky. The afternoon had begun to give way to the evening and the darkening sky brought with it an ominous mystery, a sense of foreboding which seemed fitting when examining the blade which it was said had destroyed a supernatural creature. Illuminated by the single, small bulb in the display case, and set against the scarlet velvet cushion upon which it rested, the dagger seemed to convey its own sense of mysticism, which was so acute that the myths behind the blade's history seemed not only more believable than ever but somehow entirely plausible.

Sebastian Lynch was leaning close to the glass case of the exhibit. His eyes burned with admiration but there was also a covetous malice which flickered within them. Ravenwood walked around the display case, the heels of his shoes sounding like thunderclaps in the silence of the room.

"It is magnificent," whispered Lynch. "Flawlessly magnificent."

Ravenwood's voice could not fail to hide his pleasure. "Isn't it, though? I've longed to possess it."

"Do you believe the legend?"

Ravenwood smiled. "I try not to think about it. The magic of something like this is the uncertainty."

"Not to mention the craftsmanship." Lynch's glare was transfixed on the variety of precious stones set into the hilt.

Ravenwood had moved close behind him. "A treasure such as this is beyond any monetary value. As a collector yourself, you must see that."

"That does not prevent one being impressed by the beauty of the piece in its own right."

Ravenwood conceded the point. "Perhaps not."

Lynch was looking around the private museum, taking in its impressive content as a whole. "So many fascinating things. I knew your collection was extensive, Sir James. It is famous for it, of course, but I had no idea it was so remarkable."

Ravenwood made no reply. He was of the breed of collector who prefers the collection itself to speak for him, but there was no disguising the pleasure which Lynch's words had given him.

"With so much at stake, I presume you keep this room well secured," continued Lynch.

"Naturally," replied Ravenwood. "The door is always locked, as are the windows. Only I have a key to this room and I always keep it on my person. Every other room has a spare key, but only I have access to this museum and nobody can get in here without me."

"Then, I am honoured to be allowed in," said Lynch.

Ravenwood laughed. "Anyone can come in with my permission, of course, but I never unveil a new exhibit without a little ceremony. My taste of vanity, you might say. Seeing it before the official unveiling tomorrow night is where you should feel honoured, my dear fellow. As a fellow expert, I felt you deserved the distinction."

Lynch smiled. "Do you suppose very many people share our love of the macabre, Sir James?"

Ravenwood pulled the black silk awning back over the case and turned off the light. "I think people have always been attracted to the darkness in life, whether they like to admit it to themselves or not."

"Perhaps you're right." Lynch found himself thinking about the dolls with their death's heads. "All men have secrets. And all women, come to that."

"Quite so," mumbled Ravenwood, unsure whether there had been a change in tone of the conversation. "Now, my dear fellow, how about a sherry before we change for dinner? There's just enough time."

They walked out of the exhibit room and back into the hallway. Ravenwood took his keys from his pocket and locked the door. They walked across the chequered floor and into the drawing room. After the atmospheric gloom of the museum, the drawing room seemed both cheerful and airy. It was well illuminated, the decorations were bright and inviting, and the hum of polite but sincere laughter greeted them as they entered.

It was a small company which confronted them. Two men sat in armchairs opposite each other and a third was standing by the fireplace. The three of them were drinking sherry. A woman was sitting in the corner of the settee, a cup of tea in her lap. As Ravenwood entered, with Lynch behind him, the company looked up with smiling faces. The seated men rose, one of them pushing himself to his feet with the aid of a cane. Lynch saw at once that the man was lame, but he could tell from the extravagant moustache and the neatly trimmed Imperial beard that mention of the disability would be unwelcome to a man so obviously proud of his appearance. The other was a large, well-built man, whose face was smiling but whose eyes betrayed an internal sadness.

Ravenwood introduced them. "Sebastian Lynch, may I introduce Mr Everett Carr and Jack Truscott."

The lame man with the moustache and beard shook Lynch's hand and gave a slight bow of the head. "How do you do?"

The man named Truscott gripped Lynch's hand with a strong, fierce grip. "Are you down for the unveiling, Mr Lynch?"

It was Ravenwood who replied. "Lynch is a man after my own heart."

"You are a collector, too?" asked Carr.

"I cannot boast to anything as majestic as Sir James' hoard of treasures," replied Lynch. "But I am proud of my own achievements."

Ravenwood was laughing, no doubt at the acknowledgement that his museum was the superior. "This is Miss Louisa Marston. I don't think you have met."

The woman on the settee did not rise. She was a small, meek woman with mouse-coloured hair which hung loosely and untidily around her shoulders.

She could not have been much over forty years of age, but her appearance gave the impression of much more advanced years. Her clothes were plain, her cheeks unfettered by rouge, and her skin so pale that it appeared almost translucent. The effect was so definite that even the small string of pearls around her slim neck seemed too ostentatious for her. Lynch walked over to her and held out his hand. She took it, clutching only the tips of his fingers, as though any further contact might infect her with something venomous.

"I don't believe we have met, Miss Marston," said Lynch.

"No, but I know who you are," stammered the woman.

What she meant by that was not to be learned. Ravenwood was too quick to introduce the third man in the room that any further enquiry was impossible.

"And this is Roderick Deville," said Ravenwood. "You may have read some of his detective novels, Lynch."

"R.P. Deville," said Lynch. The two men did not shake hands. "Yes, we have met before."

"Briefly, and only once," replied the young author.

"And have you read any of his books?" asked Ravenwood. "I am told they are excellent."

Lynch smiled, but it was not welcoming. "Are they indeed? I regret that I have never had the pleasure of reading one of your own books, Mr Deville. You must forgive me."

"Not at all." The young author smiled and his cheeks flushed, but his eyes refused to meet those of the older, more imposing man.

Lynch turned away from him, the smile remaining on his lips. "Who else can we expect this weekend, Ravenwood?"

"My daughter and her fiancé," replied the baronet. "A most unsuitable young man, but one must allow girls to make their own mistakes. At least that's what my dear Mary says."

"Young girls will always be attracted to men of whom their parents disapprove," observed Carr. "If a mother and father were taken by a young man, the young girl concerned would not fall for him in the first instance. The same can be said," he added, by way of qualification, "of young men.

Youth does not discriminate by gender."

Ravenwood was unimpressed by this wisdom. "Be that as it may, Carr, it does nothing for a chap's nerves when he knows his daughter is running around with a gigolo."

Lynch asked in a lowered voice: "Do you know him to be a gigolo?"

"Not exactly," confessed Ravenwood, "but a man has his instincts."

"How true," replied Everett Carr, cryptically.

"And who else can we expect?" asked Truscott. "I've met Dr Gilchrist and Miss Garrick."

"Gilchrist is a fine fellow," said Ravenwood. "A trifle cavalier in his manner, but a decent man. Miss Garrick is a very interesting woman. A friend of my daughter's."

"Dr Gilchrist, I feel I've met before, but I can't place where," said Truscott.

Carr smiled vaguely. "Perhaps you have, dear boy."

Roderick Deville helped himself to another glass of sherry and ran a hand through his unruly hair. "I heard Lady Ravenwood mention an artist also. A Miss Montgomery?"

"Eliza Montgomery," confirmed Ravenwood. "She's coming to view the museum, of course, but I also rather like her work. I thought I might commission a piece from her. A portrait, perhaps."

"So, she is blending business with pleasure, is that right?" asked Lynch.

"Something of the sort." Ravenwood poured sherry for those who accepted the offer.

It was at this moment that Lady Ravenwood stepped into the room, with a welcoming smile on her distinguished features. It had been some time since Carr had seen her but, as ever, he was struck by the elegance of her beauty. Sir James strode to the door to greet her, kissing her on the cheek with such devotion that it was clear to Carr that her husband was as aware still of her allure.

"My darling, come and have a glass of sherry," he said. "There is somebody I would like you to meet."

"I only came in to tell you, James, that Alicia and Richard have arrived."

Ravenwood dismissed the news with a wave of his hand. "They can look after each other for now. Come, let me introduce you to our new guest."

Allowing her no time to protest further, Ravenwood led his wife into the room. She was smiling, her eyes drifting around the room, as if seeing her guests assembled was a comfort to her or, just possibly, a matter of pride. Her husband was talking to her, but it seemed to Carr that she was hearing none of his words. Instead, she was consumed by indulging her own natural desire to entertain. Carr watched her glide around the assembled company, nodding further greetings to those guests whom she had already welcomed.

"And this, my dear," said Ravenwood, "is a professional rival of mine but, I hope, no less a friend for that, Mr Sebastian Lynch."

"It's a pleasure to meet you, Lady Ravenwood," said Lynch. "Sir James has often spoken of you, although he did not prepare me to meet such a beautiful woman." He bent forward and kissed her hand.

"You're very kind, Mr Lynch. And welcome to Warlock's Gate."

"I am very pleased I came, Lady Ravenwood."

She smiled briefly, removing her hand from the clasp of Lynch's own, and turned to her husband. "James, I think I should go and see Alicia."

"Of course."

She gave one more smile to the room before announcing that dinner would be served at eight o'clock. "But we shall have cocktails beforehand and I trust you will all be ready for one."

There was a general murmur of consent and, as if to seal the pact, Deville poured himself a third glass of sherry.

"Your wife is extremely beautiful, Ravenwood," said Lynch. "With an elegance too lacking in girls today."

"She's the greatest of my treasures," said Ravenwood.

"I can believe it." His eyes were fixed on the door which the lady of the house had closed behind her.

* * *

Later that evening, whilst he was dressing for dinner, Everett Carr replayed matters in his own mind. He doubted anybody else had detected the change

38

in demeanour in both Lady Ravenwood and Sebastian Lynch when they were introduced to each other, but he had been certain of it. Her usual composure had slipped, however briefly, and Lynch's cruel eyes had warmed slightly. It had been the briefest change in conduct on both their parts, but it had occurred nevertheless, of that Carr was in no doubt. He had found it merely interesting when it had occurred. Now, however, after some time had passed, it was of profound fascination to him that two people who had clearly met before in the past had found it necessary to act as if they had been introduced to each other for the first time.

Chapter Seven

The cocktails had been prepared and served. Truscott had debated whether to decline the offer of one, given his past indiscretions, but he had determined that those days of imminent dependence were behind him. His recovery was all but complete, as far as he was concerned, and he did not think that he fell into the category of those whose relationship with alcohol was so torrid that there could be no contact at all after a termination of it. If anything, indulgence now could be a test for his faith in himself and a trial of his own control.

He was standing next to Everett Carr with a Manhattan in his hand, and its effects showed no sign of taking an unholy possession of him. Carr himself was sipping a sherry, his shrewd eyes flickering around the room, and the elegant moustache and Imperial twitching with curiosity. It was evident to Truscott that something was engaging Carr's curiosity, as if he had realised a point of interest which had escaped everybody else. Truscott, unaware of what that point might be, gave it no more thought than he considered necessary and, instead, enjoyed the bitter taste of his drink.

Dr Gilchrist was talking to Helena Garrick by the fireplace. Truscott's attention had been seized by Helena as soon as she had entered the room. She was dressed in a claret gown which gave her skin a delicately pale shimmer, whilst highlighting the darkness of her hair. She had given Truscott a small but agreeable smile with her deep, scarlet lips and he had hoped, despite himself, that she would walk over to him and begin a conversation. She had not. She had engaged herself in conversation with Alicia Ravenwood and, in turn, with Dr John Gilchrist. And yet, as often as he dared, Truscott allowed himself to look over at her and smile warmly whenever she returned his gaze.

"A very beautiful woman," observed Everett Carr.

Truscott felt his neck and cheeks burn. He turned away from the room, lest Helena should witness the change in his complexion. "I suppose she is."

"I should think there is no supposition about it." Carr sipped his sherry. "You feel it would be inappropriate to get to know her, is that it?"

"Is that what?"

"The reason for your hesitation in speaking to her. Perhaps you see it as a betrayal."

Truscott bristled, but he knew it was because the truth was difficult to hear. "I still love my wife, regardless of whether she is with me or not."

"No doubt." Carr looked up at him with kindness in his onyx eyes. "But it would be unfortunate if you allowed that love to keep you alone."

Truscott was desperate to change the subject. He turned back to face the room and took a mouthful of the Manhattan. "Even if you are right, Mr Carr, I fear her attentions are elsewhere."

Carr followed his gaze to Helena and Gilchrist. He smiled gently. "My dear boy, there is no romantic interest there on either side. Take the word of an older man, if not that of your own eyes."

Truscott seemed disinclined to trust either. "I know I've seen him before."

Carr nodded. "And so you have. Your recent past has clouded the fact, that is all. Think back. There was a time when Dr Gilchrist was somewhat infamous. Even your own newspaper columns dedicated extensive copy to him." After a significant pause, Carr added: "And his wife."

The memory dislodged itself in Truscott's mind and he clicked his fingers in recognition of it. "Emily Gilchrist, of course."

"Precisely," murmured Carr. "Did you cover the story personally?"

Truscott shook his head. "No. Anything I knew about it was what I read or overheard. Gossip, really. But I don't think there is any doubt he did it."

Carr looked across at his companion, whose eyes were now fierce, fixated not so much on Helena Garrick as the doctor himself. Carr gently cleared his throat. "No charges were ever brought against him."

41

"That proves nothing, surely."

"It proves that any evidence against him was insufficient, or circumstantial at best," cautioned Carr. "Which means that any suggestion that he was guilty is speculation only and, no doubt, slanderous."

Truscott was smiling. "Don't you tell me that a man of your experience in criminal matters doesn't get an instinct, Mr Carr. As a former judge, surely you have an opinion, with or without definite evidence."

Carr shrugged. "Possibly."

"A reporter has that instinct. And mine tells me, evidence or not, that Gilchrist murdered his wife."

Carr did not reply at once. Instead, he drank more of his sherry and dabbed gently at his moustache with his handkerchief. "I rather think my instinct is keener than yours."

Truscott took the matter no further. "If he did murder his wife, I cannot say I am happy with him speaking to Miss Garrick."

Carr was shaking his head. "Dr Gilchrist is not as intriguing as Sebastian Lynch."

Truscott sneered. "He is one of those men whom I find it easy to dislike on sight. There is something about him which simply does not inspire kindly thoughts."

"You must hope that nothing serious happens to him, my boy," said Carr. "Comments such as that might land you in some deep and unpleasant waters."

Across the room, Lynch himself was in conversation with a tall, slim woman of indeterminate age, although Carr suspected that she could not have been more than halfway into her second decade. Her appearance suggested an age in advance of those years, however; the wispy hair was prematurely grey, the eyes burdened with signs of exhaustion, and, whilst her cheeks were flushed, the pallor of her face overall was sallow. Her dress was ostentatious rather than extravagant and she wore it without any suggestion of elegance or ease.

"I believe you are an artist, Miss Montgomery," Lynch was saying.

"I am trying to make a name for myself, at least," replied Eliza Montgomery. "I am hoping a commission from Sir James will help me to do so."

"Would I have seen any of your work?" Lynch took a large drink. "I tend to take an interest in art."

Eliza Montgomery smiled at him. "You may have seen some of my smaller pieces."

From his distance, Carr watched the conversation unfold. He could not hear all of it, but the pieces picked up by his ears seemed innocuous enough. It seemed to him to be little more than the banal small talk which is forced upon strangers who are thrown together in any social engagement such as this. Artists, in his experience, were fond of talking about their work and yet Eliza Montgomery seemed unwilling to do so. It was curious in itself, but it was made even more so when Carr observed the slight but distinct shaking of her hand whilst she spoke to Sebastian Lynch and to hear the gentle tinkling of the ice in her glass caused by it.

Her nerves seemed to dissipate once Sir James Ravenwood broke into their conversation.

"I see you are monopolising my artist friend, Lynch," said the baronet. "You may not paint his portrait, Miss Montgomery, until you have fulfilled my own commission. Whatever we decide that will be!"

It was Lynch who spoke in reply. "I wouldn't dream of requesting any work from Miss Montgomery which would interfere with your own, Sir James."

Eliza Montgomery smiled, but she would not allow her eyes to rest on either man. "I am not sure I could paint Mr Lynch accurately. He has such a striking face."

Ravenwood erupted into laughter. "There, Lynch, isn't that a compliment? Or is it an insult to me, Miss Montgomery? My face is not so striking that you feel unable to give the brushes an attempt at it?"

Eliza Montgomery shook her head against her embarrassment at her own indiscretion. "Sir James, I did not mean to cause any offence. Please accept my apologies."

"Nonsense, child," said Ravenwood. "Think nothing of it."

Lynch, likewise, was quick to appease the young girl. "He is pulling your leg, Miss Montgomery. Give it no more thought. Nevertheless," he added, his voice descending into a darker realm, "I wonder why you feel you could not paint my own face easily. Is it that difficult?"

Eliza Montgomery did not reply. Eventually, a smile creased her thin lips. A response might have been behind it but, if so, it never came. Instead, she retreated into herself and sipped her drink.

It was Ravenwood who saved the situation. "Let us see what she does with my own portrait, Lynch, before you begin criticising her work generally."

"By all means," conceded Lynch.

With a smile, Ravenwood walked away. Carr watched his host drift once more around the room, chatting cordially to each of the guests. During the cocktail hour, as Carr had come to expect, Lady Ravenwood had done likewise in her own fashion. It was typical of their hosting strategy, a means to allow each guest to have their individual attention. Carr had always respected the decision and it had seemed to him to make a deal of practical and social sense. And yet, on this particular evening, it struck Carr that the focal point of the room was Sebastian Lynch, as if the other members of the party, and the hosts themselves, were satellites drifting around his planet. If Carr's impression were accurate, Lynch himself seemed oblivious to it. He drank, he smoked, and he conversed, seemingly without any impression of the effect he seemed to have on others. Standing at a distance, however, Everett Carr could see the covert glares and the private snarls, the whitened knuckles and blanched cheeks of fear whenever the man spoke or looked in a particular direction.

Above all, he noticed that Lady Ravenwood entirely kept her distance from Sebastian Lynch.

So deep were his thoughts that it was some time before Everett Carr realised that the gong had sounded for dinner and the guests had begun to leave the room.

Chapter Eight

Dinner was over, brandy and cigars had been enjoyed, and the first steps had been taken to retire for the night. Gradually, the house fell silent, save for the distant chiming of the various clocks scattered around the premises. Outside, the sky had darkened and the moon had disappeared behind a cluster of thick clouds. Rain threatened to exert itself during the night but, for the present, there was no downpour, only the heavy, blackness of a starless sky.

Lady Ravenwood sat in silence in the drawing room, staring into the dying embers of the fire. The darkness outside made the cinders burn with an intensity which her ladyship found bewitching. The only other light was from a small table lamp, which offered very little illumination but which emphasised her delicate yet noble features. Ravenwood had gone up to bed but she had told him that she had found the evening rather more overwhelming than usual and she wanted a few moments of peaceful solitude. In fact, she knew well enough that her mind was anything but at peace.

She thought back to the days before the weekend, to when Ravenwood had suggested a weekend party to celebrate the purchase of this dagger of his. There had been no reason to refuse the idea and she could not have known that a ghost from her past would begin to haunt her life once more as a result of her agreement to it. If Ravenwood had told her the name of his special guest, if he had confided in her something of the man he proposed to invite, surely she could have deflected matters. If Ravenwood had not insisted on keeping such details to himself, if he had not felt the need to gloat over the acquisition of this vampire's dagger, Mary could have avoided the position in which she now found herself.

If...if...if...

If the special guest had been anyone other than Sebastian Lynch, the problem would not have arisen. It was a cruel coincidence that her husband should have met a fellow obsessive about morbid relics of the past and that this comrade should be a man whose heart she had broken.

She had never discussed her past relationships with her husband and, perhaps to his credit, he had never enquired about them. If he had, and if she had told him the truth of the affair with Lynch, she knew that Ravenwood would have considered the matter scandalous. In retrospect, perhaps she found it so herself. Certainly, in her younger days, Mary had been less restrained in her emotions and she knew it. Lynch had exploited it but she was honest enough to accept that she had not fought him very strongly. It had not been a long affair, a year perhaps, but it had burned brightly, intensely, and, above all, passionately. She did not regret it, but she did not want to resurrect it and, at all cost, she did not want her husband to discover it.

And yet, here was Sebastian Lynch, in close proximity to her after all those years and as a guest under her roof. Irrationally but uncontrollably, and despite its size and dimensions, Warlock's Gate seemed in that moment to her to be unpleasantly and fatally claustrophobic.

"Hello, Mary." His voice seized her heart with a shocking abruptness which jolted her out of her reverie. She gave an involuntary gasp.

He was standing in the open doorway, slowly closing the door behind him. In the gloom of the darkness, his size seemed overwhelming. He was little more than a looming shadow of menace, his shoulders unnaturally broad, and his presence bearing down on her with imposing insistence.

"You shouldn't be down here," she hissed.

"I had to speak to you," said Sebastian Lynch. "I wasn't sure when I would get another opportunity."

"I can't believe you are here." She rose from her seat and walked to the window. She looked out into the darkness, as if trying to find some way out of her predicament. "You shouldn't be here."

Lynch walked over to her. "How could I have known you were the lady of the house?"

"If you had known, would it have made any difference?"

He averted his gaze from her. "I cannot say."

"Now that you do know I am married to James," said Mary, her voice defiant, "will it make any difference? Will you leave in the morning?"

He looked into her eyes. "No. Not now that I've found you again."

"That's your answer, then. If you had known who James was married to, you would still have come. It would have made you even more determined to come."

"I suppose that must be right." He allowed a short pause to pass between them. "Do you blame me?"

"How can you ask me that?" She moved away from him, as if being in his company alone was a betrayal of her marriage.

"Don't tell me you don't feel the old charge between us, Mary." Lynch was behind her with almost supernatural speed and silence. She felt his breath on her neck. "Don't pretend that if I took you in my arms now, you wouldn't feel some of those feelings come back to you."

"You have no right to say things like that to me, Sebastian."

He gripped her shoulders and spun her round so that she was forced to look him in the face. The violence of the movement made her gasp. And yet, to her horror, she did experience a sudden desire for him, a spontaneous wish to feel him against her once again, to rekindle a fire which she long believed to have been extinguished.

"I still love you, Mary," he whispered urgently. "I always have. There have been others since, but they were nothing next to you."

"I love my husband," she protested.

"You still love me," he insisted. "I saw it in your eyes just now. You may have forgotten it, but you remember now. And we can begin again."

"No." She spat the syllable with a determined venom.

His grip on her shoulders tightened. "You can't turn your back on me a second time, Mary. I won't allow it."

His face was contorted with rage and something which struck her as far more sinister. It was a dark, twisted version of love. With a feral swiftness, so quick that it startled her, he slammed her against the wall, his face inches from hers. She could smell the whisky and tobacco on his breath as it hissed at her. His weight was against her, forcing the air from her lungs, and his livid eyes bored into hers, his intent etched with hideous clarity on his features. Her world now seemed to contain only him. His hands were clutching at her, his powerful leg prising hers apart, his lips fiercely exploring the flesh of her neck. A memory came back to her, a recollection of a time when he had gorged himself on her. Then, she had allowed him to do so, only because she had feared what would happen to her if she resisted him further and inflamed his rage. Now, as she felt the same terror of him rise up inside her, she knew that she could not let history repeat itself. This time, he would not take her dignity. This time, he would not please himself. She felt secure in the knowledge that a scream would bring down a household and she felt certain Lynch would realise it too. Warlock's Gate was not the cramped room in that terraced house which had formed part of her dark memory.

But she did not scream. Instead, with an effort of will, she bit down hard on the surface of his neck. He grunted in pain and loosened his grip enough for her to strike him in the face and push him away. He glared at her, barely human now, but her resistance had emboldened her and she knew that she was no longer afraid of him.

"You stay away from me, Sebastian," she hissed, "or I will bring the whole force of this house down on you."

"You belong to me, Mary," he snarled.

"I love my husband, Sebastian. That is all there is to it."

He glared at her and, for a long moment, there was no movement in the room. Lynch's breathing was short and intense, coming out in sharp blasts of furious air, whilst she remained externally calm, in direct contrast to the riot of emotions which were exploding within her. Lynch took a step towards her and, when he spoke, his voice was low as if burdened down by the weight of his menace.

"You're mine, Mary," he said. "I lost you once, but I refuse to do so again. I suggest you think about that very carefully. We belong together, and you know it as well as I do."

He raised a hand swiftly, making her recoil in sudden horror, but the violence which she had anticipated did not come. Instead, he smiled and then allowed it to break into a short, guttural laugh, as he placed his palm against her cheek and softly but menacingly stroked her flesh.

"I love you still, Mary," he whispered, "and I know you love me."

The words remained in her head after he had left the room. For a moment, she remained standing where she was, her own hand resting lightly on the cheek where he had touched her. Her mind and her heart were whirling in confusion and, as she realised slowly, fear.

She waited for a while longer, to be sure Lynch had gone back to his room, and then she made her way to the door. She opened it carefully, peering into the hallway. It was empty and there was no movement in the house. The silence was emphatic. Her blood racing in her ears, Mary ran towards the staircase and made her way swiftly upstairs.

She crept softly into her bedroom. Ravenwood was in the bed, lying on his side but facing away from her. She climbed carefully into the bed and settled down. Her husband stirred.

"Are you all right, darling?" he asked, his tone serious and concerned.

"Fine," she replied, burying her fear and fighting to control her breathing. "Go back to sleep."

"I wasn't asleep. Can't seem to settle."

"We both need some rest before your exhibition tomorrow." She kissed his head. He smiled back at her, his eyes staring deeply into hers. "I love you, James," she said at last.

His smile remained on his lips. "Follow your own advice and get some sleep."

He kissed her gently and settled down into the bed. Mary did likewise but, despite those advices, she lay awake for a while longer, the scene with Lynch playing over and over in her troubled mind. In an effort to erase it, she moved closer to her husband and placed her arm around his waist. He

49

gripped her fingers tightly and, in that moment, she felt a comforting sense of security.

And yet, still, it was some time before she succumbed to sleep.

* * *

A few seconds after Lady Ravenwood had raced up the staircase, a figure stepped out carefully into the hallway.

Helena Garrick stood for a moment in deep thought. She could make nothing of what she had witnessed. She could not fathom what might have caused Lady Ravenwood and Sebastian Lynch to be together after dark in the drawing room of Warlock's Gate. To judge from the expression of horror on Lady Ravenwood's, what had occurred between her and Lynch was not at all innocent, which made the matter all the more mysterious. As she pondered the matter of Lady Ravenwood and Sebastian Lynch further, an explanation refused to come to her and nor did she see how she could question anybody about it. To do so would surely require an explanation of why she herself was sneaking around the house in the dead of night. And that was a question which she did not wish to face. Slowly, it dawned on Helena Garrick that perhaps she was not the only person at Warlock's Gate who was hiding a dark and dangerous secret.

A clock chimed the hour from somewhere, breaking the silence of the house. Frowning, and dismissing the mystery from her mind for the present, she disappeared into the shadows once more and crept out of the house.

Chapter Nine

The following morning, Roderick Deville was sitting at the mahogany desk in the library with his head in his hands.

In front of him was a sheet of blank paper and a freshly sharpened pencil. Scattered around his feet were balls of crumpled paper of varying sizes, like little globes of failure. Deville's fingers pressed into his scalp and a low, guttural growl of frustration rumbled at the back of his throat. He removed his spectacles and dropped them on the desk, rubbing the palms of his hands into his eyes, as if doing so would allow him to see matters more clearly.

"I hope I'm not intruding."

Deville turned around in his chair, knocking his paper and pencil to the floor. Eliza Montgomery was standing in the doorway, a small smile on her lips. Deville rose from the desk.

"Not at all," he replied. "If I am honest, perhaps a break would do me some good."

"I presume you are working on a new book, Mr Deville."

He smiled. "Wrestling with it would perhaps be a more appropriate way of putting things."

"It isn't going very well?"

He conceded the point with a shrug of his shoulders. "I don't know why I do it. Only a madman would spend his life trying to conjure up intricate plots specifically designed not to be understood until the final chapter."

"I always thought it must be a hugely entertaining profession, writing detective stories. Thinking up elaborate ways to murder people and coming up with ingenious puzzles—it must be tremendous fun."

Deville sighed. "If only I had a shilling for every time someone said something like that to me, I wouldn't need to write anything. Dreaming up the crime isn't the problem—solving it in your own head is. For example, I am struggling right now to work out how in God's name Stanislaus Crane is going to deduce how a body managed to disappear from a locked church only minutes after it was discovered."

"Stanislaus Crane?"

"My detective. The problem I have is that I come up with a title first. I couldn't resist *The Corpse Fled By Moonlight* but making a story fit with it is driving me to Bedlam." He paused, suddenly conscious that he might be boring her. "I'm sorry. When I'm frustrated, I tend to talk too much."

Eliza Montgomery laughed gently. "I have every sympathy for you, Mr Deville."

His eyes warmed. "Please, call me Roderick."

She smiled at him and wondered whether he had felt the electrical charge which had seemed to pass between them. "Then you may call me Eliza. And I meant what I said. I do understand your predicament. I share similar moments of creative frustration."

"Ah, yes, you're an artist, are you not?"

"I'm someone who tries to make something beautiful for the world."

"You deal with lightness and beauty, I dabble with death and darkness."

"Art is nothing if not varied."

Deville shrugged his shoulders and looked back at the balls of paper on the floor. "I'm not at all sure what I do is art."

The door opened once more, breaking their conversation. Richard Prentice and Alicia Ravenwood walked in, whispering softly to themselves. It seemed to Deville that they had expected to find the library unoccupied, because they stopped talking abruptly when they saw Deville and Eliza, as if their presence was an intrusive one. Prentice smiled easily, Deville noticed, but Alicia was staring at them both with wide eyes. Deville was reminded of a child being caught in an illicit act of deceit.

"I see we have walked in on an artists' convention," quipped Prentice. He bowed to Eliza and shook Deville's hand. "How are you, Deville? I say, is this mess yours?"

Deville flushed at the question. He apologised frantically, stooping to pick up the discarded balls of paper. "I was just saying how difficult I'm finding this latest project of mine," he explained.

Prentice turned to Eliza. "Was he crying on your shoulder, artist to artist?"

It was clear from her face that she found Prentice's manner disagreeable. "Not at all, although I doubt you would have appreciated the conversation even if he were."

"Actually, Richard is an artist too." Alicia was quick to leap to her fiancé's defence, but she regretted the words immediately.

Eliza raised an eyebrow. "Really? In what field, Mr Prentice?"

"I don't think Miss Montgomery would call me an artist as such, Alicia," said Prentice, his eyes remaining on Eliza. "I take a few snaps here and there."

"Is photography classed as an art form?" asked Eliza, with a distinct twist of snobbery in her voice. Deville found that he was smiling at her response.

Alicia Ravenwood sat down in one of the leather armchairs which were scattered across the library. "I believe my father is looking to commission a portrait from you, Miss Montgomery."

"He's been so kind as to suggest it, yes."

Prentice looked enlightened. "So, that is why you are here, is it? I wondered why dear old Ravenwood had invited you down here. I thought his hubris about this dagger of his had properly gone out of control this time and led him to invite complete strangers to the party."

"Do you resent my presence here, Mr Prentice?" asked Eliza coldly.

Prentice took a moment to consider his position. He lowered his head and placed his hand on his heart. "Forgive me. I was being unnecessarily flippant. I meant no disrespect. If anything, I was poking fun at Ravenwood."

Alicia snorted. "You placate one woman and offend another!"

"Not doing awfully well, am I?" said Prentice with a laugh and, despite themselves, the two women laughed with him. Only Deville isolated himself from the good humour.

"Just how fabulous is this dagger?" asked Eliza, sitting down beside Alicia.

"I haven't seen it," replied the girl. "Daddy never lets anybody see his treasures until the grand unveiling."

"Is it something he does regularly? Throw parties to show off his trinkets?"

Prentice laughed heartily. "Don't let him hear you call them trinkets, Miss Montgomery. He'll throw you out of the house without missing a breath."

"And to answer your question," offered Alicia, "Daddy only hosts weekends like this when he is particularly proud of a new addition to his dreary museum."

"Dreary?" said Deville. "How can you call it that? I find the idea of a museum dedicated to the macabre absolutely fascinating."

"I suppose you would, given the sort of books you write," sneered Prentice.

"And you wouldn't find it fascinating if you were brought up hearing about it day in and day out," said Alicia. "Talking about something constantly is bound to become tiring."

Eliza had been examining a fingernail. "Might we have a look at the dagger? A sneak preview, as it were?"

The suggestion was met with a silence which suggested that it was scandalous even to exist as a thought. Eliza looked at the three of them, their eyes wide with astonishment and shock, as if she had uttered the darkest of blasphemies. Had she suggested committing a crime against the King himself, she doubted their reactions would have been so extreme.

"Surely the dagger will be locked away," said Deville, hoping to break the tension.

Alicia nodded. "Father always keeps the door locked. His museum is so precious to him that nobody is allowed in there without him. What a bore."

"Besides, you only have a couple of hours to wait until you see the dagger and the collection in all its glory," said Prentice. "The unveiling is this evening, after all, before dinner."

"I shall have to possess my soul in patience, then," smiled Eliza. Deville detected a mischief in her, both in her eyes and in the tone of her voice. She looked up at him. "Roderick, if your book is troubling you, would you like to take me for a walk?"

The question came so unexpectedly that Deville was unable to conceive of any reason why he could not and should not accept. They made their farewells and stepped out into the hall. Deville was about to speak when Eliza pressed her fingers to her lips and cautioned him into silence. For a moment, she waited and Deville knew that she was anticipating Alicia and Prentice leaving the library also. There was no movement from behind the library door, however, and Deville had the notion that whatever it had been which had consumed their conversation when they had walked into the room had been resumed.

Eliza must have had a similar thought. She smiled at Deville and took him by the arm. She led him across the hallway but it was not until they were outside the door to the museum room that Deville began to resist.

"We mustn't," he hissed.

"Where's your detective instinct?" she teased. "Just a quick look through the keyhole."

He gave it some thought, but only for a moment. He would have been lying to himself if he had denied any temptation at all, but whether it was the lure of the dagger or of the possibility of spending time alone with Eliza, he could not say. Both possibilities were attractive, but he could not help thinking that one was more so than the other. Nevertheless, something which he assumed was a sense of loyalty overcame the desire to pry. He broke free from her grip and shook her head.

"I'm terribly sorry, Eliza, but I can't," he said. "And I don't think you should either. It's offensive to our host."

She smiled. "How prudent of you, Roderick. I'm suggesting a peek through the keyhole or perhaps the window. I'm not proposing we break in or anything of that sort."

"Prentice was right. It is a matter of trust and I want no part of abusing it."

She watched him. There was something touching in his boyish refusal to offend, an earnest innocence which gave him an attractive vulnerability. She wondered in that instant what it would be like to kiss him, but the idea seemed so ridiculous that she dismissed it. He smiled foolishly at her and walked away, heading up the oak staircase which rose from the centre of the chequered floor of the hallway. His helplessness stayed with her for an instant and it attempted to compel her to turn away from the museum, but she resisted the coercion.

She dropped to her knees and peered through the lock. Ahead of her, she could see the display case with the black silk covering. As far as she could tell, it was the only exhibit to be concealed, although her view was necessarily limited. She began to fantasise about being in the room, of feeling the corner of the silk shroud between her fingers. She imagined that she could feel how delicate it was and she thought of the thrill of pulling it away from the glass case.

"What the devil do you think you are doing?"

Eliza spun her head around and leapt to her feet, her hand to her mouth and her eyes wide with fear. Ravenwood was glaring at her, his jaw clenched in suppressed rage. His cheeks were crimson with fury and Eliza noticed that his hands had balled into fists, the knuckles whitened with the tension.

"I am so sorry, Sir James," she stammered. "They warned me not to pry, but I simply couldn't resist."

"You should have listened to the warnings."

"I have no excuse other than my own curiosity."

He did not seem to be listening. "Nobody is allowed to see any exhibit until it is unveiled."

"I understand that, but—"

"If I wanted you to see it before everybody else, Miss Montgomery, I should have shown it to you," Ravenwood roared.

"I am so sorry," she repeated. "Please forgive me."

"I think we shall have to reconsider that little commission." Ravenwood's eyes were fierce. "I cannot conduct business with someone whom I cannot trust."

Tears began to well in her eyes. "Please, don't say that, I beg you. I am sorry I have offended you and, by all means, I shall stay in my room for the unveiling this evening. Or I shall leave the house now, if you prefer, but don't cancel the portrait, please. Please." This last entreaty was broken by a sob.

Ravenwood stood to one side and pointed to the door. "Get out of here."

Eliza needed no further persuasion. She walked to the door, barely resisting the desire to flee, and she could hear his more measured footsteps behind her. In the hallway, she watched him close the door and, taking a bunch of keys from his pocket which were attached to a chain to the waistband of his trousers, she watched him unlock the door. He stepped into the room and took a swift glance around it, before stepping back out and closing the door, locking it once more.

"I can only apologise once again," Eliza whispered.

Ravenwood nodded. "Perhaps we had better say no more about it. What cannot be cured, and so on. But, please," he added, his voice lowering, "do not ever breach my hospitality again."

Eliza shook her head in response, mumbling incoherent words of assurance. As Ravenwood walked away, her eyes were fixated on his back. He walked towards his study and disappeared inside. As soon as he was gone, her eyes flickered back to the door of the museum room and tears began to well inside them. Slowly, Eliza turned away from the door and made her way up the stairs.

Chapter Ten

Everett Carr sat on the terrace.

After a typically sparse breakfast, a meal in which he had seldom indulged, he had taken a stroll around the grounds of Warlock's Gate and now, in order to rest the leg which gave him perpetual trouble, he sat on one of the small stone benches which looked over the lawns at the back of the house. The morning was bright, the air brisk and clean, and there was a serenity which had settled across the break of the day. And yet, despite the beauty of his surroundings and the sound of birdsong in the distance, Carr himself was not settled.

He had become accustomed to days such as these. When they occurred, it never escaped his attention that the injury to his leg bit with a more terrible ferocity than usual whenever he missed his wife more keenly than normal. So frequently did one follow the other that it was difficult not to see a connection between the two factors. When his heart ached for the loss of his wife, the pain in his leg intensified. It was not so fanciful an idea, Carr mused at length. After all, had his knee not been shattered by a bullet from the same gun which had killed his beloved Miranda?

Painfully, but uncontrollably, his mind played back the tragedy. How long ago it seemed now, although he had known it was no more than three years. Perhaps it was a symptom of grief that allowed time to be so easily manipulated. Just as his loss had seemed to extend over a longer period than the truth, so did the impact of that day seem to him to be so immediate that it might have taken place three hours ago rather than three years. He could feel still the sharp, indescribable agony of the tearing of his flesh and the shattering of bone. He could hear the explosions of fire which had erupted from the barrel of the gun. He could smell the cordite and the burning metal; just as strongly, he could smell his own fear and shock. Above all, he could feel Miranda's weight against him as she fell dead to her feet. In life, she had been like a feather, like air, a graceful woman almost without weight. In death, she had seemed to him to be a tweed twin-set of lead. Even now, looking across the luxuriant gardens of the Ravenwood estate, Carr seemed to feel the weight of her death against him.

And, above all else, there was his own guilt of survival. Miranda had lost her life; Carr had lost only his knee.

The joint was physically painful, especially in the colder temperatures, but Carr had learned to live with it. What he had not come to terms with, and what he feared he might never be at ease with, were the associated psychological injuries. With every spasm of agony which his broken knee inflicted on him, there returned the knowledge that it should have been he who had died on that day. In his mind, Carr had grown to recognise his permanent injury as a similarly eternal reminder of his wrongful survival of that assassination attempt. In return, he had come to accept his injury as an insistent accusation that his wife had died in his place.

It was nothing less than the truth. Carr accepted that it was impossible to imagine that the Cullearn gang had targeted his wife and not him. Miranda Carr had not sentenced Doyle Cullearn to prison; her husband had done so. Miranda Carr had not made her feelings about Doyle Cullearn and his crimes known from the bench; her husband had done so. Miranda Carr had not expressed publicly her disgust at Doyle Cullearn's torture, violation, and murder of a vulnerable teenage girl; her husband had done so. Miranda Carr had not condemned Doyle Cullearn to his lawful fate at the end of the hangman's rope; her husband had done so, and he had done it with pleasure. The Cullearn gang had no desire for revenge against Miranda Carr, only against her husband.

And yet, their assassination attempt had left Miranda dead and Everett himself only permanently injured. There had been no further attempts to murder him by the Cullearn gang. Carr had long wondered about that fact.

Over time, he had come to realise the truth that, just possibly, the cruel villains knew well enough what they had achieved by their mistake. And it followed that they knew that any further violence against Carr would serve no purpose and would be no greater torture than the one he now endured.

Carr wiped what might have been a drop of rain or a snowflake away from his cheek. With a sombre smile, he noted that it was neither raining nor snowing.

His thoughts were interrupted by the sound of voices. They were clear and distinct, but Carr could sense the distance between them and his position. He knew that the terrace upon which he sat extended around both sides and the back of the house. He was sitting on the east terrace overlooking the lawns; the voices came to him from the south, at the back of the house. He recognised the voices immediately and, as a result, his interest was awakened with a keen alertness. He had thought to himself on the previous afternoon that Louisa Marston had recognised Sebastian Lynch from somewhere, even if he had not known her, and Carr felt sure that any conversation between the two now might offer him some justification of his impressions. It was rude to eavesdrop, no doubt, but Carr felt unable to lift himself from his stone seat.

"I hope you didn't mind me suggesting a little stroll around the grounds, Miss Marston," Lynch was saying.

"I would not have accepted if I minded," Louisa replied, "but I must say I cannot imagine what you could have to say to me."

Lynch laughed gently. "Forgive me but when we met yesterday, you said you knew who I was."

"What of it?" she asked.

"I am curious, that is all," said Lynch. "You see, I never forget a face and I know that we have never met, Miss Marston."

A silence descended and Carr felt an uneasiness roll beneath it, as the sound of thunder trembles beneath a darkened sky. He remained motionless, conscious that any sound from him would break the illusion of the others' privacy.

"It's true that you don't know me," said Louisa Marston at last. Her voice was so low, so timid, that Carr was forced to strain to hear them. "But you did know my father."

Lynch tried to recall. "The name Marston means nothing to me, I am sorry."

"Why should it?" Now, her voice was harsher, twisted with venom, and its timidity had hardened into bitterness. "I don't suppose you recall every man you condemn to death."

"I don't understand."

"My father was Alfred Marston. Does that name mean nothing to you?"

Carr could infer from the silence and her tragic howl of laughter that Lynch had shaken his head.

"No, why should it?" Louisa hissed. "I don't suppose you remember Edith Myers either?"

Again, Carr deduced the shake of Lynch's head.

"At least that is consistent," spat Louisa Marston. "I suppose I shouldn't be surprised that a man like you remembers neither the victim of a murder nor the man wrongly accused of it."

And, after a long moment, Lynch spoke softly, almost regretfully. "I see."

"You murdered my father." Louisa's dramatic statement was infused with the melodrama of a child's response to an event.

"I was merely the foreman of the jury," Lynch said. "I had no part in the case against him."

"It was your word which condemned him."

"You cannot blame the foreman, or even the jury, for the case brought against a man," Lynch said. His tone was didactic, as if he were lecturing a foolish and idealistic schoolgirl. In many ways, Carr supposed, he was doing exactly that. "The evidence was there and it was presented to us. The judge directed us towards a guilty verdict. It must be difficult to hear, Miss Marston, and almost impossible to accept, but it is the truth of the matter."

"There was no evidence against him." The words came with a tearful defiance.

Another silent moment passed. "How old were you when it happened, Miss Marston? Barely twenty years old?"

"I was not a child."

"Of course not."

Carr nodded his head. He knew what was passing through Lynch's mind. Louisa Marston might not have been a child in terms of her years of age, but it was not difficult to imagine her as an adolescent in her mind. Even now, she seemed shy and timid, suggesting that her experience of the world was minimal and her understanding of it wanting. Her anger in the last few moments was that of a petulant child, unable to think evil of her own father. Carr did not know the case of Edith Myers, any more than he knew the name Albert Marston, but he was disinclined to believe that an entire jury was misdirected. It was not an impossibility, but it could not be taken for granted as the normal course of events. To do so would be to dismiss one of the foundations of society and, whilst Carr could accept that justice may be flawed on occasion, it remained the best system available. He had to believe in it or else the world meant nothing. Just as a priest must believe in the Lord, Carr had to believe in justice. Therefore, his instinct was that the verdict against Louisa Marston's father had been correct, although it did not follow that his daughter would have to accept it. And that was where the present danger lay.

"I know what the truth is, Mr Lynch," Louisa said. "And so did my mother. We know what happened that day in Court."

"You cannot blame one man for an entire jury's verdict," Lynch repeated.

"Perhaps not," replied Louisa, her voice now like the blade of a knife. "But I only have that one man under the same roof as me, haven't I?"

Lynch's voice, until now measured and somewhat sympathetic, chilled with menace. "I don't take kindly to threats, Miss Marston. And I wouldn't have expected you capable of making them."

"I hate you for what you did," she said.

There was a long pause. Carr's eyes narrowed in anticipation of Lynch's response. When it came, Carr was thrown into confusion.

"Is that why you send the dolls, Miss Marston?"

She did not reply immediately, but her broken voice suggested that she shared Carr's perplexity. "Dolls?"

"I think you know what I am talking about," replied Lynch.

"I am sure I do not," protested Louisa. "What dolls?"

"The dolls with the skulls for faces. The ones with nooses around their necks. The ones you've been sending to me over the past few weeks." Lynch's tone had hardened further. "A reminder of what happened to your father, are they, designed to scare me with the memory?"

Her tears came in an instant, contorting her voice into a screech of hatred and humiliation. "I don't know what you're talking about. What are you accusing me of?"

"Just confess it to me!" roared Lynch.

"I hate you, I hate you," was her reply, a scream of fear and tragedy. "I wish you were dead."

There was the sound of running, shoes against stone, and Carr knew that Louisa had fled. He waited for a moment, wondering whether now was the moment to stand and make his way from the scene. He chose not to do so, remaining motionless, save for the gentle caressing movement of his hand against his shattered knee. His mind was alive with curiosity. The mention of dolls, skulls, and nooses had both fascinated and worried him. He was eager to learn more about them, to try to discover what it was behind them, although he doubted Lynch would be willing to discuss the matter with a stranger. Against these thoughts, there reverberated Louisa's exclamation of her wish for Lynch's death. Those words would not cease chiming inside Everett Carr's mind like the most furious and fervent church bells.

For now, his reverie was broken by the appearance of Lynch at his side. The man evidently had gathered his thoughts and walked away from the south terrace. He had determined that he would not follow Louisa Marston and so he had walked in the opposite direction to which she had fled. Naturally, this had brought him to where Everett Carr was sitting. When Lynch saw the retired judge sitting on the stone bench, his eyes had flashed with an animalistic fury. Carr prepared himself for a confrontation, to defend himself against accusations of eavesdropping or spying, but none came. Perhaps there was something about the dark, impenetrable glare which met Lynch's own which prohibited any such charges being made.

Whatever the reason, Lynch heaved his shoulders and marched back towards the front of the house.

Everett Carr remained in silence for a further half an hour, his thoughts as troubled as the expression on his face. He had been disturbed before he had heard the argument. Now, he felt a darker emotion swell within him, one which he recognised as fear: the dread not only of what might possibly occur but also at the terrible knowledge that, if it did, he would be powerless to prevent it.

Chapter Eleven

Lynch found Mary in the living room. She had been quietly reading a book, with a cup of tea by her side, and she had been enjoying the peace. The intrusion might have been unwelcome regardless of who had come into the room, but when she saw Lynch, Mary felt her stomach tighten with anxiety.

"I've been looking for you, Mary," he said. "I felt we should talk."

She laid aside her book and rose, walking to the window so that there was some distance between them. "We have nothing to say, Sebastian."

"Don't say that when you know it isn't true."

"After what you did last night, you're lucky I don't inform the police."

His cheeks burst into flames, but she could not tell if it was from anger or shame. "I was a madman last night, I realise that. And I am sorry for it. You must forgive me. I acted beyond reason, but only because I love you. Dear God, Mary, can't you see that even after all this time I still love you as fiercely as I did?"

"Fiercely," she whispered. "That is what frightens me."

He understood the implication. "I would never willingly hurt you."

She knew that she could never believe it, not now. Once, perhaps, she might have allowed herself to do so, but she was no longer the girl she had been. "I love James, Sebastian. I've told you before, that is all there is to it."

"And I've told you that isn't good enough for me."

He was beside her now and he took her hand in his. For him, it was a reminder of how delicate and gentle she was; for her, it was one of his strength and his determination. As before, her reaction was a mixed one, a curious blend of fear and desire. She felt his breath close to the nape of her neck as he leaned in to speak softly to her. His voice was low, but it was not without menace.

"I can't lose you again," he said. "It would kill me."

She knew that she should move away from him, but his closeness and his hold over her was too great. "You have to leave me alone. James will be back any moment."

"Gone out, has he?"

"Only into the village," she said.

"Far enough."

She twisted so that she was looking at him and, in doing so, she forced him to release her hand. His face was dark with a primitive impulse and she was horrified to witness it. She did not flee from it, however; instead, she confronted it with all her disgust.

"What has happened to you, Sebastian?" she hissed. "Whatever your faults once were, you were never so dangerous and monstrous as this."

"Circumstances can make a man a monster."

"What on Earth does that mean?"

"My life has not been a happy one, Mary. I have made enemies. There are people who hate me. Some of the choices I've made may have been wrong, however right they may have seemed at the time." He stepped closer to her. "But none of that matters compared to letting you go."

"I wish you wouldn't say these things." Mary was resolute. "I will not leave my husband for you, Sebastian. What we had is over. It was before; this is now."

"I won't take that for an answer," spat Lynch with violence.

Mary was prevented from making any further response by a commotion outside the room. There was a banging on the front door of the house and a clamouring on the bell. Even Lynch's attention was seized by it. Glancing back at Mary, he could see that any further discussion was redundant. Her concentration had been broken by the noise and she had no interest for any other matter. She made to make her way into the hallway and Lynch felt compelled to follow her.

Fenton had already reached the front door. When he saw her ladyship, he gave her a bow of assurance. Several others had been alarmed by the noise and had congregated in the hallway to discover its origin. Alicia and Prentice flocked naturally to Mary's side. Helena Garrick was standing on the bottom stair of the main staircase, her attention switching from the front door to Mary herself. Everett Carr was standing to one side of the hallway, his presence unobtrusive but his eyes focused on the commotion. There were other people there, but Mary's attention drifted to the door as Fenton pulled it open.

Sir James Ravenwood fell into Fenton's arms.

His appearance was unusually dishevelled. His necktie was disarranged and his waistcoat and jacket were torn. There were scuff marks on his shoes and signs of mud and grime on the knees of his trousers. Similar marks could be seen on the elbows of his jacket. His face was ashen, his hair disarranged and matted with sweat. He was shaking with nervous energy and his lungs seemed to have been emptied of sufficient air, because his breathing was short and rapid. His appearance was shocking enough, but it was made all the more horrifying by the blood which ran down his face from a contusion to his temple.

Mary let out a scream and ran towards her husband. Alicia was close behind her. Fenton placed Ravenwood's arm around his shoulder and Richard Prentice was first to assist him by doing likewise with Ravenwood's other arm. Together, they moved Ravenwood into the library, Prentice shouting to the congregated crowd that they should give them space and air. Once inside the library, they placed Ravenwood in a leather armchair and Carr had filled a glass with whisky.

"Give the man some air," he commanded, his voice now iced with authority. "Fenton, would you fetch Dr Gilchrist immediately, please. I think everyone should leave the room with the exception of Lady Ravenwood."

He made the suggestion with such force that it was difficult to argue with it and, upon his arrival, Dr Gilchrist reinforced it. Nobody objected, but Carr himself did not follow his own doctrine and, as Gilchrist got to work, Carr stood silently to one side.

"What has happened, James?" asked Mary, holding her husband's trembling hand in hers.

"I took a shortcut back to the house from the village, down by the river," was the hesitant, breathless reply. "Two men jumped out of the woods and knocked me down. Happened so quickly, it was over in seconds."

"Did you see the two men?" asked Carr.

Ravenwood shook his head. "Not really. I was on the ground before I knew it. One grabbed me from behind and the other struck me on the head. They roughed me up rather badly."

Gilchrist was cleaning the wound. "It's nothing serious. It looks worse than it is."

"It feels worse than it looks, I imagine," said Ravenwood, forcing a smile.

"Have they stolen anything?" asked Carr sombrely.

Ravenwood nodded his head. "My pocketbook and money have gone, as have my keys. We shall have to secure the house, my dear, until we can have a locksmith to change the locks."

Mary was momentarily bewildered. "Why?"

It was Carr who replied. "It is likely the attackers knew whom they were assaulting. They will have the keys to Warlock's Gate and, if the attack was premeditated, burgling the house would seem to be their primary objective."

"Dear Lord," was all Mary could say. Ravenwood tightened his grip on her hand.

"The unveiling of the Tethran Dagger cannot go ahead now," he declared. "The door is locked, as you all know."

"And your assailants have the key," concluded Carr.

"I'm afraid so," Ravenwood groaned. "What a disaster of a weekend."

Gilchrist had finished his examination and treatment. He packed away his bottles and bandages and stood in front of his patient with his hands in his pockets. "You'll live, Sir James, but stolen keys or not, I would have advised you to abandon the unveiling anyway. You need bed and sleep, for the rest of the day at least."

Ravenwood shook his head. "Nonsense, Gilchrist, I'm perfectly all right."

"You'll do as you're told, James," demanded Mary. "The guests will understand and Alicia and I can host in your place. I won't have you straining yourself."

Ravenwood rolled his eyes and patted the bandage across his head. "A knock on the head is nothing compared to the bullying I receive here. Very well, my dear, have it your way. You too, Gilchrist."

The doctor laughed. "You've always been a terrible patient, Sir James."

There was a gentle knock at the door and Alicia stepped into the room. "Is Daddy all right?"

"I'm fine, darling," was his reply, but it was barely heard over Mary's insistent voice.

"He needs to rest and he is going to rest," she declared.

Gilchrist helped Ravenwood to his feet. Mary took her husband's arm and led him to the door. As he passed Alicia, he gave her a further word of assurance and kissed her on the cheek. She smiled at him and watched her mother lead him away. The young woman turned to face Gilchrist.

"Will he be all right?"

The doctor nodded. "Right as rain."

"What happened?" Alicia asked.

It was Carr who replied. "It seems he was attacked down by the river. Two men, apparently. They stole his money and the keys to the house. We must speak to Fenton about securing the property."

"The back gate is always locked," said Alicia, "and Fenton will make sure that the doors to the rear of the property are bolted."

"Excellent," said Carr. He turned to Gilchrist. "Then we must concentrate only on the front door. It will be bolted, of course, but that will no matter if these villains have keys. We must make sure that nobody has a chance to enter the grounds at all. Tell Fenton to put one of the servants in the lodge to act as a sentry."

The doctor nodded. "Yes, indeed. I'll go and have a word with him."

He marched out of the library and pulled the door closed behind him. Carr limped over to Alicia. "Don't worry yourself, Miss Ravenwood. Your father is a strong man and he will soon be right. He's had a knock on the head and a shock, but he'll mend."

She smiled at him, but it did not extend to her eyes. "Thank you, Mr Carr. You're very kind."

"Not at all."

She left Carr alone in the library. He walked painfully across to the window and looked out onto the lawns. His mind was in turmoil, a storm of anxiety and dread breaking across his thoughts. The attack on Ravenwood was violent enough, perhaps, but Carr could not rid himself of the feeling that it was tame compared to the darker and more brutal violence which he feared would take place and against which he felt helpless. He had not spoken to anybody of his anxiety, but his instincts were burning with unease. He thought back to what he had overheard, what he had witnessed, and what he had felt. Keener than ever within him was the cold grip of the anticipation of murder.

And, as if to give form to his thoughts, Everett Carr saw Sebastian Lynch walking across the lawns, his mind deep in thought and his face twisted with malice.

Chapter Twelve

Night had fallen. Warlock's Gate had descended into silence, but it was not entirely at peace with itself.

In her room, Louisa Marston lay awake, her eyes fixed on the ceiling. In other circumstances, she might have blamed the second cup of black coffee after dinner for her wakefulness, but she knew that to do so now would be disingenuous. It was not stimulation which prevented her from drifting into slumber, but distress. She had been disturbed since her confrontation with Lynch earlier in the day. It had prevented her from enjoying dinner as much as she should have done. She had known that the food was excellent, as she had come to expect, but she had been unable to eat very much of it. She had imagined that Lynch had spent the meal staring at her and, on those occasions when she saw him in conversation with someone else, she supposed that he was discussing her. Her mind was plagued by his accusation that she had been sending him threats against his life and her spirit was strained by the directness and malice of his indictment.

She had been pleased when Mary had announced that the unveiling ceremony was cancelled, although the cause for it appalled Louisa. She would never have wished any harm to Sir James and, when she had heard of the attack, Louisa had been sickened; but the possibility of being in close proximity to Lynch during the ceremony sickened her in equal measure. She had begun to feel as though he was invading her life, like a tumour, and that she would never be free of him. Now, lying in the darkness, she felt the same sense of suffocation. Her words to Lynch, wishing his life would end, reverberated in her brain and her contempt for him swelled within her more keenly than ever.

However sinful it was, she wished Sebastian Lynch was dead.

She sat up in bed. It was pointless trying to sleep when it would never come. Her thoughts were too dark and too incessant that she was unable to divert her attention away from them. She turned on the bedside light, squinting at the sudden glare of the bulb. She lay back on her pillows, allowing her eyes to adjust to the light, although her mind remained fixated on Sebastian Lynch. She reached out to the bedside table once more and picked up the volume of collected Chekhov plays. Her hope was that reading might help to distract her from the unpleasant memory of the day.

But her spectacles were not on the bedside table. After a moment's thought, Louisa realised that she must have left them in the drawing room where she had been reading earlier in the day. With a grim smile, Louisa recalled that she had been reading when Lynch had found her and suggested the walk around the grounds which had ended so unhappily.

Clicking her tongue in irritation, Louisa threw off the bedclothes and swung out her legs. Slipping her slim feet into her satin slippers, she pulled her dressing gown from the back of the chair where she had folded it. Slowly, cautiously, she opened the bedroom door and stepped out onto the silent landing. Her eyes swiftly became accustomed to the darkness and, moving swiftly but noiselessly, Louisa made her way down the main staircase to the hallway. She crossed the chequered floor towards the drawing room. Passing both the library and the infamously locked door of the museum room, she slowly pushed open the door to the drawing room.

There was nobody in it, but she hardly expected there to be. She closed the door and turned on the light. Glancing around the room, she feared at first that her spectacles had been moved and she bit her lip in concern. But, as her eyes moved more carefully about, she saw them on the small table where she had left them. Sighing delicately in relief, she ran over to the table and grasped the delicate frames to her bosom, with an urgency which suggested that the glasses were more important to her than they ought to be.

Louisa turned off the light and stepped out into the hallway. As silently and swiftly as she had come, she retraced her steps up the stairs. Back in her room, she removed the dressing gown and placed the spectacles on the book on the bed. She did not know, and never would know, what impulse drove her to check the window to ensure it was fastened properly, but she did so. She pulled aside the curtains and took hold of the clasp. It was secure, so that the wind which was blowing rather stronger now than it had been earlier in the evening could not infiltrate or disturb her room.

It was when she gripped the curtains to close them once more that she saw the figure. Her room looked out over the rear of the house across the back lawns of the grounds. She knew from her experience of the house that those lawns culminated in a high brick wall, built into which was an iron gate. The figure was racing across the stretch of lawn from that iron gate towards the kitchen door, which was the nearest means of access to the house. Louisa watched as the figure approached the house and it seemed strange to her that anybody should be running across the gardens of the house at such an hour. Louisa peered over her shoulder at the clock on her side table and saw that it was a little after one in the morning. By the time she looked back out of the window, the figure had vanished.

Louisa ran to her door and opened it carefully. She stepped to the banister of the stairs and leaned over, so that she could see into the hallway. She thought she heard the closing of the kitchen door but it might easily have been her imagination. What she did not imagine was seeing the dark figure run across the hallway from the direction of the kitchen to the staircase. Louisa stepped back into the shadows as the figure began to ascend the stairs. Louisa backed into her room and pulled the door close to shut, keeping only a small gap open through which she could see.

It was only as the figure reached the landing that Louisa could see it clearly enough to identify it as Helena Garrick.

Louisa made her way back to bed and pondered why Helena might have been running across the lawns in the early hours of the morning and where she might have been. She reached no conclusion before passing into sleep, without even realising that she had not needed the Chekhov after all.

Chapter Thirteen

Jack Truscott awoke early on the following Saturday morning. The memories of his dreams were fragile, but not so much so that he could not recall that they had been intense and about his dead wife. He seemed to recall waking in the night, his hair matted to his head and his breath rasping in his throat, but the period of consciousness must have been short because now, in the brightness of the morning, it seemed as unreal as the fragments of dream which flitted across his mind. As if in an effort to erase the whole broken night, Truscott had thrown down a glass of water before dressing and making his way to breakfast.

Few people joined him in the meal. He knew that Everett Carr was a man who seldom enjoyed food in the morning, so his absence came as no surprise, and Truscott knew that Ravenwood himself would not make an appearance after his unfortunate experience of the previous afternoon. Those two men aside, Truscott had expected the majority of the remaining houseguests to be present to enjoy the range of dishes on offer. As it was, the dining room was almost empty.

Mary was sitting at the head of the table, her plate half-filled with untasted food. Her eyes were staring ahead of her, but their intensity and concentration suggested to Truscott that they saw nothing but what was in Mary's mind. Her noble features were heavy with anxiety and the delicacy of her skin now seemed ashen with fear. Truscott greeted her twice before she broke from her thoughts and smiled aimlessly in his direction in reply. Gilchrist was sitting further down the table. His plate showed traces of indulgence as keenly as Mary's demonstrated the reverse. He was leaning back in his chair, a cigarette in one hand and a coffee cup in the other. His handsome but insolent face was stretched into a smile but Truscott seemed to think that the greeting he gave was sincere enough. Opposite him, Louisa Marston was eating slowly, reminding Truscott of a small bird pecking on a lawn. She smiled at Truscott and returned to her eggs, but she said nothing of substance, and Truscott noticed how her hands shook and her eyes danced nervously around the room without focusing on any person in particular. There was no sign of Helena Garrick. Perhaps on account of his dreams, Truscott was pleased she was not there. To see her would have felt, somehow, like too much of a betrayal.

He helped himself to bacon, eggs, and coffee and sat beside Miss Marston. She largely ignored his attempts at conversation, but Gilchrist was typically ingratiating.

"I had expected to find more people down to breakfast," confessed Truscott.

Gilchrist inhaled on his cigarette. "Most of them don't know what they're missing, am I not right, Truscott?"

Truscott smiled. "I suppose Sir James will have his meal in his room, Lady Ravenwood."

She did not reply at once. There may as well have been nobody in the room with her. Truscott repeated his observation, stressing her name, and she once again broke her thoughts with a flicker of her eyes. "Yes, I expect so. He still needs rest. After what has happened." These last words were spoken almost as an afterthought.

"Best place for him," said Gilchrist. "Shame about last night's unveiling being cancelled though. I was rather looking forward to it."

"There will be another opportunity, no doubt," said Truscott.

Gilchrist nodded, mockingly, as if the possibility had never occurred to him. "Never thought of that."

Truscott held his gaze for a long moment before smiling thinly, but he said no more. Gilchrist allowed a silence to exert itself before he spoke again. "No sign of Miss Garrick, either."

Simultaneously, Truscott and Louisa Marston glared at him. Truscott saw the remark as a taunt, but Louisa saw it as something else. She wondered whether Dr Gilchrist also had seen the Garrick girl running across the lawns in the dead of night and this was his way of hinting as much. It seemed strange that he should mention her particular absence otherwise, although Louisa did not put her suspicions into words. She watched the doctor closely. His smile was wide but crooked, his eyes filled with gleeful mischief. She found him impossible to understand and she could not fathom what his mocking expression and his seemingly provocative remark might mean.

Truscott contemplated his food. "Perhaps she likes to sleep late."

"Or was up late," offered Louisa, her eyes fixed on the doctor. He did not react to her, but simply continued to smoke his cigarette and drink his coffee. In fact, if either of the men had taken notice of her remark, they did not acknowledge it. Perhaps, she reflected, she had said it too quietly to be heard. Or, she wondered, was it possible that she had never said it at all?

Truscott finished his breakfast in silence. Gilchrist smoked another cigarette and left the room. Louisa drank a further cup of tea and did likewise. Mary remained where she was, oblivious to their conversation, her face the same shade as frost on a winter morning. Truscott did not attempt to speak to her. Something about her demeanour suggested it would have been an unwelcome gesture. Instead, he rose slowly from the table and bade her a simple farewell.

He found that the idea of a walk around the terrace appealed to him. He stepped out onto the steps of the front door and lit a cigarette of his own, feeling that particular sense of satisfaction which a contented man feels when he has eaten well in the morning. His mind was not filled with any one train of thought and he was glad of it. The attack on Ravenwood and the resulting cancellation of the unveiling of the precious dagger were recurring images in his mind, as might be expected, and he had to confess to a similar sense of disappointment as Gilchrist that the dagger itself remained under its velvet shroud of secrecy.

Dinner on the previous evening had been somewhat muted as a result of the afternoon's events, the faces of the guests solemn with concern for their host. Carr, particularly, had seemed withdrawn, his dark eyes narrowed in anxious concentration throughout the three courses. Truscott had recognised the symptoms of a troubled mind in the older man's expression and in the nervous twitching of his moustache and Imperial, as the thin lips beneath them quivered with excitement. What it was specifically which troubled Carr, Truscott could not guess, but there had been something in the retired judge's face which betrayed his concerns.

More obvious was the cause for Mary's distress. She had managed to retain something of her dignified control of emotions during the meal, engaging her guests in conversation and responding to points put to her. Her smile might not have been as warm as usual, but it had been present and any shallowness to it might have been forgiven in view of the events of only a few hours earlier. But, this morning, it seemed to Truscott that her reaction to the attack on her husband had worsened. He had known shock to be delayed in such a fashion before, so that the feeling of horror at an event would strike hardest not in the immediate aftermath but later, when the mind had been able to analyse what had taken place. Truscott suspected something of the sort had happened to Mary and, in his private thoughts, he felt nothing but sympathy for her.

He had made his way along the east side of the house and, from his previous explorations, he knew that he was almost upon the back terrace. He was passing the broad windows on the eastern wing and, idly, he looked into each one. Through the library window, he could see Roderick Deville, sitting at the writing desk, his head once more in his hands. Whatever book it was which the young man was writing, it was testing his abilities and his patience. Sitting in one of the leather armchairs, politely distant from Deville so as to not disturb his work, Truscott saw Everett Carr. His cane was leaning against the arm of the chair and the injured leg was stretched out before him, his hand gently massaging the joint. Aside from that one movement, Carr was motionless, his head tilted back against the chair. Once again, Truscott had the impression of a troubled man, deep in thoughts which meant something only to Carr himself.

Truscott continued with his walk, passing by the window of the museum room. Here was the place where the dagger was to have been unveiled. As if in deference to the occasion which had not come to pass, Truscott paused and looked through the pane. He could see the glass cases of the various exhibits which lined the room and his mind began to wander over the years, guineas, and pounds which must have been spent building up the collection. Aside from rugby, Truscott had never had a hobby as such and he could not begin to understand the mentality of a man like Ravenwood. And yet, he felt he could still appreciate the magnificence of the hoard and the dedication it had taken to accumulate it.

In the distance, as he peered closer into the room, Truscott could see the case in which the dagger itself was displayed. It took a moment for his brain to register what was wrong with the image before him. The case was there, standing on its plinth, but something was missing. At first, Truscott could not see it but, once he did, the sequence of images which deluged his mind came swiftly and mercilessly. First, he saw that the black veil of silk which had covered the glass case had been thrown to the floor. Then, immediately, he saw that the glass door of the case had been opened and the dagger itself had vanished. His first thought, naturally enough, was of theft but his body refused to allow him to move to raise the alarm, as if his soul was screaming that there was more for him to see.

He cupped his hand over his eyes, blocking out his reflection in the glass of the window, and he narrowed his eyes, straining to see more. At once, he realised that robbery was a foolish idea. The door was locked according to Ravenwood's tradition and the key had been stolen the previous afternoon. Subconsciously almost, his hands tried to open the window but it, too, was locked.

And yet, the Tethran Dagger had gone.

His eyes wild with confusion, Truscott stared harder into the room. As if by natural instinct, his gaze fell from the empty display case to the floor. It was then that Truscott's breath caught in his lungs and his blood roared in his ears. His brain told him that what he had seen was impossible, but his eyes refused to deny what was lying there in front of them.

Truscott ran back along the east wing and into the house, his voice shouting for help. He ran across the hallway to the locked door of the museum room. His hand was on the handle of the door and he was already banging his shoulder against it. He was barely aware of the growing crowd behind him.

"Stop it!" cried Mary. "Stop it, you mustn't!"

"We must get this door down now!" roared Truscott. "Gilchrist, Prentice, lend a hand here."

There was a general murmur of confusion, questions muttered under breath and inaudible words of concern whispered in ears, as the two men joined Truscott at the door. At his command, they prepared themselves to hammer their shoulders against the wood. Mary continued to protest, her voice becoming louder and more hysterical, and Alicia ran to her side and put her arms around her mother.

"What's the alarm?" asked Deville, from a distance, but he received no reply other than the rhythmic beating against the locked door.

"What's going on down there?" bellowed a voice from above. Ravenwood was standing on the main staircase, his head bandaged and his face pale, looking like some spectre at a feast nobody wanted to attend.

Everett Carr had emerged from the library more slowly than Deville. Now, he was calmly making his way through the assembled throng. His eyes were darker than ever and his face was taut with a grim, inexorable expression of dread. He looked swiftly around the people in the hallway and up the stairs to Ravenwood. He said nothing; instead, he made his way silently and painfully to the three young men who were causing the lock of the door to groan under their combined weight. Whether the sound of the lock giving way was as loud as they remembered or whether it only seemed so in the silence which immediately followed it, nobody was prepared to say. There was a crack of wood and metal and the door swung open, causing Truscott and his two allies to stumble into the museum room.

The horror was lying on the floor in front of them. It lay on its back, the arms by its sides and the legs stretched out towards the group which had formed in the doorway. Its eyes remained open, but it was the cold, glass stare of death. There was nothing human about how it stared up at the ceiling of the room, as if simultaneously entranced and horrified by the elaborate coving and the crystal chandelier. The dinner suit, complete save for the bow tie and jacket, gave it an air of respectability which was at odds with the unnatural violence of its death. The white of the shirtfront was sullied by a large crimson sun, out of which rose the ornate hilt of the fabled Tethran Dagger. When surrounded by blood and standing proud out of the breast of what had once been a man, the weapon seemed to glisten with a majesty beyond those shining jewels, as if being used for its proper purpose had brought the thing into a grim life of its own. Except now, it had not been thrust into the heart of a vampire to give everlasting peace.

Instead, it had been used to murder the man known as Sebastian Lynch.

Chapter Fourteen

Everett Carr took control of the situation at once.

"I must ask everyone to go to the drawing room and stay there for the moment. This room must not be disturbed any more than necessary. Mr Prentice, might I ask you to find Fenton and have him bring some refreshments. Coffee, tea, whatever people wish. Alicia, please take care of your mother. Dr Gilchrist, ensuring as little contact with the body as possible, could you confirm death has occurred and estimate a time?"

The doctor was surprised. "There's no doubt the man is dead, surely?"

Carr was resolute. "It must still be stated as a medical fact, doctor, if you please. Thank you. Truscott, please go and telephone for the police immediately."

Ravenwood had forced himself to the doorway. His eyes were frantic with outrage and his skin pale with shock. The bandage around his head made him seem frail, as if he were a man older than his years. "The police?"

Carr put his hand on the baronet's arm. "We must have the police, Sir James. This is a matter of murder."

"How did anybody get in here to commit murder?" asked Gilchrist. "Come to that, how did Lynch get into the room without a key?"

"Precisely," smiled Carr. "In any case, a suicide would not commit the act with an ornate and much-discussed artefact such as this dagger. It is altogether too elaborate and public. Suicides tend to prefer privacy for their final moments. No, for the moment, I think we must assume that Mr Lynch was murdered."

Ravenwood stared into Carr's eyes for a long moment, almost incapable of understanding either the words or their meaning. Slowly, the sense of Carr's demands dawned on him and he nodded his head absently. "So, they came, after all."

"They?" Carr's eyes narrowed.

"The swine who attacked me."

Carr shook his head. "I do not think so, sir. The door was forced by the doctor, here, your daughter's fiancé, and Mr Truscott. The room was locked, just as you left it yesterday afternoon."

"Locked…?" Ravenwood stared dumbly at the retired judge. "But, then… It doesn't make any sense."

"Besides, I took the liberty of arranging for a sentry to be on guard at the lodge, to make sure that they could not get into the grounds if they did return. Nobody could have got into the grounds through the front gates?"

Ravenwood seemed not to have heard. "It makes no sense at all."

"At the moment," said Carr, softly, "it does not."

Gilchrist had knelt by the body in order to examine it. Now, he rose to his feet and stepped out of the room. He addressed Carr directly. "I'm not a pathologist, you understand, but I should say he has been dead for around seven or eight hours. No more, I wouldn't have thought, but you mustn't hold me to it."

"Somewhere between one and two o'clock in the morning, then?" Carr waited for the nod of agreement from the doctor. "When was Mr Lynch last seen alive?"

"Probably by young Deville and me," said Gilchrist. "Lynch was at dinner, as you will remember yourself, Mr Carr, and he had a last brandy in the library with Deville and me. It must have been around eleven when he left us."

"So, until we learn otherwise," mused Carr, "we can assume that the murder occurred between eleven last night and two o'clock this morning."

"Murder…" Ravenwood spoke the word so gently that it seemed incongruous, as if his disbelief of the situation had robbed the word of its terrible implications. His eyes widened a little more as he glared down at the body in front of him, before the lids fluttered and the baronet's knees trembled beneath him.

It was Gilchrist who was the quickest to respond. He grabbed Ravenwood in his arms and ordered him back to bed. He suggested that he give the patient a mild sedative and Carr nodded in agreement. As the doctor led Ravenwood back to his room, Truscott returned to the scene of the tragedy.

"The police are on their way," he announced.

"I was afraid of this." Carr's voice was deepened with regret. "I had an idea that something terrible was waiting to happen."

"How could you have known?"

"Instinct, my boy. An intuition of disaster."

Carr looked into Truscott's eyes and nodded. Then, very deliberately and gently, he stepped into the room. Truscott remained in the hallway, but he watched the older man slowly moving around the body. With some difficulty, the lame leg stretching out to the side and his weight leaning on the silver-handled cane, Carr examined the wound as closely as he felt able. His free hand stretched out to touch the dagger but it recoiled almost immediately, as if confronted by a serpent, lest any valuable evidence be disturbed. With some difficulty, he pulled himself back up to his full height and glanced over at Truscott.

"It took some strength to do that," he murmured.

"A man?"

Carr inclined his head. "Not necessarily. A passionate woman could have done it, I should imagine."

"Hard to believe a woman capable of doing such a thing," said Truscott, sadly.

Carr seemed not to hear. He was breathing heavily and his lips were pursed in confused concentration. "How did the murderer get into this room?"

"I have no idea. I tried the window when I first saw the body, but it was locked."

"You tried to open the window from outside?" Carr pointed with his cane.

"Yes. An automatic reaction, I suppose."

"Very possibly," replied Carr. "But it only deepens the mystery. The door was locked, the windows were secure, and there is no other way in or out of this room. And yet…"

"And yet, there is a body."

"Exactly."

Carr's eyes had been moving around the room during this exchange but now they fixed themselves on a single point ahead of him. From his point of view, Truscott could not see what had attracted the older man's attention, but it was evident that it was behind the door. Truscott, carefully, took a step forward and peered around the frame of the door. On the floor between the wall and one of the long exhibition cases which stretched into the room, there was a small, wooden table which had toppled over. Beneath it, there was a heap of shattered glass and marble, which once had been a lamp which had stood upon the table concerned.

"Curious," said Carr, almost to himself. "How has that lamp come to be broken?"

"Is it important?"

Carr shrugged. "Perhaps not."

"I would have thought the attack on Sir James was more important," said Truscott. "The only set of keys to this room were stolen when he was assaulted. Somehow those responsible must have returned and gained access to this room. They used the same keys to open the display case, hoping to steal the dagger. No doubt Lynch interrupted them and…"

Carr held up a finger of caution. "How is that possible? You forget that Fenton placed a guard at the lodge. Anybody coming from the outside would have to pass him and he was under orders to prevent anybody from getting inside the grounds."

"And the back doors to the house were bolted." Truscott frowned, but it came with a knowing smile. "I am getting ahead of myself, of course."

Carr smiled gently, but his eyes remained serious. "You must not gallop before you can canter, my boy. We must keep our minds open. There is much to be learned before we can begin to try to reconstruct what might have happened in this room."

Carr fell into silent thought for a few moments more before stepping back into the hallway, with Truscott close behind him. Fenton was in attendance, his expression more sombre than usual. Carr gave an instruction that nobody was to enter the museum room until the police arrived and the butler assured him that it would be so. With a word of thanks to the servant, Carr walked to the drawing room and opened the door.

The assembled group looked up at the interruption. Carr saw eyes stained with tears glaring back at him, expressions of concern pointing towards him, and unspoken questions directed at him. Lady Ravenwood was sobbing in the corner of the room and Alicia continued in her efforts to soothe her mother. Prentice was standing beside them both in a protective manner, silently smoking a cigarette with such speed and deep inhalation that it was evident his nerves were on edge. Louisa Marston kept her gaze averted, as if looking at no person in particular might shield her from any glimpse of suspicion or accusation. Eliza Montgomery and Roderick Deville were standing together at the fireplace and, whilst they were not speaking, it was clear that they had only concluded doing so at the moment Carr entered. Only Helena Garrick stood away from everybody else, noted Truscott. She was concentrating on the tip of her cigarette rather than any of her fellow guests, her thoughts her own and not to be shared with anyone at present.

Carr gestured to Deville. "I wonder if I might have a word?"

The young author stared back at him as if he had been summoned to his own execution. He tried to find words and a voice, but both failed him. He looked around the room and thought he could detect accusation in the frowns and glares which fell upon him. Only Eliza Montgomery was watching him with something approaching support and encouragement. As if galvanised by it, Deville walked across the room.

Carr led him to the library and Truscott closed the door behind them. Deville refused the offer of a seat and he remained standing by the writing desk, wringing his hands and letting his eyes shift around the room, as if searching for a means of escape.

"You don't mind if I sit down myself, do you?" asked Carr. "This damned leg of mine is an awful nuisance, not to mention a painful one."

"Of course, of course," replied Deville, not in the least placated by Carr's kindly tone.

"Would you like something to drink, Mr Deville?" asked Carr. "You seem rather unsettled."

"No, thank you."

"I do wish you would sit down. It would make us both much more comfortable."

Deville clamped his eyes closed and curled his fingers into fists. "I don't want to sit down, Mr Carr. I want you to explain what it is you want from me."

Carr did not reply immediately. He kept his eyes on Deville but his expression betrayed none of the thoughts which ran through his mind. He stroked his Imperial beard gently before smiling broadly at the young author.

"I suspect most people would expect you to be excited by a real murder," he said, "given your line of occupation. But I suppose real life is a lot more terrifying than fiction."

Whatever the intention of the remark was, it succeeded in forcing Deville to bring his nerves into check. He stopped churning his hands together and placed them behind his back and he forced himself to meet Carr's glare. He straightened his spine and raised his chin into the air. It was not a convincing performance but it was preferable to the alternative.

"What do you want, Mr Carr?" he asked.

Carr began to massage his knee. "I understand you had a final brandy last night in here with Dr Gilchrist and Mr Lynch."

"Are you questioning me, Mr Carr?" Deville's eyes narrowed. "I would have thought that was a matter for the police."

"They're on their way," replied Carr. "Obviously, you shall have to answer their questions but, quite right, you aren't obliged to answer mine. But I am sure you see no harm in satisfying an older man's curiosity."

There was something so ingratiating and self-deprecating in Carr's manner that Deville felt ashamed of himself for the minor, barely effective protest. "I'm sorry if I was rude. It's the shock. You're not wrong about real life being much more horrible than what I dream up, Mr Carr. The stark reality of murder can only ever trivialise what someone like me creates."

Carr was not inclined to get into a debate about the relationship between truth and fiction. "Did you have a brandy with Lynch last night?"

"Yes. Gilchrist and I sat with Lynch after everyone else went to bed."

"Until what time?"

"Around eleven. A little after, perhaps."

Carr smiled indistinctly. "What did you talk about, the three of you?"

"Various things, really."

"Nothing which strikes you as important in light of what has happened?"

Deville lowered his gaze. "Nothing."

"Which of the three of you was first to retire to bed?"

"Dr Gilchrist. He had finished his drink, so he left Lynch and me to do likewise in private."

Carr leaned forward in his chair. "Did Lynch say anything about the doctor after he had left?"

"No. We didn't stay here for long after Gilchrist had gone."

"Did your conversation after Gilchrist left get heated at all?"

"No." Deville looked down at his feet.

"Did you see Lynch at any time after leaving him?"

"No. I went back to my room and I tried to do some work on my book, but it was useless. I am starting to think that the whole thing is futile and beyond saving. I'm afraid I might have to jack it in and start over."

Carr's expression displayed a suitably sympathetic twist. "For how long did you wrestle with it?"

"An hour, if not more. In the end, I gave up and tried to get some sleep."

"Did you leave your room at all?"

"No."

"So, you saw nothing?"

Deville shook his head. "No, I didn't see anybody."

Carr nodded with a smile. "Thank you, Mr Deville, I greatly appreciate your help. One last thing, if you would indulge me a little longer. When we were introduced to Lynch, he said you and he had met before."

The young author was struck with indecision. His eyes shifted from Carr to Truscott and, finally, to his feet. His hands came from behind his back and clasped together in an uneasy alliance once more. If he was contemplating a negative response, he realised quickly that it would be a futile gesture. Carr's memory was more acute than his own scope for dishonesty.

"Yes. I had met him before." The solemn delivery of the reply suggested that it might well have been a confession.

"Did you know him well?"

"No," replied Deville. "We had a mutual friend. It was he who Lynch knew really, not me."

"Might I ask the name of this friend?"

Deville paused, as though afraid that saying the name might force him to choke. "Anthony Barclay."

The name meant nothing to Carr. "And it was through Mr Barclay that you met Lynch?"

Deville nodded. "Yes."

"When, exactly, did you meet Lynch?"

"A couple of years ago," said Deville. "Not long after the publication of my first book."

"I seem to remember Lynch saying he had read none of your books."

"That is correct." Deville forced a smile. "I suppose I shouldn't take that personally."

Carr smiled. "What was your opinion of the man?"

"I didn't like him. I don't have to make any secret of that. It doesn't mean I killed him."

"I don't think anyone has suggested you did," Carr pointed out. "Disliking someone, thankfully, is not a genuine motive for murder. Was there a reason you didn't like him?"

Deville held his gaze for a long moment. "He put an end to my friendship with Anthony Barclay."

Carr frowned. "How?"

"I would rather not say and I don't think I'm under any obligation to do so," replied Deville. "Is that the last of your questions, Mr Carr?"

Carr allowed the subsequent moment to stretch out between them for long enough to make Deville feel uncomfortable but not long enough for its effect to become diluted. At last, he smiled broadly at the author and gave a slight bow.

"You have been most helpful, Mr Deville," said Everett Carr. "And I thank you for it."

Deville marched to leave the room and pulled open the door. He glanced back at Carr before stepping out of the library and closing the door behind him, but it did not help to shut out the lie which had so obviously been told.

Chapter Fifteen

T ruscott had not been comfortable with Carr's suggestion that they should search Lynch's room. It had seemed to him to be an unforgivable invasion of privacy on the one hand and in extremely poor taste on the other. Quite aside from those considerations, Truscott was adamant that a search of a murder victim's room was a matter for the police. Upon hearing the objections, Carr was stubbornly casual in his dismissal of them.

"Stay down here then, my boy, if the idea turns your stomach," he said.

Truscott was insistent. "It's a matter for the police."

"We're not stopping the police from searching the room." The retired judge's dark eyes were luxuriant with mischief. "We are simply doing it before them. And why not?"

"Because it isn't right."

"Very well," replied Carr with a shrug of his shoulders.

He was barely up three of the stairs before Truscott was back by his side. "If you're going to walk all over a police investigation, I can at least make sure you don't make a complete fool of yourself."

They found the room unlocked. Once inside, they stood in silence for a moment. The room seemed to have an exaggerated sense of personality about it. Objects which might otherwise be taken for granted now seemed to both men to have a more profound and solemn importance. It seemed disconcerting to see the bed in which the dead man had slept but in which he would sleep no more. It was humbling to see the hairbrush and the shaving equipment set out on the dressing table and to think that only a relatively small length of time ago they were being used by the man who now would never use them again. The sight of his suit hanging on the doorknob of the wardrobe somehow seemed to emphasise the fact of Lynch's life in the face of his violent death. It was the normality of the items, their reminder of the trappings of life which are common to every human being, which accentuated the fact that a man who had once lived was now dead. For Truscott, at least, it was sufficient to compel him to feel like a ghoul.

These impressions only came to Truscott later. In the moment, his attention was transfixed by the state of Lynch's room. It looked as though it had been torn apart. The drawers of the dressing table had been pulled out and their contents thrown to the floor. The wardrobe doors had been pulled open and the clothes which hung inside had been pushed to one side of the rail. Lynch's suitcase was on the bed, the remaining items inside it tossed across the mattress. The bedside table was empty, the items which had been on it previously now scattered across the floor.

"Somebody has been searching for something," observed Carr.

"I wonder what," said Truscott.

Carr looked at him oddly. "I wonder about something quite different."

"What?"

"Whether they found it."

Gently, Carr walked towards the bed. With the tip of the silver handle of his cane, he sifted through the discarded belongings from the suitcase. There was a pocketbook which seemed to contain a not insubstantial sum of money, a selection of auction catalogues, a couple of novels, and a collection of papers and envelopes. Carr leaned forward over the bed, peering more closely at the papers and envelopes, trying to ascertain their nature. Some of them appeared to be bank statements and other financial documents; some appeared to be purchase orders and receipts for various *objets d'art* which Lynch had bought, presumably, Carr reasoned, from the auctions detailed by the catalogues which he had found.

As he prodded the papers with his cane, one of the envelopes caught his attention. It was beige, rather stiffer than the rest, and foolscap in size. Taking his handkerchief from his jacket pocket, Carr picked up the envelope.

91

The flap of the envelope had been torn open but it had been done with care, as if by a knife's blade. Manipulating the flap with his handkerchief, Carr peered inside and saw what were clearly photographs. He walked over to a small writing desk which was placed under the window and, in a deft movement, he emptied out the contents of the envelope. They were photographs, indeed, but what they depicted was something which Carr could never have guessed.

They were all of a young woman. As far as Carr to tell, it was the same woman in each of them. The nature of the photographs, however, were obscene. The woman was almost naked in all the images. She was dressed in a cloche hat, pulled low over her brow, stockings, and high heeled shoes. She wore nothing else, other than a string of pearls and a large, black domino mask. She had been photographed in various poses: her legs apart with her hands between them and her head thrown back in rapture; bending forward, the picture taken from the front and the back; in several, she was tied to cheap beds and even cheaper chairs. In others, she was pleasuring a man whose face was never shown. It was almost as if she were being forced into the act. In some, there was more than one man involved. The mask and hat concealed her identity, but her youth was undeniable and Carr doubted she could be much past twenty years of age. The innocence of her age made the depravity of the images all the more abhorrent.

"My God," whispered Carr. "My God..."

He turned his back on the photographs and walked to the centre of the room, to distance himself from their wickedness. Truscott walked over to the table and looked down at the scattered pictures. He could not do so for long.

"She's little more than a child," he said. "Who do you suppose the girl is?"

But Carr was beyond theorising. He had returned to the writing table and had begun to scoop up the photos, covering his hand with his handkerchief. As he picked them up, he saw a mark on the reverse side of one of them. Looking at it more closely, he saw that it was a monogram stamped in ink. He squinted at the slightly smudged ink and read the words: *Les Lentilles d'Henri Chastain*. There was an address in Soho.

"Does that address mean anything to you, Truscott?" Carr watched whilst the journalist shook his head slowly. "Well," continued the former judge, pointing to the envelope of photographs, "whoever ransacked this room clearly wasn't looking for these awful things, otherwise he would have taken them away with him. Which leads one to ask what exactly he *was* looking for."

"Do you have any idea what it might be?"

Carr shrugged. "There is something I expected to find in here, which I have not. That is curious in itself."

"What something?"

But Carr did not reply. Instead, he began to make a tour of the room. Truscott watched him move slowly, stepping with slight difficulty over the upturned drawers and discarded clothes. The dark eyes danced furiously over the scattered objects, peering out from under the heavy brows. He began to stroke the white moustache and Imperial, as if their softness was a comfort to him in his confusion and bewilderment. In turn, Carr examined every possible place of concealment: the wardrobe, the chests of drawers, the dressing table. With each inspection, Carr became increasingly irritated. Truscott would have assisted in the search, if he had known what he should be looking for, but any enquiry along those lines would have been unwelcome.

Carr sat down on the edge of the bed. He remained there for some long moments in silence, his eyes closed, and his hands gripping the silver handle of his cane with a fierce tenacity. At last, at the point when Truscott had begun to find the silence uncomfortable, Carr let out a snarl of frustration. Easing himself to the floor as painlessly as possible, he lay down on the floorboards and peered under the bed. He gave a small snigger and pulled himself back to his feet.

"Some men never truly leave behind the habits of their childhood," he said. "Hiding one's secrets under the bed is a scheme which occurs to every child at some point. Would you be so good as to shuffle under the bed, my boy? You will find a small valise tucked away under there, against the back wall, and I would be much obliged if you would drag it out for me."

Protesting was not an option. Carr's expression was sufficient persuasion of that fact. Truscott dropped to the floor and, with a slight grunt of effort, peered under the bed. The valise was silhouetted in the shadows of the bed frame and the general darkness of the space. Reaching out, Truscott grabbed hold of it and pulled it out into the light of the room. He rose to his feet and placed the valise on the mattress of the bed.

"You're not going to open it?" he asked.

"Of course."

"It is evidence, surely?"

Carr nodded. "I sincerely hope so, otherwise we are wasting our time searching it."

Before Truscott could argue further, Carr had tucked his cane under his arm and was pulling open the valise. He looked inside and allowed a slight gasp of satisfaction escape from between his gritted teeth. He smiled across at Truscott as he wrapped his handkerchief around his fingers once again. Reaching inside the bag, he pulled out the wooden dolls with the painted death's heads for faces and the cord nooses around their necks. He laid them carefully on the bed and turned to face Truscott.

"What do you make of those, my boy?"

"Are they what you were looking for?"

Carr nodded. "I overheard a disagreement between Lynch and Louisa Marston yesterday. He accused her of sending these little beauties to him. Over a period of a few weeks, he said."

"Why would she do that?"

Carr waved aside the question. "That does not matter for now. The question we must answer first is what purpose do these dolls serve?"

"The skulls and the nooses suggest death threats," said Truscott, "but it is a very melodramatic gesture. Why not send an anonymous note like everyone else?"

Carr's eyes were like polished onyx. "That, my boy, is rather the point."

Truscott frowned. "Are you suggesting you know who is responsible for them?"

"I think I can take an educated guess, at least," Carr replied. "Surely you can too. The more interesting point is why they were sent at all."

"Whoever sent these dolls must have carried out their threat," Truscott gasped, no longer listening to Carr's words. "They warned him of his death and carried out the threat."

"There is still much to learn before we can be certain of that," said Carr, smiling to himself. Any more conversation was prevented by the sound of car tyres over gravel and the screeching of brakes, suggesting an arrival at speed. Truscott strode over to the window and peered out over the driveway.

"It is the police," he said, looking back at Carr over his shoulder. "We should put everything back as we found it. The photographs, the valise, the dolls…"

Carr tutted. "Then we should certainly be caught in the act of doing so. There is not enough time for us to complete that task before the police are in this room. We cannot prevent them from discovering our search now, but it would look infinitely more suspicious if we were caught in the act of covering our traces."

Truscott sighed heavily. "What do you propose we do then?"

Carr smiled warmly and sat down on the corner of the bed once more. He rested his hands on the handle of his cane and stretched out his injured leg. The knee had begun to ache with his exertions. He looked back at Truscott, the smile still fixed impishly on his lips beneath the whiteness of his moustache.

"I say we sit here as comfortably as we can and await the arrival of the police."

He spoke with a jaunty, careless tone of voice, but the dark eyes were heavy with thought as they alternated their attention once more between the sordid photographs on the writing table and the macabre dolls which lay beside him on the bed.

Chapter Sixteen

Inspector Swift arrived on the scene in a frenzy of activity and efficiency. After the terrified stillness which had settled on the house following the discovery of Lynch's body, Swift's brisk authority seemed to be like the most ferocious of tempests. He barked orders to uniformed officers and he snapped questions at the harassed detective sergeant who had been obliged to accompany him on their mission. The younger officer tried valiantly to keep up with the demands of the Inspector, but his hand and pencil could not work or move as rapidly as Swift's voice and mouth.

If the Inspector's manner was abrupt and brusque, his appearance did nothing to compliment it. He was overall too dapper to have such a personality as he had. Where his conduct was bombastic, his grooming was ordered and pristine. His suit was neatly pressed and the knot in his tie was so precise as to be almost prim. His shoes were polished but not quite to the extent which might suggest an obsession. His dark hair was trimmed to a military perfection, swept back from a high and intelligent brow. He was clean-shaven, as if any facial hair might run the risk of seeming untidy or disarranged. He stood in the hallway with his hands clasped behind his back, his deep, commanding voice declaring his intentions and commands.

Dr Gilchrist had asserted that he should accompany Lady Ravenwood to greet the official police. She had attempted to dissuade him, but the doctor had been adamant.

"It's on my insistence that Sir James is not here to greet them himself," he had said. "The least I can do is stand in his place, if you will permit me."

Now, Gilchrist had undertaken to make the necessary introductions. Swift had listened intently but without emotion to the explanation of Ravenwood's whereabouts.

"Upstairs, sedated?" he barked. "Why is that?"

"He was attacked yesterday afternoon," said Mary. "Two men stole his house keys and what money he had on him."

"Stolen keys?" Swift had pounced on the fact like a cat on an unsuspecting mouse.

"That is why we had to break down the door," said Gilchrist. "Sir James always kept the museum locked and only he had a key. It was stolen when he was assaulted. But the thieves cannot be responsible."

"Why not?"

"The house was locked, front and back, and we had placed a sentry on guard at the lodge at the front gates, to stop anyone from getting into the grounds."

Swift digested the information with customary swiftness. "Who broke down the door, sir?"

"I did, along with Richard Prentice and Jack Truscott."

"They are…?"

"Richard is my daughter's fiancé," explained Mary. "Mr Truscott is one of our guests this weekend. This disastrous weekend," she added, tears welling in her eyes once more.

Swift, not known for handling the emotions of women with any subtlety or compassion, turned his attention back to Gilchrist. "How many people went into this room after the door was broken down?"

"Only myself and Mr Carr, as far as I know," replied the doctor. "You have Mr Carr to thank for that. He took control of the situation immediately. He asked me only to confirm death and estimate a time."

Swift's eyebrows raised. "Did he? And what time did you estimate, Dr Gilchrist?"

"Between eleven last night and two this morning. But, as I told Carr, I am not a pathologist and you mustn't take my word for it."

Swift nodded in understanding, but his expression was troubled. "And who, exactly, is this Mr Carr?"

"I don't know him personally," replied Gilchrist. "He's a retired judge, as I understand it."

"Everett Carr is a dear friend of the family," added Mary. "He and James have been friends for many years."

Swift contemplated matters for a few seconds only but, if he had drawn any preliminary conclusions, he kept them to himself. "Speaking of Sir James, I shall have to have a word with him, Lady Ravenwood. As soon as possible."

Mary nodded. "I understand, Inspector. As soon as Dr Gilchrist will allow it."

Gilchrist checked his watch. "Half an hour or so, Inspector. Not sooner."

Swift's mouth stretched into a sly, humourless smile. "Plenty for me to be doing in the meantime, doctor. I shall have to speak to everybody in turn. I will send a constable to take preliminary statements from everyone in the house."

"The guests are in the drawing room," said Mary, "and Fenton has the staff assembled in the kitchen."

"In fact, only Mr Carr and Jack Truscott are absent," said Gilchrist. "I don't know where they are."

Swift had stopped listening. "If you could go back to the drawing room yourselves, I will be with you in due course. First, I must see the body."

The examination of the scene of the murder was brisk but professional. The broken lamp registered itself in Swift's consciousness and his mind suffered a slight twist of unease at it. He had been a police detective for almost twenty years. Instinct had served him well in the past and it had been honed over the years of service to a status of certain reliability. It told him now that the overturned lamp and table held a certain significance but, in the moment, he could not delineate their importance. He stood staring down at them, but his mind would not react further. At last, turning away with a frown, he looked down at the body.

Between Gilchrist and the jewelled knife, Swift had sufficient information to ascertain how and when death had occurred, both of which were his primary concerns at any scene of murder. The pathologist would need to verify the time, but Gilchrist's estimate was sufficient for Swift's present purposes and he was grateful for the fact. Swift was not a man to linger unnecessarily over death, preferring instead to try to maintain a professional sense of detachment. And yet, despite this preference, Swift had never been able entirely to distance himself from the effect of violent death. In the end, he felt always that murder was an outrage, an act which could never be forgiven or go unpunished. He felt it now, that familiar determination to find the culprit and, with it, came the equally familiar anger that a life should be brought to a halt before its rightful end.

"Sir?"

The detective sergeant was behind him, his cheeks flushed and his eyes wide with anxiety. Swift inhaled deeply, taking a last look at the body, and turned around. "What is it, Lane?"

"The dead man's room, sir. There are two gentlemen in there."

Swift's eyes narrowed. "What two gentlemen?"

"Only one of them spoke, sir, so I only got his name." Lane checked his notebook. "A Mr Everett Carr, sir."

Swift snorted, as if the stern expulsion of air from his nostrils could blow away the name which had already begun to crawl under his skin. "What's he doing in the room of a murder victim?"

Lane stuttered over his reply until Swift's snarl forced him to find the words. "I'm not sure you're going to like this, sir."

"Try me, Lane."

"He says he's waiting for you."

Swift did not reply, but it was clear from the speed at which he marched upstairs that Lane had been correct. The Inspector had not liked the response at all.

Swift nodded briefly to the constable who was standing outside Lynch's room. The door was open and he stepped into the room with a grim determination. He was struck immediately by the chaos surrounding him: the discarded drawers, the scattered clothes, and the disarranged papers. He saw Carr sitting calmly on the edge of the bed and, behind him, Swift's eyes caught sight of the open valise and the wooden dolls. He looked around the room in initial disbelief and then in subsequent irritation. Truscott had risen when Swift had entered but, even if he had not done so out of politeness, he would have been forced to stand to attention under the command of the Inspector's glare. Carr, by contrast, showed no inclination to stand and his eyes remained fixed on Swift, a small smile breaking from behind the moustache and beard.

"Would somebody care to explain what is going on here?" asked Swift. His voice was low and restrained, not unlike, Truscott thought, the oppressive stillness in the skies before a thunderstorm broke.

"Do not upset yourself, Inspector," said Carr. "My friend and I have not made this mess. The room was like it when we came in here."

"Is that right? I suppose it would be too much to ask why you came in here at all, sir."

"I thought we could save you some time." Only now, and on his own account entirely, did Carr rise. He did so slowly, his leg protesting slightly at the effort. "And, if I may say so, I think we have."

Swift's frown had deepened, but it seemed to Truscott as if some of the fury had evaporated from it, being replaced by an effort to remember a temporarily forgotten fact. The Inspector was staring at Carr: at his face, his vivid lilac tie and handkerchief, at the black suit, the ruby-eyed skull lapel pin, and at both the injured knee and the cane. His mind was running at full speed: *Carr...retired judge...*

Carr held out his hand. "Everett Carr, Inspector."

Despite himself, Swift shook the older man's hand. "You got Doyle Cullearn hanged. That was you."

Perhaps Swift could not have known the tragedy which lay behind the memory. Perhaps the achievement of sending a dangerous man to his death had overshadowed its consequence. Carr was not offended by the recognition, nor was he angered by it, but he still felt the pain of the memory. True to form, his knee began to burn. Carr lowered his gaze and simply replied, "It was, yes."

"Even in these parts, news of that judgment was welcome," said Swift. "I doubt there's a copper in the country who didn't cheer you on account of it."

"You are very kind." It was all Carr could think to say.

A moment passed. At its end, Swift re-asserted his natural manner but it seemed to have softened slightly at its edges. "You still have no right to be in here, Mr Carr."

Carr smiled, but his eyes still betrayed something of his momentary sadness. "No doubt, Inspector, but I think you will agree that the murderer must still be in this house. I thought time was rather of the essence."

Between gritted teeth, Swift said what he felt it was his duty to say. "Which is why, at the moment, sir, everyone in the house is a suspect. Including you."

Carr tilted his head. "Don't talk nonsense, Inspector. Now that you know who I am, you no more suspect me than Truscott does."

Swift was about to say something more, but Carr did not give him the opportunity. He began to walk back towards the bed and he sat down once more, stretching out his leg. He rested his cane against his shoulder and clasped his hands in his lap. As he moved, he spoke.

"There are three points of interest in this room. First, it has been ransacked, as you see. We can conclude that must have happened in the night, otherwise, Lynch certainly would have commented on it last evening and he did not. The second point is what is inside that envelope on the table under the window. Finally, there are these dolls." Carr indicated the bizarre figures on the bed. "I presume you have ascertained a time of death, Inspector."

Swift was looking, in turn, at the photographs and the dolls. "Only from Dr Gilchrist. The pathologist has not yet arrived. I'm aware, Mr Carr," he added, slyly, "that you know what Dr Gilchrist's estimate of the time of death is."

Carr ignored the veiled rebuke. "And you know about the attack on Sir James?"

Swift nodded. "If the museum room door had to be broken into, the keys couldn't have been used. I don't see any connection between the murder and the attack."

Carr bowed his head. "I agree, up to a point."

"That leaves us with a little puzzle, does it not?" murmured Swift, his eyes fixed on Everett Carr.

"You mean how the murderer got into the room and escaped from it," observed Truscott, speaking for the first time.

Swift ignored him. He had no attention for any person other than Carr. Nevertheless, he replied to the comment with a simple, "Precisely."

Carr shook his head. "There is no mystery there."

Both Swift and Truscott glared at him. It was the Inspector who asked: "What?"

"The broken lamp is the key to that particular problem," replied Carr. He shook his head vigorously. "We mustn't get distracted by simple points when we have much more troubling mysteries to solve. I suggest, Inspector, that you examine that envelope and its contents and these dolls before we discuss anything further."

Carr shifted himself on the bed and reached behind him, taking one of the dolls in his handkerchief and passing it over to the Inspector. Swift frowned as he took in the painted skull and the makeshift noose. "Death threats?"

Carr assented with a lowering of his eyelids. "I overheard Lynch talking about these fascinating dolls yesterday."

"Who to?"

"Miss Louisa Marston." Carr took the doll back from Swift and set it back down on the bed. He folded his handkerchief and replaced it in his jacket pocket. "They had quite an argument."

"About what?"

"I think you should ask her about that yourself, Inspector." Carr smiled amicably. "The point is whether the threat conveyed by these dolls has been carried out or whether they are incidental to Lynch's murder."

"They are surely something which we have to bear in mind." Swift was walking around the room now, his hands sunk into his trouser pockets.

"Undoubtedly," replied Carr. "But it may not be a simple case of cause and effect. Come to that, it may not be that Miss Marston was guilty of sending the dolls at all."

"But Lynch suspected her?"

Carr shrugged. "I fear it was more a question of him shooting in the dark, as it were. I don't think he had proof of anything."

Swift had reached the small writing table. Taking a pencil out of his inside pocket, he nudged the pictures around, taking in their details for as long as he felt able.

"Filth," he hissed, under his breath. "Why would Lynch have this sort of muck in his possession?"

"I can think of several reasons," said Carr, softly.

Swift had picked up one of the photographs and he looked at it briefly. "There is no way of telling who any of the people in them are."

"The girl is the main focus, of course," said Carr.

"This sort of thing makes me ashamed to be a man," spat Swift, tossing the photograph aside.

Carr nodded his head slowly. "I cannot disagree with that."

"Perhaps Lynch was the man behind the camera," suggested Swift.

Truscott was emboldened to speak. "Or else he had the photographs commissioned for his own purposes."

Swift was gracious enough to give a slight nod of his head, but he made no verbal reply. "We shall have to visit this M. Chastain in Soho, of course. I'd very much like to have a couple of hours in his company," he added, more to himself than to anybody else, and his tone made it clear that the meeting would not be a sociable one.

"Everything in its place, Inspector," said Carr, standing once more. "M. Chastain is not likely to go anywhere for the present, so he can wait. There is much to learn and explain within this house before we think about trips to London."

Swift took a step towards him and pointed a finger in his face. "I appreciate that, sir, and I will learn it all. But not with your interference, Mr Carr. You are a suspect, whatever else you might think."

There was a moment of silence which passed between the two men. Swift remained adamant in his resolve, his eyes glaring into those of Carr, as if daring the older man to oppose him. Carr's own eyes danced around the Inspector's face and a smile crept over his lips.

"If I am a suspect," he said, "all the better to keep me in your sight at all times."

"You are not involving yourself in my investigation, Mr Carr," pressed Swift.

Carr's smile widened. "Naturally not."

Swift was insistent. "I must ask you to go downstairs and wait for a constable to take your statement."

"By all means, Inspector," replied Carr, "but I think it would be much more beneficial for us to interview Sir James Ravenwood first. I am sure Dr Gilchrist will sanction it now."

"Go downstairs, Mr Carr," snapped Swift.

Carr gripped the Inspector's forearm. "Time is marching against us, Inspector, and we must not allow it. Come now!"

Before Swift could protest further, Everett Carr had left the room, giving an amiable greeting to the constable who stood on guard as he passed.

Chapter Seventeen

Mary had insisted on being present when Swift spoke to her husband. The Inspector had raised no objection to her demand. It had come as no surprise to him as it was a request which was frequently made by a husband or wife in such circumstances and, to Swift's efficient mind, it was an opportunity of conducting two interrogations simultaneously. Sir James Ravenwood sat up in the bed, his back and shoulders supported by pillows. His face was pale and haggard, which made the dressing to the wound on his temple seem even more pitiable than it was. Swift stood at the foot of the bed, his hands clasped behind his back. He had given Carr a suitable warning against interference, but he had allowed him to remain in the room. As a gesture of goodwill, Carr stood by the window, as if to emphasise his role of silent spectator.

"Such a terrible thing to happen," said Ravenwood. "Strange, but people often read about murder for pleasure, in detective stories and what have you, but when the real thing intrudes in one's life, it shows the true evil of itself."

"It's horrible," said Mary under her breath.

Ravenwood gripped his wife's hand. She looked into his eyes, her own widened with shock and fear, and she reached up to caress his hair. She smiled gently at him, but she could not stop the single tear from rolling down her cheek.

"I'm sorry about this, old girl," Ravenwood whispered, looking across at her. Mary did not reply, other than to continue to smile and tighten the gripping of their hands. Ravenwood looked up at Swift. "You have questions, of course, Inspector."

Swift stood to attention. "I shall try not to keep you, sir. I know from Dr Gilchrist that you must rest a while longer."

"Gilchrist is being over-cautious. I am perfectly fine. You mustn't read too much into this wound of mine, Inspector. It looks worse than it feels."

"It can't have been a pleasant experience, sir."

"Certainly not. The only mercy of it was that it was over quickly. I barely had time to register what was happening before it was done with."

"I understand your keys were taken in the attack, sir. Including the key to the door of the museum room where the other, more tragic incident occurred." Swift chose his words carefully.

"That's correct," replied Ravenwood.

"Dr Gilchrist tells me that efforts made to secure the house, on the assumption your assailants would come here to rob you."

Carr cleared his throat. "I suggested as much to the doctor and he was to get Fenton to arrange it. A member of the staff was present in the lodge at the front gates throughout the night. The back doors were locked, as always. The house was secured."

"And this servant is trustworthy?" asked Swift.

Ravenwood interjected. "I vouch for every member of my household. If they had orders to stay in the lodge at the front gates and permit nobody to enter, they would have complied."

"Are there spare keys to the rooms in this house?"

"To all except the museum room, Inspector," replied Ravenwood. "My own foolish vanity. That room is mine alone and only I wanted control of the key to it."

"So only you could have locked it yesterday, sir?"

"Indeed."

"And entry through the back of the house was impossible?"

"There is an iron gate in the back wall, but it is locked," said Ravenwood, "as are the back doors themselves at night. Besides, the keys which were stolen did not include any of the keys to them. Nobody could gain access that way from the outside once the doors were locked."

Swift was silent for a moment. "So, to be clear, the house itself was more secure than usual, by virtue of the guard at the lodge, as well as the usual locked doors at the rear. Which means that if either of the men who attacked you did come here last night, they would not have been able to gain entry in any event."

"Correct."

"And nobody inside the house could get into the museum room, because the only key has been stolen." Swift threw a significant glance towards Carr, who simply smiled and shrugged his shoulders. "Could somebody have made a duplicate of the museum room door key without your knowledge, Sir James?"

Ravenwood shook his head emphatically. "Out of the question, Inspector."

"Granted that nobody could come in from the outside, how do you explain the fact that Mr Lynch certainly got in there and so did whoever killed him?"

His brow creasing in bewilderment, Ravenwood sighed. "It simply makes no sense. I cannot begin to explain it, Inspector."

Swift began to pace the room. "This is a very old house, is it not? It's not uncommon for such houses to have secret passages. Priest holes and the like."

"There is nothing of the sort here, Inspector Swift." Ravenwood smiled grimly. "Abraham Dyer, who built this house, was reputed to have been a warlock and a necromancer. I doubt he would have had much cause to conceal and protect Catholic priests. Besides, the house was built after the Tudor period."

If Swift interpreted the reply as mockery, he did not challenge it. "Mr Lynch was killed between the hours of eleven and two o'clock last night, sir. You will forgive the directness of my question but it is one which must be asked of everybody. Where were you between those times, Sir James?"

"I would like to say that I was in my bed, Inspector, but I'm afraid it would be a lie. I had been sleeping deeply, on account of Dr Gilchrist's administrations, but I awoke in the early hours in great pain. I could not settle, so I thought I would go and sit in the peace of the library for a while. I did not wish to wake my wife, you see, with constant tossing and turning."

"What time did you go downstairs?"

"I cannot be sure, but it must have been somewhere around one o'clock, a little before perhaps."

"Did you stay in the library for the rest of the night?"

"No. I went back to my room after half an hour or so, three quarters perhaps."

"And you saw nothing unusual whilst you were downstairs?"

Ravenwood shook his head sadly, as if his reply was in some way the cause of the disaster which had befallen the household.

Swift turned to Mary. "And your ladyship? What were you doing in the relevant period?"

She glared at the Inspector, her eyes alive with an emotion which might have been fear or outrage. It was as if she had not expected to be asked about her own movements, as if they were irrelevant to anything which had occurred in the house during the twilight hours.

"What time do you mean, Inspector?" she stammered. "Eleven and when?"

"Two o'clock."

"Of course, forgive me." She took a moment to collect her thoughts. "I was in bed, naturally."

"You did not wake when your husband left the room?"

"No."

"And you did not hear Sir James return?"

"No."

"You didn't wake yourself and go downstairs?"

"No." It was more emphatic now. "I was in bed the entire time. I am a heavy sleeper, Inspector."

She spoke with such insistent vehemence that Swift was compelled to leave the matter alone. He looked over to Everett Carr, who had been silent during the interview. He was leaning against the window frame, his cane hanging listlessly between his fingers, and his head inclined to the side. His dark eyes were intense under the furrowed brows and the thin lips were pursed in concentration. For a moment, it was as if nobody else existed in the room except himself. He seemed neither to see nor hear anybody or to have no interest in anything other than whatever thought had seemed to occur to him. At last, his eyes shimmered and the spell was broken, his gaze shifting from the point in space upon which it had been fixed to the room as a whole.

"Forgive me, Inspector," he said with a genial smile, "my mind was elsewhere. I wonder if I might ask one or two questions of my own."

"If you must," conceded the Inspector, with a smile which suggested anything other than humour.

Carr either overlooked or failed to recognise Swift's irony. "How long have you known Sebastian Lynch, Sir James?"

"We have been in correspondence for a while, but I only met him a few months ago."

"And you met as a result of your shared interest in, dare I say, the macabre?"

"Yes. Lynch was a collector like myself. We shared a fascination of the violence of man's past."

"Torture in the Middle Ages," said Carr, "executions, the various criminal punishments which were meted out through the years. One might even say the evolution of murder?"

Ravenwood shifted in his bed. "Yes, but only from a historic perspective. Our interest was purely from an academic and collecting point of view. And it was not simply the topics you mention, Carr. We both shared a love of myths and legends, of superstitions and the occult."

"You were rivals, I think you might say."

"I wouldn't put it like that. Any serious student of a subject might be classed as a competitor to a man of the same inclination, but it is always a courteous competition."

Carr smiled warmly, showing that he fully understood the point. He looked across to Mary. "I understand you did not know the dead man at all, Lady Ravenwood?"

"No, I met him for the first time yesterday. I knew James was inviting a new acquaintance this weekend, but I had no idea who it was."

Carr was smiling at her lie. "Can either of you think of a reason why anybody should want to murder this man, Lynch?"

"None at all," said Ravenwood, his voice lowering with sadness. A moment later, Mary shook her head in response.

"Were you aware of any threats against his life at all?" asked Carr nonchalantly.

"Threats?" gasped Ravenwood. "What type of threats?"

"Any type at all."

"Certainly not. I doubt he would have confided in me anyway," added Ravenwood, "but he never mentioned anything like that, no. Lynch was a private man. I never knew anything very much about him, aside from his collection and articles which he had written on our subject."

Swift stepped forward, reasserting his authority. "You know of no family?"

"He had a sister, I think, but she had died," replied Ravenwood. "He never spoke of any other family."

"No wife, no children?"

Ravenwood smiled. "Not that I know of, but I gather he had been rather wild in his youth, so I suppose it is possible."

Carr coughed gently. "If I might intrude once again, does the name Henri Chastain mean anything to either of you?"

Ravenwood exchanged a glance with his wife, but their expressions remained blank. It was Ravenwood who spoke, but Mary's shaking of the head confirmed his reply. "Never heard it before, as far as I can recall. Who is he?"

"A man of no immediate importance," replied Carr. He bowed his head in thanks to both of them. "I'm obliged."

Ravenwood leaned his head against the wall and closed his eyes. He sighed heavily and, under his breath, he muttered a word of prayer. Then, with a sudden sadness in his eyes, he looked to Swift. "The Tethran Dagger...I suppose you will have to take it away for the time being?"

"I'm afraid so, sir," said the Inspector.

"Will it be returned to me?"

"When we are done with it."

Ravenwood looked to Mary and held her gaze for a long moment. When he looked back at Swift, his eyes had hardened. "Give it to the British

Museum. Or whoever else might want it. If nobody does, throw it in the sea or bury it. Do what you like with it. I never want to see it again."

"Sir James?"

Ravenwood spoke through gritted teeth. "The thing is cursed. I don't want it anywhere near my family ever again."

Chapter Eighteen

Helena Garrick could stand the claustrophobia no more.

The drawing room had become intolerable for her. It was not that she failed to understand the reason for the sombre atmosphere or that she could not empathise with the fear and sadness which permeated through the room. On the contrary, she felt the same anxiety as the rest of the household and she could not fool herself otherwise. What disturbed her more profoundly, however, was the growing suspicion which tainted her thoughts. She found it distressing enough to be present at the discovery of a murder, but to know that the murderer was someone in close proximity to her was too terrible to contemplate. The knowledge that any one of the people in the room could have committed the crime was both bewildering and terrifying. Standing by the door to the drawing room, Helena had watched her companions as they walked around the room in suppressed distress or sat weeping without any attempt to conceal that same sense of dread. She wondered whether any of them was watching her with the same morbid suspicion that consumed her now.

It became too much for her to bear. She was seized by a desire to be out of there, to be far away, to be anywhere else, and to breathe air which did not feel contaminated by the smell of death. She pulled open the door and stepped out into the hallway. A constable was still standing outside the museum room, talking to Detective Sergeant Lane. Helena approached them with purpose.

"Can I speak to Inspector Swift, please?"

Lane looked at her with uncertain authority. "He's busy at the minute, miss. Can I help?"

Helena doubted it, but her desire to be free from the house overwhelmed any other considerations. "I can't sit in that room any longer."

"The Inspector doesn't want anyone to leave the house."

"I just want a walk around the terrace, to get some air." She looked back towards the drawing room. "It's stifling in there."

"I can't let you do that, miss." Lane looked genuinely contrite. "I'm sorry."

Helena clicked her tongue and shifted the weight on her feet, crossing her arms in defiance. She gave the matter some more thought and then smiled back at Lane. "I won't leave the terrace, Sergeant, I promise you."

"Even so, miss, I can't let you go."

Helena's cool exterior cracked and her voice rose with the same fury as the temperature of her mood. "This is ridiculous."

The detective sergeant was spared any further embarrassment by the sound of Swift's voice from the stairs. "What's the problem, Lane?"

Helena answered swiftly. "I'm suffocating in that room waiting for you, Inspector, and I need to get some air. I must insist you interview me now or else let me have a walk around the terrace."

"I'll speak to you when I'm ready, miss," replied Swift. "You may have a walk around the terrace if that will assist in calming you down before I do speak to you."

Helena looked back at Lane but replied to Swift. "Thank you."

Lane felt it prudent to defend himself. "You said nobody was to leave the house, sir."

By now, Swift was by his side and able to reply in that soft, lowered tone which was heavy with menace and which Lane recognised too well. "She's not going to go anywhere, is she, Lane? Not now we've secured the property and got men on post at all the gates."

Lane accepted the comment by staring at the floor. "No, sir."

"No, sir," mocked Swift quietly.

Helena, not wishing to lose her advantage, walked swiftly to the front door and pulled it open, stepping out onto the threshold of Warlock's Gate with a heavy sigh of relief.

She stood motionless for a moment, listening to the sound of distant birdsong and the gentle rustling of the trees in the breeze. She inhaled the smell of the outdoors, of the grass and the firs, and she listened to the faint sound of a church bell tolling the hour. It was all so soothing, a comforting reminder of normality, of a life untainted by sudden death and fearful suspicion. For those precious few seconds, Helena seemed to forget what had happened between the walls of the house behind her. It was as if she had nothing to do with any of it, as though her life was how it always had been before murder soured it. There was, in those few seconds, nothing but the trees, the birds, and the possibility of the existence of God. But the peace was only momentary. Like a shot from a gun, the memory of Lynch's blood exploded in her mind and the image of tranquillity which she had conjured up was shattered. Now, she was back in the reality of death and the cold presence of murder.

Helena walked around the pathway to the back terrace. She sat on one of the stone benches there and lit a cigarette, inhaling deeply on its soothing fumes. She tried to bring her breathing under control, to regulate its irregular rhythm, but her mind would not rid itself of those images of Lynch's lifeless body and sightless, accusing eyes. Helena closed her own eyes, but it did nothing to blind her memory to what it saw. She knew she must think about something else, that she must try to deflect her brain's attention from the details of that unique horror which she had witnessed.

Fumbling with the collar of her dress, she pulled out the golden locket which hung around her neck. Her fingers twitched with anxiety and she struggled to unfasten the clasp which kept the locket closed. On the third attempt, she succeeded. She forced her eyes to open and she allowed them to rest on the image within the locket. If the birds and the trees had soothed her earlier, the face which smiled back at her consoled her entirely. The girl's eyes shimmered with both the innocence and vigour of youth. The smile was wide, filled with promise and ambition. The tightly curled hair, worn in errant bunches on either side of her head, was unruly but it held the same vitality of spirit as the girl herself. Despite the few tears which fell, Helena felt her heart soar, but now it was with happiness rather than fear, and she felt her breathing turn into short, gasps of laughter.

She closed the locket and replaced it beneath the collar of her dress. It had calmed her better than any tonic which John Gilchrist might have been able to prescribe.

"Are you all right?"

She could not have known how long he had been standing there. His voice startled her and she wondered whether he had seen her loss of resolve or, worse, whether he had seen the photograph in the locket. She inhaled deeply once more on the cigarette and nodded vigorously.

Truscott pointed to the space on the bench beside her. "May I?"

She agreed. "Has it all got too much for you too, Mr Truscott?"

"I wish you would call me Jack." He waited for her to say something more, but she did not oblige. "Terrible thing to have happened."

Helena kept her gaze fixed on the trees ahead of her. "I couldn't stand it in there any longer. I had to come and get some air."

"I can understand that. It's difficult to know what to do or say when something like this happens."

"Are you saying that from experience?"

"Through my work."

"A crime journalist."

He was flattered that she remembered his profession, but he did not express it. "I've seen first-hand people affected by murder in the past. It's never anything but horrible."

She shifted on the bench so that she was facing him. In doing so, she moved closer to him, her legs accidentally touching his, prompting a brief and embarrassed apology. She looked at him seriously. "I suppose you never get used to it."

Truscott smiled. "You have to pray you don't. If you do, what hope is left for your humanity?"

Helena continued to stare at him. His words had pierced her. "What a remarkable thing to say."

"Is it?"

"I don't mean that offensively," she assured him. "I mean it sincerely."

Truscott bowed his head. "Not many of my colleagues share it. Most of the hacks I know salivated at the thought of a good murder. The bloodier, the better for most of them. They would say I had too weak a stomach for the job. People like them think a good crime reporter has to be immune to the shock of the crime. Or at least pretend he is."

"They would be wrong."

He looked across to her. "You don't see it as weakness?"

"Wanting to retain your humanity? Not at all."

"What would you call it?"

"Sensitivity. And you're a better man for it than your colleagues," she added, leaning in towards him. A smile had crept across her lips.

They sat together in silence for a moment. It was not an uncomfortable silence and Truscott was surprised at how much he enjoyed it. Inevitably, his mind turned to Jane and a feeling of betrayal twisted his stomach. He wondered whether he had any right to be sitting in the company of this woman when his wife was only a year deceased. He could not pretend that he felt anything approaching love for Helena Garrick; to do so would have been ridiculous. But he knew that he found her attractive and that being in her company was something he craved. Even in the wake of the tragedy of the previous night and its current aftermath, Truscott had wanted to be near her and he had found himself wondering what she was thinking and feeling. Whether any of that was a precursor to love or, possibly worse, evidence of a betrayal of his wife, Truscott could not say. But he knew that to deny his feelings would be to lie to himself and he had learned that such lies are the hardest to tell.

Helena had been thinking her own thoughts. Truscott could not have known what they were but, when she spoke, she gave no indication that they were running along similar tracks to his own.

"How did it happen?" she asked. Her brows were creased and Truscott found the imperfection in her otherwise flawless expression to be both vulnerable and alluring. "How did Lynch and his killer get into that room?"

"Carr thinks he knows."

"Is Mr Carr a friend of yours?"

Truscott shrugged. "In a manner of speaking."

"Has he confided in you?" Her voice was almost breathless with what he took to be excitement, but which might have been something else entirely. "What's his explanation of it?"

Truscott laughed and shook his head. "He won't tell me until he's ready."

"How frustrating."

"Yes, he can be. Extremely so."

Helena allowed some moments to pass whilst she summoned the courage to say what was on her mind. "Nobody could get in or out of that room."

"And yet someone did exactly that."

She looked into his eyes, pleading with him to understand her meaning without forcing her to say it aloud. She could determine from his face that he had failed to understand her wishes. She took a breath and said the words. "Whoever killed Lynch is in this house, isn't he?"

Truscott did not know immediately how to reply. He could detect her anxiety now without difficulty and, whilst he did not know her well, nor could he pretend to, he thought he could recognise a quality in her which would prefer truth to evasion. "It looks that way, yes."

She wrapped her arms around herself, as if the air had suddenly dropped in temperature. "It's just so awful. To think that one of us..."

"Had you ever met Lynch before?" It seemed as easy a diversion as any other.

"I met him a couple of times through mutual acquaintances. Alicia and Richard, for example. But to say I knew him is stretching a point. It doesn't stop his death being shocking, just because he was a stranger."

Truscott found that any reply he thought of sounded ludicrously trite in his own ears. The words he conjured in response were next to meaningless and silence seemed to be both a more prudent and sensible option. He stood up in an effort to alleviate his embarrassed discomfort. "Perhaps we should get back inside. Just in case people are looking for us."

Helena shook her head. "Five more minutes, Jack. Please."

It was impossible to refuse the plea, especially since it came more from her deep, emerald eyes rather than from her tone of voice. Truscott sat back down beside her. "Is everything all right, Helena?"

"It's just this whole murder business."

"It's a shock for everyone."

She was shaking her head even before he had finished speaking. "I don't mean that. No, I do, of course. Obviously, the murder is preying on my mind, but…"

"There's something else?" Truscott's eyes narrowed.

"I don't think I should say any more."

"Why not?" he pressed. "What is it?"

She looked at him once again. "I don't know what to do, Jack."

"Tell me what's wrong."

His eyes were gentle, his expression filled with concern, as if he was desperate for her to share her troubles with him. Helena stared back at him, wondering what she would have done if he had not been here, if he had not come for the weekend and if he had not come outside to join her. It was coincidence entirely, but without it, she feared what she might have felt. A part of her wanted to tell him what was on her mind, but another part prohibited her from doing so. Without her putting it into words, he answered her most crucial question in any event.

"You can trust me, Helena, I promise you that."

Perhaps, after all, she could. "What we were saying about the killer being somebody in the house…"

And now he was alert. His eyes hardened and his shoulders straightened, as if he were assuming an official role of authority. He moved closer to her, encouraging her to confide in him, but his voice was adamant and determined. "If you know something, anything at all, you must tell the police."

The suggestion horrified her. "I can't do that, Jack. I don't know what any of it means. It might not mean anything at all and, if it doesn't, but I've told the police anyway, I can't think what harm I would do."

"Then tell me," said Truscott.

Helena stood up and walked to the balustrade of the terrace. He allowed her some moments to gather her thoughts and, at last, she turned to face him, her mind decided.

"The night before last," she said, "I overhead Lynch arguing with someone in the drawing room. A woman. I couldn't hear what they were saying, but I could tell it was serious. Even hushed voices can have an urgency."

"Do you know who the woman was?"

Helena hesitated again, her eyes refusing to meet Truscott's. "I saw Lynch come out of the drawing room in a fearful temper and march back to his room. A few minutes later, the woman came out of the drawing room and went upstairs herself."

"Did you see her clearly enough to recognise her?"

Helena's voice broke under the strain and fell so low that Truscott had trouble hearing the words. "It was Lady Ravenwood."

Truscott glared at her in disbelief. "What would she have to argue about with Lynch?"

"I don't know," replied Helena, as if the question meant nothing to her. "But what should I do about it? I've been friends with Alicia Ravenwood since we were little girls and both Sir James and Lady Ravenwood have been so good to me over the years. What sort of thanks would it be to them if I told the police about this?"

"Helena, you must."

"I can't," she hissed, her distress soured now by a rising anger. "I can't tell them. I can't say anything to them."

"Why not?"

"Lady Ravenwood is no murderer," Helena declared, her voice more assured of the truth of her words than her eyes were. "It's ridiculous to say otherwise. There could be any number of reasons for her arguing with Lynch. Does arguing with someone make you guilty of killing them?"

"Of course not, but..." He stopped himself from protesting further. The defiance in her glare was enough to convince him to say no more. And yet, he felt he could not turn his back on the subject entirely. "You don't believe that argument was innocent, Helena. If you did, you wouldn't be so upset and troubled by witnessing it. If you can't bring yourself to speak to Inspector Swift, consider speaking to Everett Carr."

"Why him?"

Truscott shrugged. "He is taking an interest in this case for some reason. I don't know why, but he is forcing his way into the investigation. But he isn't the official police. It might not feel as much of a betrayal to you if you spoke to him instead of Swift."

She shook her head. "I've made too much out of nothing. I shouldn't have said anything to you, let alone to anybody else. Please, just forget I said anything."

He looked into her eyes once more, hoping to find some weakness in her resolve, but he was disappointed. He turned on his heel and walked away. After only a few steps, he looked back at her. "I can't force you to do the right thing, Helena. All I can do is trust you to do it of your own accord."

She watched him disappear around the corner of the house. It was only then that she realised she had been holding her breath. She expelled the air from her lungs now and took rapid, anxious gasps in order to fill them once more. She turned over in her mind all that Truscott had said and she tried to think objectively about whether he was correct or not in his advice. But any clarity of thought had been drowned by the overwhelming tide of relief which she felt because Truscott had not asked her what she had been doing in the hallway in order to be able to overhear the argument between Lynch and Lady Ravenwood at all. He had come too close to being in a position to question her about it, to probe into her secrets and, perhaps, to compel her to confess them. He had not done so, however, and the consolation she took from his oversight was immense.

And yet, as she walked back to the house, Helena's peace of mind was shattered again as she realised that her respite from any enquiry into her private affairs might be now only temporary. It would not take very much time for Truscott to appreciate what he had overlooked for the present and, she suspected, it would take Everett Carr even less time to query it.

When she walked back into the hallway, the constable on duty outside the museum room thought, sadly, that the beautiful lady with the green eyes looked more upset after her breath of air than before it.

Chapter Nineteen

Carr had retired to the library once the pathologist had arrived at Warlock's Gate. He had no interest in what the medical professional had to say. Like Swift, he took the view that the crucial details surrounding the time and method of death were self-evident. Dr Gilchrist might have insisted that his estimate of the former not be taken as definitive, but Carr was satisfied Gilchrist's caveat was little more than his personal need for caution against any potential professional embarrassment.

Carr sat in the same leather armchair as earlier, his eyes closed, savouring the silence of the room and the comfort of the leather volumes which lined the expansive shelves within it. His mind wandered idly over the facts of the tragedy, but he did not linger on any one of them for a significant length of time. He had drawn some preliminary conclusions, but they were little more than speculation and he could not feel with confidence that they explained the mystery entirely. There was still so much which he could not fathom and to which he could find no clue.

His thoughts were interrupted by the door being thrown wide and the sight of Louisa Marston peering into the room. "I am sorry, Mr Carr, I had no idea you were in here."

Carr held up a hand. "Do not apologise, dear lady. You are welcome to join me. It is quiet in here, as it should be."

"Oh, indeed. I just wanted to read my book in some peace, Mr Carr. Tempers are getting rather short, I'm afraid. Inspector Swift said I might be allowed to sit in here," she added, as justification. "I was not aware you were seeking sanctuary in here also."

"We are of one mind, miss."

Louisa seated herself, her reading glasses perched on the edge of her nose and her collected works of Chekhov open on her knees. Carr sat down in the chair opposite her and watched in silence as she read.

"You enjoy Russian drama, Miss Marston?" he asked.

"I enjoy all theatre," she confessed. "I have done since I was a little girl. I once had some aspirations to the stage, Mr Carr, but I fear I am much too stupid to make a convincing actress."

Carr felt it politic not to make too direct a reply to this criticism. "Have you ever, perhaps, attempted to write a play?"

She blushed at the idea. "Oh, I think it would be very amateurish if I did try it. I am sure I haven't got the insight into people to make any character seem convincing. And I doubt I have the patience to sit and write all those words." She gave an embarrassed, self-deprecating laugh, but it was only short-lived. A darker, more distressing thought had occurred to her. "The drama of theatre seems so artificial now that this genuine tragedy has happened." As if to demonstrate the point, she closed the book and removed her spectacles.

Carr said nothing immediately. "It is certainly a tragedy, yes. But, perhaps the artificial drama of the stage can be taken as a comforting distraction." Then, after a polite pause, he said, "Forgive me for prying, Miss Marston, but I believe you knew Mr Lynch before this weekend."

Her lips fell open and she looked away from him swiftly. Her lips made vague movements, futile attempts to form a reply, but her voice betrayed her, so that she could not help but gasp like a suffocating fish. Her eyes were widened with panic and her cheeks flushed with discomfort. Seeing the reaction his words had produced, he leaned forward and patted her knee gently, soothingly, like a kindly uncle calming a tormented child.

"Please, do not distress yourself," he said. "I have no wish to frighten or intimidate you. I am just an inquisitive old man. It's a force of habit."

"I didn't know him," she stammered, but the lie was automatic and Carr could tell as much. There was no genuine attempt to deceive.

Carr smiled. "When he was introduced to you, you told him that you knew who he was."

"I didn't know him," she repeated, with more force this time.

"My girl, I do not wish to frighten you," Carr said softly, "but, in circumstances of murder, dishonesty breeds suspicion. I have dealt with crime and its consequences for many years. I know how it can twist one's perspective and violate lives. But deceit will only ever assist crime and obstruct the truth. And it is no good lying to me about this. I overheard your argument with him yesterday. On the terrace. I heard it all."

Louisa was horrified. "You were eavesdropping?"

Carr shook his head slowly. "No, no. I was enjoying a moment of solitude, Miss Marston. It was purely by chance that you and Mr Lynch invaded it."

She was looking into his eyes, so dark that they seemed almost black, and yet she saw kindness in them. Strange, that they could be so profoundly dark and yet radiate with goodness. The moustache and beard concealed much of his lower face, but she could tell by those eyes that he was smiling at her. And, for a reason she could not explain, Louisa Marston was in no doubt that Everett Carr's smile was sympathetic, perhaps even kind.

"Do you believe in God, Mr Carr?" she asked.

The question took him by surprise and his delayed response made it seem as if he was not sure of the answer. "Of course, Miss Marston."

"Have you ever known tragedy?" She was gripping the book in her hands now with such force that she must have felt some pain from its edging and spine.

"I have," confessed Carr. "A deep loss."

It was the answer she had wanted. She looked at him now, her tears rolling freely but an expression of defiance across her face, as if she was daring him to contradict her next argument. "Do you never wonder how a God who claims to be merciful could allow such pain?"

Carr knew the route which this conversation was aiming to take and he was determined not to permit it. "Tell me about your father and Mr Lynch."

"Tell me about God's mercy," she insisted.

"I believe in God on my own terms," replied Carr. "And I must trust that He can understand that. I know nothing of His mercy or His cruelty. I try not to think of Him in those terms. I believe in God because the alternative is ever more difficult to accept."

"What alternative?"

"That we are governed by Chance. That there is no structure to the world or to our lives. That tragedy and cruelty can occur for no reason at all. Our moments of sadness must be designed for some purpose, just as our moments of goodness must be. We cannot have beauty without ugliness, Miss Marston, any more than we can have light without darkness or good without evil. One defines the other. And that cannot be the product of chaos, only of design."

He said no more and he felt there was nothing else to be said. Louisa had listened intently, her attention focused entirely on his face, and she remained as if in awe of him for several seconds after his voice had ceased to reach her. She stared at him as if there was nothing else in the world but his face and words. His eyes flickered, blinking erratically as the hypnotic effect of what he had said was broken.

"They hanged my father," she said. "On that evil man's word, they hanged my father."

"He was the foreman of the jury." Carr retained his soothing but instructive tone of voice. "He was not responsible for the verdict, the evidence, or what happened."

"He said the word. He said it out loud."

Carr knew the word she meant. He had no need to say it. He doubted Louisa could ever bring herself to say it in the context of her father.

"Lynch talked about some dolls," Carr said. "Do you know what he meant by that?"

The twist of hate in her face shifted into something more disturbing. Her head began to shake from side to side, her lips parted into an almost feral snarl, but there was nothing predatory about it. The widening of her eyes prevented any suggestion of savagery. Carr could recognise panic and fear when he witnessed it.

"I don't know anything about that, Mr Carr," she whispered, her voice cracking under the strain. "I don't know what he meant."

"Why would he think you had sent them?"

"I don't know." She pressed her knuckle into her mouth and began to bite on it, a childish display of anxiety. Carr noticed for the first time that her teeth protruded slightly from under her upper lip and he found himself wondering whether she had sucked her thumb as a child. He could not doubt it and, sadly, it seemed that she had continued the habit into adulthood.

"I don't know," she said again, but to herself now rather than to him. "I didn't do it."

"You didn't send the dolls?"

She turned on him swiftly. "I didn't *kill* him."

It was an assurance Carr could accept. It was entirely possible that she had sent the ghoulish dolls to Sebastian Lynch, he thought, but surely it was stretching his imagination too far to envisage her stabbing Lynch to the heart. It was true that the death of her father had polluted her opinion of the dead man and Carr knew well enough how the mind can function when contaminated by such toxic experiences. And yet, for all that, he could not accept that this frail, frightened, childish woman was capable of cold-bloodied murder. He watched her begin to stroke the cover of her book of collected plays and, as swiftly as his mind worked, he found himself wondering how far she had pursued her dream of working in the professional theatre. And, consequently, he found himself thinking more profoundly about whether her displays of shyness, innocence, and her apparently childish instincts were genuine or the product of a carefully constructed performance. When he contrasted them with the very real hatred in her eyes when she spoke of Sebastian Lynch, his impression of artificiality intensified.

"Did you sleep soundly last night, Miss Marston?" asked Carr, his voice more cautious now.

The change of subject seemed to disorientate her out of her apparent fear, as sharply and suddenly as a palm across her cheek. It was as if the change of subject had shaken her out of herself and its repercussion made her voice revert back to its timid uncertainty. "No. As a matter of fact, I didn't."

"And why was that?" Carr's kindness, like her nervousness, had returned.

"My mind wouldn't settle," she replied. She recalled the reason well enough, but she had no wish to resurrect the topic of her confrontation with Lynch. "I thought I would read for a while, to see if that would calm me, but I had left my spectacles downstairs in the drawing room, so. I had to come down to collect them."

"What time was that?"

She thought back. The precise time escaped her, but she knew that her more general estimate was adequate for the purpose. "One o'clock, perhaps, a little before."

If Carr had been taken aback by her answer, he was prudent enough not to show it. He felt a caress of ice on the nape of his neck, but his instinct told him that to betray his excitement would have been a mistake. Keeping his voice as controlled as possible, he said, "You had to come down into the hallway?"

"Of course."

"Did anybody see you?"

She shook her head. "Not that I know of."

"Did you see anybody?"

The question seemed to unsettle her. "Not on my way down the stairs."

Her evasion was suggestive and Carr seized its importance at once. "What about when you went back up the stairs?"

She leaned forward in her chair and lowered her voice. "It was when I went to check my window before getting back into bed. My room looks out over the rear lawns of the house. I saw someone. I couldn't see who it was at first, not at that distance, but I saw eventually that it was a woman. She was running across the garden back to the house."

"Did you see where she went?"

Louisa nodded, the rapid bowing of the head of a schoolgirl who is being coerced into betraying a friend for some misdemeanour in which she personally had not been involved. "She came into the house."

Carr frowned. "Are you sure about that, Miss Marston? You are sure she came back into the house."

"I watched her come up the staircase," said Louisa.

It was Carr's turn to lean forward, completing their complicitous tableau.

"She was one of the household?"

"I saw her clearly when she reached the landing." Louisa's voice had begun to tremble with anxiety once more. "It was Miss Garrick."

For a moment, Carr remained motionless. His eyes did not deviate from Louisa and she found his glare as oppressive as the silence which had descended upon them. After several long moments, during which her discomfort increased, Louisa began to shuffle in her seat and the movement was sufficient to force Carr to realise the effect he was having on her. He rose from his chair, smiling now, in an effort to dispel any negative effect of his previous intensity of manner.

"Can you think of any reason why someone would want to murder Mr Lynch?" he asked.

"He was an unpleasant man," she replied.

"Does that justify his death?"

"No." She shook her head, with a trace of reluctance. "And I can't think of anyone who would want to kill him. The man was a stranger to most of us."

Carr raised an eyebrow at the qualification. "Most of us?"

Louisa flustered for a moment. "He knew Sir James, of course."

"And Mr Deville," observed Carr. "I think you were there when Lynch said as much."

"I seem to remember that, yes." She nodded. "Mr Lynch said that he had not read one of Mr Deville's own books."

Carr's eyes narrowed. He had been present during the conversation in question but the specifics of Lynch's contribution to it had not fixed themselves in his mind. He had been preoccupied with other ideas and concerns. Now, taking into account what Louisa had said, he found that his attention was seized upon the point. "Were those his exact words?"

Louisa looked up at him, as if his shift in temperament had unnerved her. She seemed less certain, but it was impossible to ignore the initial impression that her memory had not failed her. "I think so."

In her attempt to be vague, Carr saw only certainty. Her recollection of the words was both accurate and precise. She shuffled in her seat and opened the book, adjusting the spectacles on her nose. Carr knew when it was prudent to let a matter rest.

One of Deville's own books...

"I have taken up far too much of your time, Miss Marston," he said, inclining his head in apology. "I shall leave you to your reading and to the intricacies of Chekhov."

He did not give her time to reply. Instead, he left the room as swiftly as his awkward and uncertain gait would allow. Once he had closed the door behind him, Carr took a moment to gather his thoughts. His mind raced with one inference after another, but he was only too aware of the danger of allowing his thoughts to chase each other in a reckless pursuit. What he had learned from Miss Marston about Helena Garrick was interesting enough, but there were secondary conclusions which he could suppose from her words which he found more intriguing than her outright responses to his questions. And yet, amongst all these colliding ideas, Carr felt certain that something much more important had come out of his interview with Louisa Marston. Something which was indicative of the identity and guilt of the murderer of Sebastian Lynch.

Like a feather on the wind, however, whatever it was which stirred his interest was borne away and out of his reach by the tumultuous winds of his imagination.

Chapter Twenty

Alicia Ravenwood disliked Swift on sight.

It might have been because of his attitude, his arrogant assumption that his position and rank would force her to treat him with the respect he felt he deserved; or it might have had more to do with the fact that this same position and rank made his presence in the house necessary. He was representative of the official law, a reminder not only of what had happened in the night but also of its imposing consequences. He was somehow the personification of her realisation that Lynch's death would not be forgotten either easily or quickly. As she sat opposite him, waiting for him to speak to her, she watched him glance over the papers which were in front of him and whose contents were never to be shared with her. It was only when he closed the file and leaned back in his chair, shifting his gaze to hers, that she realised that it was not dislike which she felt about him, after all. It was altogether something much more akin to fear.

Whether Richard Prentice felt anything of it, she could not say. Certainly, his attitude did not suggest a mutual feeling of dread in the presence of the police. Prentice was sitting back in his chair, one leg crossed languidly over the other, and the manner in which he smoked his cigarette suggested a louche lack of interest in the proceedings. If it was an act, Alicia thought, it was a remarkably proficient one. If it was genuine, Prentice was as much at ease as she herself was in turmoil.

Almost making it seem like a tactically advantageous approach, it was Alicia whom Swift addressed first. "I've spoken to your mother and father,

Miss Ravenwood. I'm sure you will want to go and see them both, so I won't detain you longer than necessary."

Alicia offered her thanks, but she had not been fooled by his apparent empathy. She knew well enough that Swift would keep her for as long as he needed to and, for that matter, for as long as he wanted to.

"Perhaps we can get the more perfunctory matters out of the way," said Swift. "Can you tell me what you were doing between eleven o'clock and two o'clock last night?"

"I was in bed."

"Alone?"

Swift asked the question without any suggestion of embarrassment and without any care about causing offence. By contrast, Alicia's cheeks flushed and her eyes flashed with a fire of outrage. "Must you ask your questions with such relish, Inspector?"

Swift was resolute. "Were you alone, Miss Ravenwood?"

"Yes." She spat the word with undisguised disgust.

Prentice cleared his throat. He was smiling sardonically, his eyes narrowed against the string of the tobacco smoke which swirled around his face. "I think we ought to tell the truth, darling."

Alicia glared at him, as if he had endangered them by this reckless display of honesty. Prentice, by way of assurance and reconciliation, touched her on the knee but he kept his eyes on Swift. "We were together, Inspector. Alicia doesn't want to admit it, because she thinks you will see it as a fabricated alibi."

Swift's expression was impassive. "Why would I do that, sir?"

"Aren't you better off asking Alicia?"

She had pushed Prentice's hand away from her knee. "You've already said so much, Richard, no doubt you can continue speaking for me."

Prentice sighed. "The sooner we tell the truth, the quicker we can get on with our lives." He turned to Swift. "The fact is, Inspector, that I went to Alicia's room a little after midnight. I stayed there for a couple of hours and went back to my own sanctum at around two."

Swift turned to Alicia. "Is that true?"

"Yes," she said. Her voice was that of a scalded child.

"Why say otherwise?" asked Swift. "Why lie about it?"

It was Prentice who replied. "You may be accustomed to dealing with murder, Inspector Swift, but we mere mortals are not. Something like this plays tricks with your mind, you know. It distorts how you see the world. It makes you do silly things."

"What is it, exactly, you're trying to say, Mr Prentice?"

"Just that Alicia panicked."

The girl had resigned herself to her fate. She sighed and, when she spoke, it was with a tone of disdain, both at herself and at the situation into which she had been forced. "I thought you might consider it too convenient that we were together when Mr Lynch was killed. I thought it would be better if we said we are alone."

"You thought no alibi was better than corroboration of your whereabouts?" Swift's manner and voice made no attempt to disguise his feelings on the matter.

"I realise it was stupid," Alicia confessed.

"Which is why I thought it best to intervene," said Prentice.

Swift watched the pair of them for a long moment. "How long have you been engaged?"

"Six months." Prentice took Alicia's hand in his.

"Long enough," said Swift.

"Long enough for what?" asked Alicia, her instincts suddenly alert.

Swift clasped his hands on the table. "To lie for each other. An alibi verified by a lover is of no more value than no alibi at all. You are not independent witnesses for each other. Mr Prentice would lie for you and you for him."

"But we were together," insisted an outraged Alicia.

"Perhaps, but, you see, Miss Ravenwood, you've done yourself a severe harm. By lying at the outset, I now have to wonder whether you are lying now. You say you were together, but you said initially you were alone. I am used to lovers lying for each other and you've confessed to lying already. So, now, I don't know what the truth is at all. You see how confusing these things can get?"

131

Swift's speech was not impressive, but the sly, almost malevolent pride he took in delivering it was. It served its purpose. Alicia shook with fearful anticipation and Prentice's usual insouciance had hardened into a granite slab of uncertainty.

"It was a foolish lie to tell," said Prentice, "but what we have said now is the truth. We can't make you believe it, but that doesn't stop it from being true."

Swift smiled slightly, an indication that better people than they had failed to fool him in the past. "What were you doing together in Miss Ravenwood's room?"

"Talking."

"About what?"

"About things people who are planning to marry tend to talk about."

Swift's smile broadened. He rose from his seat and began to pace the room. The billiard room had been requisitioned for the purpose of the police interviews. Swift, who was a skillful player, ran his fingers along the baize on the edges of the table. "How well did you both know Sebastian Lynch?"

Prentice glanced over at Alicia and crossed his legs once more. "Not all that well."

"But you knew him before he arrived this weekend?"

"We met him through a mutual friend."

"At a party," offered Alicia.

Swift had moved to a position behind their chairs. If he saw it as a psychological advantage, he did not press the point too severely. "Did your father know that you had met Lynch, Miss Ravenwood?"

"I never told him. Nor did Richard."

"Might Lynch have told him?"

Alicia lowered her gaze to the clasped hands in her lap. "I doubt it."

It seemed a strange response. "Why?"

"I just don't think it would have occurred to him to say anything to Daddy." Alicia shrugged her shoulders, as if to dismiss what she had said as something insignificant. But her attempts to belittle her response were unconvincing.

Swift watched her keenly. "Wouldn't it be a natural thing to do?"

"I don't know."

Prentice looked over his shoulder at Swift. "Of course she doesn't know. How could she tell how a man she barely knew would react to any given circumstance? Besides, people like Lynch and Ravenwood only talk about their mutual interests. The rest of the world is irrelevant to them."

Swift allowed the point to pass for the present. "Did you like him?"

"Not especially," said Prentice.

"Why not?"

"I doubt many people you speak to who knew Lynch liked him very much."

Swift sat back down opposite them. "Why?"

"He wasn't an easy man to like," said Alicia.

"Did he have any family?"

"Not that I know of," replied Prentice, obtaining a shake of the head in confirmation from Alicia.

"What about enemies?"

"I would say so."

"People who might threaten him? Kill him?"

Prentice considered his reply. "Let me say this: it would not surprise me to learn there were such people around."

"Do you know of any?"

Swift locked eyes with Prentice, daring him to lie, but Prentice was not intimidated and he maintained the gaze as he answered, "No."

Alicia leaned forward, her face paled with anxiety. "How did the murderer get into the museum room? And out of it, for that matter?"

Swift shifted his glare to her. "Do you have any ideas about that, Miss Ravenwood?"

She sat back in her chair abruptly, as though his words had stung her. "Absolutely not. Why would I have?"

"I can't say," replied Swift. "I'm interested to know why you felt the need to ask. I thought you might have had some theory about it."

"I haven't," she stated indignantly. "It's just that the whole situation is so mysterious. Isn't it natural to find it fascinating?"

133

Swift conceded the point. "Your father says there are spare keys to every room except the museum room."

"That's correct."

"Who knew about the spare keys?"

"The family, the staff, Richard, Helena Garrick. Almost anybody who is a regular visitor to the house, I would think."

"Was it common knowledge that there was no spare key to the museum room?"

Alicia laughed gently. "Everybody knows Daddy's pride in his collection."

"Does that answer my question?"

"It should do."

"Everybody knew the arrangement about the keys," said Prentice. "Is this relevant, Inspector?"

Swift smiled coldly at him. "I have to gather as much information as I can, Mr Prentice."

Prentice lit another cigarette, his fingers moving swiftly as if to mirror his increasing impatience. "Let's keep it simple. The fact is that nobody in the house could have entered the museum room, because the keys had been stolen. And nobody from outside could get in from the back of the house, because the doors were locked, or from the front, because there was a sentry on guard at the lodge. Do you agree, Inspector?"

Swift nodded. "That seems to be correct, sir."

Prentice leaned forward. "And yet, somebody managed to get into the museum room, murder Lynch, for whatever reason, and leave the room again *without being in possession of the one and only key.*"

"Can you explain all that at all, sir?"

"Not a hope." Prentice thought for a moment. "Come to that, what was Lynch doing in the museum room at all?"

Swift narrowed his eyes. "Very interesting, Mr Prentice. Do you have any ideas about that?"

Prentice shrugged casually. "Isn't that your job, Inspector? Perhaps Lynch was responsible for the attack on Ravenwood. Perhaps he knew the two men who stole the keys and arranged to meet them. They let themselves in and the three of them went into the museum room. They removed the dagger, but there was an argument. Maybe the two thieves decided Lynch was no longer needed or that he didn't deserve his share of the loot. They couldn't let him go, in case he talked, so they killed him."

"But why would they need Lynch at all?"

Prentice was warming to his theory. "He was the expert. Only he would know how valuable the dagger was. Or maybe he wanted it for himself."

"He could have stolen it on his own, if that were the case."

"True. So, we go back to the three of them stealing it for profit and there was a falling out. In the struggle, Lynch was stabbed with the very thing they had come to steal. In a panic, the thieves flee the scene." Prentice was smiling at Swift, proud of himself for beating the Inspector at his own game, and Swift found himself sneering at the other man's misplaced and lazy conceit.

"There's still the question of how anyone could have left that room, isn't there, Mr Prentice?" asked Swift.

Prentice frowned. "Yes, there is still that mystery. I can't help you there."

"And haven't you already established, sir, that these thieves could not get back into the grounds because of the sentry?"

Prentice frowned. "*Touché*, Inspector."

Swift asked several more questions, routine in nature, before allowing Alicia and Prentice to leave. Once they had gone, he spent some time in silent thought, his brow furrowed and his fingers playing with a blunt pencil. As a theory, if it were not for the mystery of the locked room, Prentice's idea would be as solid as anything which Swift could muster. He felt a grudging respect for Prentice for having conjured it in the heat of the moment and he would hardly have believed the young man capable of such swift intuition. So much so that Swift found himself wondering how long Prentice had been thinking along those lines and whether it was a spontaneous thought at all.

Swift's mind was simmering with half-conceived and incomplete thoughts. He found himself wondering whether Richard Prentice had formed this theory as an alibi for himself and whether, in fact, it had been Prentice who had plotted with Lynch to steal the dagger and, subsequently, whether it was Prentice who had quarrelled with Lynch and stabbed him in the heart with their mutual prize.

Chapter Twenty-One

D r John Gilchrist displayed no trace of nervousness or discomfort when he was summoned for his interview. He answered the call with a glib remark, extinguishing a cigarette and rising from the chair in which he had been seated with the same mischievous cheerfulness. The remaining guests in the drawing room watched him follow the constable out of the room, but none of them were sure whether his apparent lack of concern was natural or a determined effort to disguise an internal unease. More than one of the people gathered in that room wondered whether Gilchrist's attitude arose from the security of the knowledge of his own innocence or a slightly overstated but necessary camouflage of his guilt.

Sitting opposite Swift now, Gilchrist's casual approach to interrogation showed no signs of dissipating. "Am I to expect thumbscrews and the rack, Inspector, or are your methods subtler than that?"

If Swift was amused, he failed to show it. "Just straightforward questions and simple answers, Dr Gilchrist. That's all I need and want."

"Ask away."

Swift was not a man who found excessive cheerfulness contagious. To him, it was anything but infectious and, more often than not, it served only to sour his mood, as if happiness in others reminded him only of his own fatigue with the world. This negative reaction to geniality was all the more severe when Swift suspected, as he did with Gilchrist, that the joviality was forced.

"Your estimate of the time of death has been confirmed by the pathologist," Swift said.

Gilchrist smiled. "That's a relief. It could have been rather embarrassing if it had gone the other way."

"What were you doing between those times, doctor?"

Gilchrist thought back over the period in question. "Sleeping, Inspector. I was tired and it's possible I'd had one brandy too many."

"Like a drink, do you, sir?"

"I work hard, Inspector, and I like to relax properly when that work is done." Gilchrist made it sound as if it was a defence which he had been compelled to raise more than once.

"You didn't leave your room at all during the night?"

"No. I slept soundly until about six. I lay awake for half an hour or so, then got dressed, and came down for breakfast."

"You didn't hear anything or see anything in the night which strikes you now as relevant?"

"No."

Swift watched as Gilchrist lit a cigarette. Even this mundane task was undertaken with a sense of impish mischief. "Did you know Sebastian Lynch before he came here?"

"No." Gilchrist looked directly into Swift's eyes, as if in an attempt to make the lie seem to be the truth as much as to attempt to determine whether Swift had picked up on it.

"Do you know if anyone else knew him before he came here?"

"Not that I'm aware. And, even if I did know anyone who had met him before, I would say nothing about it. I am not a gossip."

Swift nodded slowly. "What was your opinion about the wound to Lynch's chest?"

"Do you mean could a woman have done it?"

"Let's assume I do."

"I'm sure your pathologist has told you all you need to know," said Gilchrist, so that Swift would appreciate that he was not dealing with a fool. "I don't see any reason to suppose a woman incapable of the deed."

"I see." Swift allowed a moment to pass before speaking again. During the silence, Gilchrist refused to look away from the Inspector's shrewd, incisive gaze. "You are very calm under interrogation by the police, Dr Gilchrist."

"I have nothing to hide, Inspector."

"I wondered whether you might have some previous experience."

It was a clumsy tactic and Swift knew it, but he made no apology for it. Gilchrist, for his part, recognised the tawdriness of the ploy also and, consequently, he expected no such apology to be made. To that extent, the two men understood each other well enough, but it was not cause for Gilchrist to bend to Swift's will.

"I have nothing to hide," said the doctor. "I know what it is you are referring to, Inspector, and it won't wash. I had nothing to hide then and I have nothing to hide now."

"Nothing was ever proven, I grant you, sir."

"Because there was nothing to prove."

Swift stood up and placed his hands in his pockets. "Being a policeman makes a man think in a particular way, doctor. It's not always a pleasant way of thinking, but this job breeds certain habits."

"Is that so, Inspector?"

Swift continued to speak as if there had been no interruption. "You don't deny, I presume, that the circumstances of your wife's death were suspicious."

Gilchrist kept the anger from his voice. He knew Swift was hoping for an outburst of some kind and the doctor was adamant that the effect would not be produced. "I do not deny it, Inspector, and I presume you do not deny that no charges were brought against me in connection with it."

"Of course not," conceded Swift, "but, in this case, Doctor, I have a man who has been involved in two suspicious deaths. To a man like me, that sort of coincidence begins to look like a pattern. Do you see my point?"

Gilchrist rose from his seat slowly. He glared into the Inspector's eyes. "No, Inspector. I don't see your point at all."

"I'm sorry to hear that, Doctor."

Swift had no more questions for the present and Gilchrist was dismissed. Swift watched him leave the billiard room and smiled. The reference to the death of Gilchrist's wife had been unkind, he could accept that, but he had wanted to see what the reaction would be. He had to accept that he had expected a more volatile outburst and he silently congratulated Gilchrist on his willpower in refusing to rise to the bait. Nevertheless, Swift had detected nothing in Gilchrist's reaction to dissuade him from his previously formed opinion that Dr Gilchrist had murdered his wife two years previously. Swift found that he was more inclined now to consider his opinion of the doctor's guilt in terms of certainty rather than hypothesis. And experience told Swift that once a man had killed, there was very little to prevent him from doing so again.

Murder, like so many other things, could become a habit.

Chapter Twenty-Two

Truscott found Carr sitting on the terrace. To a casual observer, he would have looked at peace with himself, his appearance suggesting nothing more than a man sitting in solitary contentment and enjoying the early afternoon sun. A closer examination would have dispelled the myth. Carr's dark eyes were hard with abstract thought and his heavy brows were drawn tightly over them. His fingers drummed against the silver handle of his cane and the foot of his stronger leg tapped out a similar but impatient rhythm.

"I hope I'm not interrupting you," said Truscott, standing to one side. Carr did not reply. "Inspector Swift has begun his interviews. They all come out looking less sure of themselves than when they went in."

But still, Carr did not reply. He inhaled deeply, held the breath for a moment, and then exhaled in a long, frustrated hiss. Truscott felt he was intruding and he had the impression that his presence on the terrace was a nuisance. With a muted utterance of apology, Truscott began to walk away. Only then did Carr seem to become aware of a world outside his own thoughts and he called back to Truscott, waving his hand in a plea for him to return.

"Do not go, my boy, please," he said. "I am sorry if I appeared to be ignoring you. I was possessed by my own thoughts. There are points about this whole business which I do not understand. Certain points are obvious, but some other factors remain entirely obscure."

Truscott stared at him. "I confess that none of it seems obvious to me. I still cannot fathom how anyone got into that room and left it again."

Carr smiled. "You persist in allowing yourself to be carried away by the melodrama of the situation, rather than concentrating on the logical reality of it. You see a locked room and you conjure a man capable of walking through walls, but the solution to the problem is much more mundane."

"How was it done and who is responsible?" persisted Truscott.

Carr stroked his moustache thoughtfully. "We must discover everything in order to have a complete picture. Your questions are only part of the puzzle."

Truscott considered his next comment with care. "Why are you doing this, Mr Carr? Why are you poking around in the pond?"

"Did you not hear Inspector Swift say that I am a suspect, as are you, Truscott?" replied Carr. "It is in our own interests to solve the mystery. It is a question of self-preservation."

"Surely there is something more to it than that."

"Possibly," said Carr, his voice lowering and the smile fading from his lips. "Justice must be done. The guilty must be punished and the innocent protected. It is a keystone of a civilised society that a rule of law exists and I have always wanted to do what I could to ensure it. Retirement from the bench has not erased the desire and nor has it diluted my fundamental beliefs on the subject."

"But it is the duty of the police to achieve it."

Carr smiled, a cruel and ironic twist of his lips. "Do you imagine Inspector Swift is capable of doing so?"

Truscott sneered at this minor display of arrogance. "You think he cannot solve this without your help?"

Carr shook his head, but he did not deny the charge. "I think it is my responsibility to assist the police with their enquiries wherever possible, my boy."

The sententious reply was not meant, perhaps, to be taken seriously and Truscott allowed it to pass. Carr looked at him as the silence between them lengthened.

"What do you think of Miss Garrick?" he asked, at last.

If Truscott was embarrassed by the question, he did not show it, although he did not reply immediately and his mouth moved silently, as if he was rehearsing his response to himself. When he did offer an answer, it was evasive. "Why do you ask?"

"I had the idea that you were rather taken with her," said Carr, without any hint of mockery or mischief.

"You said something of the sort last night."

"Am I so wide of the mark?"

"I think she's very attractive," said Truscott. "But it's nothing more than that."

"Do you know anything about her?"

Truscott wondered what the purpose of the question was. He had the idea that Carr was skirting around an issue, hinting at it rather than setting it out directly, and it was so unlike the man that Truscott could not help but draw an adverse conclusion from it. He leaned towards Carr and was not surprised to hear the guarded, defensive tone in his voice. "What's all this about?"

"I find her intriguing. I wondered what you knew about her, that is all."

There was an honesty to Carr's response which seemed to make Truscott's previous wariness unfounded, if not an overreaction. It had punctured Truscott's momentary enmity and he felt now that he had no option other than to comply.

"I'm not surprised you find her intriguing," he said. "As do I, although I know very little about her."

"That explains her effect on you," said Carr gently.

"She has been friends with Alicia Ravenwood for many years, I know that."

"Do you know anything of her family?"

"Nothing. I suspect that she is very private in her own way." He remembered that Gilchrist had used the word *secretive*.

"Really?"

"It is only an idea I had." Truscott wondered whether he could bring himself to betray a confidence and, with only a passing twinge of guilt, he decided that it was necessary to do so. "I was talking to her earlier about what happened here last night. She told me something, something I thought

143

she should tell the police, but she refused. I suggested she tell you instead. I don't suppose she has done."

Carr shook his head. "What could she have to tell me?"

"It's a little awkward, Mr Carr," replied Truscott. "She told me in confidence."

"Murder destroys all confidences," murmured Carr.

"It was a matter of loyalty as far as Helena was concerned, loyalty to the family." Truscott began to pick at a fingernail. "It concerned Lynch and Lady Ravenwood."

Briefly, Truscott explained what Helena had overheard. Carr listened intently. His own thoughts had been occupied by Louisa Marston's statement regarding Helena Garrick. His choice to sit in silence on the back terrace had been dictated by his desire to look at the lawns over which Helena had been seen running. Carr could see the gate in the back wall which must have been the means of access Helena had used and, above him, he had seen the window through which Louisa had been staring. He had his own ideas about what Helena might have been doing in those early hours, but how to act on them had been a decision which had eluded him. Now, here was Truscott, providing him with a perfect, almost fortuitous, reason to speak to Helena on his own terms. It was an opportunity to ingratiate himself with her, whilst simultaneously avoiding any suggestion of invading her privacy.

Truscott concluded his tale. "I can only assume Lady Ravenwood and Lynch have known each other at some time in the past."

"It would seem so," replied Carr. "It does not come as a great surprise to me."

"Why not?"

"When Lynch was introduced to Lady Ravenwood, I had the idea that they were not meeting for the first time. It struck me as odd that they should pretend to be doing so."

"Why would they want to keep it a secret?"

"Curious, is it not? It seems to me that somehow it is of enormous importance."

"Yes, I thought so, too."

Carr smiled broadly and a hushed, guttural laugh rumbled at the back of his throat. "Not for the same reason, I fear."

Truscott frowned. "Meaning what, exactly?"

For a moment, Carr fell once more into silence, his eyes darting around the lawns as swiftly as his thoughts were colliding and multiplying in his brain, like the cells of a virus in an incubated environment. At last, he gave the same, hoarse snigger.

"It might be so very simple, after all," he said. "So simple, it could easily be overlooked. And, if it is right, it would make everything seem more complex than it is."

"I don't follow you."

Carr held up a hand with such authority that Truscott felt unable to speak. Carr fell into a further moment of deep thought, during which his hand did not move and the silence was not broken. At last, he struck the stone floor of the terrace with his cane and gave an exclamation of determination. A decision had been made.

"Come, Truscott, we have work to do. We must speak with Swift first and then with your lovely Miss Garrick."

They found Swift in the billiard room, the interviews suspended for the moment. He was in conversation with Detective Sergeant Lane, although it was evident that the talk was all on Swift's side. The sergeant was far from a ruthless intellect, but he was sensible enough to know when to speak and when to remain silent. When Carr pushed open the door and stepped into the room, Swift glared at the interruption, assuming it was a recalcitrant constable intruding in a private moment of detective speculation. If possible, Swift's mood darkened further when he saw who had caused the untimely disruption.

"You've no business coming in here, Mr Carr," he said. "When I want to take your statement, I'll send for you."

Carr dismissed the professional formality of the suggestion. "Statements can wait, Inspector, we have much more important things to consider."

"Meaning what?"

"The timing of the murder," declared Carr.

Swift laughed. It was a sly, mocking sound and its humour was black, so that it did nothing to alter the disapproving expression on his face. "We know all about the time of death, Mr Carr. Dr Gilchrist estimated the time of death as being between eleven at night and two in the morning. You will remember as much. What you won't know, though, is that the pathologist has examined the body and sees no reason to contradict Gilchrist."

"That is all very interesting but the precise timing of the crime is of paramount importance," insisted Carr.

Swift's eyes narrowed. "Have you been able to narrow that period any further, Mr Carr?"

"No."

The blunt negativity of the reply, as well as its apparent irrelevance, irritated Swift. "I'm a very busy man, Mr Carr. I don't have time to dance around in circles with you."

"I assure you, Inspector, that I have never been much of a dancer."

Swift had risen to his feet. His voice, when he spoke, was restrained and professional but it was no less menacing for that. "Stop wasting my time, Mr Carr. The time of death has been established and I am satisfied about it. Now, if you don't mind, I have further interviews to conduct. I shall call you when I am ready for you," he added, hoping for an effect not only of dismissal but of disparagement.

Carr, perhaps typically, was ignorant of either. With a snort of frustration, he touched Truscott on the sleeve and made his way out of the billiard room.

Chapter Twenty-Three

Helena had retired to her room.

After her talk with Truscott, she had felt dispirited and depressed. The thought of returning to the drawing room had intensified her low mood. She had made it known where she would be, so that Swift could not accuse her of fleeing from his demands, and she had sought sanctuary in her own space, kicking off her shoes and lying on the bed. As soon as the softness of the pillow had kissed the back of her head and the comfort of the mattress had embraced her from behind, she had felt consumed by weariness. Her blood had seemed to scream in her ears and her head had begun to feel as if it were encircled by lead. Sleep had seemed a certainty and she had begun to succumb to its charms when she had heard the gentle tap on her door. For a moment, it had seemed like part of a dream but its more resolute and insistent sequel had shaken Helena out of her drowsiness.

With a sigh, she dragged herself off the bed and stumbled over to the door. She pulled it open, with the intention to send away the caller already forming on her lips, when the appearance of Everett Carr blew away the unspoken words like a strong wind through a sea mist. The unexpected sight of him smiling back at her, his benign and kindly face beaming at her from under his moustache but the dark eyes suggesting a sinister purpose, surprised her into silence.

"I am sorry to interrupt you, my dear young lady," he said, soothingly and honestly, "but I wonder if I could have a moment of your time."

"I have a very bad headache, Mr Carr."

He pressed a hand against his breast. "Five minutes only, Miss Garrick."

There was something so childishly dramatic, perhaps so naively pious, in the gesture of honesty that she found she was unable to deny him. She stepped aside and let him enter, frowning in sympathy and she watched him limp past her. She felt a sudden flame of anger at her involuntarily patronising reaction to his disability and it was perhaps an extension of this mild fury which caused her features to harden when she saw Truscott. The implication of the two of them hunting her down now was surely self-evident. Truscott had betrayed her confidence; he had taken it upon himself to tell Everett Carr what he had insisted she say herself. His arrogance was as evident to her as his repentance, which was marked out on his face by the lowered lids and pursed lips. By contrast, Everett Carr was smiling still and looking amiably around the room.

"You seem to be very comfortable here, Miss Garrick," he said. "I believe you are a regular visitor to Warlock's Gate. Do you always have the same room?"

"Yes," she replied. Her voice was polite but, conversely, the glare which she had fixed on Truscott was nothing less than hostile. "I've had this room since I first stayed here as a little girl."

"How charming." Carr pointed to a small wooden chair in the corner of the room. "I wonder, might I be permitted to sit down?"

Unconsciously, without any intention to offend, Helena's eyes glanced down at his broken knee and his cane. "Of course, please do."

Carr offered his thanks and eased himself into the chair. It was rather too low to make the exercise entirely comfortable for him and, as an additional concern, it was not entirely stable under his weight. He thought it would hold, but he decided that unnecessary movement ought to be avoided.

Helena walked slowly over to Truscott. He kept his eyes fixed on the window, refusing to meet her own, preferring instead to stare out of the window and across the lawns outside. It may have been cowardice or it may have been prudence, but Truscott was determined not to engage her in any form of argument.

"You told him," she hissed. "What I said to you was in confidence. I told you that. I shouldn't have said anything to you at all."

Despite his wishes to avoid a conflict, Truscott was unable to keep quiet. "But you did say something and what you said was important. This is a matter of murder, Helena. That has to take priority over any sort of supposed family loyalty."

"Supposed loyalty?" she sneered. "How dare you? What do you know about family, about mothers and daughters? What do you know about any of it? You had no right to tell him. No right!"

He held her gaze and, as he did so, he knew that he would hold it in any circumstances. Somehow, it had ceased to matter to him whether she was looking at him with eyes of mischief, friendship, or hostility. What mattered was that she was looking at him at all. The realisation of the fact hit him hard, but he maintained his stoicism and, if she read anything of his feelings in his expression, she gave no indication of it. He doubted she was sharing the feelings, or experiencing anything approaching them, but it suddenly seemed vital to him that he should not look away from her.

"You must not blame, Mr Truscott."

Carr's voice came over to her like the first sunlight after a frozen winter. It was gentle, calming, so full of kindness and empathy that it seemed to slice through the cold resilience of her resentment. Despite herself, she found that she had no choice other than to follow the voice back to its source, to the crippled man who sat in the corner of the room like a black shadow, whose intensity was broken only by the gaudiness of his handkerchief and tie. For the first time, she seemed to notice Everett Carr in detail and her overall impression of him was that of intense blackness. His suit, his eyes, and the lurking darkness of his expression behind the smiling lips seemed now so much more evident to her, as was the sharp contrast with not only the livid colours of his sartorial accessories but also with the softness and kindness of his voice.

"He betrayed me," she found herself whispering.

Carr shook his head slowly. "No, my dear, he saved you. If Inspector Swift had discovered the connection between Lady Ravenwood and the dead man, he would have pursued it with vigour. If he discovered later that you knew and had not divulged it, his mind would have converted your loyalty to Lady Ravenwood into deceit. Men like Swift have minds which point in only one direction at a time."

"I won't tell the police," Helena said.

"You do not have to," assured Carr. "I have been told, which is altogether better than informing the police. You may leave it all in my hands. But you must not blame my friend for doing what he knew was right."

"Will you tell the police about what I overheard, Mr Carr?"

It was a question which might easily have embarrassed him, but he showed no signs of it. He ran his finger along the ornate silver handle of his cane in an idle fashion, but the keenness of his eyes showed that his thoughts were fixed entirely on Helena. He allowed the question to hang in the air for a short while, not to disorientate her but to ensure he was satisfied with his reply.

"That remains to be seen," he replied. "If Lady Ravenwood is shown to have played no part in the murder, I see no reason to muddy the waters for the police. But if the contrary proves to be the truth, I cannot suppress it. You have my discretion, Miss Garrick, for as long as I am able to give it. If you leave the matter in my hands, you have that guarantee."

She considered the reply. It was far from the definite assurance for which she had hoped, but there was something so trustworthy about Carr's kindness that the idea that he might deceive her seemed too outlandish to credit. When she glanced over to Truscott, she saw a transparent plea in his expression for her to accept Carr's word. He seemed so keen as to be irresistible. She cursed both him and herself for the emotions he stirred within her and the effect he had begun to have over her.

"Very well, Mr Carr," Helena said, "I will trust you."

"I'm honoured," replied Carr, courteously.

"I suppose all this means I am excused from having to mention what I heard when the police eventually do question me?"

Carr frowned, but there was no genuine concern behind it. "Rather a tricky situation, I admit, Miss Garrick, but I see no reason to mention it right now. Given you had decided to say nothing anyway, it needn't trouble your conscience too greatly, of course."

"There is that," replied Helena, smiling slightly. "Thank you."

Carr continued to examine his cane. "There is a good turn you can do for me in return, miss. If I may ask as much of you, that is."

Helena felt a slight tremor of anxiety ripple through her heart. "What good turn?"

Carr's voice lost some of its amiability. "You can tell me where you went last night."

There was a momentary lapse of control on Helena's part. Her eyes flickered, her hands clasped and unclasped, and her mouth moved silently as untruth and evasion tried to form themselves into words which would not come. Carr remained motionless in his chair, his eyes averted from her, as if to look into her eyes now would galvanise her into falsehood. Truscott stared at him, unsure in the moment whether he had heard the words correctly or not and, if he had, ignorant of either their meaning or their implication.

Helena was suddenly aware that the silence she was permitting to extend between them was telling against her. "I was in here. I retired a little after half past ten. I read for a little while and then I settled down to sleep."

Carr remained impassive. "You remained in your room all night?"

"Yes."

If he was appalled or impressed by the ease with which she told the lies, Carr did not show it. He continued to run his finger along the silver handle of the cane and his eyes remained absorbed by the action, refusing still to look in her direction. The only suggestion of a response to her reply was the slight smile which crept across his lips. "You didn't, by any chance, leave the house by going through the kitchen, leaving the door unlocked to allow your return, which you effected through the back gate, crossing the lawns at the rear of the house?"

"No." The tension in her throat as she forced the lie to be told seemed to make her entire body tremble with the deceit. But then she realised that it was not only the dishonesty which unbalanced her. It was fear also: the fear that Carr knew her darkest secret. As if to deflect her attention away from it, she added: "The house had been made more secure than usual."

Carr gave the impression of a man who had been reminded of a long-forgotten fact, but it was only a momentary effect. It was gone as quickly as it had been conveyed, replaced by a cunning but stern expression of defiance. "Only at the front. There was no need to secure the back, which was always kept locked. But there were spare keys and you know the house well enough to be aware of them. In any event, I have a witness not only to the unlocked kitchen door but also to the sound of the gate being opened. And I have a witness to your return over the lawns."

It was now that Carr chose to stand. He walked slowly towards her, his eyes now seizing her attention and maintaining it. He moved with such determination that his limp now seemed not to be a weakness but a menacing and foreboding step. Helena felt as if its uneven rhythm matched the erratic beating of her heart as her nerves tingled with apprehension. Carr was still smiling, but there was now something demanding in the twist of the lips and the dark eyes seemed heavy with authority, as if daring her to attempt to deceive him anymore.

And yet, when he spoke, his voice retained its avuncular and genial tone. "Shall we have the truth now, Miss Garrick?"

It might have been the directness of the question or it could have been the shift in Carr's deportment and attitude. Perhaps it was simply the stark accusation of dishonesty disguised as a friendly, almost innocuous question. Whatever it was which unsettled her, Helena felt her cheeks begin to ignite. It was anger as much as humiliation or guilt, and the more conscious she was of it, the deeper the colour became. She was determined to tell this man nothing about herself. He was not the official police and he had no right to question her. There was no obligation or duty on her to answer him, truthfully or otherwise, but the expectant and guileful expression on Carr's face made her feel as if silence or even dismissal would be impossible. She had to say something, but she was adamant it would be something which told him nothing.

"All right, I did go out," she replied. Her voice was defiant enough to illustrate her power of will, but it was not strong enough to conceal entirely how much Carr had shaken her resolve.

"To where?"

"I don't see why I should answer that, Mr Carr. It's none of your business and it has nothing to do with the murder."

Carr smiled. "Forgive me, but I do not think that is a distinction you are able to make."

"I'm afraid I don't agree. You are not the police," she added, but it was a weak admonishment, delivered with less conviction than she had envisaged.

"The police would be able to compel you to explain yourself."

"They could try. I would give them the same answer."

Carr clicked his tongue in mild, almost mocking reproach. "Such rebellion in one so young. I admire your spirit, Miss Garrick. The police think their authority is all they require. It is a weapon as blunt as their truncheons and they wield it with even less subtlety. Inspector Swift is typical of his sort. I can well imagine that you would not want to confide anything sensitive to someone like him."

Again, his affability disconcerted her, with its almost conspiratorial approval of her obstinate silence, and she found herself thinking that it was he who remained in control of the situation. He might not be obtaining the information he wanted from her, but that did not mean he was subservient to her in any way.

"Where I went, what I did," she stammered, "they're private matters."

Carr nodded. "Indeed, I understand that. And I daresay you will not want to speak about it until you have to."

"Until I have to?"

"Until you have to explain it in order to avoid being arrested for murder." Carr was smiling, as if the strategic move he had employed pleased him immeasurably.

"I didn't kill Sebastian Lynch," she felt obliged to say.

"That remains to be seen, of course," replied Carr, "but, if it comes to it, I advise you to be less protective of your movements last night than you are being at present."

"That sounds like a threat."

Carr seemed horrified by the idea. "Goodness, no. A word of caution only."

He had unnerved her further now, to the extent that she began to wonder whether she should invent some lie to explain where she had been. Almost immediately, she dismissed the idea. Any story she told now would be too late to be credible. She had insisted on saying nothing and she knew she had to maintain her tactic of silence.

Carr gently placed a hand on her arm, like a wise uncle counselling a troubled niece with words which seemed harsh but which were meant only to be beneficial. "Whoever you are protecting, it is best to tell me the truth. I cannot force you to do it, but I can implore you to do so."

"I am protecting no-one."

Carr smiled, as if the lie was obvious to them both and so weak as to be irrelevant. "You must have your reasons for keeping your silence, Miss Garrick. All I ask is that you do not injure yourself by attempting to save another."

He held her gaze for a little while longer, his expression filled with meaning, but he said no more. He bowed politely to her and made his way slowly from the room. If he had been expecting her to call after him, or to say anything else at all, he was to be disappointed. He showed no signs of any such expectation, however, and he left the room with a dignified quiet.

Helena watched Carr step onto the landing and out of sight. She took a deep, relieved breath of air before looking back into the room. As she did so, her eyes fell on Truscott. He was looking at her with what she thought was a mixture of sadness and concern, but she was unable to deny the distinct trace of distrust which darkened his expression. He said nothing and nor did she. At last, he made his way to the door, following Carr onto the landing. As he passed her, Helena threw out an arm and blocked his way.

"Despite what I said, you told him anyway," she said. "About Lady Ravenwood and Lynch."

He looked down into her green eyes, which peered out from the contrasting paleness of her skin and the raven black of her hair. "I made no promises."

"You said I could trust you."

"You could and you can," he replied. "You can trust me to do the right thing, which is what I did. Carr said so and I agree with him."

She was beyond such sanctimonious conceit. "Don't expect me to forgive you for it."

"I don't," he said, without regret. "But I expect you to tell the truth."

They remained in their tableau for a few seconds longer until, at last, she lowered her arm and allowed him to move to the door.

"Don't speak to me again," she said, her voice only seconds away from breaking.

When she received no response, Helena looked back to the door, but he had already disappeared and could not have heard what she had said. She waited, as if expecting him to peer back around the door, to apologise for betraying her, perhaps even to walk back into the room and put his arms around her. The moments which passed seemed like hours and, as she realised that he was not coming back and that she was finally alone with herself and her thoughts, she walked over to the bed and sat down.

Her tears fell silently and her shoulders began to quiver with that particular rhythm which only sobbing can produce.

Chapter Twenty-Four

Eliza Montgomery was alone in the drawing room. Those guests who had been interviewed by Inspector Swift had not returned to the room after their ordeal and those who were yet to be subjected to it had grown impatient during the wait. Swift had permitted movement around the house and grounds and most had taken advantage of his decision. Eliza had preferred to remain where she was, seated in the window seat, her thoughts known only to herself.

She had yet to be interviewed. The delay was, incongruously, both a relief and a cause for distress. It prolonged the anxious suspense whilst simultaneously giving her time to consider what questions she might be asked and what she would say. She knew that the exercise was futile. It was impossible to predict what Swift would want to know and it was impossible to attempt to pre-empt him. And yet, it was a purely human instinct to want to be prepared for an interview which would inevitably be difficult. All this aside, the prolonged period before she was summoned for questioning gave Eliza the opportunity to decide whether she should tell the police everything she knew about the night of the murder or not.

She had poured herself a cup of coffee. Lady Ravenwood had ensured that refreshments were kept available continually and Fenton had attended to the command with customary efficiency. How long she had sat with only her own thoughts for company was made clear to her when she took a mouthful of the strong, black coffee and found it was cold. She placed the cup with its barely touched contents on the small table beside her and stared out of the window. Uniformed officers were searching the grounds,

156

their shapes seeming intensely black against the bright green of the lawns and trees. They seemed to Eliza to resemble insects on ripened fruit at a ruined picnic, dark intruders on vibrant goodness. It seemed an apt image to her and, curiously, an idea for a painting came into her mind. It would be a dark piece and, for a brief moment, she wondered whether it was a common effect of murder that one's thoughts became necessarily twisted, their sweetness inevitably soured, and their optimism inexorably darkened.

The door opened, startling her out of her contemplations, and she was grateful for the interruption. Turning to greet the newcomer, she was surprised to find that it was Everett Carr. He stepped cautiously into the room, smiling as he saw her, and Eliza saw that Jack Truscott was close behind him. Eliza noticed that Truscott seemed less at ease with himself than Carr. His unease was so clearly marked on his face that she wondered, briefly, what it was which troubled him.

"You will forgive us if we disturb your peace, Miss Montgomery?" asked Carr. He waited for her to assent. "I see there is coffee. Would you like one? I feel ready for a cup myself, certainly. Truscott," he added, turning to the journalist, "would you be so kind?"

As Truscott silently obliged, Carr limped slowly over to Eliza and sat beside her. She did not object, either to his presence or his proximity. There was something so beguiling about him that she found it impossible to refuse him.

Carr pointed out of the window at the constables in the gardens. "A waste of effort, of course, but one cannot accuse Inspector Swift of being anything other than thorough."

Eliza frowned. "Is it a waste of effort?"

"I doubt the murderer went anywhere near the lawns, so he is unlikely to have left any clues there."

"Surely he came across the lawns in order to get into the house."

Carr watched her closely. He found it incredible that she could genuinely believe that the killer had come from the outside and he wondered whether she was being deliberately obtuse or whether, in fact, it was her mind's understandable denial of the obvious as a defence against the horror of the murder.

"I do not think it is likely that the murderer came into the house," said Carr softly.

Eliza kept her eyes on the police officers and the lawns, as if they were an assurance that her reading of the tragedy was correct. "He must have done, because otherwise, it would mean…"

But she did not finish the sentence. Instead, she pulled her attention away from the outside world and onto Carr's dark eyes. He smiled, assuring her that she was now thinking correctly, and that the unpleasantness of those thoughts was better to be faced than avoided. Eliza nodded her head, lowering her gaze to her clenched hands which rested uneasily in her lap.

"I suppose I never really thought otherwise," she said.

Truscott handed her a fresh cup of coffee and she accepted it with a smile of gratitude. She held it but did not drink it. There was every possibility that, like its predecessor, it would be allowed to go cold without being tasted.

"Have the police interviewed you?" asked Truscott.

"Not yet. I think they are leaving me until last."

"They have much to establish," said Carr. "It takes time and patience is a necessity."

Eliza smiled. "I am trying not to view the delay as a sign of suspicion."

Carr seemed horrified by the idea. "And why should they suspect you? You hardly knew this man, Lynch, is that not so?"

She shifted her position slightly, crossing one leg over the other. "No, I did not know him at all."

"You met him for the first time this weekend?"

"Yes."

"That is curious."

"Is it?"

Carr shrugged, as if what he was about to say was insignificant. "I had an idea you were frightened of him."

"I didn't know him," she insisted.

"I noticed something last night when Sir James introduced you to Mr Lynch." Carr smiled gently. "Your hand was shaking."

CHAPTER TWENTY-FOUR

She looked away from him. "Was it?"

"Very definitely."

"I must have been cold." She knew the lie was inadequate for her purpose. He would know that the room was not sufficiently chilled to produce the effect. "Or nervous."

"Nervous of what?"

She seemed now to be more assured in her response. "I knew nobody here, Mr Carr. It is rather daunting to attend a weekend house party when one does not have the emotional support of a previous acquaintance."

Carr smiled and allowed the explanation to pass. "You are an artist, I believe. In my experience, people who paint, or write, or perhaps even act on stage, have very keen eyes. They notice things about people, things which they can use in creating their pieces of art. Am I right about that?"

Eliza was flattered that his general comment had been designed to include her within it. "We do have some skill in observing people, yes," she answered with a smile.

Carr spoke immediately. "And what impression did you form of Sebastian Lynch?"

He spoke with such immediacy that it seemed like a crack of a whip to Eliza and she saw now that his flattery, whilst it might well have been honest, had been designed to trap her. She let him know that she had recognised his tactic but he was unrepentant. He was smiling at her still, his head slightly nodding, and his dark eyes expectant of her answer. Eliza debated her response with herself. She could not pretend to have formed no opinion of the dead man, not when she had confessed to possessing the skill in clear and equivocal terms. But, equally, she had an instinct that anything she said now would have to be carefully considered.

"I can't say I found him very pleasant," she said. "He struck me as aggressive, overbearing. Cruel, perhaps. I wouldn't have liked to find myself on the wrong side of him."

Carr thought back to Lynch's argument with Louisa Marston, which he had overheard. He could accept Eliza's assessment of the dead man. It was not too far from the opinion he had formed himself and, having witnessed

Lynch's almost animal rage during that encounter with Louisa, he suspected that Eliza's view might not be too far removed from the truth. And yet, there was something else in her tone, a discordant note which he could not clearly define. Her voice lacked the cold detachment which he might expect from a character analysis of a stranger. He tried to define the apostate quality, but the closest he could manage was that it had been a glimmer of something he could only describe as disappointment.

"Can you think of any reason why anybody would wish to harm him?" asked Carr.

"Of course not."

"He had been receiving death threats," said Carr, carelessly.

He waited for her to show some surprise, but she did not comply. Instead, she asked simply: "What sort of threats? Anonymous letters?"

Carr shook his head slowly. "Something altogether more sinister. Wooden effigies of a hanged man."

Eliza glared at him. "That is horrible."

"Does it surprise you to learn he was receiving threats?"

She considered the question for a moment. "I cannot say it does. Certainly not in the wake of what has happened." Her face clouded, as if the reality of the situation had reasserted itself on her. Her voice trembled under the seriousness of it. "It's so awful. All of it, it's horrible."

"Murder always is, I'm afraid. That is something which can never change. You must be brave and face it."

As if to demonstrate how to do so, Carr sipped some of the coffee. It was suitably strong and bitter and he savoured in turn the taste, the smell, and the stimulating effect of it. Eliza followed his lead and he noticed again the almost imperceptible tremor of her hand as she raised the cup to her lips. He made no comment on it, but it was sufficient to convince him that she had secrets which she hoped would remain hidden. Carr wondered how many people were able to say they had no such secrets and remain assured that they were being true to themselves as well as to others.

"The police will want to know your movements last night," he said at last. "Are you able to give a clear account of them?"

If she saw through this indirect form of interrogation, she neither showed it nor resented it. She nodded swiftly. "There is very little to tell. I went to bed as soon as I came upstairs. I read for a short while, but I felt inordinately weary. I think it was the excellence of the food and wine."

Carr made a gesture of agreement. "You did not see or hear anything?"

"Nothing," replied Eliza.

It was as if she were not entirely convinced by her own reply. Her teeth bit into her bottom lip and her eyes seemed unable to focus on anything in particular. Carr, sensing that any word from him might be precipitate, remained silent. He judged that no contribution from him was either necessary or helpful. Eliza seemed anxious to say something and it was simply a question of allowing her time to summon the courage to speak.

"I don't think I saw anything important," she said at last. "I think that's what I mean to say."

Carr nodded his understanding. "It's impossible to say whether a thing is important or not until it is open for examination."

"But it might be entirely innocent."

"Equally, it might be the exact opposite."

Eliza thought for a moment longer. "I saw someone going into Lynch's bedroom."

Carr did not reply immediately. He twisted his body to face her, suppressing the instinctive excitement which swelled within him. "What time was this?"

"Around half past one."

"Can you say for certain who it was?"

Eliza shook her head. "I don't want to get anybody in trouble."

"If you withhold any information from the police, the person in the deepest trouble will be you."

Eliza was adamant. "I believe Lynch was murdered between eleven last night and two in the morning. Surely, he was dead by the time I saw this person and, even if he were not, this person I saw was nowhere near the museum room at the important time."

Carr shook his head, but he smiled kindly. "You cannot say that with any certainty, Miss Montgomery. The murder might have already been committed by the time you saw this person go into Lynch's room. After all, if whoever you saw is the killer, and if Lynch was already dead, he or she would know that there was no possibility of Lynch returning to his room."

It had been something which Eliza had not considered, possibly because she had subconsciously allowed herself to believe that what she had witnessed was unimportant, so that she would be excused for having to divulge it and any argument which contradicted her could be safely dismissed. But now, with this direct and unassailable counter-argument, put forward with gentle candour by Carr, she found that her faith in her own judgment was less assured than before.

"I hadn't thought of it in those terms," she confessed. She drained her coffee and Carr took the cup from her, handing it to Truscott to be replaced on the serving trolley.

"You see now why it is important to say who it was," said Carr, turning back to Eliza, "assuming you can identify the person without any doubt."

She nodded. "I know full well who it was. I saw him knock gently on Lynch's door and push it open when he received no answer. He stepped into the room and closed the door softly behind him. I didn't want to wait any longer so I returned to bed. I don't know how long he was in the room and I don't know what time he left it. Or what he was doing in there."

These were all important points and they had to be made, but Carr could not resist the temptation to see them as serving as a tactical delay of the inevitable. As if to prevent any further such prevarication, he said: "You saw whom, Miss Montgomery?"

Eliza looked at him with an unsettled gaze and her voice was low, as if burdened by the weight of her doubt about whether she should speak or not. At last, with her eyes closed, she said the words.

"Dr Gilchrist," she whispered. "I saw Dr Gilchrist."

As the revelation was unveiled and processed, a silence fell on the room. Eliza looked back down to the floor, as if she had caused damage which could never be repaired. Truscott stared at her, his expression a blend of excitement and disbelief. He glanced at Carr, who remained motionless in his seat, his attention also transfixed on Eliza Montgomery. He was almost entirely impassive, the only suggestion that he was profoundly interested in this development being the slight narrowing of his keen, onyx eyes.

If Eliza had been able to read his mind, she might have been surprised by his thoughts. She might have expected him to wonder why Dr John Gilchrist had entered Lynch's room during the time it was known the murder had been committed but, in fact, Carr's mind was stubbornly running in a different direction. It was not that he was disinterested in the revelation about Gilchrist; he decidedly was. But, likewise, he was wondering why Eliza Montgomery herself had been in the vicinity of Lynch's room and had been able to witness Gilchrist's movements at all.

Chapter Twenty-Five

The day's brightness was beginning to darken into evening.

The preliminary interviews with the guests and the staff had been concluded. Lynch's body had been removed to the mortuary, but the museum room remained secure. Swift and his fellow officers had left Warlock's Gate for the day, having taken details of addresses of everyone concerned. The Inspector had permitted people to leave if they wished, but they were cautioned to be available for further questions. Swift had given the command with customary authority and it had been his parting shot, so that if any of the people in the house had expected or hoped that the mood would lighten once the police intrusion had ended, they were to be disappointed. The absence of the detectives did not necessarily mean the lifting of the presence of the police. The rooms in which they had conducted their initial enquiries seemed still to reek of them; the beauty of the lawns still seemed violated by the memory of the police searches; the corridors and halls of the house seemed empty and soulless without the busy sound of professional investigations and police efficiency. The quiet which followed their activity, rather than being comforting, seemed both oppressive and malevolent.

It would come as no surprise to anyone who found him alone in the living room that thoughts such as these were passing through the mind of Dr John Gilchrist. His normally cheerful demeanour was absent and his expression of serious contemplation was so intense that any amiability might have seemed an impossibility. He held a self-prepared cocktail in one hand and the latest of several cigarettes in the other. His mind was playing over the interview with Swift and he wondered whether he had been too defensive when it came to the subject which he knew still cast such a powerful and cancerous shadow across his life.

There had been women before his wife, too many of them perhaps. He would never be able to name all of them, but he knew that he had enjoyed each of them at the time. There had been a moment in his life when he doubted marriage could ever hope to trap him and his reputation as an eligible bachelor had been keenly established. It struck him then, as it still did now, that he should be permitted to have the undeniably upright *soubriquet*. To be considered eligible brought its own sense of respectability, no doubt because it came with a definite expectation of an eventual proposal. Gilchrist had never denied or questioned the label, but he was aware that it was misplaced. He had no desire to marry, but he enjoyed women. People might say that he was eligible, but Gilchrist knew what he was in truth and, in retrospect, there was nothing reputable about it. A woman who acted as he had done would be expected to charge for her services.

And yet, from the moment he had met Emily, his attitude had changed entirely and immediately. What it had been about her which brought about this change, he had never been able to say for certain. Perhaps it was her gentleness, her innocence, her quietness. Perhaps it was her beauty, far from conventional but no less deniable for that. It was the beauty of a timid, repressed heroine of Victorian literature, like a first draft of a Hardy protagonist, and it was this timidity which captivated him so intensely. The others had known he was attractive and they had never made an attempt to conceal their attraction to him. Emily had seemed barely conscious of it, so that the girls who had preceded her had begun to seem to be constructed of nothing more than carnal desperation. It was as if the brightest sun had been burned out by the simple beauty of a candle flame, flickering in a gentle breeze.

If Emily had been aware of his past, or appalled by it, she never made reference to it and it did not prevent the marriage. It was a simple but honest ceremony, performed with maximum joy but a minimum of fuss, and they had honeymooned in a guesthouse on the Cornish coast. It had been Emily's choice, a throwback to her childhood holidays with her respectable but modestly financed parents, but Gilchrist had raised no objection. To him, it had been a quiet week by the sea, but its simplicity had been both refreshing and invigorating. The subsequent years of marriage had produced no children, but it was never a regret. Gilchrist, for one, would have found a child to be an intrusion into their lives, a barrier between him and Emily, who would naturally want to put the child before him. He had never spoken of those feelings with her, but he had suspected, hoped, and finally taken for granted that she felt the same.

And then, without warning, she had taken her own life.

Looking back now, drinking a second cocktail and smoking a further cigarette, Gilchrist supposed her death had not been as unexpected as he had once believed. There had been indications of it: the increasingly early nights and late mornings, the lack of appetite, the death of even the most routine conversation, the permanently distracted mind. Emily had ceased to be the woman he had married; she had become a husk, a collection of bones and flesh which had a passing resemblance to the woman he had loved. He had felt increasingly isolated, as her depression cruelly distanced them from each other with such aggression that it had begun to shape itself in his mind into a malignant tumour.

It was only a matter of time before the rumours began. In part, he had been to blame for them, allowing himself to be seen in his old haunts, drinking champagne and eating oysters with women he had known in the past. It might have come as no surprise that he should seek solace in his old style of life, especially when his life at home was barely deserving of the word. Speculation about adultery was initially muted and only ever conducted beyond his hearing, but he was still aware of it, dismissing it as groundless. He knew as well as the women concerned that he had never been unfaithful to his wife. But when she was reported as dying from an overdose of Veronal, the wave of rumours intensified and the denials could do nothing but drown under the force of it. The gossip became something more insidious than idle speculation of infidelity: it became a motive for the murder of Emily Gilchrist, a murder for which her husband was the only genuine suspect.

Gilchrist forced his mind into the present. His mouth was dry with the sourness of the memories. He was surprised to find that he had smoked the cigarette and finished the cocktail, but the pleasures of both he could not recall enjoying. To have a third drink would have been rudeness in the absence of his host or any other guest, but Gilchrist had no desire to conform to decency. His experience of the police and the memories it had resurrected made his tolerance of politeness less than threadbare. He mixed a third martini, lit a further cigarette, and stared again out of the window at the reflection of a man whom he barely recognised.

He was distracted from himself by the sound of the door opening. Turning to meet the intrusion, he saw Everett Carr standing in the doorway. He smiled at Gilchrist in greeting and asked politely if he might enter the room, as if Gilchrist had any control over what happened in the house or over Carr's own actions themselves. Gilchrist gave his consent with a nonchalant wave of his hand, replacing as he did so that more casual attitude which he preferred to cultivate as his natural demeanour. The darkness of mood in which he had indulged himself over the past few moments, and which he felt to be much closer to his natural character, was dismissed once more to the hidden corners of his conscience. He was honest enough with himself to accept that his careless amiability might once have been his normal self, but he was likewise candid enough to admit that it was no longer the case.

Carr approached Gilchrist slowly, with an almost reverential step, as if he had been privy somehow to the solemn thoughts which had occupied the doctor's thoughts. Gilchrist took a sip from his cocktail, bowing to propriety slightly by taking a more moderate sip than he had done in his own company. He saw Carr's dark eyes lingering over the clear liquid in its shapely glass.

"You think it inappropriate to be drinking cocktails before the accepted hour, Mr Carr?" asked Gilchrist, with a glint in his eye but the slightest trace of a blade in his voice.

"Goodness, no," replied Carr, with dignity.

Gilchrist seemed not to have heard the denial. "You may be used to people like Inspector Swift, but I'm not. He leaves a distinctly unpleasant taste in one's mouth which only a strong Martini can vanquish."

"You misunderstand me, Doctor," said Carr. "I was not sneering at your glass but admiring it. I wonder, might I impose on you to…?"

"Fix one for you?" Gilchrist was suitably impressed. "By all means."

He prepared the drink with his usual flair. Carr watched the performance and found himself appreciating not only the ease but the skill with which it was undertaken. When it was complete, Carr accepted the chilled drink with gratitude and took a sip of the cocktail. It was strong and invigorating, more so than he had expected, but its effect was welcome. Cocktails were not his chosen drink, and never had been. His preference had long since been for wine and whisky. A drink such as the one which he was enjoying now was an irregular indulgence and all the more pleasing for it.

"The place seems empty now that the police have left us in peace," said Gilchrist.

"It is only momentary, I fear." Carr allowed the truth of his remark to settle in the doctor's consciousness. "Was your interrogation particularly difficult?"

"No more than anybody else's, I suspect. It is difficult not to find it uncomfortable to be suspected of murder."

"Did they suggest you were suspected?"

"Not in so many words." Gilchrist, almost against his will, recalled Swift's barely veiled suggestion that the doctor might well have killed once and could have done so again.

"I suppose the Inspector asked you about your movements on the night of the murder," said Carr, giving as convincing an impression of casual interest as he could muster.

"Naturally," smiled Gilchrist without humour. "And I told him the truth. I had a final drink with Deville and Lynch, then went to bed. I stayed there, slept soundly, and woke early."

The lie came so easily that Carr wondered whether Gilchrist had convinced himself of its truth. He waited a moment before unsettling the doctor's assurances. "No doubt Inspector Swift was satisfied you had told him the truth."

Gilchrist turned to face him, his eyes like steel. "That suggests you are not satisfied of it, Mr Carr."

Carr returned the gaze with equal mettle. "What were you looking for in Lynch's room last night?"

"I think you have said quite enough."

Carr was not so convinced. "Lynch's room has been ransacked. Drawers overturned, suitcases rifled, private papers searched. It was obvious at once that somebody was looking for something and, later, I hear that you were seen going into his room in the early hours of the morning."

"Seen by whom?"

"That hardly matters," purred Carr. "What is important is why you were in the dead man's room. I can speculate, of course, but I would rather you told me willingly."

Gilchrist smiled thinly and drank deeply. "Speculate away."

Carr raised an eyebrow in disappointment. "I was once a criminal barrister, Dr Gilchrist, and latterly a judge. I am retired now, of course, but my occupation meant I was always keenly aware of cases of murder. Known cases and suspected cases, if you understand me."

Gilchrist's grip on his glass tightened, the knuckles whitening, as if he were about to launch it across the room like a grenade. He said nothing, but his reaction to Carr's words demonstrated his understanding of the older man's meaning.

"It is idle guesswork, of course," continued Carr, "but one can hardly do anything else in these circumstances. It seems likely to me, though, that if you were searching for something in Lynch's room last night, it is somehow connected with your recent past. And your wife," he added, with meaning.

"Very interesting," said Gilchrist sourly.

"Was Lynch blackmailing you, doctor?"

The question was so stark that it startled Gilchrist into a short burst of laughter. "Blackmail?"

"I wondered whether he might have threatened you with some information about the death of your wife."

Gilchrist was laughing no more and he was aware that any suggestion of humour was, paradoxically, the product of unease. "The death of my wife is my business."

"Is that what you told Lynch?"

"He has nothing to do with my wife and I have nothing to do with his murder."

"Then what were you looking for in his room?"

Gilchrist took a step closer to Carr, towering over him, his proximity designed to intimidate. Carr remained fixed to the spot and, if he was supposed to feel threatened by the doctor's posture and expression of flint, he did not oblige. Gilchrist recognised as much and, in that moment, he began to realise that the man whom he had dismissed as a foolish, crippled dandy might be something else entirely. As if for the first time, he saw more than the luxuriant moustache and Imperial beard, more than the gaudy necktie and handkerchief, more than the ornate skull lapel pin with its ruby eyes, and more than the lame leg. Now, he saw only those dark eyes, like black pools of determination, and he was conscious of a new feeling that a man he had thought of as insignificant and preening was something altogether more dangerous.

"I didn't kill my wife, Mr Carr," he said, his voice as low and respectful as it might have been in the confessional.

"There are many who believe otherwise."

"I'm aware of that. Are you one of them?"

"If my opinion is of any relevance at all, I can say that I am not. I doubt you would have been capable of killing the woman who changed your life."

Gilchrist smiled and, this time, it was genuine. It seemed to Carr that it was the first truthful show of good humour which he had seen from the doctor. His usual cordiality and cheerfulness had previously struck Carr as too emphasised to be entirely credible. Now, however, he saw what he considered to be an honest display of happiness.

"Emily did change my life," Gilchrist was saying, "and I cannot deny it. I don't need to tell you what sort of man I was before she came into my life. The newspapers at the time were full of it. Perhaps I don't need to tell you what sort of man I am now she has left it."

Carr sat down slowly, stretching out his defective leg, his eyes remaining fixed on the doctor. "What happened?"

Gilchrist inhaled deeply, as if the following confession was likely to require all the breath in his body. "She killed herself, Mr Carr. That's the simple, brutal, cruel truth. The police were correct about everything except their final conclusion. The Veronal which was in her system was from my medical supply. I had begun to seek a life elsewhere, because my marriage had become nothing more than a meaningless, sterile existence. But I did not seek solace with another woman and I did not administer the Veronal to my wife in order to facilitate a new relationship. I had no intention of committing adultery, let alone murder, and I had no plans to desert my wife for another woman. To do so would have made a lie of our whole life together. Her depression was suffocating us both. All I needed was some air, some distance from it. I would always return to her."

"Why did she do it?" Carr asked the question with a gentle sympathy.

A single tear had welled in the doctor's right eye. He seemed unaware of it and Carr wondered whether Gilchrist had reached the point where tears over his wife were so frequent that they had lost all meaning, their frequency diluting their significance.

"It was her brother," whispered Gilchrist. "Can suicide be hereditary? If so, Emily and her brother had both inherited the trait. He took a rope and hanged himself from his own bannisters and she filled her body with Veronal on our settee as a result." His venomous cynicism was a protection against the tragedy of it all.

"The poison of deep grief," quoted Carr. "Your wife never recovered from the death of her brother?"

"And she followed in his footsteps."

Carr took a moment to contemplate this double tragedy. He was no stranger to the same poison of grief. There had been times after Miranda's death when he had wondered whether it was worth continuing with his own life and it had only been the knowledge that Miranda herself would have objected to such defeatist self-pity that he had refused to succumb to the temptation. He contemplated a word of condolence to Gilchrist, but he knew that it would sound trite and that the doctor would be able to accept it only as a futile gesture of polite sympathy, no matter how well-intended it may be. Instead, and in order to save them both from the embarrassment, Carr allowed a grave and respectful moment of silence to pass.

"Tell me about her brother," he said at last. It was a gently made command, spoken so earnestly that to refuse to comply with it would have seemed unreasonably obstructive.

"He was betrayed," said Gilchrist. "He wasn't a strong man. Emotionally, I mean. He was the sort of man who took things to heart. So, when he found that he had been deceived, it broke him."

"How was he betrayed?"

"Perhaps that is putting it too strongly, but it was certainly how Anthony saw it. He was a failed novelist, the sort of artist who is cursed with genius but has only a mediocre talent to express it. He was a very poor writer, but he could never accept it. No amount of rejection and adverse criticism could dampen his ambition." Gilchrist lowered his head in memory. "No, it took the theft of one of his ideas to break his spirit."

Carr felt a memory stir, but he could not bring it into focus. "I take it that the stolen idea was turned into a success."

"How do you know that?"

"Your story must end with his tragedy, doctor. It is not too much of a stretch for the imagination to understand what happened."

"The success should have been Anthony's, no doubt," said Gilchrist. "That was how people explained what he did. I have my doubts."

"How so?"

"I think it was the final acceptance that he could never have achieved the success on his own terms. The idea had proved itself, but only in someone else's hands. In his hands, it would have been another failure. I think it was the realisation of that fact which led him to do what he did."

Carr nodded in agreement. Plagiarism in itself was a matter for legal action but not for something so terrible as suicide. That required a much deeper motive and the acceptance of one's own uselessness and insignificance would be such a motive. "Do you know who stole the idea?"

CHAPTER TWENTY-FIVE

"I never enquired. It never seemed to matter very much to me."

"Did your wife know?"

"Not that I'm aware of. The death of her brother mattered more than the reason, perhaps. He was dead. What did it matter why he was dead?"

Carr could not help but disagree, although to argue the fact would have been neither tactful nor helpful. "Had Lynch discovered the truth? Is that why you were searching his room, to see if he had proof of it?"

Gilchrist shook his head. "No. It wasn't that. Lynch had discovered what happened and it had been he who told Anthony that his idea had been stolen. But that wasn't why I was searching his room."

The indirect confession went by without comment from Carr, but he had not failed to notice and remember it. "What, then?"

"He claimed he had some proof that I had murdered my wife."

"Blackmail?"

Gilchrist shrugged. "He was capable of it, I have no doubt about that, but there was never any request for money. I think it was the feeling of power over me which he enjoyed. Perhaps that was its own reward."

"Did he threaten to go to the police with this new evidence?"

"He gave the impression that he could do so if he wanted to. I think that was the point."

Carr could accept the suggestion as truth. "You could not have taken that threat seriously, though, surely? After all, you know your own innocence."

"Of course, but that did not stop me wanting to find out what this apparent evidence was. False proof can be as harmful as legitimate proof. To one's reputation, if nothing else."

Carr conceded the point with a taste of the cocktail. "Did you find any of this supposed evidence in his room?"

"No."

"Did Lynch tell you what it was?"

"Only in general terms. He claimed to have made contact with a woman who told him that she was my confederate in the plot and that she was going to marry me."

"Surely he could hardly have expected you to believe that?"

Gilchrist demurred. "I think you are wrong there, Mr Carr. I didn't believe it, naturally, but I doubt that is the point. The woman concerned is real and has wanted to get her sly claws into me for years. I think Lynch believed her lies about me and, in turn, felt he had something on me."

"But it would be easily disproved," argued Carr.

"Granted, but it would have opened up the old wounds and the speculation might well have been twice as vitriolic second time around." Gilchrist finished his own drink and contemplated another, neither his power of will nor his dignity persuading him otherwise. "Besides, the woman in question is a devious and vindictive little minx. I could not know what tactics she had used, or what lies she had told, to persuade Lynch of my guilt. If he had been fooled by whatever it was, other people might be similarly duped. I had to make sure."

"When you failed, did you try to find him? He was obviously not in his room."

"He wasn't, no, but I didn't feel the need to search for him."

"You did not go downstairs at all?"

"No." Gilchrist stared into Carr's eyes, as if daring him to contradict the reply. "I went back to my room and tried to sleep."

"Did you see anyone on your way?"

"No."

Carr saw no reason to disbelieve him and it meant that Eliza Montgomery had been telling the truth when she had said she returned to her own room after seeing Gilchrist enter Lynch's. "Did you hear any noises downstairs?"

"You mean did I hear Lynch being murdered?" Gilchrist regretted the fatuousness of the remark. "No, I did not. I had no idea what had happened until the body was discovered."

Carr knew that he could accept the truth that Gilchrist had returned immediately to his room after his futile search for this doubtlessly fabricated evidence against him. But that did not mean that he was innocent of murder. Eliza Montgomery had said she saw Gilchrist enter Lynch's room at half past one. As Carr had explained to her, Gilchrist could have murdered Lynch before she saw him on the landing. There was more than sufficient time for

Gilchrist to have committed the crime and searched the room afterwards. However candid Gilchrist had been over the past quarter of an hour, Carr could not feel confident that he could be excluded from suspicion of the murder itself. There was the question of motive. Carr doubted that Gilchrist had anything to fear from the unquestionably false evidence of a plot to murder his wife, regardless of whatever damage Lynch himself had believed he could do with it. But Gilchrist might have held Lynch responsible for the suicide of his brother-in-law, on account of the exposure of the plagiarism. If so, he may well blame Lynch, however indirectly, for the death of his own and beloved wife.

There was motive for murder there on the part of Dr John Gilchrist. And, unless he was much mistaken, Carr felt that Gilchrist's tragedy provided an equally persuasive motive for another guest to have committed the murder at Warlock's Gate.

Chapter Twenty-Six

As they left the library, Carr and Gilchrist found Ravenwood coming down the stairs. He looked better for his period of rest, but his face remained pale and haggard, and the dressing on the wound to his head lent a melodramatic quality to his overall appearance, whilst simultaneously emphasising the seriousness of his injury. Like Carr and Gilchrist, he had dressed for dinner and his suit was immaculate, the bow tie imperfect enough to show the mark of a true gentleman, but the excellence of his dress only served to exaggerate the injury and its protective gauze. It had a similar effect as if a small tear had been detected in the canvas of a pre-Raphaelite masterpiece.

When he saw Gilchrist, Ravenwood held up a warning hand. "Don't preach to me, Gilchrist. You may think I need to stay in bed forevermore, but I want a decent dinner with all its comforting formality. I like routine almost as much as I need it. Besides," he added, jerking his head behind him, "my good lady has already voiced sufficient protest for you both."

Resplendent in a burgundy gown whose colour was so intense that it made the diamonds which accompanied it seem even more dazzling than they were, Lady Ravenwood was a couple of steps behind her husband. Carr admired her, as he always did, but her delicate beauty seemed now to be more fragile than ever. There were no traces of tears, but Carr had the instinctive impression that she had been crying. It was only her composure and the usual calm dignity of her voice when she spoke which made him think he had been mistaken.

"My husband is a stubborn man, Dr Gilchrist, as you well know," she said.

"Once he has decided to act, there is no hope of dissuading him."

Gilchrist smiled and kissed her hand politely in the accepted form of greeting. Carr did likewise, upon her invitation, but he was not smiling. His mind was distracted, as if haunted by an impression and idea which he could not remember and which he might not understand if he could.

Ravenwood shook hands with both men. "I'm dying for a White Lady. What do you say, Gilchrist? Will my constitution survive it?"

"I daresay it will, sir."

Ravenwood turned to his wife. "You see, darling? Doctor's orders are a drink!"

They found a party of guests in the drawing room. Alicia was sitting beside the fireplace but, as Ravenwood entered, she ran to him and embraced him. He kissed her gently on the head and, in answer to her rapid succession of questions, assured her that he was feeling fine. A look to her mother gave Alicia the confirmation she clearly required. Following his fiancée's lead, Prentice greeted Ravenwood with a firm shake of the hand and kissed Lady Ravenwood delicately and formally on the cheek.

Ravenwood turned to Gilchrist. "You're the king of cocktails, doctor. I've yet to meet anyone better. Do me the honour of preparing me one."

"Of course," said Gilchrist. "Anything for you, Lady Ravenwood?"

"A sherry, please, nothing stronger."

Gilchrist attended to the requests. Carr refused a further drink when asked, and made his way to the corner of the room in which Truscott was standing. Helena Garrick was sitting on the settee with Louisa Marston, concentrating too deeply perhaps on their conversation, so that it was self-evident that she was avoiding Truscott's gaze, just as it was clear that he was hoping to break her concentration by the intensity of his stare. She could not possibly be unaware of it but, at present, her resolve was unbroken. Only when Gilchrist offered to pour her a drink did she allow her attention to shift and, when she had declined the offer, she was unable to prevent a swift, almost imperceptible glance in Truscott's direction. To him, her look seemed almost dismissive, as if it had been a regrettable accident, and it was enough to convince him to avert his eyes from her.

Carr was smiling up at him. "You remain intoxicated by Miss Garrick."

"She's as infuriating as she is beautiful."

"Take comfort in the fact that she was unable to stop herself looking in your direction," said Carr, touching Truscott's arm. "You should not give her any scope to believe you are pandering to her. Women like her do not appreciate it and they are never impressed by it."

Truscott was about to respond but he saw that Carr's attention had been seized by something else. Following his stare, Truscott saw that Carr was looking directly at Roderick Deville and Eliza Montgomery, sitting together on the window seat. They were in deep conversation, their heads bowed, as if their shared words were precious secrets which only the two of them deserved to know.

"Those two have been by each other's side all day," Truscott said.

"Interesting," observed Carr, almost to himself.

"Artists flocking together, perhaps. One is a writer and the other a painter, but I suppose they still share some common ideas."

"Very possibly," murmured Carr, "but I think there is something more sensitive even than art blossoming there."

"Do you think so?" asked Truscott, his tone of voice suggesting strongly that he did not share the point of view.

"I wonder if it explains why she was on the landing at the time of the murder," mused Carr. "Deville was outside the house, so I wonder if he was waiting for Miss Montgomery. It is an idea."

Truscott frowned. "Miss Montgomery was on the landing at the time of the murder?"

Carr considered him for a moment before laughing silently to himself. "My apologies, dear boy, but there is much I must tell you."

What Carr had to tell Truscott, it seemed, would have to wait. Their attention had been caught by the conversation taking place in the centre of the room. Carr made a small gesture to Truscott and they stepped closer towards the centre of the room.

"I suppose everyone has had the pleasure of Inspector Swift," Ravenwood was saying.

"That is not the word I would have used," said Prentice. He gripped Alicia's hand and kissed it. "I suppose we were fortunate to be interviewed together."

"It didn't make it any easier to cope with," replied Alicia, her flesh dimpling at the memory. "He's a horrible little beast of a man."

"He is doing his job, Alicia," said Mary seriously. "No doubt he has to perform many unpleasant duties."

Gilchrist laughed. "I should think Inspector Swift enjoys them immensely."

"Must you be so cynical all the time, John?" asked Helena sourly. "It can be tiresome at times."

"Forgive me," he replied. "I would hate to trample on your feelings. I hadn't realised you were an admirer of the dogged detective and his flattened feet."

She sneered in response and turned away from him, drawing deeply on the cigarette which was held between her slim fingers. Again, as she did so, her eyes fell to Truscott and, this time, they held his own for a longer period of time. He did not permit himself any sense of hope from it, but it did not leave him feeling anything approaching rejection.

"He did not seem to discover anything to help solve this terrible business," said Louisa. Her voice was hesitant, as if her opinion barely deserved the words which formed it.

"You cannot know what he has or has not discovered," said Carr. "And he will not divulge anything which he does not want to be known."

Roderick Deville rose from the window seat and walked slowly towards Carr, running his fingers through his unruly hair. "What about you, Mr Carr? Have you discovered anything? You seem to be conducting your own enquiry, after all."

Carr smiled at him, but the pressure of the glares which now descended on him was impossible to deny. He allowed himself a small shrug of the shoulders. "We are all suspects, Mr Deville. I am a naturally inquisitive man, but I am also a man with some experience of justice and its demands. I have no wish to be a suspect in a murder enquiry for longer than necessary."

Gilchrist gave an exclamation of agreement and raised his glass. "So, Mr Carr, your plan is to solve the thing before you are arrested for it, is that the idea?"

Carr smiled. "Something of the sort."

"But what can you hope to discover?"

It was Alicia who spoke and her words seemed to fascinate the room. A silence fell whilst Carr considered his answer. As he looked around at them, he saw with interest that some of them did not share Alicia's incredulity. Helena Garrick, recalling her own encounter with Carr, did not look at him. Deville, now regretting the consequences of his question, put his hands slowly and deliberately into his pockets. Louisa was looking up at him, her eyes widened in alarm, as if she were terrified that he might in some way betray a confidence or make an accusation towards her.

Carr spoke finally, his voice gentle and measured. "I have discovered very little."

Alicia was insistent. "Does Inspector Swift know you have been making these enquiries?"

"I have hidden nothing from him," replied Carr, judiciously.

She could see that she would have to be satisfied with the reply. "Do you know who committed the murder?"

Carr shook his head. "I cannot say for certain."

"But you have suspicions?" Alicia's voice was seeking to sound careless and amused, but it was only succeeding with a great effort.

"I have several."

"Won't you share them?" She laughed now, looking around the room, but the burst of humour was shrill rather than disarming.

Carr waved aside the suggestion. "They are ideas only, idle thoughts of a member of the public who is himself a suspect. My ideas are no better or more valid than anyone else's in this room."

Prentice began to laugh, as he walked over to them and put his arm around Alicia's waist. "I had no idea you were some sort of amateur sleuth, Mr Carr."

"I can hardly pretend to be anything so exciting, Mr Prentice."

Gilchrist joined in the laughter. "Still, I wouldn't put any money on Swift solving it before you do, Mr Carr."

The two men's good humour lifted the mood of the room and Carr was thankful for it. Conversations were commenced between individual groups of people and the quiet hum of polite discussions began to emanate through the room. The uneasy silence which had followed Deville's question to Carr had dissipated and it did not appear to have left behind it any trace of paranoia or suspicion. Deville walked away from Carr and back to Eliza Montgomery. They began to talk once again, their heads close, and their glances back to Carr seemed innocent if frequent.

Ravenwood was at his side in an instant, offering him a glass of whisky. "You look as if you need that."

Carr did not argue. "I'm grateful."

Ravenwood watched him savour the drink. "Have you really been poking around in this business?"

Carr bowed his head and stroked some remaining drops of whisky from his moustache. "Mr Deville makes too much of a trifle."

"Be that as it may, if you are trying to get one up on the police, you're a better man than me, Carr. This business of the locked room, and how the culprit got in and out of the house, it is all too much for me. I just cannot understand it, I've said so all along."

Carr clicked his tongue. "You are like my friend, Truscott, who cannot see past that mystery, when I have assured him that the solution to that part of the puzzle is so simple."

"Simple?"

But, as he had with Truscott and Swift, Carr dismissed the baronet's astonishment. "Precisely how well did you know Lynch? I understood your acquaintance with him was not recent but nor was it long-standing."

"A fair assessment. I've been corresponding with him for some time, but we never met until a few months ago."

"Your wife never met him?"

Ravenwood looked over to Mary. "No. She had never met him until this weekend."

"I had an idea she recognised him." Carr spoke softly.

Ravenwood looked at him and shook his head. "You know Mary. She is always ingratiating."

"Just so," agreed Carr. "Was Lynch interested in photography, at all?"

Ravenwood frowned. "Photography? Not that I know of. Why do you ask?"

Carr shrugged. "An idea, nothing more. I think you said Lynch had a sister, who had died?"

"I understood so, yes."

"Did he ever tell you anything about her?"

Ravenwood shook his head. "He wasn't the type to divulge very much about his private life. She was some years younger than Lynch, as I understand it, and she had died naturally when she was still fairly young. The Spanish flu, I believe."

"The Spanish flu," muttered Carr. "A terrible business."

"Other than this sister," continued Ravenwood, "I don't think there was any other family. He had come close to marriage once, he said, but he had avoided it."

"Avoided it?"

Ravenwood lowered his voice. "Not to gossip, you understand, but I think the woman in question was somewhat demanding."

Carr's eyes narrowed. "Did he ever mention any other love affairs?"

"No." Ravenwood drank some of the whisky.

Carr did likewise, savouring the effect of the spirit. "I wanted to ask you something, Sir James. Will you indulge me for a moment?"

"My dear chap, of course."

"If I recall correctly, you were in the library on the night of the murder, having been unable to sleep."

"That's right."

"And it was, I think you said, close to one o'clock in the morning?" Carr watched Ravenwood nod in agreement. "You sat there for half an hour or so?"

"Three quarters, perhaps."

Carr nodded, gratified that his memory of Swift's initial interview with Ravenwood and Lady Ravenwood had not betrayed him. His mind was drifting in another direction now. "Did you see or hear anybody moving around the in hallway? Going up the stairs, perhaps?"

Ravenwood gave the question the consideration he felt it deserved. "No, not that I can recall."

"You are certain?"

"As certain as I can be." He tapped the dressing on his temple. "This damned thing plays havoc with one's head, naturally, but I am fairly sure I heard nothing and saw nobody."

And yet, Carr was thinking, so many of the people concerned had been moving around at various times during those early hours of that tragic morning. Helena Garrick, on her mysterious mission; Roderick Deville, possibly waiting for Eliza Montgomery; Gilchrist undertaking his search of Lynch's room; Louisa Marston fetching her spectacles; Ravenwood sitting in silence in the library. It was the purest chance, he reasoned, that one or other of them did not witness anything. And, in the midst of it all, Lynch had been stabbed in the heart by an unknown assassin who had eluded them all and vanished into nothing.

"It is all so fascinating," said Carr to himself, "and so very complex."

Ravenwood was about to speak but any further comment was prevented by a raucous, intrusive burst of laughter from the far corner of the room. Richard Prentice had been so amused by something said by Gilchrist that his eyes had dampened and his cheeks had risen in colour. Helena Garrick was smiling also, but her humour was more controlled than Prentice's own. The noise which had erupted from him was lewd, almost indecent, and it ended with a brief fit of coughing. Alicia handed him a glass of water but he refused it, preferring instead to clear his throat with his Manhattan. Ravenwood watched the scene with distaste and, once it had subsided, he turned his attention back to Carr.

"You will forgive my honesty, Carr," he said, "but I cannot stand that man. It may not be done to say so, given I have agreed to allow him to marry my daughter, but there it is."

Carr was careful with his reply. "He seems an excitable young man. Rather too much, perhaps. But we were all young once, Sir James, and our own tempers no doubt seemed too spirited to our elders."

Reluctantly, Ravenwood accepted the point, but he questioned the relevance of it. "I had someone look into him, you know. Private detective chap, I mean. Seedy little man, not much more respectable than the people he tracks down, I shouldn't wonder."

Carr's interest was piqued. "And did he discover anything?"

"Very little." Ravenwood seemed disappointed, but whether it was on account of the lack of information or the money wasted in obtaining that result was impossible to know. "Certainly nothing I could prove, but the indications were that Prentice is a player. There were rumours a few years ago that he was making a living cheating at cards. Nothing was ever proved, of course, and it doesn't do for a chap to go around hurling accusations without evidence. Also, he had been linked to fraudulent business deals, handling dope, and there was even a suggestion that he was involved in the peddling of sordid material."

"Dear me," purred Carr.

"I don't need to tell you the sort of thing, I mean, Carr. Disgusting."

"It's remarkable that Miss Alicia was ever able to meet such a man."

"That's the devil of it. He's a climber. Racketeers like him often are, you know that. They like the life people like us lead but they don't have the means to support it. So, they inveigle their way into it and live on the back of others."

"They met at a party, I understand?"

"Some of Alicia's acquaintances are a lively bunch."

"You put it so delicately," smiled Carr. "Not so long ago, we would have called them Bright Young Things, is that not so?"

"That's the measure of them." Ravenwood flashed a cautious glance at Carr. "Not that my Alicia was ever like that, you understand. Too much of her mother in her to fall for all that nonsense, but it didn't stop her being in the centre of such people. She called it living, God help her."

"And it was through these people that she met Mr Prentice?"

"Yes," drawled Ravenwood.

Carr contemplated what had been said for a long moment. "I am surprised you have elected to allow the marriage to proceed."

"How could I stop it?" Ravenwood threw a disapproving glance back at

Prentice. "Obviously, with proof, I could have intervened, but I had none. So, I took Prentice to one side and had it out with him."

Carr's eyebrows raised. "And what was his defence?"

Ravenwood laughed, despite himself. "Admission, would you believe? He said he had been reckless, even disgraceful, in the past, but meeting Alicia had tamed him. That was the very word he used. I was sceptical, of course, but the parties ceased, his propensity for scandal evaporated, and he became dutiful both to Alicia and my wife. If I had objected to the wedding, you can imagine how I would have seemed."

"So, you capitulated?"

"I took Prentice at his word. I don't have to like the man but, to be decent to him, he seems to have given me the truth."

"Perhaps," murmured Carr. "And yet, the truth is so difficult to tell."

At that moment, as if to punctuate the significance of Carr's philosophical statement, the gong sounded for dinner. Ravenwood drained his glass and went to his wife, taking her arm to escort her into the dining room. The assembled group slowly dissipated, but Carr remained motionless for a long moment, his eyes fixed on the floor.

As people left the room, like the shrouds of mist blowing away on a cold, winter evening, they cleared his range of vision and only then did he see Louisa Marston. She was sitting alone on the settee now, glaring up at him with a mixture of confusion and alarm.

"Miss Marston?" he said. "Is something the matter?"

"Sisters," she said to herself, so quietly that Carr had to strain to hear it. "You said something about sisters..."

"Mr Lynch had a sister, yes."

"And, of course, there is Protopopov."

"Who?"

His voice seemed to break some sort of abstract spell and she shook herself back into reality. She rose uncertainly, her lips moving silently and her eyes flickering around the room in a measure of distress which belied her words of assurance to the contrary.

"Forgive me, Mr Carr, I was away with the fairies. I had a thought about something, but it has gone now. I am so scatter-brained." She made an attempt to laugh, to reassure him of her peace of mind. It did not succeed, although he did not say so, and he found himself wondering whether she had been trying to convince him or herself.

As she left the room, Carr thought back to the conversation with Ravenwood. It was clear that Miss Marston had heard something in it which she had thought was important. Ravenwood had said that Lynch had a sister who had died and her reference to sisters seemed to connect with that fact. But if she had seen some importance in it, Carr failed to recognise it himself. His own mind had seized upon something else entirely, a fact which he knew was important and upon which he would have to act swiftly, but now he wondered if he had overlooked something else of importance, something which had struck Louisa Marston so resolutely. He replayed the conversation with Ravenwood in his mind, but the elusive point failed to come into focus.

At last, with a sudden awareness, he realised that he was alone in the room. His absence from the dining room would have been noticed and it would be unwise to prolong it. He forced himself to leave the room and he began to make his way slowly to the door, his mind preoccupied with frustrating and indefinable thoughts about twilight assignations, photographs, dead sisters, and murder.

Chapter Twenty-Seven

The night air was still, without the cruel bite of the usual autumn wind, and so quiet that the violence and horror of the previous couple of days might have been forgotten. The night was so complete in its darkness and tranquillity that it seemed impossible to connect Warlock's Gate with any type of dark mystery. The moon was full and it cast its nocturnal light over the lawns and terraces of the house, covering them in a spectral glow in which the shadows seemed to possess an ethereal beauty of their own. The silver sheen of moonlight emphasised, yet complimented, the pure black of the night sky, like pearls against a velvet gown, and the gentle rustling of the trees on the subtly chilled breeze was both soothing and enchanting. From somewhere in the distance a lonely owl let out a succession of rapid, solemn notes.

Everett Carr was standing on the rear terrace with a glass of port and his thoughts. He had barely eaten at dinner, but he was suffering no ill effects from his lack of food. His mind was too preoccupied with the various mysteries which he had set himself to unravel, just as it had been when he had picked at the otherwise excellent guinea fowl which had been served as the main course. Until now, he had been sure that his conclusions were generally accurate. He had been confident that he knew not only how and why the murder had been carried out, but also who had committed it. There were a number of extraneous mysteries surrounding the central problem and these, also, Carr had felt confident were within his grasp. But, as Ravenwood had said, albeit in different circumstances, it was all a question of proof.

And yet, now, his confidence had suffered a shipwreck and Louisa Marston was to blame. What had it been, Carr wondered, that she had gleaned from the mention of Lynch's sister? What connection could that sister, long since in her grave, have with the death of Lynch himself? Carr could find no place for her in his theories and, if his ideas were accurate, he could not explain why Lynch's sister, alive or dead, should be of such importance. A simple answer to the conundrum was that his conclusions were wrong and he should re-evaluate the position, a thought which both sickened and depressed him. With an impatient gesture, he dismissed the idea. His conclusions could not be wrong, not least because there was no other way of reconciling all the facts of the murder. And yet, as matters stood, there was no place for this dead sister in any of those speculations. Perhaps, then, it had been Louisa who had made the mistake, which was a more soothing thought, but one which would leave her reaction inexplicable. Carr closed his eyes in frustration. His brain ran in circles, like a serpent eating its tail, and he could see no means of breaking the chain of confusion.

Carr whispered a low, brutal curse and, as if disgusted with himself, he rinsed his mouth with the port.

"Enjoying the evening air, Mr Carr?"

Richard Prentice stepped out onto the terrace and lit a cigar. Ravenwood's words in connection with him returned to Carr's memory and, in a moment of fancy, it seemed to Carr that they were capable of twisting Prentice's handsome features or, alternatively, corrupt Carr's own assessment of those features. Where once he might have considered Alicia's fiancé suave and charming, he seemed now able only to see him as manipulative and unctuous. The face was still attractive, but Ravenwood's words had imposed a dangerous darkness to the man's magnetism.

"Just enjoying five minutes of solitary thought, Mr Prentice," replied Carr.

"I am sorry," said Prentice, suddenly contrite. "I am disturbing you."

Carr held out a hand to the young man's arm. "Not at all, Mr Prentice, not at all. Solitary thought quickly becomes lonely thought and I am glad of the company."

"Well, if you are sure, sir."

"Has Miss Alicia retired for the evening?"

Prentice shook his head. "No, she is chatting with Helena over coffee."

"It is a shame she should not experience such a beautiful night as this." Carr waved his hand towards the clear night sky.

Prentice smiled. "You may be right, Mr Carr."

"Fetch her," said Carr, unexpectedly. "Bring her here and let us enjoy a few peaceful moments together."

If Prentice thought the request was strange, he was polite enough not to show it. There was something so earnest and insistent in Carr's tone that declining the suggestion never seemed to Prentice to be a valid response. He smiled and nodded, exclaiming that it was a sound idea and that Alicia herself would appreciate it. Carr returned the ingratiating smile but, as soon as Prentice was out of sight, Carr's lips straightened into a serious line and his eyes crystallised, all trace of geniality removed from them.

Prentice was absent no longer than a couple of minutes and, when he returned, he was holding Alicia by the hand. Dressed in an emerald-coloured dress of chiffon, which accentuated her slim figure to seductive effect yet without inviting accusations of indecency, Alicia was as radiant and ethereal as the moonlight itself. Her skin was so delicate that it seemed as fragile as her dress and the brightness of the moon seemed to give her blonde hair a strangely supernatural glow. If ever it was clear why a man could love a woman, it was when Alicia Ravenwood stepped into the twilight.

Carr kissed her gently on both cheeks. "My dear, you are lovely. I hope that Mr Prentice understands his good fortune."

"I am sure he does." She looked up at the man in question, as if appreciating yet again her own good luck in securing his love.

Prentice kissed her hand. "You are a daily reminder of it."

She looked out over the gardens. "What a beautiful evening."

"Isn't it?" Carr looked up to the sky and the few stars which were visible in it. "My wife used to love clear night skies such as these. She found them both beautiful and mysterious. Maybe she found the mystery of them beautiful or maybe it was the other way around, but she adored them. I find I love them all the more now that she is above them herself."

It was a lyrical and emotional soliloquy and both Prentice and Alicia allowed themselves a moment of silence to savour it. It was made all the more impressive to both of them by the unexpected honesty of it. Alicia, who had never before viewed Carr as anything other than an eccentric friend of her father's, saw for the first time a sadness and sensitivity in him which she found unusually touching. She had never assumed that someone like Carr, with his dandified appearance and overstated moustache and beard, might have known emotions such as love, tenderness, or grief. Suddenly, he was no longer just the strange man who attended weekend parties; he was gentle, delicate, and tragic.

Prentice leaned against the balustrade which edged the terrace. "I suppose the police will be back in the saddle tomorrow, crawling all over the place again."

"I hope they leave us alone," said Alicia. She turned to Carr. "They called us liars, you know."

Prentice cautioned her. "You must remember that we did plot to lie to them, Alicia, and you were prepared to go ahead with the idea. You would have done so too, if I hadn't stopped you."

"What lie was this?" asked Carr.

"That we were both in our own beds at the time of the murder," said Prentice. "Only we weren't. We were together, which I thought was a much better story to tell, not least because it was true."

"You are all about truth, are you, Mr Prentice?" asked Carr carefully.

Before he could obtain any response, Alicia had begun to speak. "Telling the truth is all very well and good, of course, except when it does you more harm than good."

"Do you really believe that, my child?" asked Carr.

The girl's eyes widened with disbelief and disgust. "That awful Inspector said our alibi was worthless, because we are engaged."

"What my darling Alicia means," said Prentice, "is that the cynical Inspector said that we were the only ones able to corroborate each other's stories and, naturally, we would be anxious to do so."

Carr smiled. He could well believe that Swift's mind had travelled along such tracks. "I fear the good Inspector will prove to be his own worst enemy when it comes to tying himself in knots."

"Does that mean you believe us?" asked Alicia.

Carr tilted his head obligingly. "I can imagine that you both had good cause to be together. I suspect you have had much to discuss since Lynch's arrival."

Alicia glanced over to Prentice. He reflected her expression of shock, as if he too had dismissed Carr as a harmless irrelevance. He had not felt any warming of feeling towards him after his reminiscence about his wife's love of night skies, but he had recognised it in Alicia. Now, however, he saw nothing in her eyes but confirmation that she was afraid of this strange man who sat smiling back at the pair of them.

Prentice tried to dissemble, as if doing so might be taken for control of the situation. "I'm not sure we had anything to talk about as far as Lynch was concerned."

Carr retained his good humour, the smile still fixed on his lips, but the dark eyes were hard. "Would it surprise you to learn that Lynch was a blackmailer?"

Alicia let out a small gasp, barely audible, and Prentice's charming self-assurance cracked, only slightly, under the weight of the question and its insinuation. He swallowed before answering. "A blackmailer?"

Carr shrugged. "I've certainly formed that view. Lynch gave the impression to one of the guests that he had some incriminating evidence against him regarding a certain circumstance and that he could use it against that person if necessary."

"Who do you mean?"

Carr shook his head. "That is not for me to say, Mr Prentice, and it is scarcely the point. The relevance of it is that Lynch had a propensity for blackmail. Not in the conventional sense, perhaps, of demanding money in return for silence, although I wouldn't put that past him, but he certainly enjoyed having power over other people."

Prentice drew heavily on his cigar. "I never did like the man."

"I imagine not," said Carr. It was a seemingly insignificant remark, but it was heavy with meaning and it would have been foolish for Prentice to pretend he had not picked up on the fact.

"Do you have something to say to us, Mr Carr?"

Carr did not reply immediately. Instead, he waited for the silence to oppress Prentice and compel him to speak for himself. But, if Carr thought he could manipulate the younger man so easily, he was to be mistaken. In retrospect, he wondered whether he had expected Prentice to be so malleable. If Ravenwood was to be believed, Prentice would have learned to defend himself and resist intimidation from worse men than Carr. Alicia, less experienced in such matters, was more easily terrorised by the silence and her paleness of skin, which had seemed so alluring moments earlier, now appeared to be the product of something much more dreadful.

Carr had no wish to prolong her agony, although the subject which he wished to discuss did not seem to be one which he could raise without careful consideration.

"There was a certain topic which I wanted to talk over with you, Mr Prentice," said Carr finally.

"What might that be?"

"Photography."

Again, the word was spoken innocently, but the look in his eyes spoke of a darker meaning. Even under their glare, Prentice refused to assist. With a sigh, Carr realised that he would have to speak alone. He glanced at Alicia, at her widened eyes and tightened lips, and he smiled softly at her, as if to assure her that he meant her no harm by the words which would follow.

"You are a photographer of some skill, I believe, Mr Prentice," he said. "You told Miss Eliza Montgomery as much, as I understand it."

"I've made no secret of it."

Carr nodded. "After we had discovered Lynch's body, I took it upon myself to have a look around his room. It was not ethical, perhaps, but I felt it was important to do so. I found several things which interested me, but only one which I think is relevant right now."

"Really?" Prentice feigned disinterest, but the restlessness of his fingers suggested otherwise.

"It was an envelope, stamped with the legend *Les Lentilles d'Henri Chastain* and an address in Soho. I don't suppose that address means anything to you." Carr waited for a reply but, once again, he received only silence in return. "I have not had the opportunity to visit M. Chastain's establishment, but I can imagine what sort of place it is. The photographs which were in the envelope were sufficient to give me the correct impression."

"How so?" Prentice had been unable to resist the enquiry.

Carr glanced at Alicia. "They were of a particular type, you understand. I don't wish to say too much in the company of Miss Ravenwood, but you will understand me if I say they were designed for a certain breed of gentleman. They showed a lady and always the same lady. That was obvious, despite the mask she was wearing in each of the images. She wore very little else. Some of the photographs might be described as portraits of her. Others, unhappily, were much more salacious, not to say depraved. In these latter pictures, the masked lady was not alone. A man, sometimes more than one, was with her and various acts were being undertaken, the nature of which I am afraid I shall have to leave to your imagination."

Prentice looked over to Alicia. "Go inside."

Carr turned to face her too. "I think it best not to leave us, Miss Ravenwood."

Alicia, alternating her wild gaze from one to the other of them, stuttered her reply. "I shall stay. I have to stay."

"I think that is wise," said Carr with a smile. "My friend, Mr Truscott, asked why Lynch should have had these distasteful photographs with him. I did not give him any answers, but several suggested themselves to me. He might have them for his own gratification. Or he might have taken them himself. But, if either of those ideas were correct, I would not have expected Lynch to have them on his person. It would have made much more sense for him to keep them secret in the privacy of his own house."

"That is guesswork," said Prentice.

"True enough," conceded Carr with a bow, "but I think we can say it is educated speculation. And, as if to put the matter beyond all doubt in my own mind, I learned that Lynch had this inclination towards blackmail which I have suggested to you already. That seemed to be the answer. If Lynch had these scandalous photographs with him and he was capable of blackmail, it seemed to me as if it was all a matter of cause and effect. You see my point?"

Prentice extinguished his cigar, slowly and deliberately. "Lynch knew who the girl was, or who took the photographs, or both."

"Precisely."

"And he planned on blackmailing one or both of them."

Carr held up a finger. "Or else he planned *to continue* doing so. Now, quite naturally, I asked myself who the girl might have been. Even with the mask, it was clear she was young and attractive. Helena Garrick might have been the girl but, somehow, I doubted it. Miss Garrick strikes me as being too self-assured, too fiercely protective of her own privacy to abandon it so completely in a series of lewd photographs. For similar reasons, I could not envisage Miss Montgomery making herself the object of, shall we say, a piece of art and not the creator of it."

He paused for a moment and took a sip of the port. "I had already convinced myself that it was you in the images, Miss Ravenwood, and that Mr Prentice had taken them. I had no proof and I still have none, but your father put the matter beyond all doubt in my mind."

Alicia had begun to tremble with fear but the mention of Ravenwood made her knees buckle beneath her. Prentice caught her and eased her into one of the seats which were set out on the terrace. Weakly, she whispered, "My father?"

Carr patted her knee gently. "He knows nothing about the photographs, you can be sure of that. But he told me certain things which convinced me that I was right about your part in them. Firstly, and you must forgive me, Mr Prentice, he told me that you were somewhat reckless in your youth and that you acted in questionable ways before."

Prentice, though outraged, maintained his composure. "He told you about the private detective?"

Carr nodded. "And about your confession and redemption. Except, I think that your absolution is not quite as complete as Ravenwood believes."

CHAPTER TWENTY-SEVEN

"What else did he tell you?"

"That the pair of you had once been Bright Young Things. The qualifications for inclusion into that scion of society is well-known: unconventionality, excess, careless abandon, behaviour designed to shock."

"It is called living," said Alicia, with feeling. "It is being alive, in touch with one's senses."

Carr's face had hardened. "Is it also about prostituting one's fiancée, Mr Prentice?"

The young man's eyes blazed with indignation. His fingers balled into fists and his body trembled with suppressed fury, the pressure of which forced the veins in his neck to stand out like executioner's rope. Carr remained still, retaining his disapproving expression, and he offered no further comment. Alicia had begun to weep silently, her head hung in shame and her cheeks crimson with degradation.

"It is all my fault, Mr Carr," she said, her voice cracking with sobs.

"Don't say anything else, for God's sake," hissed Prentice.

Alicia shook her head. "What does it matter now, Richard? Lynch is dead, but Mr Carr knows the truth. We can't hide anymore."

"I am not in the business of blackmail, Miss Ravenwood," Carr said. "What you tell me will be in confidence, assuming it has nothing directly to do with the murder."

She shook her head. "We didn't kill him, Mr Carr. I swear we didn't and what we told Inspector Swift was true. We were together, Richard and I, just as we said."

"We were trying to decide what to do about Lynch," confessed Prentice, "but our ideas did not stretch to murder."

Carr nodded. "He was blackmailing you about the photographs, is that not so?"

"He had been for months."

Alicia's sobbing had intensified, so that her words were barely intelligible. "I blame myself for everything. It was all my fault."

Prentice put his arms around her and kissed her gently on the head. He looked up at Carr. "What she means, sir, is that what I said to Sir James was

195

true. I did want to turn my back on my past and start again. I was tired of being a heel, of being something people despised, and of being associated with all manner of sordid things. I wanted to be respectable. I still do. I am trying to be," he added uselessly.

Alicia pulled her face from his chest and looked up at Carr with pleading eyes. "I have never been anything other than respectable. Always expected to be upright, so morally perfect, never to make any social misjudgements or errors. When I met Richard, who was the opposite entirely, I thought he was so exciting, so dangerous. Have you any idea how attractive that can be to someone like me, Mr Carr?"

He looked down at her, his emotions conflicting with shock and pity. "Are you saying that you wanted to continue living scandalously but Mr Prentice wanted to convert to respectability?"

"Yes." She nodded, but the voice was filled with shame.

Carr spoke softly. "The photographs, then, were your idea?"

Alicia nodded again, but now there were only tears and no words of affirmation were necessary. Prentice's hold on her tightened and he closed his eyes in a sense of shared pain at her agony. For a moment, the tableau was undisturbed by any sound except Alicia's muffled weeping until, after a moment, Prentice looked up at Carr.

"I had known Henri Chastain from the past," he said. "On the surface, he is a reputable photographer but, for additional money from those who desire such things, he can accommodate more unconventional tastes. A friend of ours had commissioned some photographs like the ones we're talking about and he showed them at one of our parties. There was a time when I would have been salivating over them as much as everybody else, but I found them hideous. I cannot explain my change of heart other than to say that I would have hated Alicia to be exploited in the same way as the women in those photos which were being passed around. It would have sickened me. What I didn't know was that Alicia herself was thinking the opposite."

"I am hateful," she spat. "Hateful!"

Neither man acknowledged her self-reproach, but it was Prentice who continued to speak. "I tried to dissuade her, but she was adamant. She had loved the idea of being exposed, put on show, exhibited. God help us both, she had been thrilled by it all."

"And the physical abuse in the photographs?"

"It was consensual."

As Prentice replied in a dejected, debased monotone, Alicia howled with disgust at herself, before forcing herself to speak. "I can see now how sordid and offensive I was. How selfish and ridiculous. But, at the time, it was so wicked that it was better than any drug. The thrill of the indecency of it, of doing something shocking and beyond conventional taste, was impossible to resist. I can't explain it, other than to say that it was so intoxicating that it drove me out of my wits. The sheer vulgarity of it, the gross impropriety of it... it was so hypnotic."

Carr looked at Prentice. "And you went along with it?"

He nodded. "I can never refuse her. And, perhaps some of her enthusiasm rubbed off on me. I should have flatly declined, but she would have gone ahead with it in any event."

Alicia's tears intensified, as if hearing Prentice's certainty about the point had deepened her shame, not only by his knowledge of it but by her realisation of it. If Carr was appalled by the sordid confession of Alicia's baser desires, he did not show it. He handed his glass of port to Prentice and indicated it should be given to Alicia to restore her composure. Prentice put the glass to her lips and she drank awkwardly, each mouthful easing her tension and calming her mood. Carr waited for the tormented sobs to subside before he spoke again.

"How did Lynch find out about what you had been doing?" he asked.

"He and Chastain had been at the same party one time," replied Prentice. "One of the Frenchman's less desirable customers had also been invited. It's amazing how many apparently respectable men in society share the same base tastes. I wonder whether any of us are truly honourable."

Carr did not consider it prudent to debate the point. "I take it that Chastain and this particular customer of his were talking and Lynch overheard?"

Prentice nodded. "Chastain had been speaking in hushed tones, of course, but that is obviously redundant if you allow names to slip out."

Carr nodded. "And, of course, Lynch knew the name Ravenwood well enough from his own dealings with Sir James?"

"That was where our troubles began," said Prentice. "He had bought the photographs from Chastain and he got in touch with us. You can imagine the conversation and what followed, no doubt."

"Sufficiently well," said Carr. "He threatened to tell Sir James?"

"And the newspapers." Prentice, despite himself, smiled. "When we learned that Lynch was going to be here this weekend, Alicia was terrified. I tried to reassure her, but she was convinced he would expose our secret to her father."

Carr shook his head. "He would not have cut off a supply of funds needlessly."

"I tried to placate her, but she wanted something to be done." Prentice seemed to understand the connotations of his remark immediately and he stammered a denial. "I don't mean murder. Dear God, no. We were going to pay him double his latest demand and insist on having back the photos."

"And burn them?" Carr waited for the nod of confirmation. "It would never have worked. Blackmailers are not so easily deterred. He would have had more than one set of the photographs and the ones I found would be dispensable. He would never have released you. Not until he had depleted you completely and, even then, he would have released the pictures in any event."

Prentice conceded the argument with a bow of the head. "We were desperate and it was all I could think of."

"But then someone solved the problem for you," observed Carr.

Alicia had stopped the flow of tears. Her eyes betrayed the traces of her anguish, the scarlet aftermath of grief burning brightly around them. But there was something more than sorrow in her eyes now. There remained a distinct sadness and, similarly, a profound shame, but Carr thought that he could now detect a strong sense of entreaty, as if her survival and redemption were entirely in his hands.

"We did not kill him, Mr Carr," she whispered. "The rest of it is all true but we didn't murder him. I swear to you, it was nothing to do with us."

Carr, touched by her desperation, shared something of her sadness. "No, Miss Ravenwood, I think I know that. Your sin lies elsewhere, as does Mr Prentice's. You must deal with your own conscience, but I do not think murder lies there."

Now, as if exhausted by the relief at hearing this judgment, Alicia sank into Prentice's arms. He held her solidly and his eyes, when they looked up at Carr, were filled with gratitude and honesty. "Thank you, sir. Thank you."

"The police have the photographs," Carr said cautiously. "They are evidence. I cannot do anything other than advise you, but I would confess everything to Swift if I were you. He is bound to visit Chastain and, if that man is indiscreet enough to allow your secret to fall into Lynch's hands, you can be sure he will not be any more cautious when questioned by the police."

Alicia looked up at Prentice, the fear returning to her eyes. Prentice smiled down at her and, perhaps for the first time, Carr believed in the man's change of character. There was nobility in the features now and protective love in his eyes. He stroked her cheek. "I will speak to Swift. You won't have to say anything."

Carr stepped forward. "If I can assist in supporting your version of events on the night of the murder, I shall do so."

Alicia spoke with an effort. "I don't deserve any of this."

"You lost your way, dear lady," said Carr soothingly. "It happens to us all. You were seduced by temptation and succumbed. But you have learned from it and you will overcome it. There are worse sins in the world than yours. You must learn to forgive yourself and, perhaps, each other."

He smiled down at her and patted her gently on the shoulder. Prentice eased Alicia out of his grip and stood up. He held out his hand and said, frankly, "Thank you, Mr Carr."

Carr took the hand which had been offered and shook it. "Be good to her. She will need your strength in the future."

If Prentice required any clarification of the comment, he was not to be given time to seek it. Carr bowed courteously and offered a final smile, before turning his back on the wayward lovers and leaving them alone to face their past evils under the moonlit sky.

Chapter Twenty-Eight

Truscott rose early on Sunday morning and found that he was alone for breakfast. He was not sorry about it. If anything, he was glad of the solitude. His mood was low and his mind distracted, so that his ability to concentrate either on the meal or any polite conversation over it was questionable. He had slept badly and what rest he had succumbed to had been plagued so heavily with dreams that it was little more than a shallow doze. In the life which seemed so long ago to him now, but which was in fact only that of his recent past, he would not have been troubled by lack of sleep. The effects of excess alcohol the previous evening and the desire, bordering on a requirement, for more of the same in order to function on the following day would have overpowered any natural sense of exhaustion. But now, with his closeness to dependency curbed and his blood cleared of it, the fatigue was overpowering and the effect of it was a shortened temper and frayed nerves.

The cause of his restless night persisted in ruining his morning, like the incessant pain of a knife in the back or a broken heart. He forced himself to confront a plate of eggs and ham, but they remained untouched once he had taken his seat, as the recollection of the conversation on the previous evening repeated itself in his memory, like the whispers of a restless spirit in the consciousness of the gullible.

It had been after dinner that he had approached her, making sure that she was alone, so that there had been no opportunity of her making any excuse to avoid him. She had been seated between Gilchrist and Deville at dinner and it was to the latter that she had explained that she had left her cigarettes in the drawing room. Truscott had waited for her to leave to retrieve them and he had followed her into the room.

She had turned to face him as he closed the door and leaned against it. "I came for my cigarettes. I can't abide after dinner coffee without a cigarette."

"I wanted to talk to you, Helena."

She had taken a step towards him, as if assured that his gentleman's propriety would compel him to make way for her, but if he had any such decency then it had temporarily deserted him. Her shock at the realisation of it had widened her eyes, not in shock but in fury. "Are you trapping me in this room, Jack?"

"Of course not."

"You will be late for brandy and cigars in the library and I shall be late for coffee in the lounge."

"The coffee will still be hot and the brandy just as good in five minutes' time," he had replied. "You've avoided me all day, so I think you can give me some time now."

She had lit a cigarette and placed her weight on one foot in an attitude of defiance. "What makes you think you deserve any time?"

"I won't apologise for confiding in Carr and I won't continue to justify what I did. It was the right thing to do and you will have to live with it. If you cannot accept that, I want to hear you say it to my face."

"Don't be so melodramatic."

He had refused to be shamed into submission. "Say it to my face, Helena. Tell me you can't get over what happened. If you can, I'll believe you and I'll leave you alone."

She had been unable to retain contact with his eyes and she had hidden her face in a cloud of tobacco smoke. For Truscott, it had been enough of an answer.

"You don't want me to leave you alone," he had dared to say. "You know it as well as I do. You're overreacting to what I did because it means something to you, something more than a stranger gossiping about you."

"I refuse to be dragged into this nonsense." It had been a valiant effort, but it had fooled neither of them.

"I can't explain what's happened to me," he had said. "I never thought I would feel like this again, not after the death of my wife, and I'm not even sure what I'm feeling is at all like that. God knows what it is, but it's something. And you know it is."

She had not agreed, any more than she had disagreed. She had said nothing. She had shaken her head and rolled her eyes at him, letting out a short and shrill laugh of indignation. In that moment, any doubts about her had evaporated. Her subtle mockery of him, her insolence, her refusal to expose her emotions even to the limited extent which he had done himself had all impressed him so keenly that he had no longer been able to assure himself of any doubt about her. He had pushed himself away from the door and stepped towards her. Barely in control of himself, he had taken her by the shoulders and pulled her towards him. She had opened her mouth to protest but no words ever came. When their lips connected, it had been with a sudden mixture of urgency and nervousness. Truscott had felt the surge of something which might have been relief or might have been anxious passion and, in that single point of time, it had been as if there was nothing else in the world but her. Helena had stiffened but, whether she would accept it later or not, she had settled into the kiss, her body relaxing against his. It had been a momentary surrender, however, and, almost as soon as it had been given, it had been retracted. She had pulled herself away from him and glared at him, as if betrayal of her was the only achievement of which he was capable and the only treatment of her which he could offer.

Breathing heavily, she had run a finger along her lips, as though in an effort to erase the memory and taste of him. He had remained steadfast, refusing to apologise for acting on the impulse which he knew he could never have denied forever. She had touched her hair and smoothed out invisible creases in her dress, before drawing heavily on the cigarette. The smoke had blurred her features, a convenient mask behind which to hide. She had smiled, again insolent but without the previous trace of mockery, and she had walked out of the room. This time, he had permitted her to do it.

No further words had been spoken and he had not seen her again that night. And, now, he came to himself and the breakfast had gone cold.

The morning was brisk and the skies were unfalteringly blue, despite the lateness of the year. The extreme clarity of the weather seemed to cleanse his own brain and, under the influence of such lucidity, Truscott could not help but feel that his impulse on the previous night had been foolish. In its moment, it had seemed the only thing to do, but the kiss now struck him as arrogant, presumptuous, and unwisely impetuous. He cursed himself for it, silently initially but then with a coarser verbal assault, and yet, despite it, he knew that he could not bring himself to regret it.

It was as he rose from the table to make his exit that he saw her.

The window of the dining room looked out over the front lawns of the garden. The long driveway which led from the main gates of the grounds to the front door was just visible from where Truscott was standing, although it was slightly shaded by the shadows of the impressive oaks which lined the approach to the house. Truscott walked swiftly to the broad windows and craned his neck, getting as clear a view as possible. It was undoubtedly her. She was dressed in a floral house dress and low-heeled shoes, her hat pulled down over one side of her face, but Truscott could recognise not only the sway of her figure as she walked but also the determined attitude which accompanied it.

He ran from the dining room and into the hall, pulling open the front door with a sudden lack of control. He stood on the threshold and watched her walk past the small lodge at the end of the driveway and through the gates onto the road which led down into the village. Without quite knowing why, Truscott pulled the door closed behind him and ran swiftly over the gravel pathway after her. He did not call her name. To do so would have alerted her to his presence and, with a sudden and unexpected return of his journalistic intuition, he felt that it would be better if Helena Garrick did not know of his pursuit. Not, at least, until he was ready to expose it.

He kept a safe distance behind her as she walked with purpose through the village. With the natural paranoia of someone acting covertly, he felt that every pair of eyes was fixed on him and that he might be given away at any moment. In reality, his concerns were unfounded and none of the scrutiny he feared was imposed on him. The village went about its business without any interest in Jack Truscott: the early morning shopping was in progress as evidenced by the delicate tinkling of the bells of shops doors, the smell of baking bread filled the air whilst accompanied by the more robust but no less uplifting peal of church bells, and the rapid movement of lips and tongues suggested that the pulse of healthy gossip was very much alive. To Truscott, it all seemed so tranquil and idyllic that the memory of murder and violence could almost be forgotten, were it not for the sight of Helena Garrick ahead of him, who served as a reminder of the intrusion of that unique crime into the subconscious of the village.

These thoughts occupied his mind only transiently and not for much longer than a few seconds. His attention was riveted primarily on Helena. Only once during this walk had she looked back on herself, causing Truscott to turn swiftly on his heel and walk in the opposite direction for a few seconds. It had been a moment of panic for him but it had come to nothing and he prided himself on being able to dissimilate sufficiently to arouse no suspicion on her part. Apart from this one incident, Helena had walked without interruption, which suggested to Truscott that she had no fear that she might be shadowed.

He had followed her over a small wooden bridge, which spanned the brook which trickled its way through the furthest perimeter of the village, and, from there, he had watched her disappear down a narrow, tree-lined lane. On one side of the lane were hedges, in front of which was a low stone wall. Opposite, there was a row of unprepossessing cottages. They were small but respectable, compact rather than cosy, but there was an honesty about them which seemed to override any deficiencies in appearance or construction.

From the end of the lane, concealed behind the trunk of a large oak, Truscott watched Helena stop outside the cottage at the end of the terrace and glance in his direction in order to satisfy herself that she was alone. She reached into the small bag which she carried and took out a key, which she used to gain entry into the property. For a moment, Truscott hesitated, unsure how to proceed. What business she could have in this lowly cottage at the end of this undistinguished lane was a mystery, but it was clearly a matter of privacy and Truscott had a momentary concern that he was invading into that privacy without any justification, beyond his own selfish concerns. Determining that he had come far enough to validate concluding his mission, Truscott stepped out into the lane and made his way to the front door of the far cottage.

Delicately, he tested the handle but the door had been locked once more. Truscott deliberated, although he was certain what steps he would take. To that extent, the delay was little more than a display of polite consideration. Having allowed it to pass, he knocked on the door with a rhythm and innocence which he hoped might suggest a passing tradesman. During the wait for an answer, Truscott readied himself for what had to follow if he was to gain entry. In a short space of time, shorter perhaps than he had expected, he heard the key in the lock. As soon as the bolt had been released and the handle began to turn, Truscott threw himself against the door, forcing it back against its hinges. Thrown slightly off balance by the effort and recoil, Truscott stumbled over the threshold.

He found himself in a narrow hallway. It was cheaply but cheerfully decorated: the wallpaper was dotted with delicately painted cornflowers, interrupted only by a succession of paintings depicting meadows, beaches, woodland forests. A middle-aged woman stood to one side, glaring at him with a furious but shocked expression, her dark eyes alive with outrage. Behind her, Truscott could see a staircase leading up to a small landing above him. Ahead of him, there was an open door, through which he could see the basic elements of a rudimentary kitchen. A door led off the hall, to the right, which he supposed opened onto a parlour, which was no doubt as simple as the rest of the house, whilst likewise trying to maintain the same impression of domestic cosiness.

Before he could say anything by way of explanation to the maid, his attention was caught by a swirl of colour on his peripheral vision. It was the hem of a dress, swaying in its natural way as the legs beneath it made their way slowly and authoritatively down the stairs. The maid, who had been on the verge of remonstrating at his forced entry, was silenced by the sound of the dress and the low heels on the wooden steps of the staircase. Anything she might have been on the point of saying was now redundant and, as if to assure Truscott of that fact, she closed her lips tightly against any words which they might have formed.

"It's all right, Annie. Perhaps you could make some tea." Helena had reached the bottom of the stairs. She addressed the maid, but her attention was fixed on Truscott, which was explanation enough for the tone of granite with which the words were spoken. She pointed to the door which Truscott had noticed to his right. "In there."

Truscott gestured that he would follow her into the room. After only a couple of hesitant seconds, Helena marched past him and opened the door. She walked into the room and allowed him to follow. He did so, closing the door behind him.

It was a parlour, as he surmised. There was a small settee and a single chair, but very little other furniture, save a cheap bureau and a low coffee table set in front of a rudimentary hearth. There were the necessary trappings of a living space but none of the domesticity or warmth of a working home. It was not necessarily clinical but it lacked personality and Truscott could not imagine any laughter or conversation over tea in front of that cold, impersonal fireplace. Helena did not sit and Truscott declined the offer of either the armchair or the settee. Nothing was said until the tea had been delivered, although Truscott's mind was brimming with questions and concerns.

"Would you like tea?" asked Helena, without any pretence of hospitality.

"I don't want tea."

She raised an eyebrow at the refusal. The arch of the brow emphasised the frigidity of her detachment. She crossed her arms and leaned against the modest mantelpiece. In the mirror behind her, Truscott could see the face of a man who might have been himself, were the features not so twisted with concern, guilt, and suspicion.

"You persist in betraying my trust, Jack," said Helena. "Perhaps I should stop being surprised by it."

"I don't set out to do it," he replied. "You give me no choice."

"It's my fault, is it?"

"I'm trying to understand you." He looked around the room. "To understand all this. Do you live here?"

She debated deceit but his expression dissuaded her. Instead, she lowered her head. "No."

"Then why are you here?" He received no reply. "Is this where you came on the night of Lynch's murder?"

"I don't have to answer any of your questions," she replied, but the words had more confidence than the voice which spoke them.

Truscott ignored the failed rebuke. When he repeated the question, his voice was harder, more insistent. "Is this where you came, Helena?"

Her green eyes shimmered with emotion, but he was not sure precisely what it was. His instinct was that it was anger, but something deeper within him wondered if it was not fear which he saw within them. "Whatever trouble you're in, Helena, I want to help."

"I'm not in any trouble."

He was beyond hearing her lies. "Won't you trust me?"

She laughed. It was short and shrill, and any humour emanating from it was dark and bleak. She was fighting tears now and, to his personal distress, Truscott saw that she was losing the battle. She must have known it too, but she refused to surrender entirely and her voice strove for a note of defiance.

"Trust you?" she spat. "What have you done to make me think that was at all possible?"

The words stung him more than any palm across his cheek, any nails down his face, or any rejection from her lips. Perhaps it was the offensive nature of them or perhaps it was their brutal honesty, but they seemed so cruel and sharp that his ears might have bled from hearing them. If she had hoped he would be broken by them, however, she was to be disappointed. They had the reverse effect. Truscott felt galvanised by them, as if this were the final roll of the dice and that any hope of her love now had been gambled away. If he had lost the game, Truscott thought, he had lost everything and he could do himself no more harm. He held her glare for a moment longer and then nodded his head curtly.

CHAPTER TWENTY-EIGHT

"Very well," he hissed. "Goodbye, Helena."

He marched out of the room. As she watched him leave, Helena was surprised to find she was trembling. She might have been shaking all through the interview but it was only now, with those words of blunt finality, that she became aware of it. She wondered for a moment whether she should run after him, but she found she could not move. Her legs had abandoned her and the shock of it seemed to have drained her awareness of any other sound or vision.

She was brought back to her senses by the realisation that she had not heard the front door open or close. Her stomach rolled with a sudden nausea and she ran from the room. Only as her feet began to clatter across the floor did she recognise that similar noise which had broken her trance. It had been the sound of his feet on the stairs. Howling his name in anguish, Helena raced after him, the maid stumbling into the hallway from the kitchen. Helena ran up the stairs, his name coming from her lips in a curious, almost inhuman croak which was a blend of anger and sadness. By the time she reached the landing, the last hope that she had retained her secrets ebbed out of her.

He was standing in the doorway of the spare bedroom. He was motionless, his shoulders slumped and his face drained of colour. Helena sank to her knees and sat on the top step, the tears now rolling freely down her cheeks. She was saying his name over and over, as if by doing so she could plead with him to forget what he had seen and, simultaneously, erase the recent past entirely.

He seemed not to have heard her, his attention captivated by whatever he had seen inside the room. At last, he moved, turning his head to look at her over his shoulder. She looked up into his eyes, neither stern nor saddened, and she spoke his name once more.

"Oh God, Jack…"

Whatever else she might have said seemed to be lost amid the sound of the breaking of her heart.

Chapter Twenty-Nine

Roderick Deville was sitting at the writing table in the library when he saw Truscott running down the gravel driveway. If he had made any connection between the sight and the departure of Helena Garrick a few moments previously, he showed no sign of it. It was doubtful whether he would have displayed any interest in that connection even if he had made it. His thoughts were entirely his own and they seemed to be monopolising his attention. His eyes were locked onto nothing in particular and the careless gnawing of a thumbnail suggested a lack of interest in any matters beyond those thoughts which consumed his mind.

The situation was entirely unforeseen and no less complicated for it. It had all been coincidence, of course. Deville would certainly never have planned matters as they had occurred. He had come to Warlock's Gate for his own reasons, not entirely fulfilled as yet, but those plans which he had made prior to his arrival had never taken into account everything which had come to pass. He wondered what might have happened if he had postponed his visit. Research on the latest novel would have been just as effective if undertaken a month later than planned and, if he had done so, he would not have come face to face once again with Sebastian Lynch. Moreover, he would never have fallen in love.

He supposed that was what had happened to him. He could not be sure, having never truly been overwhelmed by his heart, but if this was not love, then he could not explain what it was. He had written about it many times, of course, and he had always considered that he had done so convincingly. At heart, he was a romantic. He had always thought a writer must be a romantic somewhere in his soul and he wondered whether this curse of temperament had tainted his understanding of true love, so that his view of it had become too idealistic to be true. It was the only explanation for the way he felt now. If what he felt was that deepest of emotions, he now realised that his descriptions of it had been not only inadequate but unforgivably inaccurate. He had never imagined that it would be so disorientating, so entirely consuming to the extent that his self-awareness and grasp of reality would both be lost to him. And yet, he had never imagined that it could possibly make a man feel so wretched and terrified as he felt now.

It was possible that he was being harsh to himself. It was just as easy to blame this corrosive opinion of his emotions on circumstance as on his own personality. There was no question that the reality of murder had twisted Deville's point of view. His writing, his plots, his characters now seemed to him to be irretrievably false, pallid constructions which could not hope to reflect the horror of the genuine crime. Similarly, if his view of his own work had been polluted by the murder, his feelings towards a love affair had become no less corrupted. What should have been uplifting was now depressing; what ought to have been a cause for celebration and happiness was, instead, an invitation to disaster.

Deville rose from the desk and put his hands in his pockets. He began to pace the room, his gaze lowered, and his mind refusing to silence itself. He was surprised to discover that he was missing his own flat, with its comforting untidiness and familiar disarrangement. It had none of the grandeur of Warlock's Gate and, for the moment, Deville coveted the lack of pretension, as if a return to a world he understood might be capable of erasing the recent past. It was a futile wish, he knew as much, but it was irresistible and he began to allow himself to believe it.

His thoughts had become this erratic when the door opened and Everett Carr walked into the room. Deville was not irritated by the distraction and nor did he resent it. Perhaps he would have done so in other circumstances, but the company of Carr was less acidic than the company of Deville's own thoughts.

Carr was typically polite in his intrusion. "Am I interrupting your work?"

"I can't put two words together at the moment, Mr Carr," Deville replied, "so you are interrupting nothing."

"I suppose it is difficult to concentrate with everything that has happened."

How Carr had been able to penetrate his deepest thoughts and insecurities, Deville could not say and, he thought, it was not something which should be thought about too deeply. "The police will be back today, I suppose."

Carr nodded. "There is no doubt about that, I'm afraid."

Deville grunted, a low growl of acknowledgement that the return of Swift and his colleagues was inevitable. In the short silence which followed, Carr took the opportunity to sit down in one of the leather armchairs. Deville walked slowly across the room and stood over him.

"Have you any idea who killed Lynch, Mr Carr?"

If the question was unexpected, Carr showed no sign of any surprise. He smiled in response, but it was circumspect. "I have many ideas, Mr Deville."

"I suppose I have no right to seek your confidence," replied the author without hostility.

"It is not a question of confidence, Mr Deville, rather one of evidence."

"Meaning you have none to support these ideas of yours?"

Carr smiled in submission. "And without proof, ideas are of little value."

"I suppose not." Deville sighed softly. "Thinking of clues and proof is extremely difficult."

Carr made no comment on this reference to the troubles of detective fiction. Instead, he allowed the moment to pass before changing the subject with a subtle sleight of hand. "Have you seen Miss Montgomery this morning?"

Deville, without any choice in the matter, flushed at the mention of her. "We had breakfast together."

"Do you know where she is at the moment?"

"I believe she and Sir James are discussing his commission."

Carr made a gesture of comprehension. "Ah, yes, his portrait. No doubt she thinks such a discussion will take her mind off the terrible events of the other night."

"I wish I could do likewise," muttered Deville.

It seemed the moment for Carr to strike. "Yesterday, I was reminded of something which Lynch said to you on that first night. Strange, isn't it, how long ago that seems now?"

Deville ignored the conversational aside. "Reminded of what?"

"When Lynch was introduced to you, he stated you had met before. We have talked about that together previously."

"I remember."

"But he said something else. I had overlooked it at the time, I confess, and it was Louisa Marston who reminded me of it. Lynch said he had never read one of your own books."

"I am not conceited enough to suppose that everyone has read my work, Mr Carr."

"Does the wording not strike you as strange?"

"The wording?"

Carr let the matter pass. "I was talking to Dr Gilchrist yesterday evening. He told me about a particular tragedy in his life. In doing so, he said something of the sadness of his late wife."

"What has any of this to do with me?"

Carr held up a hand, begging for patient indulgence. "His wife had a brother, who took his own life. He had literary ambitions, Mr Deville, but he did not have the skill to realise them. This was not sufficient to lead him to kill himself, of course, but the knowledge that someone else had stolen one of his ideas and turned it into a success was more than enough cause for him to do so."

Deville's eyes had widened slightly and his cheeks had lost their colour. "I don't know what you're talking about."

Carr did not give any credit to the denial. "Dr Gilchrist's brother-in-law was called Anthony. I did not ask him what his wife's maiden name was, but I suspect that, if I did ask, he would tell me that it was Barclay. And Anthony Barclay was also the name of the man who introduced you to Lynch. You told me as much, if you recall."

Deville now had begun to shiver. He gripped the back of the chair opposite Carr and steadied himself, his legs threatening to fold under him. Carr said nothing and made no effort to assist the younger man to sit down in the chair. The dark eyes watched the slow progress of the motion, unblinking in their accusatory glare, and it was only when Deville was hunched in his seat that Carr spoke once more.

"Lynch had discovered your plagiarism, hadn't he?" He watched Deville nod. "The peculiar wording of his greeting to you was a concealed reminder to you that he had that hold over you. He had never read one of your own books because, in his mind, everything you wrote was indebted to Anthony Barclay."

"Yes," whimpered Deville.

"Was Lynch blackmailing you?"

"He asked for money on some occasions, but I don't think it was ever about that. It was the power of the knowledge which excited him, the ability to expose you whenever he chose. It was having you at his mercy which he enjoyed, like having an insect caught under a glass."

Carr recalled Gilchrist had said something similar. "You said Lynch was the reason your friendship with Anthony Barclay ended. Was that true?"

Deville nodded sadly. "It was Lynch who told Anthony what I had done. Between us, Lynch and I killed one of the kindest men you could ever meet. Not that Lynch would see it that way."

Carr made no comment on this dissemination of blame. "And, no doubt, you thought that Barclay's suicide would mean any exposure of your part in it would be even more destructive to you?"

Again, there was a solemn bowing of the head. "Does Dr Gilchrist know about me?"

"If he does, he has not said as much to me." Carr read the unasked question in Deville's eyes. "It is not for me to tell him anything about it and I have not done so."

Deville leaned back in the chair, suddenly seeming exhausted. Carr could recognise the symptoms of that peculiar sense of reprieve whenever a burden is lifted. "Not a day goes by that I don't blame myself for what happened."

Carr clasped his hands in his lap, resting his cane against his leg. "Whatever you say to me shall be in confidence, Mr Deville, assuming it is not connected to the murder."

Deville's eyes were imploring. "I didn't murder Lynch, Mr Carr. God knows, I had reason to and I can see that. I'm not a complete fool."

"On the night of Lynch's murder, you said you were in your room, struggling with your novel, am I correct?"

"Yes." A thought struck Deville with horrifying clarity. "And nobody saw me. Which means I have a motive and the opportunity."

Carr was unmoved. "You saw somebody on that night, did you not? You opened your door and saw someone on the landing."

"No."

"I asked if you had seen anything. Do you remember your reply? You said that you did not see *anybody*. A subtle difference, Mr Deville, but a crucial one."

"I saw nothing and nobody," insisted Deville.

Carr glared at him but he could see no further benefit in pressing the point. "Tell me about Anthony Barclay."

"You know most of it, no doubt. We had been friends for years, since university actually. He had always wanted to be a writer, but he was plagued by a contradiction in his brain, namely that he was never short of fascinating ideas but he did not have the capability to execute them. He lacked the narrative flair but, even if he had possessed it, he didn't have the patience and discipline to complete a project. He would get so far through a story or a book and lose energy."

"He could never have achieved his ambition?"

"Sadly, no." Deville's expression twisted into one of disgust, at himself as much as anything else. "That makes what I did even worse."

"Then why did you do it?"

The disgust intensified. "Because I'm selfish. And greedy. At the time, I thought it was tragic that such a good idea could be conceived but not realised. Now, I can see it was nothing short of opportunism. Surprising what you learn about yourself when you're forced to confront your secrets."

Carr paid no attention to this display of contrition. "The idea which you stole was what, exactly?"

Deville shrugged. "It hardly matters now. Read my first novel, *The Spectre of Death*, and you will see it in its glory. And it was the only idea I stole. The rest of my work is mine."

"What was the stolen idea?" pressed Carr.

"In essence, it was a conjuring trick. Anthony had come up with a particularly cunning locked room mystery, whose solution was impossible to guess. Certainly, nobody who read it solved it before the solution was given."

Carr made no comment on the validity of this literary boast and wondered whether he would be able to solve the conundrum if he devoted any time to reading the novel concerned. "Perhaps you see some irony in the fact that Lynch himself was murdered in a locked room."

Deville shook his head, as if to admit to such an idea would be to make some sort of admission of guilt. "I can't explain that."

Carr smiled. "It is a conjuring trick in its own right, is it not? And, like all magic, its solution is very prosaic."

Deville stared in disbelief. "You don't mean to say you know how it was done?"

"I knew immediately," replied Carr without any trace of egotism in his voice, "but it is of no importance."

Deville's astonishment suggested that he disagreed with Carr on the point, but there was something about Carr's attitude which decreed that further discussion of it would be fruitless. Even if Deville had dared to probe further, Carr would have given no reply. His smile lingered under the impressive moustache and he pulled himself out of the chair.

"If you will permit me to offer you some advice, Mr Deville, you should speak to Miss Montgomery. What I suspect you fear from her reaction will not trouble you and you will no doubt feel better about yourself for saying it."

Deville stared in bewilderment. "What do you mean?"

"I think you know, my boy," said Carr. "Trust her with your emotions, Mr Deville. She may yet surprise you."

Carr said no more. With a polite bow, he limped slowly to the door and pulled it open. Deville called after him and he turned around to face the author.

"I did not murder Lynch," Deville said. "On my soul, I didn't do it."

Carr contemplated the younger man for a long while. "So you have said."

"Do you believe me?"

Carr did not reply. In his own mind, he was satisfied about Deville's guilt or innocence, but the persistent demand for reassurance unsettled him. He stroked the moustache thoughtfully, his dark eyes narrowing. Deville stared back at him expectantly, anxious for some sort of reply. But Carr had no more words for him. With a grave nod of his head in farewell, Carr stepped out of the room and closed the door behind him. To Deville, it seemed to have the cruel finality of a judge's black cap after the delivery of a verdict of guilty.

Chapter Thirty

Helena recovered something of her previous composure and pulled herself up to her full height. She marched past Truscott, still standing motionless in the small room, his brain whirling at the meaning of what he had discovered. As Helena brushed past him, he came back to his senses and he was able to see the room as a whole. He saw the rocking horse, the building blocks, the small collection of stuffed animal toys scattered across the single bed in the corner, like an unruly and chaotic menagerie. He saw the dressing table and chair in one corner of the room and the doll's pram in the opposite one. He saw, in minute detail, the wallpaper decorated with delicately painted roses and the soft pink curtains which covered the small window in the far wall.

But, eventually, his attention was drawn back to the centre of the room. Standing there, staring up at him, was the little girl. She was no more than six years old, dressed in a blue dress with a nautical twist, her tightly curled, unruly hair fashioned into two bunches on either side of her head. Her skin was as pale and delicate as Helena's and the eyes burned with the same vibrant green. There, the resemblance ended. The child's features were beamed with innocence and vitality, but the eyes were enlarged and slanted upwards to reveal folds of skin on the inner corner. The bridge of the nose was flattened and the mouth was stretched open to show a line of uneven teeth through which protruded a thick, fissured tongue. Despite its natural flaws, the face retained its endearing appeal and the eager happiness of the smile which reached from those thin lips to the almond eyes deflected any negative reaction to the features themselves. The girl had smiled at him when he had burst into the room and she was smiling still, the happy innocence of it contrasting dramatically with the anguished glare of Helena herself. She had knelt down beside the child and had put her arms protectively around the small shoulders. Now, she stood up and faced Truscott, keeping the girl's hand in her grasp.

"You had no right to force your way into this house," she said, "let alone this room."

Truscott was not interested in the rebuke. "Who is she?"

Helena faltered in her reply. Her tongue had dried in her mouth and it seemed too large to be able to form the words. "Her name is Rosie."

Truscott was staring at the girl's green eyes and the pale skin of her face. His eyes flickered as his gaze shifted from the girl back to Helena. He had drawn a conclusion, but he could barely bring himself to believe it and, when he spoke, the words came out in a strangled, hoarse whisper. "Your daughter?"

Helena's reaction to the question was pained, as if the words had been bullets aimed at her heart. She felt the tears sting her eyes and she knew that her voice would desert her if she attempted any speech. Instead, she nodded her head and clamped shut her eyes, so that she could protect herself from his reaction. Simultaneously, she pulled Rosie towards her and clasped her arms around her in a similarly protective gesture. What the reaction she feared might have been, Truscott could not say, but he supposed she had expected something terrible. He did not know whether he could understand the expectation or not and, he could admit to himself, he did not know how he should be expected to react. Perhaps it was this uncertainty as much as the shock of the discovery which forced him only to sigh, before looking away from the mother and child and, finally, leaving the room completely.

He walked back down the stairs, passing the maid in the hallway but ignoring her look of reproachful indignation. He walked into the parlour and sat down on the small settee, his eyes focusing on nothing in particular and his mind unable to consider anything other than the revelation which he had experienced. How long he sat alone he could not say and, when Helena finally entered the room alone, he barely acknowledged her presence. She spoke his name, but he did not reply. She demanded some strong, sweet tea from the maid and, the order given, she lit a cigarette and sat down opposite him.

"Please don't sit there in silence, Jack," she pleaded. "I can't stand silence."

He did not say anything for the moment and, seeing that he would welcome no pressure to do so, she did not insist on it. She suffered the brief silence with the sort of remorseful stoicism which a castigated child might adopt whilst waiting for a disapproving adult to accept an apology for some misdemeanour. She smoked, to have something to do with her hands as much as from any need to calm her nerves. The tea arrived but none of it was poured.

"I've read about Langdon Down's researches and conclusions into human characteristics," Truscott said at last.

"But never met anyone afflicted by them?"

Truscott answered only with a shake of the head. "Where is her father?"

The question was asked with a voice which was heavy with something Helena thought was indignation but which might equally have been trepidation.

"I don't know," she confessed. "And I don't much care."

He was unable to disguise his shock. "You don't know?"

She breathed deeply on the cigarette. "Don't look so outraged, Jack. I know who he is but he wants nothing to do with us and the feeling is entirely mutual."

"I don't understand," said Jack, entirely truthfully.

Helena finished the cigarette with regret and, conscious of the admission she would have to make, she contemplated another. She restrained her desire, however, preferring not to give him any more reason to be disgusted with her.

"He was a married man, Jack."

The truth was out, part of it at least. She waited for him to make some remark in response, an expression of reproach, but none came. He simply rose from his seat and placed his hands in his pockets. He began to walk around the room and Helena had the impression that his gesture was a substitute for another, more violent one.

"He made the usual promises of divorce and sacrifice, of course," said Helena, realising that it would be better if she continued talking instead of giving him any opportunity to question her. "Perhaps he even believed them himself at first. I certainly did," she added, in a voice which showed how foolish she now realised such a belief had been. "If he had believed what he said, Rosie changed his mind. He made it plain he wanted nothing to do with a child. Suddenly, he had a conscience which could be pricked. Adultery was one thing, fatherhood quite another."

"He turned his back on you?"

She nodded. "He was rich, both titled and entitled. He had enjoyed the fun but the responsibility of the consequences were mine entirely. There was never any doubt about that."

"And when Rosie was born...as she was?"

Helena was offended by the clumsiness of his words but she did not express it. "A child was bad enough to him, but Rosie was unforgivable. He was disgusted from the first sight of her."

Truscott gave no indication of his thoughts or reactions to what she was saying or how her previous lover had acted. His face was nothing less than granite, the brows furrowed and the jaw clenched against any betrayal of emotion. "Who was he?"

"Does that matter?" countered Helena.

He conceded the point with a shrug of the shoulders. "Have you brought her up entirely on her own? Her father has contributed nothing?"

"Not a shilling, not a birthday card, not a kiss."

Truscott stared out of the parlour's small, grimy window. "Why the secrecy? Are you ashamed of her too?"

And now her fury was uncontrollable. Her eyes burned with a toxic mixture of anguish and outrage and her cheeks, normally so pale and delicate, were singed by the flames of a similar anger. She ran over to him and slapped his face with an instinctive reflex of retribution. When she spoke, her voice was a screech of wrathful resentment, so violent that she flecked his face with spittle.

"Ashamed of her? How dare you, Jack? I love that girl. I love her more than anything else in the world. I never thought I could love anything or anyone as much. I'd die before I let anything happen to her. You all think I'm strong, sassy, composed, always in control. You don't know me at all, any of you. I never thought my life meant very much but she makes everything worthwhile. I have nobody in this world, Jack. My father drank himself to death and my mother died of grief. I was brought up by relatives who resented me and I made friends with a girl who knew nothing but privilege. All those trips to Warlock's Gate, all the parties and dances—all they did was remind me of how worthless I was. Then, suddenly, I had Rosie. Everything changed. The world wasn't so bad, nor was life. So what if she was slower than others, looked different, or needed more care than a normal child? She loved me without question. Just as I loved her. Ashamed of her? You've got no idea. No idea at all."

"Then why the secrecy?"

"Don't be naïve." The anger had twisted into scorn. "What do you suppose would happen to her? They'd lock her away in an institution, keep her strapped to her bed, isolated from anyone else. People like her aren't treated like you and me, Jack. They're nothing less than animals. If they're not shut away and forgotten, they're beaten and maltreated, starved, broken, neglected. Do you know what some people think? That girls like Rosie are a curse on the mother, a punishment for previous wrongdoings, sent by Satan himself."

"That's ridiculous."

"That doesn't stop it being true." She had exhausted herself with her venom and her shoulders were heaving now, her voice breathless. "And, on top of all that, she's illegitimate. I couldn't ever bring myself to let all that badness hurt her."

"You can't keep her hidden forever," he said.

She shrugged helplessly. "Maybe not, Jack."

"What will you do when she's older?" he demanded.

"I don't know," she whispered, the defeat evident in her voice. "For now, it's all I can do."

"Is this your permanent home?" He looked around the place.

She shook her head. "We live in London. Whenever I come down here to see the Ravenwoods, I rent this place. I can't leave Rosie and it's not fair to expect Annie to look after her for a whole weekend."

Truscott stepped closer to her. "You did come here on the night of Lynch's murder, didn't you? You left the house through the kitchen using one of the spare keys and you returned the same way."

"I had to see Rosie." She spoke with an undercurrent of desperation. "She gets frightened if she thinks I have left her. And I missed her. You can't understand how much."

A silence fell between them. For her part, Helena felt she had no more to say. For his, Truscott was coming to terms not only with the story he had been told, but also the possibility that if Helena had been visiting her daughter in secret on the night of the murder then she was unlikely to have been guilty of it. The maid would be able to confirm Helena's presence in the house and Louisa Marston could vouch for Helena's return. There would be very little time left for the murder to have been committed by her. And, of course, there was no sign of any motive, unless Lynch had discovered the existence of Rosie.

"I don't suppose Lynch knew about this place, did he?" He asked the question with caution, anxious not to upset her further.

"Of course not." It was clear the question had perplexed her. "Why would he?"

But Truscott only shrugged, suddenly aware that he felt intensely tired. He took Helena's hand in his and, to his pleasure, she did not protest.

"Did you love the father?" He looked into the green eyes. "Tell me the truth."

She returned the glare with candour and nodded slowly. "Very much. If he had kept any one of his promises, I would be with him now."

Truscott nodded. "But you're not."

She held his gaze. "No."

"Thank God."

She did not react to his divine gratitude. "I know what you want me to say, Jack. Perhaps part of me even wants to say it, but I don't know if I can. He broke me in two when he walked out on us, Jack, and I don't know if I can put myself together again. He left me humiliated and disgusted with myself. I won't ever let a man do that to me again."

"Is that why you have been distant to me?" If it sounded petulant, he did not regret saying it.

"I won't allow myself to be hurt again."

"Even at the expense of your or anyone else's happiness?"

"Even then."

Truscott shook his head. "It all makes sense now. Your reaction to Carr being told about you seeing Lynch and Lady Ravenwood together, your sense of betrayal, ignoring me—you were scared, weren't you? Scared of how you were feeling, afraid your emotions were losing control. I'm right, aren't I?"

She shook her head, crying silently. "Don't make me say it, Jack."

"Everything else was a reaction against that fear."

She looked up at him, her eyes resigned to the truth. "Yes, yes. There, I've said it. Are you happy now?"

He did not rise to the challenge. "And Rosie?"

She lowered her gaze once more. "Nobody will want her and they can't have me without her. I can't allow my feelings, whatever they are, to matter more than her."

Truscott did not reply. After a moment of contemplation, during which his eyes did not move from hers, he took her hand and led her from the room. They ascended the stairs, back to the child's room. Suddenly aware of his intention, Helena tried to stop him, but he dismissed her remonstrances. Gently, he pushed open the door and stepped into the nursery. Rosie looked up at him and smiled. When she saw Helena, she waved frantically, the smile broadening when her mother returned the gesture. Truscott walked over to the girl and slowly lowered himself to the floor beside her. He watched her stroke the fur of a small stuffed bear and waited for her to look up at him and smile once more.

"Hello, Rosie," he said. "My name's Jack. I'm a friend of your mummy's."

Rosie looked into his eyes. "Hello, Jack."

She handed him the bear and he began to stroke it. He looked only at Rosie as she continued to play with the collection of stuffed animals, so that he did not see the tears which ran freely and silently from Helena's proud, but astonished, green eyes.

Chapter Thirty-One

It was over lunch that Ravenwood made his announcement. He had waited until the meal was over, although little food had been eaten. The reappearance of Swift and his team had eroded the collective appetite, as if each mouthful was soured by guilt. Swift had not summoned anyone for further questioning as yet, but there was an overbearing sense of inevitability which had descended upon the house as soon as he had entered it once again. Only Everett Carr seemed unaffected by the resurgence of the police presence, Ravenwood noticed, as if they were of no concern to him at all. He sat in silence at the table, sipping a delicate white wine, and eating the turbot with small, bird-like motions. There was a faint smile across his lips, although his dark eyes were heavy with concentration, but nothing to show what it was which occupied his mind so profoundly.

There was no sign of Truscott and Helena. Swift had been disgruntled by their absence, but he did not express it. He had given permission for people to leave the house and to go back on his command would have been foolish and inconsistent. If Swift regretted the order, he was not prepared to admit it. He had gone to the billiard room, which remained commandeered for his purposes, and he had declined the offer of lunch. The rest of the house had assembled for the meal in the dining room. Now, Dr Gilchrist had finished eating and was standing by the window, smoking a cigarette. Eliza Montgomery and Roderick Deville were seated together and, opposite them, Alicia and Prentice were eating in a desultory and perfunctory fashion. Mary was beside them and, with a note of sadness in his breast, Ravenwood noted that she had eaten nothing at all. Louisa Marston was putting down her knife and fork and dabbing her lips with the napkin in her lap when Ravenwood spoke.

"This will be our final lunch together," he declared, "so there is something I want to say to you all. The police have agreed that you can all return to your own homes and I am sure some of you will want to do so, although everyone is welcome to stay. Of course, you have to be available to speak to Inspector Swift whenever he wishes it and I am sure you will all assist him." He stopped speaking, as if he had forgotten his point and needed time to recall it. "What I wanted to say was this. I wanted to apologise to you all. This is my house, after all, and you are my guests. I cannot help but feel responsible for the terrible thing which has happened here."

There was a general murmur of disagreement, but it was Gilchrist who spoke. "It's not your fault, Sir James. It's a magnanimous gesture to make, but you cannot blame yourself. And I doubt any of us do either."

"Of course not," said Prentice. "There's no denying the atmosphere in the house is dark, but we can only blame one person for that. And I don't mean Inspector Swift," he added with a crooked smile.

"You mean the murderer," said Deville.

Before Prentice could nod his response, Mary slammed her palm against the table. "Must we talk about it? Can't we leave the subject alone for once? It's bad enough having the house infested by police without constantly reminding ourselves of why they are here. God knows, that awful Inspector is reminder enough!"

Ravenwood rose to his feet and walked swiftly to her. He placed his hands on her shoulders in a display of reassurance, but Mary shrugged them off with a violent twist of her spine. She hissed words which suggested that the attention was unnecessary, but they were futile attempts to suggest that she was in control of her emotions. She rose from the table, breathing heavily and closing her eyes in an external demonstration of the calming of her nerves.

"I'm sorry," she said. "It's just that this is all so horrible. So horrible."

She attempted to smile but it was too forced to be genuine and, without another word but with an apologetic bow of the head, she left the room.

Ravenwood stood impotently for a moment, staring after her with an indecisive hopelessness in his eyes, until he became aware of the ridiculous embarrassment of his position. He turned back to the table and smiled, with as little genuine humour as his wife.

"I'm terribly sorry," he said. "My wife has not been sleeping very well. You can imagine what this has done to her. Please, help yourselves to anything you like and Fenton will attend to you all."

He looked as if he might say something more, but he did not and, instead, he left the room as swiftly as Mary had done. Once he had gone, the room remained silent for a few seconds, as if nobody dared break the startled effect of the scene. Carr had watched the outburst with interest, although the serenity of his features did nothing to suggest the thoughts which passed through his mind. It would have been too much to say that he had anticipated Lady Ravenwood's hysterics, but they had confirmed an idea which he had formed almost as soon as the murder had been discovered. He had no time to deliberate further, however, because Alicia had begun to speak.

"I'm sorry about all that too," she said, evidently thinking that, as the only member of the family present, she was obliged to say something. "It's not like Mummy to get so upset."

Prentice took hold of her hand. "She's never had to deal with a murder before, though, has she?"

"No, I suppose not," said Alicia, as if the point had not occurred to her. "Poor Mummy."

"Poor Ravenwood, too," said Gilchrist, extinguishing his cigarette and sitting down. "Things like this can have serious and far-reaching effects. People have long memories and they are not always anxious to forget any association with violent crime."

"Are you talking from experience?" asked Prentice.

Gilchrist glared at him, until a smile formed slowly across his lips. "In a manner of speaking."

Alicia was leaning forward in her chair, her eyes widened with horror. "Are you saying they might never recover from all this?"

Gilchrist, immediately aware that he had spoken unwisely, shook his head with emphasis. "No, of course not, Miss Ravenwood. I just meant that things like this have serious consequences and they are difficult to cope with. I was saying it must be a strain on both of your parents, so if they show the strain then it is only to be expected. I assure you, I meant no offence."

Alicia leaned back in her chair. She seemed placated, but there remained a remnant of her previous horror in the wide, pale eyes. Gilchrist lit another cigarette, an effort to occupy himself without having to speak further, and he ensured that he did not look back into Alicia's eyes. He was embarrassed and it had never been an emotion he had managed successfully, so he had no desire to fuel it further.

Carr sipped some of his wine. "You are correct in what you say, Mr Prentice. There is only one person to blame for what has happened and for its consequences. The murderer."

Deville turned his attention to him. "You know who it is, don't you?"

Gilchrist broke free from his personal spell. "You can't possibly know who it is."

Carr rose from the table. Placing his hands behind his back, he latticed his fingers and began to pace the room. "There is something I must make clear. Some of you know that Mr Lynch was receiving threats against his life. Wooden figures with skeletal faces and nooses around the necks. The police know about the threats, so there is no harm in me telling you about it."

"Threats?" asked Prentice, his interest aroused. "You mean, whoever was threatening him carried out their plan?"

Carr held up a finger. "That is precisely my point. I think I know who was sending these figures and it is to that person I speak now."

"You mean whoever sent them is in this room?" asked Deville, his voice a blend of excitement and fear.

Carr nodded. "That person must listen to me carefully. What the police think about the connection between the threats and the murder need not matter. What ought to matter to you is that I know who you are and, more importantly, I know that the threats are *not* connected with the murder itself. Listen to me and believe me—the threats are incidental to the murder.

The longer you remain hidden, the worse your position is. Trust me and I will help you."

The speech had been delivered with a calm authority and addressed to the room in general. In its wake, those people assembled around the table darted glances at each other. The expressions of the group varied, from candid fascination to curious concern, but Carr's statement produced nothing in the way of any admissions. It would have been reasonable to assume that the failure to elicit any further information about the wooden dolls might have disappointed Carr, but his reaction was rather more one of sadness. His dark eyes were dimmed with regret and his arms raised and fell in a gesture of failed indignation. Looking at him closely, Gilchrist, for one, had the impression that the sadness was aimed not at Carr himself but at the person of whom he had spoken. The idea was crystallised when Carr spoke once more, his voice heavy with warning.

"A shame. If I cannot persuade the person concerned to speak, I am helpless to protect them. I can only ask again that the person behind these dolls reconsiders in private and I stress that it would be better to put your trust in me."

It appeared to be a form of dismissal and, as if to enforce the idea, Carr turned his back on the group and stared out of the window. The hands, clasped behind his back, tightened their grip on each other and his brows knitted over the dark eyes. The moustache and beard bristled with the impatient and anxious pursing of the lips beneath them. The sound of the chairs being pushed out from the table and the muted sounds of the exiting of the assembled diners did not disturb him from his internal struggles. It was only when Louisa Marston wished him a good afternoon that Carr sparked into life once more.

"I would like a very quick work, Miss Marston, if I may," he said.

She seemed unwilling to comply, but her natural politeness would never have permitted her to refuse. Even if this were not the truth, the hypnotic allure of those dark eyes which stared at her now would have forbidden any excuse to avoid submission. Louisa smiled, but her discomfort was only too evident. "If you insist, Mr Carr."

"I shall keep you no longer than a minute or two. What I have to say will not take long."

Louisa's grip on the book in her hand intensified. "What could you have to say to me?"

"I wish to give you a very definite warning, Miss Marston."

"Warning?" She aimed for casual dismissal of the idea but neither her voice nor her eyes could give credence to the effect. "A warning about what?"

"I think you know."

"I'm sure I do not," she stated as forcefully as she could manage. Then, as if an idea had occurred to her, she looked back into his eyes. "Are you suggesting I sent those dolls? You have tried to persuade whoever is responsible to confide in you but the attempt failed. Are you now trying to frighten a confession out of the person involved? And you think that person is me?"

Her voice had risen with her increasing anger and Carr was obliged to raise a hand to quieten her. As he did so, his lips spread in a gentle smile of reassurance, although his eyes retained the intense gravity which had been prevalent throughout the luncheon. "I do not think you are responsible for the dolls, Miss Marston, and I am quite sure you have no knowledge of them at all. Be assured of that, I beg you."

"Then what warning do you mean?"

"It is a far more serious warning I give to you. The sending of the dolls is malicious but there was no actual danger behind them. But you are walking through a very definite peril, Miss Marston, I am convinced of it."

"I don't know what you mean." Her voice and the naivety behind the pale blue eyes suggested that the statement was true.

Carr took a step nearer to her, his voice so calm that it was almost unnerving in its command. He looked down at the smaller woman, as if daring her to contradict him. "I think you have realised something about the murder, Miss Marston. If I had to guess, I would say that whatever has occurred to you has in some way suggested the murderer's identity to you."

She was shaking her head. "I have no clue to what you're talking about."

Carr smiled at the denial but he did not address it. "What you have realised

231

puts you in danger, Miss Marston. If the murderer learns about it, you are a threat which cannot be permitted to exist. I implore you, tell me what has occurred to you and I can protect you."

There was something so earnest in his manner that, for an instant, Louisa felt transfixed by it. She glared at him, conscious suddenly that she had never seen him look so serious and so intense. She had never felt able to take him as seriously as she did now and, in that single moment, she wondered if she had learned something important after all. She had been sure that the idea which had drifted into her mind was irrelevant, a mistake of some sort, but Carr's certainty now threatened to convince her otherwise. But, as soon as the moment passed, the spell was broken, as if a cobweb had been swept away from a long-neglected mirror. Suddenly, Louisa saw matters clearly and she knew that her initial instinct about what had occurred to her had been correct. Carr's warning now seemed to her to be foolishly melodramatic, his manner as extravagant as the gaudy necktie and handkerchief, his concerns as elaborate as the white moustache.

"I'm sorry, Mr Carr, but you are mistaken," she said with a gentle laugh. "I haven't any clue who the murderer is and I cannot for the life of me understand why you should think I had."

Carr did not flinch. "You must trust me."

"I do trust you, Mr Carr, but on this, you are quite wrong, I do assure you." She placed a hand on his forearm. "You must trust *me*, Mr Carr."

She smiled at him and gave him another word of comfort before walking out of the room. If she had attempted to placate his fears, she had failed. His instincts were burning with foreboding and no words from the naïve woman he had tried to help could extinguish the flames. He shook his head, conscious of the weight of expectation which troubled his conscience but, more keenly, disturbed by the knowledge that he was powerless to prevent his fears from being realised. He placed his hand on his breast and lowered his head.

"Miranda, my love," he whispered, "what am I to do?"

No words came from beyond the grave, but his shattered knee ached in reply. Opening his eyes, Carr limped to the window and stared out of it. His mood was low, his thoughts bleak, but a smile drifted incongruously over his lips, like a shaft of sunlight on a winter's morning, as he saw Truscott and Helena walking up the driveway, their hands locked together and their eyes fixed on nothing but each other.

Chapter Thirty-Two

It was late evening when Louisa settled down in her own cottage with a small sherry and the book of Chekhov. It had been a satisfactory day all around and she felt that the indulgence of the small drink and an evening of quiet solitude was well deserved. The fire had been lit and she stretched her legs out towards it, feeling the gentle heat of the flames behind the grille. She was contented, as if the warmth of the fire had penetrated to the depths of her soul. It was not only that her mind had been set at rest, but also that she was back in the comfortable security of her own home.

The cottage was on the outskirts of the village, within walking distance of Warlock's Gate itself. It was hers outright, a legacy following the death of her beloved parents. After they had passed, she had wondered initially whether she could remain in the home she had shared with them but she began to consider that if she sold the house in which they had raised her and, subsequently, bequeathed to her, it would be the worst kind of betrayal. They had wanted her to continue living in it, just as she had done with them, and it was not for Louisa to deny them one of their final wishes. She had taken no steps to make the house exclusively hers. The furnishings and the decorations had not been altered and, whilst there had been the necessity to decorate, the newly chosen wallpaper had not differed overmuch from its predecessor. As if to allow them to see how far she had preserved their memory, she had placed a photograph of the two of them on the mantel over the fire. It was a sentimental gesture, perhaps, but it seemed to Louisa to be more than appropriate and, if the overall appearance of the cottage seemed too old-fashioned for a woman of her age, it did not trouble her.

There was never any abundance of visitors to raise the criticism and, in any event, the loyalty to her parents was of more concern to her than an outsider's approval.

She had arrived home at a little after four in the afternoon. The awful Inspector Swift had summoned them all altogether once again and Louisa had feared more questions and further accusations. Neither had materialised, however, and the purpose of the Inspector's meeting was only to advise them once more that they were free to leave Warlock's Gate, albeit on the strict understanding that they were all to be available for interview at any given moment. To Louisa, it had seemed as if they were all prisoners of the police, if not in body then in spirit. They were free to move, free to go about their business, but the hold of the police was over them all, so that the freedom seemed only transitory. Only now, in the familiar and soothing environment of her own home, did Louisa feel that the presence of the police was far behind her.

Before leaving Warlock's Gate, Louisa had known that she had to put her mind at rest on that specific point about which Mr Carr had tried to question her. She remembered how serious Carr had been when he had tried to convince her to confide in him and she smiled at the memory. It was only something trivial which she had realised about the night of the murder and it could not possibly lead to any danger. She had no doubt that Mr Carr was overstating the matter, perhaps succumbing to a taste for the sensational, and any doubts she had about it herself, however fleeting, were dispelled after that other brief and friendly interview she had conducted before she departed Warlock's Gate. She had given the matter no further thought. She had cooked a simple supper of liver and bacon, which she had enjoyed immensely, and now she sat quietly in her armchair.

She opened the Chekhov book and began to read. As her eyes drifted over the dialogue and the stage directions, she began to change her mind about the chosen play. She flicked back through the pages of the book and found *The Three Sisters*. With a smile at the play's appositeness in light of current events, she settled down to the lives and loves of Olga, Marsha, and Irina. The sherry was a luxuriant accompaniment and, in that moment, Louisa's mind was free from darkness and her recent experiences of violent murder were a distant memory.

The knock at the door was so delicate that it was barely audible. It was only on the third series of taps that she was roused from the light sleep into which she had fallen. Momentarily disorientated, Louisa was slow to pull herself out of the armchair and the glow from the fire now seemed to have intensified into a stifling heat. The knocking on the door had become more insistent and she was already apologising before she had opened the door completely.

"I am so sorry, I must have dozed off," she was saying. Her words were cut short when she saw who stood on her doorstep.

"May I come in?"

Louisa did not reply at once. Only after the question was repeated did she realise how rude she must seem. She stepped to one side and pulled the door further open, allowing access. "Please do. I am so sorry."

An offer of a drink was refused and Louisa did not touch the remainder of her sherry. To do so now seemed inappropriate. One should not drink when a guest abstained. Whether or not it was an accepted social doctrine she did not know, but her own sense of respectability suggested that it should be and, indeed, probably was. She picked up her glass and took it back through to the kitchen. She would pour the remainder of the sherry back into the bottle when she was alone once more. For now, she went back into the parlour.

"I'm surprised to see you here," she said, "and so soon after our last chat."

The eyes which turned to greet her had altered. Now, there was no warmth of amiability and no trace of kind-hearted friendship. They were cold, cruel, and uncompromising. The lips were pulled downwards in a grim frown of violence. The dying flames of the fire flickered across the features and, as she stared back at them in horror, Louisa felt as if she were staring into the eyes of Satan himself. In a moment of oddly clear thought, Louisa seemed to know that this was death and, in that isolated moment of time, she was strangely unaffected by it, as if the realisation that her life was about to end in violence had increased her mind's capability for philosophical detachment.

And yet, when the hands closed around her throat, her senses came rapidly back to her. Now, there was no objectivity about her predicament. There was only fear, panic, and shock. She tried to scream but the sound which came out of her mouth was only a guttural and indistinct noise, barely human, and it only added to her horror and confusion. She looked at the twisted, determined features which loomed over her and she saw the wild, fierce eyes which seemed to will her to die. In tandem, like a terrible symphony, the fingers tightened around her neck. Death, the great neutral, was nearly here now, bringing with it a blessed relief from the pain and torment of the moment. Louisa knew that it was not the room which was getting darker around her but that it was the darkness of death engulfing her.

In her final moments, Louisa Marston surrendered to the shadows and struggled no longer. Murder had overpowered her. As she sank to her knees, her eyes rolling into their sockets and her tongue swelling in her mouth, the darkness gave way to a brilliant and blinding light which lasted only for a second, until, finally, there was nothing left to see or feel. The silence which followed was unnaturally profound, pervading the house, and, under the strain of it, the photograph of Louisa's parents on the mantel stared helplessly and uselessly over the body of their daughter. It was now only a picture, no longer of relevance to anyone, nothing more than a faded image of two strangers, dumb witnesses to the murder of the girl who had tried so keenly to keep their memory alive.

Chapter Thirty-Three

C arr heard the news the following morning.

The alarm had been raised by a postman, who had passed Louisa's cottage and found the front door ajar. He had alerted the local police who, upon investigation, had discovered Louisa's body. A message had been sent immediately to Warlock's Gate and Swift had responded with efficient urgency. Pressing though the summons had been, it was equally indiscreet. The fact of Louisa's death spread through the house with impunity and, as he was taking morning coffee, it became known to Carr.

He had wasted no time in getting to the cottage. He had been unable to find Truscott and so he made his way to the village alone. The serenity of the morning was broken by the intrusive presence of the police in the high street. The black cars, as bleak as they were official, seemed incongruous against the quaint cottages which were scattered throughout the centre of the village and the sombre figures of the uniformed officers, going about their preliminary enquiries, seemed more foreboding than reassuring. Carr watched them from a distance for a moment before walking slowly to the cottage itself. A police constable blocked his way, but the obstruction was only temporary, because Swift appeared on the small pathway and beckoned Carr into the house.

"I saw you through the front window," explained Swift. "I suppose it would only be a waste of effort fighting to keep you away."

Carr did not reply. His thoughts were confined to the tragedy which had occurred. He stepped into the parlour, his attention immediately seized by the horror which lay before him. He was barely aware of Swift at his side and whatever the words were which the Inspector was speaking went unheeded. Carr felt a weight of sadness descend upon him but, as his eyes drifted over the corpse, it was soon displaced by a rising fury. It was not the fact of the death which enraged him. In many respects, he had anticipated it. Rather, it was the manner of the death itself which outraged him.

Louisa was lying on her back, her head turned to one side. Carr saw the livid, purple bruises around her throat, their colour deepened by the pale white of the surrounding flesh, like a hideous and gaudy necklace. They told their own story of the cause of death, as did the unnaturally protruding eyes. The mouth was slack and, if he had been able to see it, Carr would have taken note of the swollen tongue which, in itself, would have given the cause of death as surely as the eyes and the bruises. But the tongue was concealed and, as he took in the details of it, Carr's anger surged, entwining itself with a sudden feeling of disgust. Inside the mouth, compacted tightly into the void, there was a coiled stocking. Instinctively, Carr's eyes drifted to the legs of the body and, sickeningly, he saw that one leg was covered by the stocking's brother and the other was naked. The inference was unmistakable. Carr could see it all clearly in his mind's eye and, from there, he watched as the killer pushed up the dead woman's skirt, unfastened the stocking, and rolled it down the motionless leg, before rolling it into a ball and stuffing it into the gaping mouth. It was a cruel, mocking gesture in its own right but, equally, it was an intrusive violation of her intimacy. Carr found that his lip had curled in revulsion and he became aware suddenly that he was breathing heavily.

"The person responsible for this shall hang," he whispered, to himself as much as to Swift. "I shall see to it."

"Whoever did this must have killed Lynch. I assume you don't think otherwise."

Carr shook his head. "The same person is responsible. Miss Marston had realised something about Lynch's murder. Whatever it was, it was dangerous enough to the killer for her death to be necessary."

"Realised what?"

"I do not know," replied Carr, his tone suggesting that the lack of knowledge was a personal failure. "I warned her. I begged her only yesterday to confide in me what it was she had learned, but she refused. She must not have considered it important. To her, it must have seemed insignificant, something which she did not think was connected to the murder but, in fact, it was vital."

"She gave you no clue at all?"

"Nothing." Carr turned to Swift. "But she must have discussed it with the murderer. That is why she now lies dead. She told the killer whatever she had learned and she must have thought that was an end to the matter."

"But it sealed her death warrant."

Carr lowered himself to his knees, his shattered leg stretched out to the side. He pointed to the wounds on the neck. "Could a woman have done that?"

Swift nodded. "According to the doctor, yes. Be that as it may, the murderer must be a man."

Carr's eyes narrowed. "Why do you say that?"

"The stocking." Swift's jaw tightened. "That suggests a sexual motive to me."

"Did the doctor find any traces of sexual interference?"

"No," admitted Swift. "Whoever chummy is, he tried to overpower her for the purpose, but she struggled, so he began to strangle her. When she died, he panicked and fled."

"Does that sound credible to you?"

"It's a start."

Carr rose to his feet. "Look around you, my good Inspector. Do you see any signs of this struggle of yours?"

"No," admitted Swift. "But that doesn't mean I'm not right. He might have subdued her easily, forced her to the ground, and prepared himself for what was to follow. She was still struggling, so he stopped her. Permanently. A struggle doesn't have to be so violent that it disturbs all the furniture."

Carr clicked his tongue with impatience. "In order to attack her as you suggest, and if his intention was as you suggest, he did not need to remove a single stocking to accomplish it. No, no, Swift. The stocking serves an entirely different purpose."

This last comment was said with such feeling that it startled Swift. When he looked at Carr, he saw an expression of intense dislike and, once again, there was the grim frown of disgust across his lips. "Are you all right, Mr Carr?"

"It is such a wicked, contemptuous, mocking gesture." The words came in short, feral spasms.

He glanced at Swift, his eyes almost brutal with determination, as if Swift himself were responsible for the horror. Swift said no more, fearing that the topic of the stocking was no longer one to be pursued. Carr had walked to the armchair in which Louisa had been sitting. The Chekhov volume was still open on the arm, her spectacles resting on the upturned spine. Taking his extravagantly coloured handkerchief from his top pocket, Carr moved the spectacles to one side and picked up the book, turning it round to read the words within.

"She was a great lover of Russian drama," he said in reflection. "She told me as much a few days ago. It seems so much longer than that, somehow."

Swift, who had never experienced Russian drama and doubted the fact would ever alter, did not respond. Instead, he turned to his notebook and refreshed his memory on more practical matters. "The doctor estimates time of death as being between nine o'clock and midnight last night. We shall have to ask everybody still at Warlock's Gate where they were between those times, of course."

"I can tell you that I was alone in the library after dinner until around ten o'clock," said Carr. "There was a somewhat sombre mood all evening. The idea of polite conversation over post-prandial brandy held no appeal to any of us."

"Why's that?"

Carr looked over to him, his smile faint and without humour. "Not everyone is as immune to the effect of murder as you, Inspector."

He was staring at the book in his hands with a concentration which was evidenced not only by the intensity of the dark eyes but also by the clenched jaw and the whitened skin of the knuckles. It was as if a catastrophe would befall him if he let go of the volume of plays which the dead woman had been reading before her life was taken away. Swift spoke his name more than once, but it had no effect. At last, as if the trance had been broken by a sound only he could hear, Carr inhaled deeply and looked to the ceiling. He made an exclamation to God under his breath and, with a curiously sinister undertone, he chuckled to himself. Then, with a wild flash of victory in his eyes, he looked back to the chair. He picked up Miss Marston's spectacles and turned them over in his hands, the smile broadening beneath the heavy moustache.

"You realised it, did you not, dear lady?" he said softly, looking down at the body. "And now, I understand it too and, I promise, you shall have justice."

Swift stepped into Carr's path of vision, forcing the older man to meet his gaze. "You understand what?"

Carr's dark eyes glistened, both with a sudden comprehension and, more vehemently, with a definite purpose. "Everything, Inspector. There is only one piece of the puzzle left to uncover and I think I know where it will be found. Really, when I think of it, it cannot be anywhere else."

Swift was growing irritated. "What are you talking about?"

Carr held up the book and the spectacles. "Miss Marston was reading Chekhov, Inspector. More specifically, she was reading *The Three Sisters*. And, most crucial of all, she needed her spectacles to do so."

Swift sighed heavily, now repentant for ever allowing the ridiculous old man to enter the scene of the murder. He had thought Carr was an intrusion in the first place and, now, standing listening to these irrelevancies, he was sure of it. His anger at Carr was matched only by his fury at himself for not standing by his own instincts. It was only the fierce look of determination in his expression which convinced Swift that Carr had not lost what intelligence he might have had. What he was saying might not make any immediate sense, but Carr's resolve was impossible to deny and it suggested strongly that he was to be taken seriously. And yet, Swift was adamant that he would not be upstaged in his own enquiry.

"See here, Mr Carr," he said with as much dignity as he could manage. "I don't know if you're playing me for a fool or not, but I think enough is enough. A book and a pair of spectacles are not going to solve this case."

Carr glared at the objects in his hand. "Not on their own, Inspector, no. There are other fundamental points to consider."

Despite his irritation, Swift was unable to resist the temptation to respond. "Other points?"

With a slight nod of his head, Carr spoke with as much gentleness as he could muster. "You will forgive me, Inspector, but I do not think you have identified the most pertinent facts of this case. Once you do, you will see that only one person could have committed these murders."

"What are these fundamental points?" asked Swift with no small degree of confrontation in his voice and expression.

Carr, undeterred, counted the points on his fingers. "You must consider the timing of the murder, the museum room key, the broken lamp, Miss Marston's stocking, her spectacles, and the Chekhov book. Those points are all suggestive in their own right but, taken together, they are damning."

Swift was unconvinced and it was only when Carr explained the points in more detail that the Inspector wondered why he had not seen the importance of them from the outset.

Chapter Thirty-Four

T ruscott found Carr in the library. He was sitting in silence, his hands clasped loosely in his lap and his eyes gently closed, so that he might have been in the deepest of slumbers were it not for his immediate reaction to the disturbance. His eyes snapped open and he sat up in the leather armchair, his mouth breaking into a smile. And yet, as soon as he recognised Truscott, his smile faded and he sank back down into the depth of the chair.

"You were not the person I was expecting, my boy," he explained, his voice heavy with disappointment.

Truscott laughed. "I'm sorry to upset you. Can I ask who you were waiting to come?"

"I have arranged to meet someone of particular importance to the mystery."

"The murderer?" asked Truscott impetuously. Carr merely smiled and closed his eyes once more. Truscott, realising that any display of impatient petulance on his part would be inappropriate, resigned himself to mystery. "We have all heard the news about Louisa Marston. Needless to say, everyone is appalled by it. A terrible business."

Carr's jaw clenched. "There is no justification for her death. I can almost justify Lynch's murder to myself, but not Miss Marston's. Her killer will not escape justice, Truscott. You have my word on that."

"You know who killed the two of them, don't you?"

"I do."

Truscott straightened his spine, as if readying himself for a confrontation.

"I don't know in which direction your suspicions point, Mr Carr, but I can assure you that Helena is not the murderer."

"Miss Garrick?"

"She is innocent, Mr Carr."

"You are sure of that, my boy?"

"Positively so. I know she lied about her movements on the night of Lynch's death, but she had good reason. You see, I know where she went."

Carr held up a hand in caution. "Be careful. If you say too much to me, she may not thank you for it. You have witnessed her react badly to your trust in me before."

Truscott smiled. "I'm speaking now with her blessing. We have resolved our differences."

The flush of his cheeks was not lost on Carr. "I am pleased to hear it."

"I've been engaged in my own investigations, Mr Carr. I have discovered that Helena has rented a cottage in the village and it was there that she went on the night of Lynch's murder."

"To visit the illegitimate daughter, whom she keeps secret from the world?"

The words forced the air out of Truscott's lungs with as much force as a blow to the stomach. "You know about Rosie?"

Carr shrugged. "I hazarded a guess only, but it was an educated one."

"How could you possibly have known?"

"Do you recall when we spoke to Miss Garrick in her room about seeing Lady Ravenwood and Lynch together on the night of the murder?" He watched Truscott nod his head. "During her rebuke to you for confiding in me about what she had seen, she asked what you could know about family loyalty. You recall that?"

"Yes."

"She asked what you could know about mothers and daughters. Why specific mention of those particular members of a family? It struck me as strange at the time and it seemed to me that the idea of mothers and daughters were prominent in Miss Garrick's mind. Why else would she particularise them so readily? When I learned that she had been seen leaving and returning to the house at night, I wondered whether it might have been to meet with a member of her family. Her words to you that day convinced me that Miss Garrick was visiting her own daughter and, moreover, that the visits were necessarily in secret."

"What made you think it was in secret?"

Carr smiled. "Why else would she never visit in the daylight and only sneak out at night to do so? Furthermore, it seemed to me that it would make more sense for someone to keep a child secret than a parent. There might be many reasons why someone would wish to keep their child's existence hidden, of course, but illegitimacy seemed to me the most likely. I made my gamble."

Truscott nodded slowly and, when he spoke, his voice was tinged with sympathy. "There is a little more to her reasons than that."

What those reasons were, however, Carr was not to hear, as there was a gentle knock at the door. Truscott threw a glance at Carr, whose dark eyes had narrowed at the sound. He remained motionless in his chair, save for the slow and deliberate movement of placing his finger against his lips, whilst Truscott leapt to his feet in expectation. The knock had come, surely, from the person whom Carr had expected and, in that moment, Truscott felt a surge of electricity charge through him as he realised that, finally, the identity of the murderer would now be revealed to him. If Carr shared any of the excited energy, he did not display it. Instead, with an inhuman calmness, he commanded entry into the library.

Who Truscott had expected to see, he was not entirely sure, even in his own mind. Accordingly, when Eliza Montgomery stepped into the room, he could not say whether he was surprised or not. She stood in the doorway, looking from one to the other of them, her cheeks pale and her eyes alive with anxiety. Carr beckoned her into the room and she closed the door behind her.

"I had hoped this might be a conversation in confidence, Mr Carr," she said.

"You must excise Mr Truscott," he replied. "He has been telling me of some adventures of his own. He will leave us alone if you wish it."

"Of course," said Truscott.

Eliza sat down opposite Carr. "I suppose it has to come out eventually. Everybody will know what I have done soon enough, so it makes no difference whether he stays or not."

And so here it was, thought Truscott. A confession, a statement of the facts of Sebastian Lynch's murder, an explanation of the mystery of Warlock's Gate. He prepared himself for the revelations, restraining his eagerness for the story to unfold, but in the same instant, Carr turned those expectations to ashes.

"I know the identity of the murderer," he said, "and, later this afternoon, it will be known to everyone. Yesterday, I told those people who were still in the house that I knew that the murder and the threatening dolls which Lynch received were not connected. I remain of that view and it is correct, is it not, dear lady?"

He waited for her to say something in response, but she did not do so. She looked at him with cold eyes, as if conscious of the inevitability of the outcome of this interview but still refusing to permit it to pass with impunity. Carr waited in silence, allowing as long as he dared for her to speak. When he was satisfied that she would not speak willingly, he sighed gently and rose from his chair, leaning heavily on his silver-handled cane.

"Will you not speak of your own accord?" he asked. "Even when I am striving to protect you from suspicion of murder?"

"Protect me? You want to incriminate me." Her eyes blazed with an obstinate fury.

"That is not so." Carr's tone was patiently benevolent, but his expression was darkly serious. "I tell you, Miss Montgomery, that I know who murdered Lynch and why. I tell you yet again that the dolls and the murder are not connected. Therefore, knowing what I know already about the murder, I need you to explain only why you sent those macabre dolls to Mr Lynch."

Eliza flushed with indignation. She attempted to give the impression of affront but her terrified eyes and bared teeth showed only too clearly the fear which his words instilled in her. She stammered a series of denials, none of them complete or close to effective, and Carr held up his hand to stem their tide.

"We do not have much time, Miss Montgomery," he said. "I know you sent those dolls and, in order to clear up all extraneous points of this matter, I must know why."

Her defence was obstinacy. "I did not send those dolls."

Carr, with some difficulty, raised himself out of his chair. "You do yourself no good, miss. The time for evasion and lies is over. This is now the time for truth. The truth is that, for reasons of your own, you instigated a campaign against Mr Lynch. I have seen the dolls with my own eyes. I may not be an expert, but I can appreciate artistic skill when I see it. The dolls have painted skulls on their faces and a tightly constructed noose, made from string, around their necks. The paintwork and the dexterity required to fashion those tiny knots suggested at once someone with more than average artistic ability. And, this point aside, there is something overtly melodramatic about them. It suggested an imaginative rather than a scientific mind."

"I don't know what you are talking about."

Carr paid her no heed. "Now, only two people in this house can boast of any creative skill. You and Mr Deville. Given the type of books Mr Deville writes, I considered him a strong possibility for the sender of the dolls and I did so for a long time. However, events have taken over my theories and I have learned that Mr Deville may not be as inventive as he pretends."

She threw him an inquisitive, almost animalistic glare. "What do you mean by that?"

Carr waved aside the question with an impatient swipe of his hand. "I will not be distracted by irrelevant matters, Miss Montgomery. Suffice it to say that I stopped suspecting Mr Deville of being behind the dolls, which left me only with you. And, then, I remembered something you said to Lynch when you were first introduced to him. He asked whether he would be familiar with your work and you gave him rather a strange reply. Do you remember what you said, dear lady?"

Eliza lowered her gaze. "I said he might have seen some of my smaller pieces."

"Precisely," said Carr, with some satisfaction in his voice. "And what, exactly, did you mean by that? I could think of only one explanation. The dolls. If these smaller pieces had been innocent, you would not have been so guarded in your response. You would have spoken freely about them."

A silence followed. Once it had passed, Eliza gave a small, silent laugh of defeat. Her eyebrows rose, as if a physical display of her capitulation was necessary, and, slowly, she stood up, readying herself to confront her guilt. "You are right, Mr Carr. I did send that odious man the dolls. It wasn't only the dolls, however. I also made nuisance telephone calls to him, always from public boxes, and I poured acid over his motor car. I'm ashamed to say it all out loud. In the wake of what happened to him, they seem utterly spiteful and ineffectual. But, at one time, I thought they would serve a very definite purpose."

"What purpose?"

"Sebastian Lynch was my father, Mr Carr."

Her words were so dramatic and unexpected that they hardly seemed credible. She had said them with her back to him and he could not bring himself to believe her claim but, when she turned and looked into his dark eyes, he saw a clarity of vision and there was no longer any attempt by her to disguise the truth.

"You find it hard to believe," she said, "but it is true. He never married my mother, of course, and he refused to accept me as his daughter, but that didn't alter the fact that I was."

Carr's memory had stirred. "Sir James said that Lynch had been wild in his youth. He said it was always possible that Lynch had fathered children, although he did not know it for sure, and that he had come close to marriage. He meant marriage to your mother."

Eliza was smiling, but it was wicked and vindictive. "Perhaps Sir James knew Lynch better than he thought. My mother says that Lynch was everything a woman should fear—handsome, charming, but cruel. She fell into his trap as easily as any foolish woman. I quote her directly, you understand. She begged him to marry her, but he refused, of course. He blamed her for the pregnancy, left her to deal with it herself. Do you know what that would do to a woman, what shame it would bring on her? Lynch's refusal could well have ruined my mother."

Truscott was thinking about Helena and her own betrayal by a man who had claimed to love her. He cursed under his breath so vehemently that it surprised Eliza so much that she realised she had forgotten his presence in the room.

"Forgive me, Miss Montgomery," he said. "Men abandoning women with whom they have had their fun disgust me."

Her eyes flickered, as if she had realised something about him which she had never noticed previously and was surprised, though endeared, by it. "You and I can agree about that, Mr Truscott."

"How did your mother avoid any scandal?" asked Carr.

"For the first twenty-one years of my life, I was brought up as if I were the daughter of my own grandparents. My mother had to endure the torment of watching me grow up as a sister to her, never engaging with me as a mother should with her first-born child. When I came of age, she told me the truth. I think she expected me to hate her for the deceit, but I didn't. I couldn't."

Carr nodded slowly. "Your hate was directed elsewhere."

"Yes," she spat. "And there are times when I wanted to murder him myself. Whoever did it has my eternal gratitude."

Her pale cheeks brightened with venom and Carr saw clearly the effect of her suppressed rage being allowed to surface. He began to understand, perhaps even sympathise, with her motivation for sending the dolls. "What did you hope to achieve by sending those ghoulish effigies?"

She spoke through clenched teeth, as if she dared not express the full depth of her emotions on the point. "I wanted him to suffer. I wanted him to live in fear, to look over his shoulder every day, and to lose his grasp of control over his life. I wanted him to know what it feels like not to be in charge of your existence, to have it taken out of your hands. That was how he had made my mother feel and I wanted him to experience it too. I wanted him to suffer, so badly that it hurt."

The depth of hatred seemed to have exhausted her. She began to breathe heavily, her shoulders heaving with the effort of her confession, her eyes wild with untamed loathing. Her hair seemed wilder than normal, her nostrils flared, and her teeth were exposed from between the lips, like a representation of the Erinyes painted entirely with malice. Witnessing the ferocity of her emotion, Carr could envisage with ease how her mind had corrupted itself as the plan of vengeance formed within it. As if to counter, to provide a balance to it, his voice was low and controlled, his manner gentle and soothing.

"When you saw Dr Gilchrist going into Lynch's room on the night of the murder," he said, "I believe you were seen yourself. By Mr Deville."

"Roderick?"

"I asked him if he had seen anything and he replied that he had seen nobody. An insignificant point, you might say, but I say it is vital. A slip of the tongue which speaks volumes. I think he was protecting you."

"Why would he do that?"

"Is there not a growing tenderness between you?" Carr replied softly.

Eliza suppressed the urge to scream. "Roderick has nothing to do with any of this."

Carr nodded in assurance. "No, no, of course not. But he did see you as you were making your way to Lynch's room. You were going there to leave another of the dolls, were you not? But Gilchrist's presence prevented you from doing so."

Eliza nodded. It was a heavy lowering of the head, as if the final arrow of truth had been fired into her body. "I could not risk the doctor seeing me, so I rushed back to my room."

"In telling me that you had seen him, of course, you proved also that you were in the vicinity of Lynch's room yourself."

"I did not kill him, Mr Carr. I sent the dolls, I made the calls, and I vandalised his car, but I did not murder him. I wanted him to suffer for what he had done to me and my mother. Perhaps I even wanted him dead. But I didn't kill him."

Carr placed his hands on her shoulders. "Have I not said to you that I know that the dolls and the murder are not connected? And have I not said that I know who the killer is?"

"Do you know? For certain?"

Carr nodded. "I have known for some time. And now, with what you have told me, I know everything."

She tried to find some indication in his expression that he was lying to her, but she found none. She saw only the earnest glimmer of honesty in his deep, dark eyes and the smile on his lips beneath the luxuriant moustache was both broad and genuine. Her eyes did not mist but she felt that, if she had lived a different life, she might have cried at his kindness and assurances. As it was, she simply said, "Thank you, Mr Carr."

"Go to your Mr Deville and tell him everything," he said.

Only when she smiled at him did he release his grip on her shoulders. She smiled once more, as he bowed courteously and watched her walk out of the room.

Chapter Thirty-Five

Swift returned to Warlock's Gate in the early evening. He made his presence known but he did not summon any of the guests for further interviews. An invitation to dine was declined, but he requested a plate of sandwiches and a pot of coffee, which, he assured Ravenwood, would be sufficient for his needs. As the remainder of the house went into dinner, Swift pulled Carr to one side.

"Did you find them?" he asked with some urgency.

Carr nodded. "I did. I searched her room this afternoon. They were in her dressing table."

"So, you were right. It was her in the museum room that night."

Carr inclined his head once more. "It was her. After dinner, we shall all retire to the library, at my request. You will join us, Inspector?"

"Damned right, I'll be there."

Dinner was a muted affair. There was a definite sense of trepidation amongst the diners, an unmistakable feeling of mutual suspicion which was so strong that it smothered much of the collective appetites. Only Carr seemed to be at ease, although he ate sparingly, his onyx eyes glancing intermittently across the pale, anxious faces around the table. Time moved slowly and furtively, like a thief in the shadows, and the overwhelming sense of inevitable foreboding seemed to chime with every quarter-hour. Once the meal was over, the party rose from the table and made their way to the library. Ravenwood ordered after-dinner drinks and coffee and, once delivered, they took their seats. Carr stood in front of the fireplace and Swift sat in the far corner of the room, an official observer only, although it was he who spoke first.

"I have asked Mr Carr to address you all in my place. He has made some interesting and pertinent observations during the course of this investigation and it is only right that he be given the opportunity to elaborate on them for your benefit. I would ask you to allow him to speak and not interrupt."

Eyes turned from the Inspector to Carr, their expressions a mixture of distrust, fascinated interest, and anxiety. Carr looked at nobody in particular, but his dark eyes drifted purposefully across the assembled group. When he spoke, his voice was calm but not without a measure of regret.

"I must thank you all for your indulgence," Carr said. "What I have to tell you will not be pleasant, I fear, and I assure you that I take no joy from saying it. I must do so, however, if the truth is to come out, and I ask you all to forgive me for speaking plainly if bluntly. I can say that I have discovered the truth about both the murder and its tragic sequel, although I felt that there were a number of other problems which had to be solved before I could set out my conclusions.

"A review of the circumstances of the crime might well be helpful. Sebastian Lynch was stabbed to death in the museum with the Tethran Dagger, which itself was due to be unveiled that evening. The ceremony was prevented by the assault on Sir James in the afternoon, during which the *only key* to the museum was stolen. Consequently, as well as locking the front door, a member of the staff was placed on guard in the lodge at the front gates. That sentry remained in place at all times and continues to do so. The windows to the museum were locked, as Mr Truscott can testify, having tried to open them when he saw the body through them. Similarly, as was the custom, the door to the museum was locked and, as I say, the only key to it had been stolen. Nobody could have gained access to that room and yet, somehow, Lynch was killed there and the murderer escaped."

"But how was that done?" asked Truscott.

Carr held up a finger and commanded silence. "Each point in its turn, dear boy. First, we must consider not how the murder was committed, but why. I was not entirely surprised to learn that almost everybody in the house had a reason to murder Lynch. It will not be pleasant, I'm afraid, but it is necessary to set out those motives, so that the one pivotal fact in the matter which convinced me of the identity of the murderer becomes clear.

"It seems natural to begin with the threats on Lynch's life. For some months, as well as bogus telephone calls and attacks on his property, Lynch had been receiving wooden dolls with painted, skeletal features, and string nooses hanging around the necks. He was unaware of the identity of the person responsible but, within earshot of myself, he accused Miss Louisa Marston of sending them. Her father had been executed for murder and Lynch had been the foreman of the jury which convicted him, wrongly so in her view. She detested Lynch and he had concluded that this hatred had prompted her to send the dolls. I could not agree. The death of her father might have given Louisa a motive for Lynch's murder, but I could not believe that she had sent the dolls.

"The figurines struck me both with their melodramatic nature and artistic competence. To my mind, only someone with an imaginative and creative streak could have constructed them. Of the people in the house, only Mr Deville and Miss Montgomery could be said to be truly creative. However, when I talked with Dr Gilchrist, I learned a very interesting story about the tragic death of his wife's brother and her own subsequent demise. But Mr Deville also told me that he had been close friends with a man who had killed himself and, when I considered the point, the coincidence struck me as too great to be plausible. Two people in the house with a connection to a suicide? No, it was too much to accept. Instead, I suspected that Mr Deville's friend and Dr Gilchrist's brother-in-law were the same man, and when I discovered that the name Anthony was common to them both, I became sure of it." He turned to Gilchrist. "It pains me, Doctor, to have to ask this, but your wife's maiden name was Barclay, was it not? Her brother was Anthony Barclay and, although you did not know it, he was friends with Roderick Deville."

Gilchrist glared at Deville. "You, who stole Anthony's ideas?"

The author, his face ashen and his eyes wild with guilt, nodded. "I never believed he would take his own life. It was Lynch who told him that I had betrayed him. That's why he did it. Lynch was just as much to blame for what happened to Anthony as I was."

Gilchrist's eyes blazed with fury. "It killed my wife. I was suspected of her murder. Do you have any idea what that did to me?"

Carr was compelled to intervene. "You must reserve your anger for another time, Doctor. Now is not the moment."

Gilchrist sat back in his chair and lit a cigarette. His hands shook but he said no more. Carr rested his hand on the man's shoulder for a moment and then continued.

"The importance of Dr Gilchrist's tragedy," he said, "is that it showed that Mr Deville's imagination was less constructive than he had claimed. He was a plagiarist but that stigma did not apply to my other artistic suspect, Miss Montgomery. It was much more likely, therefore, that she had sent the dolls and, a short time ago, she confessed it."

"Sebastian Lynch was my father," Eliza said, aware of the eyes on her. "He ruined my mother's life. The dolls were a revenge, a persecution, and a punishment for the torture of my mother."

"But you said that the sending of the dolls was not done by the killer," said Prentice. "So, Miss Montgomery did not kill Lynch."

Carr nodded his head. "Precisely, but the point is that she had a reason to do so, just as Mr Deville had cause to want Lynch dead. He had betrayed Deville to Anthony Barclay and caused that poor man to end his life, a death whose effects also gave Dr Gilchrist a motive to kill Lynch. On the night of the murder, Miss Montgomery was on her way to leave another of the dolls in Lynch's room and she had been seen by Mr Deville, although he denied the fact. Similarly, Miss Montgomery herself witnessed Dr Gilchrist entering Lynch's room, although she fled from the scene before he could see her.

"Dr Gilchrist was searching for evidence which Lynch claimed to have that would prove Gilchrist had murdered his wife. The doctor, I hope, will forgive me for explaining that Lynch had been taunting him with this supposed evidence for some time. This love of the thrill of having power over another person was in Lynch's character. It was something he craved, something he relished, and Dr Gilchrist was not the only victim of it, no more was Mr Deville." He had been walking slowly in a circle as he spoke and, now, he stepped across the room to Alicia and Prentice. "Lynch had a hold over you both, also, but it was not simply the power which he wielded over you. No, in your case, he went further—to actual blackmail."

Ravenwood roared. "Blackmail?"

"I am sorry to have to reveal matters in this way," complained Carr, "but it is essential. You were wrong, Sir James, to suspect that Mr Prentice was an adverse influence over your daughter. True, Mr Prentice had been wild in his younger days, but the attraction of excessive and scandalous living had burned itself out. Meeting Miss Ravenwood showed him that he craved respectability, to become an honourable man of standing. Unfortunately, she had been seduced by his previous life. She saw it not as immoral or outrageous but as exciting and alluring. She had permitted certain photographs to be taken of her, images which were developed by M. Henri Chastain of Soho. They were of such content that no innocent girl would wish her parents to see them and I must say, in her defence, that she regrets them bitterly. Mr Prentice had been complicit in the photographs, but only as a means of ensuring Miss Alicia came to no actual harm. He was sickened by the business, just as she was thrilled by it, but he had to be involved because he wanted to protect the girl he loved."

Alicia was shamed and tearful. "I am so sorry, Daddy."

"This is monstrous," hissed Ravenwood. "I cannot believe it."

"Nevertheless, I am sorry to say that it is true," said Carr. "Lynch discovered their secret and used it to extort money out of them."

"A prime motive," declared Swift.

Alicia screamed, her eyes filling now with chastened tears. "But we didn't kill him. We told you that."

Carr placated her with a finger to his lips. "Calm yourself, my dear girl. I make no accusations as yet. I am showing only that there were people in this house with a reason to kill. In a short space of time, I had established that Mr Deville, Miss Montgomery, Miss Marston, Dr Gilchrist, and both you and Mr Prentice all had reason to wish Sebastian Lynch dead. Who else might have had cause to turn to murder?"

"Miss Garrick had no motive to kill Lynch." Truscott had felt the need to speak and, when he did so, Helena took hold of his hand in gratitude.

Carr smiled, as if he were dealing with a stubborn but foolish child. "But Miss Garrick has secrets of her own. Louisa Marston had witnessed her running across the lawns in the dead of night and Miss Garrick had lied about her movements on the night of the murder. When confronted about it, she refused to explain herself. The purpose of these nightly journeys was unknown to me, but I had surmised that she was visiting someone close to her, a person whose existence was kept secret for reasons which only Miss Garrick herself could clarify. I was proven correct in that analysis, Truscott, as you know. It was possible that Lynch had found out and, if he had done so, it was not unreasonable to assume that he would have levied blackmail against her also. It would be a suitable motive, but I have found no evidence of it. On balance, I am satisfied that Miss Garrick had little or no motive for murder.

"Nevertheless, and this is crucial, what she did know was that someone else might have had cause to kill Lynch. Miss Garrick was an important witness, because she saw something which showed that there had been a history between Lynch and someone in the house which had never even been suspected, let alone confessed. One night, Miss Garrick overheard a man and a woman arguing in the drawing room. She heard enough to assume that these two people had once been lovers. As Miss Garrick watched from the shadows, she saw them leave the room once the quarrel had ended and she was bewildered to discover that the two people were Lynch and Lady Ravenwood."

There was a collective intake of breath, like a basket of vipers, which broke the command which Carr held over the room. Mary was quivering with emotion, her eyes wild with fear, as if Carr was a dangerous animal which had cornered her. He walked slowly towards her, staring down at her from under lower lids, as though he had a supernatural hold over her.

"It is true, is it not, my lady?" he asked.

Alicia had risen from her chair. "Mother, what is he talking about? It isn't true, it can't be. Tell me it isn't."

Mary did not reply. She was unable to pull her gaze away from Carr's sympathetic and encouraging glare. He replied for her, repeating his question. "I know it is painful, but it is better to be frank. Is what I say true?"

"I knew Sebastian years ago, long before my marriage. We were lovers. That's what you wanted to hear, isn't it, Mr Carr?" She spat his name.

He seemed unmoved by her outrage. "Lynch wanted to resume the relationship. He was threatening your marriage by ignoring your rejection of him. You knew that he would not let you slip away from him for a second time. Your Eden now had its serpent and it had to be banished."

Mary began to weep. She seemed to have deflated, lessened in stature and dignity, but if Carr felt any regret about causing the change, he did not show it. Instead, he turned his back on her and addressed the room once more.

"I suggested to Inspector Swift that the *timing* of the murder was vital," he declared. "He thought that I was referring to the time of death, but he misunderstood my point. You see, a question had occurred to me – why was Sebastian Lynch murdered *at this particular time?* I have been at pains to explain to you how the majority of people in this room had a motive to commit his murder and, no matter how unpalatable it was to me, it was important that I did so in order to demonstrate the fact that those reasons were all long-established. The resentments I have elucidated, those hatreds and desires for revenge, had been in existence for extended periods of time. If any of those people with motives wanted to murder Lynch, they could have done so long before now. So, why did the murderer decide to kill Lynch at *this specific point in time?*

"The answer is obvious. *It was because the murderer did not know that he had a motive to kill Lynch until this very weekend.* Prior to now, the murderer had no reason to kill or, at least, he or she was unaware of it. But, when a motive suddenly appeared, the murderer knew that Lynch had to die." He stressed the final three words with a macabre emphasis. "The love affair between Lynch and Lady Ravenwood was the only motive for murder which came to light this weekend and whose existence was unknown previously. That fact alone persuaded me that their previous relationship was central to the mystery."

He paused. Nobody filled the silence, either because they expected him to continue or, possibly, because none of them had any words which appeared relevant. Mary was gently sobbing now, her head sunk onto her breast and her hands clasped in her lap. The knuckles were whitened, as if she was holding onto her previous happiness with as much tenacity as she could muster. Carr reached into his pocket and, his eyes on her, took out a set of keys. He allowed them to hang loosely from his fingers, swaying gently like a hypnotist's watch, and Mary glared at them with horror.

"Where did you get those?" she gasped.

"What are they?" Gilchrist asked.

"They are Sir James' stolen keys," said Carr. "I found them, my lady, in your dressing table."

Ravenwood rose to his feet, his face flushed with anger. "Enough, Carr. This charade has gone on too long. Just say what you need to say and get it over with."

Carr looked queerly at him, as if seeing him for the first time. It was Swift who spoke, walking towards the tableau with a determined, official step.

"I doubt there is any more to be said, Sir James," he declared. "I think we have all the answers now."

"Meaning what?" barked Ravenwood.

Swift's voice was devoid of emotion. "Lady Ravenwood, you arranged the attack on your husband and you planned for his keys to be stolen, so that only you could have access to the museum room. The keys being in your dressing table is sufficient proof of that."

Alicia sprang from her seat. "Why would she attack my father when she could have taken the keys at any time?"

Swift was undeterred. "She could not simply take them without arousing Sir James' suspicions."

Gilchrist leaned forward. "But why would she want to create that elaborate locked room nonsense?"

The Inspector, devoid of any explanation, ignored the interruption and kept his focus on Mary. "You murdered Lynch to stop him from interfering with your marriage. When Miss Marston found out about it, you had to kill her. Is that not so, Lady Ravenwood?"

Only now did Carr speak and, when he did, it was with a voice as sharp and ruthless as the sword of Justice herself. "That is not so, Inspector. Lady Ravenwood did not commit the murder. She is guilty only of protecting who did."

Mary sobbed helplessly. "Please, say no more..."

But Carr had not heard her. He was staring intently at her husband. "Why should she protect the murderer? Simply because she loves him. She has always loved him. No, Inspector, Lady Ravenwood is not the killer. The man who murdered Lynch was, in fact, her husband—*Sir James Ravenwood.*"

Chapter Thirty-Six

Ravenwood sank slowly back into his chair. "I suppose you know everything, Carr."

"I believe so, yes."

"Then I shall not stand in your way."

It was an invitation to continue speaking, without interruption, and Carr accepted it without argument. "It was not only Helena Garrick who overheard that argument between your wife and Lynch. You had been restless and you had woken to find that Lady Ravenwood was not in bed. You went in search of her and you heard them arguing."

Helena made an exclamation. "But I would have seen him, surely."

Carr turned to her. "Were you looking out into the hallway for the entire time?"

"No, I didn't want to be discovered."

"If you had looked out a moment sooner or a minute later, you would no doubt have seen him. He was there and he had heard the same as you. He ran back up the stairs to bed as soon as he heard his wife and Lynch preparing to leave the drawing room."

Mary stared at her husband. "You said you were not asleep when I got back into bed."

"I wasn't," said Ravenwood softly.

"And you heard everything?" She watched him nod a confirmation. "I had no idea."

"I didn't want you to know. I should have confronted him at that moment, thrown him out of the house, but I didn't."

"No," purred Carr. "Something altogether more dreadful occurred to you."

Swift pointed to the keys in Carr's hand. "But how do you explain those being found in Lady Ravenwood's dressing table? And the locked room?"

Carr smiled gently. "The whole mystery of the locked room was impenetrable to you all because you were carried away by the melodrama of it. A magic trick is only impressive because of its mystery, but if you look at any illusion with a sceptical eye then you will find they are all easily explained. You will recall, Inspector, that the shattered lamp in the museum was one of those six points to which I drew your attention. I was struck immediately by its importance."

"Yes, I remember you mentioned it at the time," said Truscott.

Carr smiled at him. "How do we explain the shattered lamp and overturned table? It might have suggested a struggle of some sort, but there was no other evidence of any such altercation. I could only think that someone had stumbled against the table and knocked over the lamp. If I was right, someone had been in that museum room with the body at some point during the night and they had been shocked by what they had seen. It might have been the killer reacting to the horror of what he had done, but I was convinced that the murder itself had been carefully planned, which surely meant that it was inconsistent to assume that the killer would then lose control of himself and begin knocking over ornaments. I was inclined to the notion that an innocent party had stumbled onto the scene of the murder and, shocked by it, had reacted accordingly.

"The Tethran Dagger was the weapon and, as we all knew, it had been locked in a display case but, when the body was discovered, that case was open. The key to the display case was on the same ring as the door key and they had been stolen. Nevertheless, the door was locked, the display case was open, and the lamp was shattered. How had the doors and the display case been locked and unlocked in turn without keys? And how was I to reconcile all these facts?

"You may have heard of the mathematic principle of Occam's Razor, a theory put forward by a fourteenth-century friar and theologian. It is most readily explained as determining that the simplest answer to a problem is often the correct one. Now, what is the simplest solution to the question of entering a locked room?"

"The use of a key," replied Helena.

Carr bowed to her. "Just so, dear lady. Whoever entered and left the museum room on the night of the murder must have done so by using the only key in existence. You will say that this cannot be so, because the key was stolen and the thieves could not possibly have gained access back into the house."

"But that is true," declared Swift.

Carr held up a warning finger. "Is it? Whose account do we have about that assault? Only Sir James'. Who says that the keys were ever taken from him? Only he does. What witnesses do we have to the attack? None. To put it another way, we only have Sir James' word that he was ever attacked at all."

Gilchrist laughed. "Look at the wound on his head. I examined it myself. It is not fake, I assure you."

"I do not say that it is fake, Doctor," said Carr. "But I do say that there is no evidence it was caused by a third party, just as there is nothing to say for certain that it was not *self-inflicted*. As a matter of undeniable fact, there is no evidence of the attack at all. The details of it come only from Sir James. Once you accept that he staged the attack on himself and that the key to the museum room never left his possession, that impossibility of the locked room mystery is easily explained."

"But what about the keys being found in Lady Ravenwood's dressing table?" pressed Swift, his mind reeling at Carr's revelations.

"In order to answer those points, Inspector, it is necessary to understand matters from Sir James' point of view." Carr took a sip of whiskey and indulged himself in its reviving quality. "If my suspicions were accurate and he had staged the attack on himself, he had to have a reason for pretending that the keys had been stolen. You will recall that when Sir James learned that the body had been discovered in a locked room with no sign of the key, he stated very definitely that it did not make sense. He said it upon the initial discovery and, again, Swift, when we questioned him in his bedroom.

"What exactly did not make sense? It seemed as if he meant the impossibility of the murder but, remember, Sir James knew that the keys had *not* been stolen. So, surely, he could easily explain why the room was locked if he had the only key in his possession. What, then, made no sense about the room being locked? It was simply this—*he had expected the door to be open and the keys in the lock.* As it was, however, he was confronted with a locked room and missing keys, neither of which he was in a position to explain. It was that which he could not understand and, in his confusion, he failed to suppress his surprise.

"You will recall, Swift, that I said that I agreed with you up to a point when you said that there was no connection between the attack and the murder. They were not connected with each other because the attack was not designed to obtain the keys to this house for the purpose of robbery. But they were connected insofar as the attack gave Sir James an alibi.

"I think that a careful plan was made and it went wrong. Sir James planned to give the impression that he had been attacked and his keys stolen. His idea was that these imaginary thieves would then infiltrate the house in order to steal some of the notable Ravenwood collection of curios. They would gain access to the room and the display case, using the stolen keys, they would steal the knife, but then be caught in the act by Lynch. They would kill him and, in a panic, flee from the scene, leaving the keys behind in their haste. Remember that it was my idea to post a sentry at the lodge. Sir James knew nothing about it until the following day. In his original plan, a thief would have been able to get into the house through the front gates, come up to the house, use his stolen keys to get into the museum room, commit the burglary and the murder, then flee.

"All of which means that on the morning after the murder, Ravenwood expected to find the museum room and display case open with the keys in the lock, Lynch's body waiting to be discovered, and an interrupted burglary as the likely solution to the matter. The murder would have been attached to two mythical thieves of whom Sir James could only give a fleeting description.

"What went wrong? The answer again is very simple. Ravenwood had decoyed Lynch to the museum room under false pretences. He could have told Lynch any number of stories to entice him to the room and, remember, Lynch had no reason to suspect that Ravenwood wanted to kill him. Once in the room, Ravenwood stabbed Lynch with the dagger, left the display case open and the keys in its lock, and returned to bed.

"At some point after the murder, Lady Ravenwood awoke. She could not go back to sleep and she went downstairs. She saw the museum room door was open and she investigated. In doing so, she discovered the body. Almost instantly, she must have realised what had happened and the keys betrayed her husband's guilt. In her bewildered fear, she stumbled against the table and knocked over the lamp. It shattered on the floor and alarmed her further. In her panic, she fled, locking the door and taking away the keys. I doubt she even thought about her actions. Irrespective of whether she consciously realised that her husband was responsible or whether she acted entirely on impulse, she locked the door and took away the keys. In doing so, she left behind her, entirely unwittingly, a seemingly impossible scene of murder."

Swift was nodding. "She hid the keys in the dressing table, knowing nobody would search there."

Carr conceded the point. "And, also, because she could not dispose of them. She could not return them to her husband without revealing her suspicions of him. She was not ready or willing to do that."

The attention of the people assembled in the library was focused on the Ravenwoods. Neither returned the glare and nor did they look at each other. Swift stepped slowly towards Carr and spoke with serious authority.

"What about the remainder of your six points of interest?" he asked. "Miss Marston's stocking and spectacles? And why did you keep going on about her reading Chekhov?"

Carr's eyes hardened. "The murder of Lynch was perhaps understandable, but killing Miss Marston was unforgivable. The malicious, spiteful gesture of stuffing a stocking into her mouth, and the violation of her intimate privacy in removing the stocking for that purpose, was despicable."

Ravenwood raised his hand and wiped away a tear from his cheek. "I am sorry. Not for Lynch, he was a monster. But I am sorry about Louisa."

"She had realised you had lied about your movements," explained Carr. "You had told Inspector Swift that you had been unable to sleep and had gone to the library to read. What you did not know was that Louisa Marston, in a similar bout of wakefulness, had gone to the drawing room to collect her spectacles. She had left them there earlier in the day and she needed them in order to read. To get to the drawing room, she had to pass the library. She heard me asking you about your movements on the night of the murder and it struck her that she had not seen you in here and that the light was not on. She knew that there was nobody in here, no matter what you said to the contrary. In truth, I must confess that I had my suspicions that you were lying about your whereabouts because, when I asked you if you had seen anyone in the hallway at that time, you said you had not. But you would surely have seen Miss Garrick returning from her nightly visit to her daughter, just as Miss Marston herself had done. Why had you not seen her? For the same reason Miss Marston had not seen you—*because you were not there.*

"And it was then that the importance of Chekhov occurred to me. Miss Marston had been a lover of Russian drama generally but, specifically, she had been reading *The Three Sisters*. I had been struck by her reaction to learning that Lynch himself had once had a sister who had died and I mistakenly thought the existence of this sister was important, but I was wrong. The relevance of a sister was only that it reminded Louisa Marston of the play. Her mind segued from the reference to a single sister to a play about three of them. Something about that play caused her to realise that Ravenwood had not been in the library when he claimed."

"But what was it?" demanded Swift.

"*The Three Sisters* has a character in it called Protopopov, the head of the local council. Miss Marston even said his name to me, but I was too slow to see its significance. The importance of the character for our present purposes is that *he is never seen on stage*. He is part of the drama but he is never there. Just as you, Sir James, were part of the drama in this house but you were not there in the library as you should have been."

Ravenwood sighed heavily. "I wondered what it was which made her realise."

"I warned her to tell me what she had realised," said Carr, "but, in her own mind, what she had realised was unimportant and insignificant. She had nothing to fear from it. Why? Because she considered Sir James free from reproach. He was not where he claimed to be, but she felt sure that there must be an innocent explanation for it. It never occurred to the poor, naïve woman that he was a murderer or that she was a danger to him. She told him that she knew he was not in the library and, as she had expected, he reassured her on the point. But she remained dangerous to him and he could take no chances. He went to her cottage last night and strangled her."

"And the stocking was used as a gag," said Swift, now understanding. "It served only as an acknowledgement of the need to silence her."

Carr nodded. "But she would never have betrayed you, Sir James. The gag was a contemptible, insulting, and unnecessary gesture. It sickens me to think of you degrading the poor woman after her death. For that vile and mocking act alone, I will ensure that you hang, sir. And I wish for no mercy on your soul."

Ravenwood got to his feet. "I don't ask for mercy. What you have said is all true, Mr Carr. I have no regrets about Lynch but I am truly sorry about Louisa. You may be right about her. She might never have said anything about not seeing me and, even if she had, it would not have been through malice. Still, the more I thought about it, the more of a threat she seemed to be. I don't know what came over me with the stocking. A temporary madness, I suppose. I think I have been half-mad from the moment I discovered the truth about Lynch and Mary."

Swift interrupted him. "Say no more, Sir James. You will require legal representation."

Ravenwood smiled. "Don't worry, Inspector. I shall be no trouble to you."

He looked back at Carr. If he felt any malice, he did not express it and none of it showed in his expression. "You are left with a strange, indescribable feeling once you have killed, Mr Carr. You can never be the same man again. You look different to yourself in the mirror. Your hands seem to belong to somebody else. Every thought you have is cursed with a paranoia which you cannot imagine. You do not simply take the life of the man you kill. You take your own life too, because it can never be the same again. It is no longer your own. Now, it belongs to what you've done. Can you understand that?"

Carr looked deeply into the guilty man's eyes. "No, sir. I cannot understand that at all."

It appeared as if Ravenwood was about to speak, but no words came. He turned back to his wife and held out his hand. She gripped it and pressed her lips against it, her tears dampening the back of it. He pulled himself free and walked away, crossing the room to Alicia. He tried to take her hand but she held them behind her back. Her eyes were wild with horror and anger, as if she were seeing him as his true self for the first time. He was now no longer her father. He was something else, something she could not comprehend. Ravenwood understood and, in that moment of realisation, his last trace of fear at the hangman's noose seemed to evaporate. In a muted, barely human voice, he said simply, "I am so sorry, Alicia."

As he was escorted from the room, Mary screamed and ran after him. There was a brief struggle between her and Swift, which managed to seem both tragic and inappropriate, as she was held back from embracing the man she loved. Truscott and Gilchrist assisted in pulling her away from Ravenwood and, almost immediately, she collapsed against them in exhaustion.

"I love you, Mary," Ravenwood said. "He would never have left you alone. He would have plagued us forever. I couldn't allow that."

Her reply was only to sob with more ferocity than before and she sank to her knees as the man who had killed to protect her was taken away to make his statement, to be put on trial, and, ultimately, to die.

Chapter Thirty-Seven

Carr followed Mary out onto the terrace. The air was sharp but not uncomfortable, the slight breeze only gently kissing the tips of the trees which were illuminated by the severe moonlight. The night was peaceful, almost profoundly so, and Carr wondered whether it was because the stillness contrasted so dramatically with the drama inside the house. It was a romantic notion, he was aware of that, as was the almost simultaneous idea that the tranquillity of the night echoed the gap in the house which Ravenwood's arrest had produced. Neither idea was appropriate and Carr dismissed them even before Mary spoke.

"Lynch was a wicked man, Mr Carr," she said. "I do not pretend it is an excuse for what James has done. I say it only because it is true."

"Even the most wicked of men has a right to live his life to its natural end."

She considered the argument. "I wish I could see things as clearly as you."

It was a reply borne not out of genuine belief but out of a form of protection against what had happened. Justifying Ravenwood's actions might give her temporary peace of mind, but Carr knew well enough that the protection would break down and she would be left with the stark reality of his guilt. "Would Lynch ever have been able to persuade you to flee with him?"

Mary looked into his eyes. "I have asked myself that question. Whichever answer I give, we lose. If I say he could have persuaded me, I vindicate what James did, but it means that my marriage meant nothing to me. How could it, if I was willing to leave my husband for another man? But, if I say there was never any chance of leaving with Sebastian, it means James killed him for nothing."

"The same would have to apply for Louisa Marston," Carr felt obliged to say.

Mary lowered her head. "James felt he had no choice in that matter."

"A few days ago, I recall, you said that, once he had decided to act, nothing would stop your husband from carrying out his wishes." He watched her nod at the memory. "I was struck at once by the words. They confirmed my suspicions, you see."

"How?"

"They assured me that, if your husband had discovered Lynch's threat to your marriage and decided to eliminate that threat, nothing would dissuade him from his course of action."

She did not respond. A moment of silence passed between them, with only the gentle whispers of the leaves and bushes of the gardens interrupting it.

At last, Mary spoke. "Was Sebastian truly blackmailing my daughter?"

"I am afraid so. She made a terrible mistake and Mr Prentice did not stop her, although his reasons were arguably sound. She has learned from it."

"Where are these photographs now?"

"Swift has them. I suspect M. Chastain will receive an official visit in the next few days."

"Were the pictures very awful?" Mary waited for Carr to nod. "I suppose you think our family is cursed, Mr Carr. A slatternly daughter and a husband who is a murderer."

"I make no such judgments, my lady."

"Perhaps I should not be surprised about Alicia. In my younger days, I was far more liberated than I am now. I am sure my own mother thought I was beyond redemption. Perhaps my daughter is no more so than I was myself."

Carr shook his head against her tone of reproach. "Miss Alicia's wickedness was of the moment and she has repented. Your husband, I fear, is not capable of atonement. For Lynch's death, at least."

"James called Sebastian a monster. Perhaps he was. I told him myself that he never used to be as cruel as he had become. I only saw the devil in him once." She saw Carr's expression tighten with interest. "I have said I was less restrained than I am now, Mr Carr, and it is true. Sebastian took advantage of it once. He gorged himself on me. I hadn't wanted it, but I did not stop it. I could not."

"Did Sir James know what happened?"

"No." She smiled, but the effort taken was only too obvious. "He had no more motive than the one he confessed. I'm telling you about it only because it shows why I could never go back to him."

"But Lynch would never have accepted that?"

"Never." She stared up at the moon. "James has saved me from that persecution, even if he has left me with a different but stronger one. People will never look at me with respect again. They will shun me, scorn me, and they will always say I must have been complicit."

Carr shook his head. "You must put your faith in people, my lady. You will find they are not as cynical as you fear."

If she believed him, either his words or their sentiment, her expression did not demonstrate the belief, but he did not press the point. She would discover whether his optimism was deserved or not in due course and he had no control over when, if at all, her enlightenment would come. His attention was caught by a brief shimmer of satin and, turning to face it, he saw Alicia Ravenwood standing behind them. Mary also must have been distracted by the flicker of moonlight against the oyster-coloured dress and she opened her arms to her daughter. The two women embraced.

"I am so sorry, Mummy," said the girl. "For everything."

Mary stroked her daughter's hair. "It is all over now."

"I keep thinking about Daddy's face when he was taken away. In my head, it isn't him anymore. He is someone else, someone horrible, someone evil. I don't know him anymore."

"He is still your father," soothed Mary.

"My father would never have hurt anybody," insisted Alicia. "I can't explain how I feel."

"I know how you feel. I feel it too." She cupped the girl's face in her hands and stared earnestly into her eyes. "We have all learned things about each other and we have to adjust to what we know. We may not like what we've come to know about the people we love and dealing with it all might seem too difficult to contemplate. But maybe it will be easier if we do it together. If I help you to adjust, Alicia, will you and Richard help me?"

The girl's tearful answer was to embrace her mother. Her grip was so tight that it seemed as though she felt that she must never relinquish it, because to do so would be to lose her mother entirely. Carr wondered whether, after all, Lady Ravenwood would come to realise that his opinion of people was justified. Murder had occurred and her husband had been responsible for it and Carr was keenly aware that murder changed everything. It changed lives, perspectives, and loyalties. It invaded people's existence without invitation and it left its crimson mark forever, but it could not be allowed to triumph indefinitely. There had to come a time, he was sure of it, when people would triumph over the effects of violent death.

For now, Carr felt his presence was an embarrassing one and, with delicacy, he walked away. When the two women turned to speak to him once more, they found he had gone but they had heard nothing of his departure.

Chapter Thirty-Eight

Early on the following morning, Eliza and Deville watched the flames dancing over the wooden figures and the ball of string. As the last remnants of her campaign against Lynch blackened and split in the fire, Deville threw his notebooks and pencils into the mixture of heat and smoke.

"You shouldn't destroy your work," she said.

He shook his head. "It isn't my work. It is Anthony's. I may have only stolen one idea from him, but everything I have achieved since has been based on that first, fundamental lie. I can't write another word with a clear conscience."

"Will you stop writing altogether?"

Deville shrugged. "I just need to take some time. I need to re-assess my approach to it all. If I can find a project which is entirely mine, something I can use to make amends to Anthony, I could pursue it. It would be honest. Does that make sense?"

Gently, she kissed him on the cheek. "Perfect sense."

After a moment, he turned to face her. "Mr Carr was right. I did see you. I was going to go and sit in the drawing room for a while but, when I opened the door, I saw you on the landing."

"I wish you had said something to me. I was so frightened, even before I knew that he was dead."

Deville took her hand. "I am sorry about how he treated you and your mother. And that it came out in such a public fashion."

"He is dead," she replied, her voice hardening. "He cannot hurt anyone anymore."

"Would you have carried out your threats?"

She shook her head almost immediately. She had needed no time to consider the question. "I could never have done it. No more than you could."

They remained silent for several minutes. At last, Deville looked into her eyes. "May I ask you something?"

"Of course."

"Would you help me search for a project I can call my own?"

She smiled warmly at him, the reflected flames flickering in her eyes. "Be your muse, you mean?"

"Be everything." He said the words with more courage than he felt.

Her eyes widened. "Is that a proposal?"

Deville laughed coyly. "That might be a plot twist too far."

She found his laughter contagious and she cut it off with a kiss to his lips. It was followed by another, a third, and then a longer, more meaningful fourth.

From the window of the library, Carr watched them, a gentle smile across his face. Dr Gilchrist was beside him, a cigarette clenched between his lips. Carr glanced over at him and saw the handsome features frozen with contempt. Gilchrist inhaled deeply on his cigarette and blew the smoke through his nostrils.

"Nice to see somebody happy," he said.

"You don't resent their happiness, do you?" Carr's tone was accusatory.

"You can't expect me to like the man, Mr Carr."

Carr shrugged. "Perhaps not. But you should remember this, Dr Gilchrist – you and he were both victims of Sebastian Lynch. He tormented you both in the same way, exerting a power over you for his own pleasure. I suspect Lynch was the sort of child who pulled off the wings of butterflies."

"Are you saying that Deville and I are butterflies?"

"I am saying that Lynch was a cruel and vindictive man. He corrupted people. Perhaps it was his exposure of Deville's plagiarism which caused the tragedy, not the plagiarism itself. If so, Mr Deville is not an enemy, but a kindred spirit."

"You are an idealist, Mr Carr." To Gilchrist, it was evidently a weakness.

Carr smiled thinly. "One cannot live in darkness forever, doctor. One day, the sun must shine over the horizon."

Gilchrist had no reply. He looked back out of the window at Eliza and Deville and smoked in silence. Carr followed his gaze and allowed himself an assured smile. Looking up at the skies, he was satisfied to see that the initial grey of the morning was now giving way to a clear blue and a strident shaft of sunlight which forced its way through the clouds.

He left the doctor to his thoughts and stepped out into the hallway. Truscott and Helena were coming in from a short walk in the gardens. At the sight of Carr, they smiled and approached him.

"Are you ready to leave, Mr Carr?" asked Truscott.

Carr consulted his watch. "Very soon now. I have a few official matters to discuss with Inspector Swift, but I shall be on the noon train back to London."

Helena took his hand in hers. "I had hoped you would be able to meet Rosie, Mr Carr."

"As I had hoped to, dear lady. There will, I hope, be another time."

Truscott put his arm around Helena's waist. She looked up into his eyes and smiled. "I think there is very likely to be many times," she said. "Funny, but I never thought things would turn out like this."

Truscott kissed her on the cheek. "That is what makes it so special."

Carr looked sternly into their eyes. "Allow an old man to give you some advice. Do not allow anything to come between you. Have no secrets, share everything. You have been given one of the greatest gifts in life. Treasure it and it shall reward you."

Helena leaned forward and kissed him. It was a caring gesture, but there was a profound seriousness in her eyes. "We shall, Mr Carr. I give you my word."

Gilchrist stepped out into the hallway. Seeing Helena and Truscott, he laughed. "My word, Helena, have you managed to find someone brave enough to take you on? Be careful, Truscott, she's a warrior."

"Don't be an idiot, John," said Helena.

"You must like a challenge, Truscott," goaded Gilchrist. "Well, good luck to you. Send me an invitation when the time comes."

He marched away, pulling open the front door and stepping out into the garden. Truscott clicked his tongue.

"The man's an idiot."

Carr shook his head. "No, no. I think he is only a man who has seen the sun rise over the horizon."

Truscott insisted on accompanying Carr to the small station at Vale Thorn. Together, they stood on the platform, the scenery no less impressive than it had been when Truscott had first arrived. The dark incidents of the weekend had been unable to twist or corrupt the beauty of the landscape.

"I just wanted to say thank you, Mr Carr," he declared, "for being supportive of me and Helena."

"She is a fine woman, dear boy. Treat her well."

"I shall." Truscott paused for a moment. "And Rosie. She's a lovely girl, like her mother."

Carr bowed his head. "Perhaps they have found a match in you."

Truscott's expression darkened. "I feel no guilt about it. Am I betraying Jane?"

"No." Carr's voice was stern. "You are young and your heart belongs to the living. The dead can look after themselves."

"Do you truly believe that?"

The implication was not lost on Carr. A vision of Miranda flashed across his mind. "I do, my friend. But the dead can only be allowed to look after themselves when the living have the courage to permit them."

Truscott did not respond, save to smile and turn away as Carr wiped a gloved finger across the rim of both eyes. In the distance, there was the sound of a faint rumbling and a vibrating tower of steam came into view.

"Your train," observed Truscott. "I'm sorry to see you go. I shall look you up when I return to town, if I may."

"Of course. We shall dine together."

"A strange few days," said Truscott. "It's been thrilling, watching you unravel this mystery, I must say. I would say you have a talent for it."

"A talent for murder?" Carr smiled. "It is not one I would relish possessing. I do not envisage repeating the experience."

"One can never say what will happen in the future."

"True, but one can take steps to avoid unpleasantness."

"As you wish," said Truscott.

"I assure you, dear boy, I aim to leave the cruelty and violence of murder far behind me."

They shared a smile and shook hands while watching the train grind to a halt before them. Truscott carried Carr's suitcases into the carriage and lifted them into the overhead racking. He stepped back onto the platform as Carr relieved himself of his coat and gloves, before settling into his seat. There was a short burst of a guard's whistle and, with a loud and mechanical cough, the steam engulfed the engine, as the train moved slowly on its way.

Truscott waved a final farewell and Everett Carr reciprocated. At last, the train picked up speed and finally disappeared from view.

About the Author

As a lifelong aficionado and expert on Sherlock Holmes, Matthew Booth is the author of several books and short stories about the famous detective. He wrote a number of scripts for a Holmes radio series produced by Jim French Productions in Seattle, as well as creating his own series about a disgraced former barrister investigating crimes for the same production company.

He is the creator of Everett Carr, an amateur sleuth in the traditional mould, who appears in his debut investigation in the book, *A Talent for Murder*, a traditional whodunit, which offers a contemporary twist on the format.

An expert in crime and supernatural fiction, Matthew has provided a number of academic talks on such subjects as Sherlock Holmes, the works of Agatha Christie, crime fiction, Count Dracula, and the facts and theories concerning the crimes of Jack the Ripper.

He is a member of the Crime Writers' Association and is the editor of its monthly magazine, *Red Herrings*. He lives with his wife in Manchester, England.

SOCIAL MEDIA HANDLES:
  Twitter: @HolmesBooth
  Instagram: @matthewboothauthor

Also by Matthew Booth

When Anthony Rathe Investigates (Sparkling Books)

The Further Exploits of Sherlock Holmes (Sparkling Books)

Sherlock Holmes & the Giant's Hand (Breese Books)

Lightning Source UK Ltd.
Milton Keynes UK
UKHW010628180122
397340UK00001B/24